3 4143 10159 6177

KT-500-456

Praise for the author

ANNE O'BRIEN

'... has everything—royalty, scandal,
fascinating historical politics.'
—*Cosmopolitan*

'A fascinating and surprisingly female-focused look at one
of the most turbulent periods of English history.'
—*Publishers Weekly*

'Better than Philippa Gregory'
—*The Bookseller*

'Another excellent read from the ever-reliable Anne O'Brien'
—*The Bookbag*

'Anne O'Brien is fast becoming one of Britain's
most popular and talented writers.'
—*Lancashire Evening Post*

'A must-read for any historical fiction fan'
—*The Examiner*

'Brings the origins of the most famous royal
dynasty to vibrant life'
—*Candis*

'Her writing is highly evocative of the time period…
O'Brien has produced an epic tale.'
—*Historical Novel Society*

'A fast-paced historical drama that is full of suspense'
—*Essentials*

'Flawlessly written and well researched'
—*Birmingham Post*

'Packed with love, loss and intrigue'
—*Sunday Express S Magazine*

Also by

ANNE
O'BRIEN

VIRGIN WIDOW

DEVIL'S CONSORT

THE KING'S CONCUBINE

THE FORBIDDEN QUEEN

THE SCANDALOUS DUCHESS

ANNE O'BRIEN

The KING'S SISTER

HARLEQUIN®MIRA®

All rights reserved including the right of reproduction in whole or in part in any form. This edition is published by arrangement with Harlequin Books S.A.

This is a work of fiction. Names, characters, places, locations and incidents are purely fictional and bear no relationship to any real life individuals, living or dead, or to any actual places, business establishments, locations, events or incidents. Any resemblance is entirely coincidental.

This book is sold subject to the condition that it shall not, by way of trade or otherwise, be lent, resold, hired out or otherwise circulated without the prior consent of the publisher in any form of binding or cover other than that in which it is published and without a similar condition including this condition being imposed on the subsequent purchaser.

Harlequin MIRA is a registered trademark of Harlequin Enterprises Limited, used under licence.

Published in Great Britain 2015
by Harlequin MIRA, an imprint of Harlequin (UK) Limited,
Eton House, 18-24 Paradise Road,
Richmond, Surrey, TW9 1SR

© 2014 Anne O'Brien

ISBN 978-1-848-45366-1

58-0215

Harlequin (UK) Limited's policy is to use papers that are natural, renewable and recyclable products and made from wood grown in sustainable forests. The logging and manufacturing processes conform to the legal environmental regulations of the country of origin.

Printed and bound by
CPI Group (UK) Ltd, Croydon, CR0 4YY

Descendants of Edward III and the Claims to the English Throne

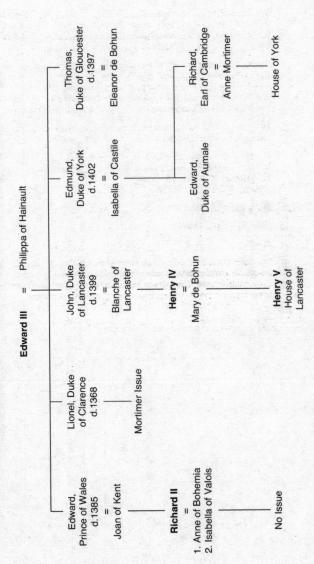

The Holland Family

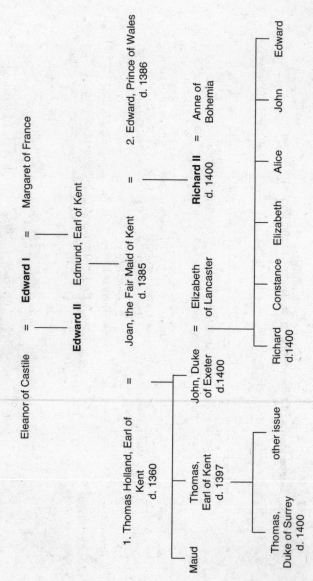

The House of Lancaster

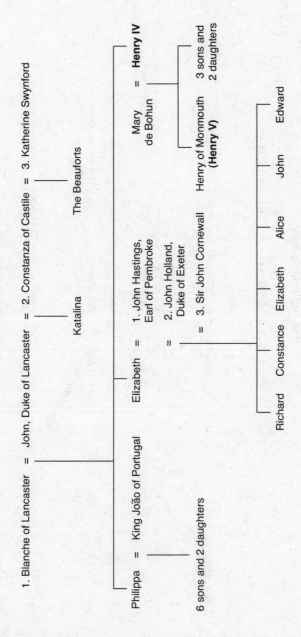

 **Anne O'Brien** was born in the West Riding of Yorkshire. After gaining a BA Honours degree at Manchester University and a Master's at Hull, she lived in the East Riding for many years as a teacher of history. After leaving teaching, Anne decided to turn to novel writing and give voice to the women in history who fascinated her the most. Today Anne lives in an eighteenth-century cottage in Herefordshire, an area full of inspiration for her work.

Visit Anne online at www.anneobrienbooks.com. Find Anne on Facebook and follow her on Twitter @anne_obrien

For George, with love and thanks. Who else could I persuade to travel the length and breadth of the country with me, in search of people who lived six hundred years ago?

And in memory of my father, Jack Garfitt, 1923-2014. His love of history first fired my imagination.

'…He (John Holland) was struck down passionately, so that day and night he sought her (Elizabeth) out.'
—Ranulph Higden, *The Universal Chronicle of
Ranulph Higden*

'When (Elizabeth) took a tearful leave of her
husband[…]Holland reproached her bitterly for
having, despite his own gloom, rejoiced and
made merry when Henry had arrested Richard
and himself[…]'
—R A Griffiths, *Oxford Dictionary of National
Biography*

'For what is wedlock forced but a hell,
An age of discord and continual strife?
Whereas the contrary bringeth bliss,
And is a pattern of celestial peace.'
—William Shakespeare, *Henry VI, Part I*

Chapter One

1380, Kenilworth Castle

'What's afoot?' Henry asked, loping along the wall walk, sliding to a standstill beside us.

It all began as a family gathering: a meeting of almost everyone I knew in the lush setting of Kenilworth where my father's building plans had provided room after spacious room in which we could enjoy a summer sojourn. Intriguingly, though, the intimate number of acquaintances was soon extended with a constant arrival of guests. So, I considered. What indeed was afoot? A most prestigious occasion. From elders to children, aristocratic families from the length and breadth of the land rode up to our gates, filing across the causeway that kept their feet dry from the inundations of the mere.

Philippa and I watched them with keen anticipation, now in the company of our younger brother Henry, an energetic, raucous lad, whose shrill voice more often than not filled the courtyards as he engaged in games with other boys of the household—dangerous games in which he pummelled and rolled with the best of them in combat *à l'outrance*. Even now he bore the testimony of a fading black eye. But today Henry was buffed and polished and on his best behaviour. As the thirteen-year-old heir of Lancaster, he knew his worth.

'Something momentous,' Philippa surmised.

'With music and dancing,' I suggested hopefully.

My father's royal brothers, the Dukes of Gloucester and York, together with their wives, made up a suitably ostentatious display of royal power. The vast connection of FitzAlans and the Northumberland Percies were there, heraldic badges making a bright splash of colour. There was Edward, our cousin of York, kicking at the flanks of a tolerant pony. Thin and wiry, Edward was still too much of a child for even Henry to notice. The only one notably absent was the King.

'We'll not miss him overmuch,' croaked Henry, on the cusp of adolescence.

True enough. Of an age with Henry, what would Richard add to the proceedings, other than a spirit of sharp mischief that seemed to have developed of late? There was little love lost between my brother and royal cousin.

The noble guests continued to arrive with much laughter and comment.

I was not one for being sensitive to tension in the air when I might be considering which dress would become me most, but on this occasion it rippled along my skin like the brush of a goose feather quill. Chiefly because there were far too many eyes turned in my direction for comfort. It seemed to me that I was an object of some interest over and above the usual friendly comment on the rare beauty and precocious talents of the Duke of Lancaster's younger daughter. What's more, on that particular morning, I had been dressed by my women with extraordinary care.

Not that I had demurred. My sideless surcoat, of a particularly becoming blue silk damask, hushed expensively as I walked. My hair had been plaited into an intricate coronet, covered with a veil as transparent as one of the high clouds that barely masked the sun.

'Is it a celebration?' I mused. 'Have we made peace with France?'

'I doubt it. But it's a celebration for something.' My sister's mind was as engaged as mine as the FitzAlan Countess of Hereford and her opulent entourage arrived in the courtyard, soon followed by the Beauchamp contingent of the Earl of Warwick.

'It's a marriage alliance. A betrothal. It has to be,' I announced to Philippa, for surely this was the obvious cause for so great a foregathering, and one of such high-blooded grandeur festooned in sun-bright jewels and rich velvets. 'The Duke is bringing your new husband to meet with you.'

'A husband for me? If that's so, why is it that you are the one to be clad like a Twelfth Night gift?' Philippa said, eyeing my apparel. 'I am not clad for a betrothal. This is my second best gown, and the hem is becoming worn. While *you* are wearing my new undertunic.'

Which was true. And Philippa more waspish than her wont since my borrowed garment was of finest silk with gold stitching at hem and neck and the tiniest of buttons from elbow to wrist, yet despite her animadversions on her second best gown, Philippa looked positively regal in a deep red cote-hardie that would never have suited me. A prospective husband would never look beyond her face to notice the hem. If the honoured guest was invited here as a suitable match, he must be intended for my sister. As the elder by three years, Philippa would wed first. Did not older sisters always marry before younger ones? I stared at her familiar features, so like my own, marvelling at her serenity. There was still no husband for her, not even a betrothal of long standing, at twenty years. No husband had been attracted by her dark hair and darker eyes, inherited from our father. It was high time, as daughter of the royal Duke of Lancaster as well as first cousin to King Richard himself, even if he was only a tiresome boy, that she was sought and won by some powerful bridegroom.

Of course this would be her day.

I sighed that it behoved me to wait, for marriage to a handsome knight or illustrious prince was an elevation to which I aspired. The songs and tales of the troubadours, of fair maidens lost and won through chivalric deeds and noble self-sacrifice, had made a strong impression in my youthful heart. But today was no day for sighing.

'I have been counting all the unwed heirs of the English aristocracy who will make suitable husbands for you,' I said, to make Philippa smile. 'I have a tally of at least a dozen to choose from.'

It was Henry who grunted a laugh. 'But how many of them are either senile or imbecile?'

I stepped smartly and might have punched his shoulder but Henry was agile, putting distance between us. And because we were finely dressed, he did not retaliate. I turned my back on him.

'He could be a foreign prince, of course.' This was Philippa, ever serious.

'So he could.' I turned back to the carpet of richly-hued velvet and silk below, imagining such an eventuality. Would I enjoy leaving England, living far away from my family, those I had known and loved all my life? 'I don't think I would like that.'

'I would not mind.' Philippa lifted her shoulders in a little shrug.

'You will do whatever you are told to do.'

Her arm, in sisterly affection, slid round my waist. 'As will you.'

It did not need the saying. I might be wrapped in girlhood dreams of romantic notions of knights errant, but I had been raised since birth to know the role I must play in my father's schemes. Alliances were all important, friendships and connections built on shared interests and the disposition of daughters. Henry might be the heir, and much prized as a promising son, but Philippa and I were valuable commodities in furthering the ambitions of Lancaster. My husband would, assuredly, be a man of high status and proud name. He would be an owner of vast estates and significant wealth, possessing an extensive web of connections of his own to meld with those of the Duke into one overarching structure of power. He would have significance at the royal court, where I would take my place, glowing from his reflected authority and, I hoped, glamour. There was nothing so attractive as a powerful man, as I well knew. And, of course, this man would be worthy of my Plantagenet blood. I would never be given away to a mere nobody, a man without distinction.

When my woman combed my hair to braid it for the night and I inspected my features in my looking glass I knew that my husband would have an affection for me. Was it possible for a man of perception not to fall in love with a face as perfectly proportioned as mine? There was the elegant Plantagenet nose, the dark hooded eyes that suggested a mine of secrets to be explored. My lips were quick to smile, my brows, surprisingly dark and nicely arched, and my hair, unlike Philippa's, the same lustrous fairness of my mother whose memory faded from me as the years passed. It was a face that promised romance and passion, I decided. No, my husband would be unable to resist and would continue to indulge my desires in formidable style. I was destined to enjoy my future life.

When a shout of laughter went up from one of the groups in the courtyard—enticing Henry to condemn us as dull company and leave us, bounding down the steps to join the throng—I too descended from our high vantage point in search of enlightenment, and discovered Dame Katherine Swynford. Our governess and much more than a mere member of the Lancaster household, she was as close as an oyster, preoccupied with some matter to do with the guests, although why it should fall to her I could not fathom. Did

we not employ a steward, a chamberlain, a vast array of servants to oversee every aspect of life at Kenilworth? Indeed I
was interested to see a brief shadow flit over her face, a sudden discomfiture that I suspected had no connection with
her own illicit and highly scandalous relationship with the
Duke.

'What is it?' I asked. No point in subtlety as yet another
festive group arrived.

When Dame Katherine, intent on speeding away, shook
her head so that her veils shivered, suspicions began to flutter in my belly. There was something here that she did not
wish to discuss with me.

'What is it that you know, Dame Katherine, and that I
will not like?'

'Nothing, to my knowledge. What should there be?'
Lightly said but her eye did not quite meet mine.

'What are we celebrating?'

'The Duke does not tell me everything, Elizabeth.'

I frowned, not believing her for one moment. I would
swear that Dame Katherine could read my father's mind,
and what she could not read she could inveigle him into telling her when she seduced him into moments of love. Or he
seduced her. I thought there were no secrets between them
now that she had been my father's mistress for eight years.
She was quick to take me to task.

'Go and wait with your sister, Elizabeth, and show
patience. All you need to know is that we look for an important guest. He comes with your father.'

'And who is this important guest?' I asked, grasping her
trailing oversleeve with no care for its embroidered edge,

determined to prevent her escape, so that she sighed and at last turned to face me. I thought there was trouble in her face.

'It is John Hastings. He is the Earl of Pembroke.' It meant nothing to me. If I had ever met the Earl of Pembroke I could not recall. 'He is coming here for a betrothal.'

I smiled. 'So I thought,' I admitted. 'For my sister.'

'Oh no. For you, Elizabeth.'

'For me? Why me?' How gauche I sounded in sudden consternation, and felt my cheeks flush.

'Because it will be a valuable alliance. He is the grandson of the Countess of Norfolk.'

'Will I like him?' Was that the only thought in my mind? At that moment all my powers of reasoned thought were hopelessly awry.

'Your father will never choose anyone you dislike.' Dame Katherine was brisk, enough to quell any further discussion. 'When has he ever used the whip or the spur to take you to task?'

And then, an aura of unease still palpable, she was forcing a path through the throng with an urgent, muttered instruction for the poulterer.

A marriage. I was too delighted to be anxious. This unknown Earl would soon be riding across the causeway and then I could see for myself. If he was an Earl how could he not make me a desirable husband? With the Countess of Norfolk as his grandmother, his importance was guaranteed. For a long moment I simply stood and breathed in the excitement of my future until it seemed that my whole body was suffused with it. Soon, very soon, I would see him for myself.

Why was everyone so reluctant to talk about this dynastically vital occurrence?

Joyful expectancy stamped out any concerns as I rejoined my sister, saying nothing more of my discovery. It would only hurt Philippa that I had been chosen over her for this match. And then when it was becoming more and more impossible to keep my lips tight, my blood sparkling with the opening of this new window in my life, there was warning of the arrival.

'Come with me!' I seized Philippa's hand and dragged her with me, running down the steps into the courtyard.

'Why?' she asked, laughing and breathless.

'You'll see!'

'Elizabeth…!' Dame Katherine called after me as we threaded our way through all the chattering ranks of the nobility of England.

'Later,' I called back. Whatever it was, it could wait. Everything could wait. Here was the superbly well-connected man with whom I would spend the rest of my life. I shook out my skirts, smoothed the deeply embroidered panels, ensured that my light veil fell in seemly folds about my face, and prepared to meet my future.

★

The gates were already open to receive the impressive entourage with mounted retainers, a curtained palanquin, and various wagons loaded with the necessities for a lengthy stay. Most prominent on pennon and flag was the flowing red sleeve, accompanied by a cluster of red martlets on silver and blue, which I took to belong to the Earl of Pembroke. Mightily impressive, I decided, although nothing to compare with my father's royal leopards, his standards snapping in red and gold and blue in the brisk wind.

I straightened my spine, lifted my chin. The Earl of Pembroke must be aware of the jewel he was getting with marriage to a daughter of Lancaster, first cousin to King Richard himself. If the solid might and luxury of Kenilworth did not impress him—and how could it not? —then *I* certainly would.

I wondered fleetingly why I had no recall of meeting him before this, since most of the high nobility had come within my orbit at Richard's coronation three years ago. Perhaps he had been fighting in France. Perhaps he had a high reputation as a knight on the battlefield or in the tournament like my father. I would like that.

And then there was quite a fuss as two ladies were helped to step from the cumbersome travelling litters. The Countess of Norfolk, whom I knew: as thin and acerbic as vinegar, her hair severely contained in the metal and jewelled coils much in fashion when she was a girl. And a lady, younger, whom I did not. But where was he?

'Where is the Earl?' I whispered, when I could wait no longer.

Dame Katherine, who had come to watch with us, stepped behind me, her hands closing lightly on my shoulders.

'There,' she remarked softly. 'There he is. John Hastings, Earl of Pembroke.'

I could not see. I looked back at her, to follow the direction of her gaze. I could see no Earl of Pembroke, no man dressed finely, or mounted on a blood horse, who had come to wed me, but I felt no presentiment. Until, behind me I heard my governess sigh and her fingers tightened just a little.

'There is he. Just dismounting,' Dame Katherine repeated. 'With his grandmother, the Countess of Norfolk, and his mother, the Dowager Countess of Pembroke.'

And so I saw him, in the act of leaping down from his horse.

I sucked in a breath of air, every muscle in my body taut. My lips parted. And at that moment I felt Dame Katherine's palm press down firmly on my shoulder. She knew. She knew me well enough to know what I might do, what I might say in a moment of wilful passion. My head whipped round to read her expression, and the pressure, increasing, was enough to anchor me into all the courtesy and good manners in which I had been raised.

'Say it later,' she whispered. 'Not now. Now it is all about the impression you make. Consider what is due to your birth and your breeding, and to your father's pride.'

And so I sank into the required obeisance before our well-born guests.

The women of Norfolk and Pembroke returned the greeting. The Earl bowed. Then scuffed the toe of his boot on the stones, rubbing his chin with his fist.

'He is younger than Henry,' I whispered back in disbelief, in a mounting horror, when I could.

He was a boy. A child.

'Yes, he is,' Dame Katherine murmured back with a weight of compassion in her reply. 'He is eight years old.'

And I was seventeen. I could not look at Philippa. I could not bear the pity I knew I would read in her face.

*

As I expected, I was summoned to my father's private chamber within the hour, allowing me only the opportunity to gulp down a cup of ale and endure a strict lecture from Dame Katherine on the exquisite good manners expected of a Plantagenet lady—whatever the perceived provocation. I promised I would keep her advice well in my mind. So far I seemed to be unable to utter a word.

How could he do this to me? How could my father inflict a boy not out of his first decade on me as my husband? The thoughts revolved and revolved with no resolution. He had done it. At least Philippa did not attempt to console me with bright platitudes. Her kiss on my cheek said it all.

Now I curtsied before Constanza, my father's Castilian wife, who sat in chilly pre-eminence, her feet on a little footstool. Then to the rest of the party: the Countess of Norfolk, the Countess of Pembroke, the youthful Earl who was watching me bright-eyed. And there was my father coming towards me, a smile of welcome lighting his features. Tall but lightly built, he was every inch a royal prince, and his gaze commanded me.

'Elizabeth.' He took my hand to lead me forward and make the introductions. 'Allow me to present Elizabeth to you. My well beloved daughter.'

The Countess of Norfolk, of matriarchal proportions and inordinate pride—as befitted a granddaughter of the first King Edward and thus Countess in her own right—regarded me, and saw fit to smile on me, the silk of her veils shimmering with emotion. The widowed Countess of Pembroke too smiled, as well she might. Did we not all know that my hand in marriage was a formidable achievement for any household, however noble? Constanza stood and kissed my cheek in as maternal a manner as she could accommodate. Meanwhile the Earl, the boy, stood stiffly to well-drilled attention and watched the proceedings with a fleeting interest. It made me wonder what he had been told of this visit. How much did he understand of its significance?

And I?

I smiled with every ounce of grace I could summon, even when my face felt like the panel of buckram that stiffened Constanza's bodice in the old Castilian style that she often resorted to in moments of stress. Dame Katherine would have been proud of me as I acknowledged all the greetings. But below my composure I seethed with impotent anger, laced through with fear at what such a marriage would hold in store for me. Was I not old enough for a true marriage, in flesh as well as in spirit? Wallowing in the troubadours' songs of love and passion, my blood ran hot as I yearned for my own knowledge of such desire. How could I find it with a child?

'Allow me to present you to John, my lord of Pembroke.'

This boy would not make my heart flutter like a trapped

bird. My blood, cold as winter rain, ran thin as I smiled more brightly still, allowing the boy to take my hand and press his lips to my knuckles with a neat little bow.

Certainly he had been as well instructed in the arts of chivalry.

'This is your betrothed husband.'

I swallowed. 'Yes, my lord. It pleases me to meet you,' to the boy. 'I am honoured that you would wish to wed me.'

No! I wished to shriek. I am not pleased, I am not honoured. I am in despair. But daughters of Lancaster did not shriek. Plantagenet princesses did not defy their father's wishes.

'I will endeavour to make you a good wife.'

He was a child, barely released from the control of his nurses. How could I wed such a one as this? I had always known that I would wed at my father's dictates but never that he would choose a boy who had not yet learned to wield a sword, who was certainly not of an age to live with me as man and wife. There would be no consummation of this marriage after the ceremony.

'It is I who am honoured that you would accept my hand in marriage,' the boy replied, pronouncing each word carefully. So he had been informed and trained to it, much like our parrot.

'When will we be wed, sir?' The Earl looked up at my father, who smiled.

'Tomorrow. It is all arranged. It will be a day of great celebration, followed by a tournament where you will be able to display your new skills.'

Tomorrow!

The boy John of Pembroke beamed.

I took a ragged breath.

So soon. So final. Could my father not see my anxieties? Could he not see into my mind and know that this was not what I wanted? If he could, my wishes were as inconsequential as leaves blasted into the corners of the courtyard by a winter gale. My life as an indulged daughter had come to a breathless halt.

'Give me your hand, Elizabeth,' the Duke said softly.

I complied.

Onto my finger, the Duke pushed a ring. A beautiful thing of gold set with a ruby of vast proportions that glowed in the light. An object I would have coveted, but in the circumstances roused no emotion at all beyond the thought that the chains of a marriage I did not want were being fastened around me with this valuable gift. The ring was heavy on my finger.

'A gift to commemorate this auspicious day. It belonged to your mother, my beloved Duchess Blanche. I thought it was fitting that, as a married woman, you should now wear it.'

'Thank you, sir.'

Never had I said so little when in receipt of a valuable gift, when normally I might have been tiresomely effusive. Today I was as wooden as the figure on the quintain on the practice field.

'I have made arrangements for your new household. You will receive moneys befitting your status…'

But the Earl was fast losing interest in such detail, his eye straying to a minor commotion in the window embrasure, and my father laughed.

'Such matters can be dealt with tomorrow. There is no hurry. You have all your lives together after today.' His eye slid to mine as the ice in my belly solidified into a hard ball of dismay. 'Why not introduce Lord John to what has taken his attention.'

'Of course, sir.'

I looked away, fearing that he might read the rebellion in my mind, beckoning to the boy to follow me, trying not to hear the laughter and comment behind me as my espousal was celebrated. I was ashamed of the unexpected threat of tears as the chatter reached me.

'It is good that they get to know each other.'

'They will make an impressive pair.'

No, we would not. I towered over him by a good three hand spans.

But I dutifully led the Earl as instructed to where a parrot sat morosely on a perch in the window. Much like I felt. It was large and iridescently green with snapping black eyes and a beak to be wary of. It was never cowed by its soft imprisonment, and it came to me that I might learn a thing or two from this ill-tempered, beautiful bird. By the time we stood before it, my weak tears were a thing of the past. This was the platter placed before me and I must sup from it.

Utterly oblivious to the underlying currents in the chamber, and certainly to my thoughts, the boy became animated, circling the stand to which the bird was chained.

'What is it?'

'A popinjay. Have you not seen one before?'

But then I could not imagine the Countess of Norfolk allowing such a bird in her solar. A popinjay represented erotic love rather than the romantic or sentimental.

'Does it speak?' the Earl demanded.

'Sometimes.'

'What does it say?'

'*Benedicamus Domine*. And then it sneezes.'

'Why?'

'Because it is what Father Thomas, our priest, says. He tries to teach it better ways. And Father Thomas sneezes a lot.'

The boy perused the bird. 'Is it an ill-mannered creature then?'

'They say popinjays are excessively lecherous.'

Which meant nothing to the spritely Earl. 'Can I teach him to speak?'

'If you wish.'

He reached out a bold hand to run his fingers along the feathers of the bird's back.

'It bites,' I warned.

'It won't bite me!'

It did.

'God's Blood!' The boy sucked his afflicted knuckle while I could not help but laugh, wondering where he had picked up the phrase that sat so quaintly with his immaturity.

'I warned you.'

'It doesn't matter.' Undeterred, he tried again and managed to stroke the bird without harm. 'What's its name?'

'Pierre.'

'Why?'

'All our parrots have been called Pierre.'

'Is it male? Or female?'

'I don't know.'

'Can I have one?'

'If you wish.'

'I do. And it will wear a gold collar.'

It made me laugh again, perhaps with a touch of hysteria. The bird was more to his taste than I was. He was certainly much taken with it.

'I will buy you one.'

'Will you? When you are my wife?'

'Yes.' My heart thudded. By this time tomorrow I would be Countess of Pembroke.

'Can I call you Elizabeth?'

'Yes.'

'And I am John.' His gaze returned to the bird that proceeded to bite at its claws. 'Perhaps I will call my parrot Elizabeth. If it is female of course.'

What a child he was. Eyes as brown as the chestnut fruit, his bowl of hair rich and curling of a similar hue, he was incongruously charming.

'Do you wish to wed me?' I asked, willing to be intrigued by his reply. I had no idea what an eight-year-old child would think of marriage.

The boy thought about it while observing the parrot's attentions to its toes.

'I suppose so.' His smile, directed at me, was thoroughly ingenuous. 'You are very pretty. And a parrot as a marriage gift would be perfect. Or a falcon. Or even a hound. I would really like a hound. A white one, a hunting dog, if you could. Did you know that if you carry a black dog's tooth in your palm, then dogs will not bark at you?'

'No. I did not know that.' So my affianced husband was an expert in the magical properties of animals.

'It's true, so they say. I've not tried it for myself.' He tilted his head, on an afterthought. 'What should I give you for a wedding gift, Madam Elizabeth?'

I had no idea.

As the welcome audience drew to a rapid close and our guests were shown to their accommodations, my father beckoned me, and in that brief moment when we were alone and out of earshot, I let my frustrations escape even though I knew I should not. Even though I knew in my heart that it would have no effect, my worries poured out in a low-voiced torrent.

'How can I wed a child? How can I talk to this boy? I would have a husband who shares my love of the old tales, of poetry and song. I would have a husband who can dance with me, who can talk to me about the royal court, about the King and the foreign ambassadors who visit, of the distant countries they come from. You have given me a callow boy. I beg of you, sir. Change your mind and find me a man of talent and skill and learning. You found such a woman in my mother. Would you not allow me the same blessing in my marriage? I beg of you…'

I expected anger in my father's face as I questioned his judgement, but there was none, rather an understanding, and his implacable reply was gentle enough.

'It cannot be, Elizabeth. You must accept what cannot be changed.'

I bowed my head. 'All he can talk about is parrots and hunting dogs!' I heard the timbre of my voice rise a little and strove to harness my dismay. 'He has given me a list of things he would like as a wedding gift. They are all furred and feathered.'

'He will make a good husband. He will grow. It may be that John Hastings will become everything you hope for in a husband.'

The ghost of a smile in my father's lips dried my complaint, and made me feel unworthy. It was clear that he would not listen.

'Yes, my lord,' I said.

Of course the Earl of Pembroke would grow. But not soon enough for me.

★

When I could, I fled to my bedchamber, where my command over any vitriolic outburst vanished like mist before the morning sun in June.

'I won't do it! How can my father ask me to wed a child?'

I wiped away tears of fury and despair with my sleeve, regardless of the superlative quality of the fur, snatching my hands away when Dame Katherine tried to take hold of them. I was not in the mood to be consoled, but equally my governess was in no mood to be thwarted, seizing my wrists and dragging me to sit beside her on my bed. I had fled to my own room so there was no need for me to put on a brave face before my royal aunts and uncles.

'Make him change his mind,' I demanded. 'He will do it, if you ask him.'

'No, he will not.' She was adamant. 'The Duke is decided. It is an important marriage.'

'If it is so important, why not my sister? Why not Philippa? She is the elder. Why not her?'

'Your father looks for a marriage with a European power. To bind an alliance against Castile. That was always his planning.'

I heard the sympathy in her voice and resisted it. I had had enough of pity for one day.

'So I am to be sacrificed to a child.'

'It is not the first time a daughter of an aristocratic house has been wed to a youth not yet considered a man.'

'A man? His is barely out of his mother's jurisdiction.'

'Nonsense! It is time you accepted the inevitable. Listen to me and I will tell you why this is of such importance.'

I huffed disparagingly. 'I expect he has land.'

'Of course. The Earl will be influential. He is extraordinarily well connected, and his estates extensive. His grandmother is the Countess of Norfolk. They are linked with the Earl of Warwick. Their allegiance is vital to challenge the voices raised against the Duke. Before God, there are enough who resent his influence over the King and would do all they could to undermine his position. Your father needs powerful allies. This boy may be a child in your eyes, but he is heir to the whole Pembroke inheritance, with royal blood from Edward the First through his grandmother the Countess. It is indeed an excellent match, and will make you Countess of Pembroke. Do you understand?'

'Yes. Of course I understand. It may all be as you say.' I looked at her candidly. 'But how can he be my husband in

more than name? How long before I am a wife?' Passion
beat heavily in my blood, and I frowned. I needed to explain
my heightened humours, but how could I with any degree
of delicacy?

'You are of an age to be a wife now.' Dame Katherine, it
seemed, understood perfectly. 'You must be patient. In the
eyes of the church, John Hastings will be your husband, but
physically, there will be no intimacy between you. You will
live apart to all intents and purposes until John is of an age
to be the husband who takes you to his bed.'

'And when will that be?'

Did I not already know the answer?

'When he is sixteen years old. Perhaps fifteen if he comes
to early maturity.'

'Another seven years at best. I will be twenty-four by
then. It will be like being a widow. Or a nun.'

'It will not be so very bad. The years will pass.'

'And my hair will become silver while I wait to know a
man's touch. While I wait for a man who is not one of my
family to kiss me with more than affection.' My dissatisfac-
tion with John Hastings was not based merely on my inabil-
ity to hold an informed conversation with him.

'Is it so important to you?'

'Yes!' I smacked my hands together, a sharp explosion in
the quiet room. 'How can you ask such a question of me,
born of the passion between the Duke and Blanche?' All
notions of delicacy had vanished. 'When the…the intimacy
between a man and a woman has been important enough
to drive you back to my father's bed even when you were
labelled whore and witch by the monk Walsingham. You

could not live without a man's touch. Nor, I think, can I!'

Dame Katherine paled, and I, hearing the enormity of what I had said, flushed from the embroidered border of my neckline to the roots of my hair.

'We will pretend that you did not say that, Elizabeth.'

'But it is true. Physical intimacy has branded you with sin. Yet my father would condemn me to live without it until I lose my youth.'

Which drove Dame Katherine to stand and put distance and a distinct chill between us. To ward it off, I snatched up my lute and plucked unmusically at the strings.

'Stop that!' my governess said, so that I cast the instrument aside. 'That is not the way for you. You will not consider it, speak of it. You will honour the memory of your mother and your royal forebears. What would your grandmother Queen Philippa say if she were alive to hear you now?'

Contrition was beyond me. 'I know not. I barely remember her.'

'Then I will tell you what she would say,' returning to clasp my wrists, imprisoning me as she belaboured me with everything I knew by heart about duty and compliance, courtesy and the role of Plantagenet daughters. Halfway through, contrition had reared its uncomfortable head. I might not always find it easy to admit fault, but Dame Katherine left me in no doubt of my sins of pride and selfwill.

'Forgive me.' At the end. 'I regret what I said.'

'I will forgive you. I always forgive you, Elizabeth.' Yet

still she was stern. 'Because as your erstwhile governess it is my role to forgive you. You might consider that your behaviour reflects on me as much as it paints you in colours of intolerance and sin. It is your duty to make your father proud of you. You will have your own household. You should know that an annual sum of one hundred pounds has been granted for its maintenance.'

'Because I will be Countess of Pembroke.'

My erstwhile governess nodded, releasing my wrists at last.

'It is your father's will, Elizabeth. It will be a good marriage. And when you are twenty-five years old, John will be sixteen, far closer to being an excellent knight and husband. Handsome enough too, I warrant.'

Another eight years to wait. I could not contemplate it.

'He admired the parrot more than he admired me,' I stated, furious with the bitterness I could not hide.

'Then you will have to work hard to change that.'

I stalked to the window to look out at the spread of Lancaster acres, for it was as if the walls of my chamber had suddenly closed in on me, curtailing my freedom, as this marriage would imprison me within an unpalatable situation. Would it matter whether the Earl of Pembroke liked me or not? Since our marriage would be in name only for almost a decade, I could not see the purpose in cultivating the affection of a child. Then another thought struck home and I stopped.

'Why did you not tell me earlier? Why did you not tell me before you actually had to?'

'Because I knew that you would not like it,' she replied without pause.

'You thought I would make a fuss.'

'Yes.'

I did not like the implied criticism. 'Would you have told Philippa? If the Earl had come for her?'

'Yes. Because she would have the charity in her to make things easy for the boy.'

'And I wouldn't.'

Dame Katherine's raised brows said it all. I did not like the implication. Was I selfish, thoughtless, mindless of the feelings of those around me? I had not thought so.

At that moment I was too cross to give my failings even a passing thought.

★

On the morning of the following day I stood next to John Hastings before the altar in the chapel at Kenilworth. Not for us a wedding at the church door. My father had wed Blanche beneath a gilded canopy held by four lords at Reading Abbey, in the presence of the old King Edward the Third. No such ostentatious splendour for me and the child Earl, but both of us, and the chapel, were dressed for high ceremonial. As were the guests who crowded in to witness our joining in this auspicious union. The robes of my father's chaplain were spectacular with red silk and gold thread. The banners of Lancaster and Pembroke all but covered the warm hue of the stonework.

My hand, resting lightly in the boy's, where my father had placed it as a sign that he was giving me into the young Earl's keeping, was ice cold: the boy's was unpleasantly warm and clammy. I glanced at my betrothed, ridiculously elegant in gleaming silk tunic, knowing that he wished himself anywhere but in the chapel. Yet I could not fault his rigid stance, his solemn concentration.

I tried to concentrate on the sacred words but failed miserably, conscious only of the child at my side, and disturbed that Dame Katherine should find my behaviour a cause for concern. Was I always as selfish, as careless of the feelings of others, as she perceived? Assuredly I would prove her wrong today. My demeanour would be faultless. I looked across and smiled at the boy, receiving a beaming grin in return.

Yes, I would be kind to him.

The chaplain, austere with the weight of the burden on his frail shoulders, was frowning at me, reminding me that I had responses to make. And so I did, accepting this boy as my husband as the consecration was brought to an end, trying not to think how ridiculous we might appear together in spite of the outward magnificence of silk and satin and jewelled borders. John Hasting's head barely reached my elbow.

So it was done. I would never again, in public, wear my hair loose in virginal purity. The boy, with surprising dexterity, pushed a gold ring onto my finger. We kissed each other formally on one cheek and then the other. Then fleetingly on the lips. We were man and wife. I was Countess of Pembroke.

'Will I be allowed to go to the stables now?' my husband whispered as I bent to salute him.

'Soon,' I whispered back.

'How long is soon?'

I sighed a little as we joined hands and walked between our well-wishers, out of God's holy presence into the trials of real life.

★

We were kissed and patted, feted and feasted, which I tolerated far better than my lord who squirmed with embarrassment and, in the end, with surly boredom, face flushed and eyes stormy. Conducted to the place of honour at the high table, our steward presented the grace cup first to us. My father's carver carved the venison for us. The festive dishes were placed before us to taste and select before the throng stripped the table bare.

This should have been one of the happiest, most exhilarating days of my life. Instead I was torn between pleasure at my new status as a married, titled lady with the money to pay for a household of my own, and dismay that I had no knight to share it with me. I would have liked my husband to woo me, to show admiration for my person. To enjoy my company, whether to dance or sing or read the French tales of love. Of course he would go to war, win glory in tournaments, take his rightful place at court, but he would return to me. He would give me gifts and express a desire to spend time in my company. My husband too would be elegant and charming, well versed in the art of seduction with words and music, gracious and sophisticated.

At least he would have admired the dress that had been stitched for my marriage—for how long had my father known of this union with Pembroke? —with the symbols of Lancaster and Pembroke twining together along hem and the edges of my oversleeves. Such a magnificent heraldic achievement could not go unnoticed by the lord for whose new pre-eminence it was created.

John Hastings paid no heed.

'My lady! What is it that I am expected to do now?' the sibilants hissed *sotto voce*, the boy at my side rubbing the bridge of his nose with his finger, without grace or elegance, and looking hunted after our steward had bowed before him with yet another platter of aromatic meat for him to taste.

I was sure that he had been taught how to conduct himself, but he had not yet been sent to be a page in some noble household, and the heavy significance of the occasion robbed him of any immature confidence that might have been instilled in him by his lady mother. I tried not to sigh. It was not his fault.

'We eat first,' I explained. 'The feast is for us.'

'Good.' His eye brightened a little. 'I will have some of that…'

And, served by our steward, he tucked in to a dish of spiced peacock, spoon akimbo in his fist, as if he had not been fed for a se'enight. I was left to choose my own repast and converse with my uncle of Gloucester on my left, who subjected me to a rambling description of a run after an impressive stag and my uncle's ultimate success in bringing it down.

I made suitable noises of appreciation. The minstrels sang of love requited, which was patently ridiculous, but I enjoyed the words and the music. My lord ate through another platter that had caught his eye, of frytourys lumbard stuffed with plums, and then drew patterns in the fair cloth with his knife until his mother caught his eye and frowned at him.

The toasts were made, and our health was drunk once more.

Then came the dancing.

The disparity in our heights made even the simplest steps more complicated as we, the newly wedded couple, led the formal procession that wound around the dancing chamber.

Think of him as your brother. Imagine it is Henry. You've suffered his prancing attempts often enough.

So I did, relieved that my lord did not caper and skip as Henry was often tempted to do out of wanton mischief. We made, I decided, as seemly a performance as could be expected when the groom had to count the number of steps he took before he bowed and retraced the movement, counting again.

Holy Virgin!

No one laughed aloud. They would not dare, but I could not fail to see the smiles. It might be a political marriage made in the chambers of power, but I could detect pity and condescension as amused eyes slid from mine. I kept my own smile firmly in place as if it were the most enjoyable experience in the world. I had too much pride to bear loss of dignity well, but I had strength of will to hold it at bay.

Returning to our seats, the processing done, the musicians drawing breath and wiping their foreheads, I became aware of the boy's fierce regard.

'What?' I asked.

'Will you enjoy being wed to me, Elizabeth?' he asked,

surprising me, his eyes as bright as a hunting spaniel on the scent, and not at all shy.

'I have no idea,' I replied honestly, immediately regretful as his face fell. 'I suppose I will. Will you enjoy being wed to me?'

'Yes.' He beamed with open-hearted pleasure. 'I have decided. I will like it above all things.' My brows must have risen. 'Why wouldn't I?'

I shook my head, unable to see why a young boy was so vehement in his admiration for our married status when it would mean nothing to him for years to come.

'I will enjoy living here,' he announced.

Which surprised me even more.

'Do you not go home with your mother? Or grand-mother?'

'No. I am to live here. At Kenilworth.' His eyes glowed with fervour, his cheeks flushed from the cup of wine with which he had been allowed to toast me in good form. 'I am to learn to be a knight. I am to join Henry in my studies. I will keep my horse here and I can have as many hounds as I wish. I will learn to kill with my sword. And I will go hunt-ing. I would like a raptor of my own, as well as the parrot...'

As I smiled at his enthusiasms—for who could resist? — I had to acknowledge this new fact, that I would see him every day. Rather than live apart until he grew into adult-hood to become my husband in more than name, we would have to play husband and wife in all matters of day-to-day living. I had understood that I could dispense with his com-pany until at least he had the presence of a man. Living in the same household, we would rub shoulders daily. I wondered if his enthusiasms for all things with fur or feathers would pall on me.

'…and then I will have a whole stable full of horses,' he continued to inform me. 'As Earl of Pembroke it is my right. Do you know that I have been Earl since before I was three years old? I wish to take part in a tournament. Do you suppose they will let me?'

'I think you will have to wait a few years.'

'Well, I quite see that I must. I will be very busy, I expect. You won't mind if I don't come and see you every day, will you?'

'I think I can withstand the disappointment.'

'I will find time if you wish, of course. And will you call me Jonty, as my nurse does?'

He chattered on. How self-absorbed he was. It could be worse. He could have been loud and boorish, which he was not. But I was not sure that I liked the idea of having him under my feet like a pet dog.

'If I cannot yet fight in a tournament, will they let me have one of the brache puppies?'

I looked across the table to Dame Katherine for succour, but knew I could do that no longer. I was a married woman and must make my own decisions, even though my husband could not.

★

The feast and music reaching its apogee, with a flourish and a fanfare the Earl of Pembroke and I were led from the room with minstrels going before in procession, the guests following behind.

'Now where are we going?' the boy asked, his hand clutching mine. 'Can I go and see the brache bitch and puppies now?'

'No. We must go first to one of the bedchambers.'

His brow furrowed. 'It's too early to go to bed.'

'But today is special. We are to be blessed.'

And I prayed it would be soon over.

The bed was huge, its hangings intimidating in blue and silver, once again festive with Lancaster and Pembroke emblazoning. With no pretence that we would be man and wife in anything but name, the boy and I were helped to sit against the pillows, side by side with a vast expanse of embroidered coverlet between us and no disrobing. Not an inch of extra flesh was revealed as our chaplain approached, bearing his bowl of holy water, and proceeded to sprinkle it over us and the bed.

'We ask God's blessing on these two young people who represent the great families of England, Lancaster and Pembroke. We pray that they may grow in grace until they are of an age to be truly united in God's name.'

There was much more to the same effect until our garments and the bed were all sufficiently doused.

'Monseigneur…' The chaplain looked to my father for guidance. 'It is often considered necessary for the bridegroom to touch the bride's leg with his foot. Flesh against flesh, my lord. As a mark of what will be fulfilled by my lord the Earl when he reaches maturity.'

I imagined the scene. The boy being divested of his hose, my skirts being lifted to my knees to accommodate the ceremony. My fingers interwove and locked as I prayed that it need not be. And perhaps the Duke read the rigidity in my limbs.

'I think it will not be necessary. John and Elizabeth are here together. There is no evidence that they seek to escape each other's company.'

The guests who had crowded in to witness our enjoyment of our married state smiled and murmured. Everyone seemed to do nothing but smile.

'What do we do now?' the Earl asked.

'Nothing. Nothing at all,' my father replied. 'That will all be for the future.'

I did not know whether to laugh or weep.

We stepped down from the bed, on opposite sides. My husband was taken off to his accommodations by his mother, the dowager countess now, who saluted my cheeks and welcomed me as her daughter by law. I returned to my chamber, where Philippa awaited me with my women to help me disrobe.

Instead, Philippa waved the servants away and we stood and looked at each other.

'Do you know what my husband will be doing as soon as he has removed his wedding finery?' I asked.

She shook her head.

'He will be down in the mews because he wants a hawk of his own, or in the stables because he wants one of the brache's litter. He tells me that he will enjoy living at Kenilworth—did you know he was to stay here? —because he can wield a sword against Henry and take part in a tournament.'

Philippa smiled.

So did I, the muscles of my face aching.

'He—Jonty—says that he doesn't mind if he does not see me every day. He will be quite busy with his own affairs to turn him into the perfect knight.'

I began to laugh. So did Philippa, but without the hysterical edge that coloured mine.

'He says he will make an effort to come and see me, if I find that I miss him.'

We fell into each other's arms, some tears mixed in, but a release at last in the shared laughter.

'If it were you,' I asked at last, 'what would you do?'

'Treat him just like Henry, I suppose'.

Which was all good sense. Pure Philippa. And indeed what I had decided for myself.

'You mean pretend he isn't there when he is a nuisance, comfort him when he has fallen from his horse and slap his hands when he steals my sweetmeats.'

But Henry liked books and reading, he liked the poetry and songs of our minstrels, as did I. Jonty seemed to have nothing in his head but warfare and hunting.

'Something like that.' Philippa did not see my despair. 'You can't treat him like a husband.'

'No. Obedience and honour.' I wrinkled my nose.

'You can't ignore him, Elizabeth. He'll be living here under your nose.'

'How true.' My laughter had faded at last. 'Philippa—I wish you a better wedding night.'

She wrapped her arms around me for a moment, then began to remove the layers of silk and miniver until I stood once more in my shift, the jewels removed from my hair, standing as unadorned as might any young woman on any uneventful day of her life.

We did not talk any more of my marriage. What was there to say?

I gave my husband a magnificently illuminated book telling the magical tales of King Arthur and his knights, as well as a parrot of his own as wedding gifts. To my dismay, the book was pushed aside while Jonty pounced on the parrot with noisy delight. He called it Gilbert rather than Elizabeth, after his governor who had taught him his letters. I was not sorry.

★

'Does your husband not keep you company this morning, Elizabeth?'

Some would say it was a perfectly ordinary question to a new wife. If the husband in question were not eight years old. So some would say that perhaps there was amusement in the smooth tones.

I knew better. Isabella, Duchess of York, sister to Constanza, my father's Castilian wife, owned an abrasive spirit beneath her outward elegance, as well as an unexpectedly lascivious temperament. Constanza's ambition for restoration of the crown of Castile to her handsome head had been transmuted into a need for self-gratification in her younger sibling, who had come to England with her and promptly married my uncle of York. I was fascinated by the manner in which Isabella pleased herself and no one else, but I did not like her, nor did I think she liked me. Her expression might be blandly interested, but her eye was avid for detail as she made herself comfortable beside me in the solar as if with a cosy chat in mind.

'Learning to read and write I expect,' I replied lightly. 'His governor does not allow him to neglect these skills, even though his mind is in the tilt-yard.'

She nodded equably. 'How old will *you* be, dear Elizabeth, when he becomes a man at last?'

'Twenty-four years, at the last count.'

'Another seven years?' Isabella mused. 'How will you exist without a man between your sheets?'

Her presumption nettled me. Everyone might be aware of the situation, but did not talk about it. 'We are not all driven to excess, my lady.'

I observed her striking features, wondering how she would reply. Isabella had, by reputation, taken more than one lover since her arrival in England and her marriage to my royal uncle of York, but she remained coolly unperturbed, apart from the sting in reply.

'Of course not. I will offer up a novena for your patience.'

Because I did not wish to continue this conversation, I stood, curtsied, answering with a studied elegance that Dame Katherine would have praised. 'I am honoured, my lady, for your interest in my peace of mind.'

'To live as a nun is not to everyone's taste,' she continued, standing to walk with me. 'Nor is it entirely necessary. I thought you had more spirit, my dear.'

I would not be discomfited. 'Yes, I have spirit. I also have virtue as befits my rank, my lady.'

Isabella showed her sharp little teeth in a smile of great

charm. 'Tell me if virtue—excellent in itself—becomes too wearisome for you, won't you, dear Elizabeth.'

I angled my head, wondering how much she would confess of her own life. I had heard the rumours in astonishing detail from the women in our solar.

'I have so many excellent remedies against terminal boredom,' she added, touching my hand lightly with beautifully be-ringed fingers. 'You would enjoy them.'

'I will consider it, my lady.'

My nails dug into my palms as she walked away, leaving the solar to practice her skills on any man but her husband. How infuriating that her observations held so much truth. Waiting until I was twenty-four years to experience marital bliss gnawed at my sacred vows, for my youthful blood rioted and my desires were aflame. Would I dare what Dame Katherine had done, taking a lover to fill the cold bed of her widowhood? Or Duchess Isabella, so blatant, a scarlet woman beneath her fine gowns?

No, I decided, I would not, as the Duchess's laughter filled the antechamber where she had found someone to entertain her. I had too much pride for that. I would not put myself into Duchess Isabella's way of life. I would tolerate the boredom if I must and I would go to my marriage bed a virgin. Solemnised in the sight of God and every aristocratic family in the land, my marriage was sacrosanct. Sprinkled with holy water in our marital bed, even if we had exchanged nothing but a chaste kiss, Jonty and I were indivisible. To step along the thorny path of immorality was too painful, as my family well knew. Neither the life that Dame Katherine had chosen, nor the louche flirtations of

Duchess Isabelle outside the marriage bed was a choice for me.

Yet I could dream. What woman would not dream? And so I did, allowing my thoughts to stray pleasurably to another man, one who was the epitome of my chivalric dreams. A courtier, superbly well connected, with a handsome face and aristocratic birth, our paths had crossed on a multitude of occasions at Windsor and Westminster. A man with a smile that could light up a room. A man whose skill with sword and lance and polished wit outshone every other knight. This was the man I could desire in marriage, and my heart throbbed a little at the thought of what might have been.

Until harsh reality sank its teeth into my flesh. For this object of my admiration was also a man of grim reputation and high temper. My father would never have desired an alliance with such an adventurer whose irresponsible behaviour was thoroughly condemned.

'He is as riddled with ambition as an old cheese with maggots!' my father had censured, when the object of my admiration had paraded in peacock silks at my cousin Richard's coronation.

So my knight errant was consigned to moments of wistful imaginings, as he should be, for a Pembroke connection was my father's wish, and as part of the great plan to consolidate the House of Lancaster, I accepted it. This was my destiny. All I must do was exercise patience, living out the next handful of years until Jonty caught up with me in maturity and experience. He might even, in the spirit of the troubadours, offer a poem to the beauty of my hair.

'Could I clasp whom I adore
On the forest's leafy floor,'

Sang Hubert, the lovelorn minstrel who knelt at my feet, seducing me with images of more than courtly love.

'How I'd kiss her—Oh and more!
Dulcis amor!'

Turning my face away, wishing misty-eyed Hubert would take his songs and his sentiments and shut himself in the stables out of my hearing, I shivered. And not for Jonty's embrace on a forest floor. My tempestuous virginal dreams did not involve Jonty.

★

I tried. I really tried in those first days when the festivities continued and the new Earl and Countess of Pembroke were under scrutiny. Taking Dame Katherine's advice to heart, I tried, like a good wife, to seduce Jonty into liking me more than he liked the parrot. I hunted with him. I rode out with a hawk on my fist, a pastime I enjoyed for its own merit. I played games, trying not to beat him too often at Fox and Geese. But he was just a boy and would rather spend his boisterous time and energy with Henry or the other lads of high blood who came to learn their knightly skills under my father's aegis.

'What do you expect?' Philippa observed as, lingering on the steps leading up to the new range of family apartments, we watched him escape his mother's clutches and race across the courtyard towards the bellows and clashes of yet another bout of practice warfare.

'I expect nothing more or less. He is a boy.' I grimaced a

little. 'It is his mother and grandmother who expect me to dance attendance on him more than I see fit. I can feel their eyes on me. Is it not enough that we sit together at dinner? That we kneel together to hear Mass? If I have to discuss the respective merits of birds of prey one more time, I'll…'

My words dried as Jonty came to a halt under the archway, spun on his heel and seeing us as the only audience, waved furiously in our direction, both arms above his head.

'My lady,' he shouted in a piercing treble.

'My lord,' I replied at a lesser volume.

Jonty bowed. I curtsied. He bowed again, and I saw the compact, graceful young man he would one day become. Then:

'Did you see me, Elizabeth? Did you see?' His excitement echoed from the stonework.

I descended and walked towards him, reluctant to continue the conversation at shouting pitch, which he was quite likely to do, scowling at Philippa to stop her laughing. What had he been doing today that I had not seen? In the tilt-yard probably. Practising archery or swordplay? I made a guess, based on his sweat-streaked face and scuffed clothing. His hair resembled nothing so much as a rat's nest.

'Indeed I did see you.' Now I was within speaking distance. 'You rode at the quintain as if you were born in the saddle.'

'The Master at Arms says I'll be a knight in about twenty years.'

He did not see the irony of it yet.

'But that seems a very long time to wait…'

Or perhaps he did.

'Will you come and watch me, Elizabeth? If I try every day it may not take me twenty years.'

I did and applauded his valiant efforts. Henry, who had come to stand at my side, swiftly vanished in the direction of the mews when Jonty dismounted at last and bore down on us. Even Henry grew weary of Jonty's exuberance.

'I'd run for it if I were you. His tongue is like a bell-clapper.'

It was indeed like owning a pet dog, I decided. I could not dislike him. He was lively and cheerful with the ability to chatter endlessly when the mood took him. His manners were impeccable with an inbred courtesy that I could not fault.

But he was no husband.

Being Countess of Pembroke palled when I had no knight to squire me or write verses to my beauty. Jonty was brave and bold but quickly proved to have no interest in poetry and possessed the singing voice of a corn-crake. Although he counted his steps less obviously when we danced, it was obvious that he would rather be in the saddle.

So, as it must be, when his family returned to their far-flung castles, I left Jonty to his own devices and returned to the pattern of my old life. A wife but not a wife. Countess of Pembroke, yet no different from Elizabeth of Lancaster, except that my carefree adolescence had been stripped away in that exchange of vows and sprinkling of holy water. I was part of the grand order of alliance and dynastic marriage.

But when I received an invitation to spend time at

Richard's court, I lost no time in ordering my coffers to be packed. While waiting for her husband to become a man, the Countess of Pembroke would shine in her new setting.

Chapter Two

January 1382, Westminster

In these days after the Great Rising had been laid to rest, there was a glitter about the King. Richard: no longer the child who wailed when Henry teased him, or when we, as children, refused to allow him the respect he considered his due. He had been a boy easy to tease. Now there was a bright, hard brilliance that I did not recall, almost febrile. The days when he was no more than a terrified youth before he rode off to face to the rebels and quell the revolt at Mile End were long gone, even though it was a mere matter of months. I curtsied low before him and his new wife.

Anne. A foreign princess, come all the way from Bohemia, with an extreme taste in Bohemian head-dresses. This was the most extravagant yet, its wired extremities almost wider than her hips, its veiling reminiscent of bed-curtains.

'My Lady of Pembroke,' Richard, seated on a throne draped in gold cloth, purred in greeting.

'Sire.' I rose from my obeisance, our eyes fortunately on a level since Richard had had the forethought to have the thrones placed on a low dais. He would not have approved of my superior height, for I had my father's inches. Richard, to his chagrin, was not quite full-grown at fifteen years in spite of his autocratic air.

'Allow me to make you known to my new wife, Queen Anne.' He turned to the lady at his side. 'This is my cousin Elizabeth of Lancaster, Countess of Pembroke.' His eyes glinted with heady delight in the candlelight. 'She and her family are dear to me.'

So formal from a boy I had known since his infancy, a boy I recalled clinging to my skirts, demanding that I allow him to fly my new merlin when it was quite clear that she was still in heavy moult, but I followed the desired ceremony as was his wish. Richard was recently seduced by ceremonial and grandeur. All because he had been given the Crown of England at so young an age, Henry frequently observed, interlarded with colourful epithets. Being the King of England when he was barely breeched had given him a damned superior attitude that he had yet to earn. Henry was more interested in tournaments than ceremony and tended to sneer when Richard wasn't looking—and sometimes even when he was, but it was no longer wise to do so now. Richard was beginning to flex his regal muscles.

So I curtsied again, head bent as was seemly, to Queen Anne.

'My lady. I am honoured,' I murmured.

Queen Anne smiled with a knowing acceptance of this piece of foolery. A year older than Richard, she looked to be little more than a child, a tiny scrap of humanity, but with a sharp eye and a tendency to laugh at the ridiculous. She also had a will of iron beneath her formal robes. There was nothing of a child in Queen Anne despite her lack of presence. Which pleased me.

'We are most pleased to welcome you, Madam Elizabeth,' she said graciously, indicating with a curl of her fingers that I should rise.

Richard stepped down at last, to salute me formally on each cheek. 'I know that you will be a good friend to my wife, Cousin.'

'I will be honoured, Sire.' I tried successfully not to laugh. How remarkably pompous he sounded for a lad whom I had rescued from the carp pond at Kenilworth where Henry had pushed him.

'And be pleased to give her advice until she becomes familiar with English ways,' he added.

And as I caught Queen Anne's eye, we laughed. The whole introduction had been unnecessary. Richard, with a flash of eye between us, froze.

'We already know each other very well, Richard,' the Queen explained gently, as she came to stand with him, a hand on his arm.

'We have already discussed fashion, horseflesh and men and what to wear for the tournament tomorrow,' I added, and took a risk, but a small one. 'And when did you last address me as my lady or even cousin?'

Richard thought about this, I could see the workings of

his mind behind his stare, tension hard in his spare shoulders. Encased in cloth of gold and enough ermine to coat four-score of the little creatures, he looked like one of our grand-father's knights got up in frivolous costume for a Twelfth Night mummers' performance. Pride held him rigid, until he took a step back onto the dais, so I must look up into his face.

'Elizabeth will be my friend,' Queen Anne murmured. 'As she is yours.'

'Of course she will. Do we not order it?'

'Richard! You cannot treat her like a diplomat from Cathay. You have known her all your life! She will be my friend and to me she will be Elizabeth, even if you continue to address her as Countess. And how foolish that will sound. Now greet her properly, my dear husband.'

And when Anne stepped up to kiss Richard's cheek, and laughed openly at him, so did he smile and all the tension was broken.

'Welcome, Elizabeth,' he said gruffly.

'I am so happy for you, Richard.'

And we were restored to a close-knit family group.

The days after the fright of the attack on the Tower had not been easy for any of us, but now all was smoothed over. A new year and new beginnings with this foreign bride. Leaving my husband to continue his growing up at Kenil-worth, I had come with Henry to Richard's marriage cel-ebrations. How it pleased me, this new delight in outward appearances, in feasts and dancing and ceremonial. And as close family to the King, Henry and I had been given the honour to receive the new Queen into London in the cold of days of January. My father, too, was restored to grace, escorting her from Dover to London. The dire lash of Walsingham's tongue against the Duke who had brought all the evils of defeat and rebellion tumbling down onto England's head had been obliterated by Richard's acceptance of the family closest to him.

Not that I was without complaint. It was not in my nature to be content. How could I be so, for here we were, celebrating a potentially happy marriage, which I did not have, a marriage in more than name and promises for the next decade. Despite the remarkable headdress she was wearing, surely hot and cumbersome, Richard was beaming at the new Queen as if he were already in love with her, while Anne, undoubtedly pretty, knew how to manage Richard's strange humours.

Jonty continued to be more enamoured of his horse, his tiercel, his new hauberk since he was growing like a spring shoot, and even a pair of shoes with riskily extreme toes that caused him some loss of dignity, than he was of me.

'We will talk after supper,' the Queen said, a gleam in her eye. 'Come to my room, Elizabeth, and see what I will wear tomorrow, when I am Queen of the Lists.' She tugged on Richard's arm. 'I think it would be an excellent idea if you choose Elizabeth to step into my shoes for the second day. She is *my* cousin now, is she not?'

'I think I will do whatever pleases you on our marriage day.'

'Then it is decided.'

Richard took his wife's hand, regarding her as if she were some precious object that he had acquired and must keep safe from harm or disappointment. 'We must speak with my uncles who are waiting to greet you.' Then to me, as the musicians tuned their instruments, looking over my shoulder to whomever it was who had approached: 'I'll leave you in the care of my brother. John, come and entertain Elizabeth. And if you don't wish to talk to her, you can always dance. I'll guarantee she'll not tread on your toes.' And to me, with a strange slide from ceremony to rude familiar: 'My brother has a reputation for entertaining beautiful women. But don't believe all he says…'

With a particularly un-regal smirk, Richard led Queen Anne to the little knot of Plantagenet uncles of Lancaster, York and Gloucester, who stood in an enclave, deep in discussion. This marriage was not popular with everyone. Anne had proved to be an expensive bride, with no personal dower worth mentioning and few diplomatic benefits for England.

Meanwhile a soft laugh reached me, stilled me. Slowly, I turned, knowing who I would find. Here, filling my vision, was my father's old cheese, riddled with maggots. A less appropriate comment I could not envisage for this courtier, resplendent in court silks heavy with gold stitching, impeccably presented from his well-shaped hair to his extravagantly long-toed shoes. Every sense in my body leapt into softly humming life, like clever fingers strumming lightly across the strings of a lute.

Sir John Holland, illustrious half-brother to King Richard, with whom he shared a mother in the dramatic form of Princess Joan, once the Fair Maid of Kent. He had made a reputation for the charm of his smile, for the wit and sparkle of his conversation, for his legendary temper, as well as for his unquestionably handsome face. Some men were wary of him, for he made much of the value of his royal connections, employing a smooth arrogance. He was ambitious for power, but that was no deterrent in my eye. As half-brother to King Richard, why should he not wield authority at the King's side?

But that was not all. He was thirty years old, with an impossibly seductive glamour. Even to me, he had a court gloss that intrigued me. When he smiled his face lit with a wild lustre, and I sighed with youthful longing, for this brilliance was irresistible. The last time I spent any length of time in the company of Sir John Holland, he had been wielding a blood-stained sword, while I had been shivering with terror, gripping his arms as if I were a child in the midst of a nightmare and he could shield me from the dark torments. Now the situation was very different. Sir John bowed. I curtsied. How superlatively decorous we were, as I surveyed him and he surveyed me. I could not read the mind behind those remarkable features, but as I acknowledged the intensity of his gaze that took in every detail of my apparel, memory came flooding back.

It had been in the previous year, when what we had come to call the Great Rising had erupted, drenching us all in fear. Peasants' mobs from Kent and Essex, vociferous in their complaints, had turned their ire on my father as royal counsellor and the instrument of all their woes, and since he was on a diplomatic mission to Scotland they vented their wrath on all connected with Lancaster. My brother Henry had been dispatched to the Tower of London to take refuge with Richard's court, newly come from Windsor, and I accompanied him, anticipating safety behind the impregnable walls until my father could return with an army to rescue us.

But then all unimaginable horrors overtook us when the garrison opened the gates of the Tower to the rebels fuelled with blood-lust. Brutal violence and fire and death descended on us, creating the nightmare that troubled me long after. Hopelessly manhandled, pushed and dragged, Henry fought back but I was beside myself with speechless terror. Were we destined to join the Archbishop and royal Treasurer as well as my father's physician on Tower Hill for summary execution?

And then in the hot centre of my fear, a new hand closed on my arm, hard and remorseless. I wrenched away, but it held tight.

'Quietly!' a voice said in my ear.

'I'll not die quietly!' I retorted, speech fast returning, as defiant as my brother, only then realising that Henry and I had been carefully separated from the rest of the prisoners.

'Be silent!' The same voice. The grip on my arm tightened even further. 'If you draw attention, we're lost.'

I whirled round, fury taking control in my mind, in my heart. 'Take your filthy hands off me. I'm meat for no lawless rabble.'

'They are filthy. But they are at your service, if you've the sense to accept it! Be still, girl!' my captor snapped back.

And I saw that I knew him, and that we were surrounded by a small body of soldiers. My furious response died on my lips as he began to issue orders to his men.

'Here, Ferrour! Take him!' he ordered. 'Hide him if you must. But keep him safe. At all costs.' And Henry was snatched up and pushed into the arms of one of the soldiers who nodded and dragged him away.

'Henry!' I called, not understanding, now beyond fear. 'In God's name…!'

The hand on my arm shook me into obedience. 'We must get the boy out of here or he'll surely die. As Lancaster's heir, this rabble will execute first and ask questions later.'

But I cried out, unable to take in what was happening. The horror of the past minutes had robbed me of all sense. 'He is my brother. I can't let him go.'

'You must. Listen to me, Elizabeth.' I tensed as his demand cut through my panic. He knew my name… 'Elizabeth.' An attempt to soften his voice. 'Stop shrieking in my ear. And listen…'

'Yes,' I said, but without clear thought. 'I don't know what to do.'

'It's me, Elizabeth. John Holland. Look at me. You know me. Henry will be safe. Now we have to get you out of here. This is what you do. You go with these men…'

To my astonishment, in the midst of all the violence and squalor around us, he grabbed at my hand, lifting it briskly to his lips in a beautifully punctilious salutation as if I were some court lady, not the bedraggled figure I knew myself to be. My gaze snapped to his, and for the moment it took to draw a breath, our eyes held, before his moved slowly over me, from my head to my feet. I could sense him taking in my ruined skirts, my hair tumbled down my back, then as his gaze focused, he seized my hand and lifted my arm.

'Is it your blood?'

I looked with surprise as he pushed back my sleeve, where it had been wrenched apart, to reveal a short but deep scratch above my wrist. I had not been aware, and the blood had now dried. I had not even felt it in the heat of the moment.

Abruptly he allowed me to go free.

'Get one of my mother's women to tend it for you. It would be a tragedy if you were scarred. Now go. And fast, or I'll use the flat of my sword to encourage you.'

I fled with my escort, to be thrust ignominiously into Princess Joan's barge, the impression of his kiss still viable against my skin. My first meeting of any tangible quality with John Holland. He had undoubtedly saved me from violent, terrible death.

He had done more than that.

This man's reputation was not merely one of military prowess, for Sir John had a name for attacking the defences of beautiful women, and with great success. His striking features won him the laurels, and not all on the battlefield or at the tournament. There was one particular rumour of a torrid affair that set the court about its ears. He had no reticence in casting his net as high as he liked when persuading a lovely woman to his bed.

Yet this did not stop him from being the knight whose vivid, volatile features I could summon into my mind as accurately as I could see my own in my looking glass, the dark-haired man who invaded my thoughts and my dreams.

★

What would it be like, I pondered, if he would see me as a woman rather than a child? What would it be like to dance with such a man, our bodies moving in unison or counterpoint? What would it be like to flirt, to spar verbally, discovering some understanding that would touch both heart and mind? To converse about something of more consequence than a hunting hound? Even now, it might be my avowed intention to remain a virgin bride until Jonty was ready to put that to rights, rather than a boy rolling in the dust in a wrestling match with his peers, but I thought I would enjoy the company and esteem of a knight who was a man, and talented withal.

And here he was, bowing with extravagant grace, and with a gallant turn of his wrist inviting me to join him as if he had no recall of me in an extremity of pure terror, of which I was not proud.

'Will you dance, my lady?'

I loved dancing. Being adept at every complicated step and simple procession it was on my lips to leap at the opportunity, for this was the *carole* that I particularly enjoyed. Then I decided that I really had no wish to dance, or not yet, knowing full well how impossible it was to hold a conversation when one's partner was hopping at some distance. Here was a man who stirred my blood. Here was a man I wished to talk with.

A man I wished to impress?

But of course, I admitted as into my mind came the image

of how he had seen me last. Frightened, blood-smeared and filthy. I wanted him to see me as I was now: finely clad, in command of my senses and my conversation, adept in the fine art of courtly love. I had been woefully ignorant, but five months at court had done much for my education. Recalling his final flamboyant gesture of a courtly kiss, I wanted to see if it had been a mere passing gesture in the enhanced emotions of the moment. Or perhaps John Holland might be persuaded to repeat the experience.

Despite my eagerness, however, I would take utmost care. There would be no scandal attached to my blood and proud name. I knew all about his reputation, more now since I had gossiped during the wedding celebrations. I was not the only woman to have an interest in John Holland—even now eyes were following his every move—but I determined to hide it better than some.

'Well?' he asked, brows flattening into a black bar when I hesitated far too long for polite refusal. 'I didn't think my invitation to dance would call for such deep contemplation. Unless you have no energy for it, you being so advanced in years.' His face remained grave. 'Or perhaps you have taken a dislike of me, in the manner of any capricious woman.'

'No, Sir John, not being capricious I have not taken you in dislike,' I replied promptly now, 'although I might if you frown at me.' Knowing full well that he was mocking me, I placed my fingers on his arm, walking with him as if I would allow him to lead me into the newly forming circle. 'Is it possible for you to dance in those?' I gestured to his hazardous footwear.

'Assuredly, lady. If you can manage the bolt of cloth in

that ostentatious garment you're wearing without tripping over it.'

I smiled pityingly, for who was he to point the finger? Used as I was to brother Henry's taste in ostentation—was he not even now enveloped in gold damask and gold lions? —here beside me was lavish resplendence. John Holland's formal calf-length houppelande, dagged and heavily trimmed with silk at hem and neck, the blood-red of its hue not a colour that flattered many, swirled and fell into heavy folds. As he moved the burden of expensive perfume—something foreign and costly such as the heady note of ambergris, I thought—surprised me, teasing at my senses. It would be no easy task for him to caper with dexterity, but I was in no doubt that he could. Determined to give no sign of any appreciation of this vision who had sought my company, I replied with comparable solemnity.

'Then I fear that you must find another partner, Sir John. I find that I do not wish to dance after all.'

'Well, that's forthright enough.' He stopped. So did I, glancing up at him. It pleased me that he was taller. 'I'll stop frowning. What do you wish to do instead?' There was a gleam in his eye.

'I would like a cup of wine and somewhere to sit. I have been on my feet since I rose from my bed at dawn.'

'And were you alone in your bed, before you rose?' His thumb brushed over my knuckles.

So! I took a breath. 'Sir John?'

'Madam Countess?'

Since this was a level of familiarity even beyond my

improved experience, I felt hot blood rise in my cheeks, but I held his stare. 'Of course, alone.'

'Is your husband not present?' he asked, all gentle malice.

'He is here. He is in my father's retinue.' Jonty had come for the wedding, as was fitting.

John Holland showed his teeth in a smile. 'Poor Elizabeth!'

I knew his sly reference to my half-wed state. Enough of this, I thought. 'I would not be such a poor thing if you would find a cup of wine for me.'

'Your wish will be my command, my lady.'

He led me to one of the cushioned stools placed against the wall, far enough from the crowd to allow us a little privacy, where he bowed me to take my seat and disappeared in search of sustenance. I watched him go, without making it too obvious, my heart still beating harder than my sitting at a court reception would engender.

John Holland, I mused, was all I remembered him to be, and all I had recently discovered. A man of hidden depths, a bold companion, but probably a dangerous enemy. But ambition and ability in the tilting field was not what intrigued me. Apart from the sheer force of his presence whenever he entered a room, what fascinated me was that John Holland had been enveloped in rumour and scandal since the day of his birth. Or more accurately, the scandal that was of Princess Joan's making.

As we all knew the salacious details of it—how Philippa and I had enjoyed dissecting these early years of the Fair Maid of Kent's life! Princess Joan was first married when very young to Sir Thomas Holland, something of a clandestine event but certainly legal. But Sir Thomas went off on Crusade, leaving Joan behind to be forced—in her own words—into a second marriage with the Earl of Salisbury. When Sir Thomas returned, it was to discover his wife wed to the Earl in an undoubtedly bigamous union. And Sir Thomas, from some strange motivation, took up a position as steward in their household.

Such a delicious *ménage à trois*!

But Sir Thomas wanted his wife back, and got her when he appealed to the Pope that Joan had promised herself to him and shared his bed. Did Joan prefer Sir Thomas to the hapless Earl of Salisbury? Who was to know? She and Sir Thomas had five children together before Sir Thomas died, leaving Joan a widow and free to wed again to Prince Edward. It might have been against the wishes of King Edward and Queen Philippa, for Joan was no innocent virgin, but she had achieved her heart's desire, and here was her royal son Richard, wearing the crown.

And here, working his path through the crowd was John Holland, her youngest child by that first marriage, now a Knight of the Garter, thirty years old, darkly beautiful to my mind with none of the fairness of Richard. A man who was creating his own glamour, his own scandals. He was unlike any other man I knew.

I watched him make his way in leisurely fashion, a smile here, a comment there, a pause as some acquaintance exchanged an opinion or a jibe, an appropriate inclination of his head towards one of the dowagers. He had all the poise, all the courtly aplomb in the world, and, as the King's brother, no one would be unwise enough to rebuff him. When he finally approached me again, he smiled, and, unable to prevent myself, I discovered that I was smiling back.

You are playing with fire, a voice of common sense warned, disconcertingly in the tones of Dame Katherine who was no longer one of our number. After the debacle of the Great Rising, my father had dedicated himself to a life of sinless morality to achieve God's blessing on England.

But how pleasant to be a little singed, I replied, wishing that she were here. *What right have you to advise me on such matters?* As my father's mistress, dubbed a whore by Walsingham for leading my father into sin, I thought she had no right to be critical.

But she would not be put in her place. *Take care he does not burn you to cinders. Some men, as I know to my cost, are impossible to withstand.*

All I intended was to practice the arts of courtly love. And with so personable a man. I had no intention of being a burnt offering on the altar of John Holland's male pride.

So have many women said. Particularly, of late, the Duchess of…

I cut off the voice before it could say more, and then he was returned with loose-limbed grace, the perfect protagonist upon whom to polish my female skills. Was I lovestruck? Certainly not. Merely enjoying my first experiences under the power of a flattering tongue, spreading my wings in the company of a man of many talents.

I smiled at my sister who was watching me from across the chamber, brows arched. I knew that expression, and looked away.

'You look pleased to see me return,' John Holland observed. 'Did you think I would abandon you?'

'I am pleased. I am thirsty, and I knew you would not leave me desolate, Sir John. Did not our King command you to entertain me? Not even you would dare disobey him on this most auspicious of days.'

'Do you say?'

'Yes. Are you going to give me that cup of wine? You may as well be of use to me.' I managed a perfect air of abstraction.

'Which puts me in my place. Since you need to sit, I will sit with you.' He hooked a foot round a stool, pulled it close and sat.

Which suited me very well. I had the energy to dance through the night but with our previous meeting in mind I sipped, smiled my thanks, smoothing the folds of my oversleeves so they draped in elegant contours to the floor, wondering if he would remind me. There were some elements of it, such as my own appearance and demeanour, I would rather remain buried in the past. And so I would select a different direction for our conversation, and, if possible, puncture his self-possession a little.

'Have you been absent from court, sir?' I knew very well that he had.

'Yes. I have a new lordship in Gascony to oversee, as well as recent grants of estates in England. Did you not miss me?'

I was prepared for this. 'No, sir.' Inspecting the contents of my cup. 'I have been much occupied.'

'I see that you have put your time here at Westminster to excellent use.' I looked up. Of course he remembered.

How would it be possible for him to forget such a cataclysmic event that brought us all close to disaster? 'A marked improvement on the last time we met. I must commend you.' He raised his cup in a toast, which I returned, with insouciance.

'In what respect, sir?' I risked.

'In respect of the radiant Countess of Pembroke.' There was a challenge that glimmered in his eye. 'Dishevelled, terrified and tearful, as I recall, and undoubtedly sharp-tongued. Today you are become one of the most beautiful women in this tedious gathering.' I felt his appraisal, which, to my chagrin, brought colour to my cheeks, as did his fulsome compliment. 'You were less than presentable when I saw you last.'

'Can you blame me, Sir John? But I deny that I was tearful.' Did he need to remind me? I raised my chin a little, even as the beat of my heart lurched and I sought for a mature response to an event that still had the power to distress me. I had no intention of being seduced by clever accolades, but I would enjoy them.

'Perhaps I was mistaken.' He inclined his head graciously. 'You had been tossed into an impossible situation.'

'From which you rescued me,' I said, eyes cast once more demurely down to my wine cup, anticipation rife, sensing that this man was at his most dangerous when smoothly compliant.

'Despite your reluctance to be rescued.' An innocuous reply.

'I must thank you for your forbearance if I seemed less than amenable.'

'I have to say, Madam Elizabeth,' he responded promptly, 'that it is not only your appearance that has undergone a transformation. Today your tongue is touched with honey.'

I knew my eyes sparkled. I would not rise to that bait, like a salmon snatching at a mayfly, only to be dragged to land by an enterprising fisherman. Instead I cast my own bait on the choppy waters.

What an enjoyable conversation this was becoming.

'I am astonished,' I observed, 'that Richard agreed to receive you at court, Sir John, if what I hear is true.'

With alacrity the bait was snapped up. Would nothing disconcert him? 'Admirable! You have reverted to your acerbic mood, I note. And at my expense. Take care, Madam Elizabeth. Would you do battle with me?'

'Yes, when you avoid my question.'

'You did not ask a question. You made an observation. Which is patently untrue. My brother is always pleased to have me close.'

'Even with the recent scandal? Causing waves to unsettle the whole family?'

'I see no waves.' Straightening, he swept a wide gesture to encompass the chattering throng. Indeed there were none, everyone present intent on nothing but enjoyment, but I pursued my quarry, since he was proving to be a willing combatant.

'My father the Duke was most displeased.'

'Are you sure, Countess? The Duke has been nothing but grateful for my recent services in his expedition to besiege St Malo. Even if it was destined to failure.'

A fast lunge and parry. A rapid cut and thrust. How exhilarating it was to talk with a man in this fashion. Would I ever have such conversation with Jonty? I knew that I never would.

'As for waves...' I mused. 'Perhaps they are only invisible because the lady in question is not here to stir them into life.' I too looked around the vast chamber, feigning astonished interest at the absence of the woman in question. 'But I expect she will announce herself very soon, and then we will see...'

'Do you spend all your days listening to gossip?' he interrupted, those dark eyes wide with innocence, unless one looked too closely and was tempted to fall into their depths. Quickly I looked away, taking another sip of wine.

'Yes. What else is there for me to do? I fear your reputation has sunk you in the mire, Sir John.'

'You shouldn't believe all you hear, Madam Elizabeth.'

'Is it not true, then? The court has been awash with it.'

'I'll not tell you.'

'I see.' I looked at him through my lashes as once more I took a sip of wine. 'Are you already suffering remorse, perhaps? Intending to confess your sins and mend your ways?' I leaned a little towards him. 'You can tell me, you know. I can be most discreet.'

'When is a young woman ever discreet? And I don't believe I've ever suffered a moment's remorse in all my life.' He laughed again, a rich attractive sound that drew eyes. 'I'll not tell you my thoughts, because you're too young for such salacious gossip.'

'What would I not know? I am nineteen years old. And wed.'

'To a husband who does not share your bed. Thus making you a charmingly innocent virgin wife. And,' he added, with no warning at all, 'I would like nothing better than to rob you of that innocence.'

Which effectively silenced me. Even more when, before I could prevent it, he had snatched up my free hand in his and raised it to press his lips to my fingers. This was far more outspoken, more particular, than I had expected, but had I not goaded him? I had asked for this riposte. Casting a hasty glance over our courtly companions, it was a relief to see that his attentions were unobserved, but a ripple of awareness, and not a little fear, ran over my nape as my hand was not released.

'You must not, sir. Do you wish to make me the subject of similar gossip?'

Upon which John Holland's smile vanished like the sun behind a particularly virulent storm cloud, and he became broodingly brisk and businesslike, defying me to follow his moods.

'Don't worry, Countess. I've not impugned your honour. It's only a kiss between family. Your father would have my skin nailed to the flag-pole at Kenilworth if he thought I had shown you any disrespect, and I can't afford to antagonise Lancaster, can I? I'm in receipt of his livery. It was my mistake to single you out in such a manner. As for you, Cousin, if you are going to wield a weapon, you must do so against someone of your own weight. Otherwise you will be wounded.'

Although my face was afire, I could not prevent an arch response. 'I am no cousin of yours. There is no blood connection.'

'So you are not, Lady of Pembroke, but near enough. Accept this as a cousinly salute.'

And there was pressure of his mouth on my knuckles again, trivial enough but startling by the implied intimacy so that I stiffened, and he must have caught a sense of it.

'What is it? Have I seriously unsettled you? I had thought you to be more worldly wise, mistress. I was wrong. You must forgive me.'

The timbre of his voice was suddenly dry enough to warn me that he had abandoned his previous trifling, and lurking at the edge of his disclaimer was the undoubted provocation. *You can trust me or not, as you wish. I don't care.* Nor did he, but I would not allow him to discomfit me. I recovered fast to display condescension when he half rose to leave. I did not want him to go. Not yet, and assuredly not on his terms where he had presumed me to be naïve.

'I am not wounded. Did you think you drew blood?' I asked, tugging my hand free but replying with a show of serenity as I spread my arms wide. 'See. I am unharmed. The Earl of Pembroke does not share my bed until he is of age. It is no secret. And it is not in your power to rob me of my innocence.'

Settling back on the stool, he perused me, much like a well-fed hawk would watch a mouse in the long grass, undecided whether to make the effort to pounce or abandon it for more worthy prey. Something in my expression, or perhaps in my picking up on his outrageous threat, made him observe: 'I doubt the situation satisfies you, whatever you say. How old is he?'

'Jonty has reached his tenth year.'

He lifted a shoulder in a little shrug. 'So you have decided to wait to enjoy the pleasures of the bedchamber under the auspices of holy matrimony…'

This unnerved me all over again but I was improving in smart retaliation. 'Of course I will wait. I make no complaint. Now *you* it seems do not need a wife at all. Unless it's someone else's.'

'I see you have not been imbued with *politesse*, Madam Elizabeth.'

'My social graces are excellent, Sir John.'

'You have wit and charm, certainly.'

To my satisfaction, he had begun to smile again. 'Is that all, Sir John?'

'Are you perhaps fishing for compliments, Madam Elizabeth?'

'No, indeed. I have no need to do so. I receive many compliments.'

'I expect you do. How could you not with your illustrious parentage? Some of us are not so fortunate, and must work harder for it…' His mouth acquired a derisive twist, even a hint of temper, that caught my interest. Then, with smooth transition, so that I might have thought I imagined the whole: 'Do you stay at court long, madam?'

A superlatively rapid *volte face*. So he had no wish to stir the mud in that particular pond of his troubled parentage, but he had given me an insight I had not expected. I let it go for now, and followed his direction into calmer waters.

'Yes. That is, I hope so. And what of you?'

'My plans are fluid.'

'Perhaps our paths will cross again.'

'Would you wish them to?'

'I might.'

'It may be that I go to Ireland in August as the newly appointed Lord Lieutenant.'

'Oh'. It was not what I had hoped to hear, certainly.

'Would you miss me now, if I were absent from court?'

Oh, I had his measure. 'How would I? Do you fight tomorrow in the tournament?'

'I will if you will be there to watch me win against all comers.'

'Such self-deprecation, Sir John. I will be there to wager on your losing.'

'You would lose, so don't risk wagering that exceptional ring you are wearing. How could I resist displaying my skills before so critical an audience? If you lost that jewel I might feel compelled to buy you another.'

'I doubt you could afford one of this value. It was a gift from my father.' And I spread the fingers of my right hand so that the ruby glowed blood-red in its heart, as red as the tunic that flattered John Holland's colouring so perfectly.

'I would willingly spend all I have to make you smile at me. As I will fight to win your praises.'

I was flattered, of course, as he intended. Except that I knew he had no intention of spending all he had, and would participate in the tournament whether I was there or not. And would probably win.

'Perhaps you will ask me to dance again afterwards?' I suggested.

'I might.'

'And I might accept.'

'I doubt if you could refuse me.'

'I will have many offers.'

He stood and offered his hand to bring me to my feet.

'You will not refuse, Elizabeth, because you see the danger in accepting my offer. How could you resist the desire that sparkles through your blood even now? I can see it as clearly as if written on velum with a monkish pen.'

This time I was the one who frowned. Did I wish to acknowledge this uncannily accurate reading of my response to him? Again he had pushed ahead far too quickly and into unknown territory.

'I could resist,' I said. 'I have amazing willpower.'

'Then perhaps we will put it to the test.'

He bowed, took my empty cup, only to abandon it on the floor. Seizing my wrist, he turned back the edging of my oversleeve, and stopped, fingers stilled, assessing the immediate problem.

'I can get no further with this,' he remarked.

'And why would you wish to?'

The sleeve of my undergown was tightly buttoned almost to my knuckles.

'To see if your wrist was scarred by the rebel's knife.' The words were curt, the consonants bitten off. 'I regretted that.'

Uncertain of this brief emergence of irritation when it seemed unnecessary, I misunderstood. 'But it was not your fault, sir.'

He was not smiling, and his clasp was firmer than the occasion warranted. 'It should not have happened. I should have been there sooner to ensure your safety. Your brother was unharmed, but you suffered. You are too beautiful to carry any blemish. I would not have it so.'

And my heart tripped a little, because I thought, of all the words we had exchanged that day, his contrition was genuine, and he had phrased it so neatly with the artistry of any troubadour. But my flattering knight bowed abruptly, released me and turned to walk away as if he had received a royal summons that demanded urgent action.

'Sir John…' I called, disconcerted. 'There is no scar.'

He halted, and returned abruptly so that we were face to face.

'How could I forget you?' he asked, as if I had only just that minute asked him the question, as if it were the one thought uppermost in his mind that angered him beyond measure. 'I swear you are the most compelling woman I have ever met. I wish it were not so, but you have inveigled your way into my thoughts from that first day I noticed you.' Clearly he was not pleased with the prospect. 'Since then I have found it impossible to remove you. You're like a burr caught in a saddlecloth, lethal to horse and rider.'

'You bundled me into a barge with your mother,' I retaliated, recalling the occasion all too vividly. 'And that was after you told me to stop shrieking in your ear because it would draw attention to us. I don't think you realised how terrified I was…'

'Of course I did.'

I became haughty. 'You were lacking in compassion, sir.'

'My compassion, as you put it, was directed at getting you and your brother out of a situation that could have been certain death for all of us. What would you have had me do? Stay to bandy words of admiration and dalliance?' He made an economic gesture of acceptance. And then there was the slow smile as his breathing eased. 'Before God, I did admire you, Elizabeth. You were bold and brave and deliciously unforgettable. Never doubt it, you are a jewel of incomparable value. Am I not a connoisseur of women?' The smile became imbued with warm malice. 'Married or otherwise.'

Then he was striding off through the gathering, leaving me feeling alive and vibrant and vividly aware of my surroundings. I was as breathless as if I had been riding hard after the hunt. What a play of emotions in this mercurial royal brother, and how my own had responded to his. It seemed that I had won his regard and his admiration, as he surely had mine.

Did I enjoy flirting with danger?

There was no danger here, I asserted. Merely an exchange of opinion with an uncommonly quick-witted man. Not one of which my late lamented mother would have approved, but why not? He had taken my eye, appealing to my curiosity, and that exchange had been harmlessly teasing rather than dangerous. He had called me cousin. There was nothing here but the closeness of family.

Did I believe my simplistic dissection of our lively exchange, when every one of my senses had leaped and danced? If I did not, if I knew we had enjoyed far more than a courtly conversation over a cup of wine, I was not prepared to confess it, even to myself.

I made my way towards the group containing Philippa and Henry, turning over the content of the past minutes, discovering one thing to ponder. John Holland's sharp retreat from any discussion of his own parentage. The instability of his background was well known, even the sly accusations of illegitimacy, product of Princess Joan's disgracefully bigamous ownership of two husbands before her royal marriage. Was he sensitive to that? I did not think so, for it was generally agreed that there was no truth in it, and I suspected that Sir John was not sensitive to anything but his own desires. What was as clear as glass to me was that he had ambitions to make his own name, not simply as the King's brother. It was impossible not to recognise in him an appetite, a ruthlessness to savour every dish in the banquet and drink life dry. He might be aware of the shadows, perhaps resenting them, but would be inexorable in sweeping them aside if they stood in his path. Already he was acquiring land to match his enhanced status as a prestigious Knight of the Garter, at Richard's creation.

For the past ten minutes he had made me the object of his potent, exhilarating, undivided attention, and I had gloried in it.

'Flexing your talons?' Philippa observed, a critical observer who made no attempt to hide her dismay. 'As long as you don't get hurt.'

'I will not. Nor will I hurt others. And, before you level the accusation, dearest sister, I will certainly not harm Jonty.'

I could barely wait for the tournament to begin.

Chapter Three

Before such fanfare and panoply, the court was called upon to welcome Princess Joan herself, and what an appearance she made as a majestic plumed palanquin, complete with outriders, an army of servants and a half dozen pack animals, all deemed necessary for a lengthy stay, made its ponderous way into the inner courtyard where it lurched to a halt. It was not necessary to draw back the curtains for the occupant to be recognisable, or for her importance to be appreciated. Heraldic achievements aflutter and pinned to every minion's breast, here was Joan, Fair Maid of Kent, Dowager Princess of Wales, King's Mother.

The lady was handed out by two of her women, enabling her to stand and survey the hastily assembled welcoming party, irritation written in every line of her body. Positioned as I was behind a little knot of courtiers, I could barely see her short figure, only the wide padded role of the chaplet that concealed every lock of her hair and supported an all-enveloping veil, but I could hear her explosion of anger.

'God's Blood! Where is my son?'

Sensibly Richard had made himself available, with as many members of his court as he could muster when the Princess's proximity was announced. Now he emerged from the royal apartments, walking in stately fashion down the steps, only to be seized in the Princess's arms and dragged into a close embrace as if he were still a small boy, while I slid my way between shoulders and overlapping skirts until it was easy for me to see the strange pair they made in this reunion. Richard, young and angelically fair, had grown tall in recent months, over-reaching his mother who had become so stout that even climbing the steps at his side made her catch her breath. Once, before my birth in the reign of the old King, Joan had been acknowledged as the most beautiful woman in England, and led a scandal-ridden life that made the most of her undoubted charms. Now her broad features and less than svelte figure proclaimed a woman who was a shadow of that former beauty.

But her eyes, although they might be swathed in little mounds of flesh, were still keen and beautifully sharp, and the timbre of her voice was mellifluous even though it could cut like a knife. As it did.

'Holy Virgin! That journey was a nightmare from start to finish. The state of the roads between here and Wallingford is a disgrace, Richard. You must do something about it. And the riff-raff that use them. I have come to meet the bride. I should have been here yesterday.'

'I would have sent my own escort, Madam,' Richard said, not pleased at being taken to task.

'That would hardly shorten my journey.'

'You appear to have travelled in comfort,' Richard observed with an eye to the equipage being led away.

The Princess waved this irrelevance aside but her complaint ground to a halt as, noticing them in the crowd, she graciously extended her hand for her two sons by her first marriage to Thomas Holland, Earl of Kent, to kiss. Which I noticed they did with alacrity, yet much affection, even if they were now grown men and royal counsellors.

'Thomas…' she said. 'And John…'

'My wife is within,' Richard announced, intent on reclaiming his mother's attention.

'In a moment…'

The Princess's eye, still quartering the crowd like a huntsman searching out its prey, fell on me. Since she saw fit to snap her fingers in imperious command, I approached and curtsied again, wishing Philippa was with me. I might be Elizabeth of Lancaster but this lady, my aunt by marriage, was the King's Mother and of vast consequence. She was also a person of hasty temper and trenchant opinions. Besides, she had more affection for Philippa than she held for me.

'So you're here too, Elizabeth. Of course you are. And your father? Where's Constanza? Not that it matters. She'll do as she chooses—she always has. You'd better join my ladies. I have need of an intelligent woman about me.' She looked me over from head to foot with a surprising degree of speculation. 'Come with me. I need to regain my strength before I make the acquaintance of my new daughter. You can be of use.'

So I followed Princess Joan who walked without hesitation to the chambers usually allotted to her when she stayed at Westminster, her habitual accommodation and my own obedience presumed with royal hauteur. And that was the manner in which, for a short period of time, I became a member of Princess Joan's demanding household. An unnerving experience, all in all, as the lady, her colour high, dismissed her own women, piled her outer garments into my arms, instructed me to send for wine and food, then handed me a comb as she removed the complication of her hair-covering. And I complied. Princess Joan, not a woman blessed with tolerance, appeared to be in a mood of high volatility.

Eventually she was settled to her liking on a bank of pillows, eating sweetmeats and drinking honeyed wine to recover from her ordeal. Disposed on a low stool at her side, waiting for the moment when she would command me to comb her hair, I sighed at the third telling of the stresses of her travelling. Hearing me, the Princess stared, before directing her attention fully to my appearance.

'Fine feathers, my girl.'

I was no finer than the Princess, heated and opulent in a high necked robe with fur at neck and cuffs, the complex pattern of leaves and flowers rioting over her bulk so that she resembled a vast spring meadow.

'Yes, my lady.'

'And why not? Enjoy your youth while you may. It dies fast enough. And then there is nought to look forward to but old age when those around you ignore you.' Which I could not imagine for one moment had been the Princess's experience. Continuing to regard me, her chin tilted. 'Now tell me. Is your marriage to young Pembroke satisfactory?'

'Yes, my lady.' I might resent such peremptory questioning, but to answer briefly and politely would be circumspect and invoke no criticism.

'Not consummated yet, I take it.'

'No, my lady.'

'Is Pembroke here?'

'Yes, my lady.'

The Princess's stare sharpened. 'I've a word of advice for you. I trust you'll not use this occasion of merriment to cause gossip. He's very young and you're of an age to look for more than a boy can offer.'

I stiffened, hand clenching around the comb, at the unwarranted attack. 'My demeanour will be beyond criticism, my lady.'

'Good. Because beautiful young women always cause gossip, even when they are innocent of all charges. And don't look at me as if I had no knowledge of what goes on when the court is in flamboyant mood. I caused scandal enough in my youth. Although I was not always innocent…' She paused to sip the wine and dispatch another plum, chewing energetically. 'But listen to me, madam. I called you here because you are young and lovely and ripe for mischief. Don't deny it…' As I opened my mouth to do so. 'You must curb your passions. It would be dangerous for your father if any further scandal were to be attached to his name at this juncture. His position is too precarious. That monkish weasel Walsingham might be prepared to sing the Duke of Lancaster's praises again, but he still has more enemies than is healthy. It is essential that you remain alert for those who would wound him. You and your sister must live exemplary lives.'

'I do. We both do.'

'No need to be affronted, Elizabeth.' Her lips stretched into a thin smile. 'So you were not conversing for too long and in too intimate a fashion with my son, under the eye of the whole court? Don't look so astonished. Court intrigue spreads faster than poison from a snake-bite.'

I sought for a reply, thoughts racing through my mind. It was like holding a master swordsman at bay. And I was indeed astonished. Where had that piece of gossip originated? There was no blame for which I needed to apologise.

'I was in conversation with Sir John, my lady,' I admitted lightly. 'But there was nothing untoward. We did not even dance. He brought me wine, entertained me and addressed me as cousin. I would never indulge in intrigue.'

'Good.' She held out her cup for me to refill. 'Now I must also say…'

'Why do they hate my father so much, my lady?' I interrupted, hoping to deflect the Princess from yet another attack on my character, and it was a subject that had impressed itself on me since the terrible events of the previous year.

It certainly caught her attention, but not in the manner I had hoped for. Her eyes almost stripped the flesh from my bones as she regarded me. 'Are you telling me that you don't know?'

I shook my head.

'Well, you should. What have you been doing all your life?' I thought her eyes flashed with a species of disdain, but perhaps it was merely the candlelight flickering in a draught. 'Filling your head with nothing but frivolities and your new husband, I wager, when the country's being torn asunder around us. Shame on you. And you an intelligent young woman. How old are you?' Then without waiting for a reply. 'You must learn, my dear Elizabeth, to keep your wits about you. To keep your political sense in tune, like your favourite lute. Would you allow its strings to become flat? Of course you would not! Knowledge is strength, my girl. Knowledge is power. If you know nothing, it will cast you into the hands of your enemies.'

I have no enemies.

Once I would have said that with conviction, but since the previous year I knew it not to be true, and so I must bury my pride. Joan's warning had fallen on fertile ground, forcing me to realise that there was much I had never contemplated in my world of cushioned luxury. In the days of the Great Rising any man who bore the livery of Lancaster had feared for his life. Henry and I had escaped but my father's much-loved physician had been executed on Tower Hill. As for the magnificent Savoy Palace, that most beloved of childhood homes, it had been utterly destroyed. Not one stone was left standing and all its contents were laid waste in a rage of revenge. I had shed tears for the blood and the destruction. I could no longer pretend ignorance. Being an intimate member of the King's family would not protect me from those who despised us

'So tell me, Madam.' Still I bridled a little. 'It seems I have been foolishly ignorant. Tell me why my father is so detested.'

The Princess needed no encouragement.

'Where do I begin? All is not good for England. Where are the noble victories of the past? The glories of Crécy and Poitiers? We flounder in defeat after defeat, yet the tax is high to pay for it. The Poll Tax is heavy on the peasants while the law holds down their wages. Do they blame my son the King? How can they? He is too young to blame. They need a scapegoat, and who better than Lancaster who stands at the King's side and orders his affairs? They pile their grievances on his head. He has already proved he is not the war leader his brother was.' Momentarily her eyes softened at the memory of the military exploits of Prince Edward, her much lamented late husband, but only momentarily. Once again they were fiercely focused on me. 'The rebels last year would have had your father's blood. As for Lancaster's heir—they'd have strung your brother up from the nearest tree as soon as look at him.'

'I know this. We all lived through the horrors. But surely all is well again. My father made reparation.'

Surprising me, the Princess reached with her free hand, fingers honey-smeared, to touch my arm.

'He did, and should be honoured for it.'

A terrible reparation it had been. Accepting God's punishment for his immorality as the cause of England's troubles, my father had made a public confession, ending with a rejection of Dame Katherine, banishing her from his life. It had filled the household with grief. It had, I suspected, broken my father's heart. It had certainly destroyed Dame Katherine's reputation since Walsingham saw fit to damn her as whore and witch. Such an admission to make, such a wrenching apart of their relationship, to restore peace and confidence to Richard's tottering government, but the Duke had done it because duty to the Crown and his nephew demanded it.

'But all is not well,' Princess Joan continued, dusting her fingers before returning to her sweetmeats. 'On the surface you father is restored to favour, the rebels put down, but there are those who still resent his power as my son's counsellor. There are too many with their eyes open for any excuse to attack and remove him from Richard's side. Don't give anyone a weapon to use against him, Elizabeth.'

This reading of court politics clutched at my belly, for I had seen no dangerous undercurrents. But what possible effect would it have on the direction of my life?

'I do not see, my lady, that my speaking with your son would give anyone ammunition against my father,' I said.

'Perhaps not. But it's good policy to be discreet and circumspect. Lancaster needs no divisions with the Pembroke faction if you appear less than a loyal wife.' She squeezed my arm again with sticky emphasis, and some residue of humour. 'I'll not say don't enjoy yourself but it would be advantageous for you to keep my warnings in mind. Richard is growing fast to maturity. How long will he need his ageing uncles at his side, chastising and advising and pushing him in directions he does not wish to go? He'll want to be rid of them. He'll listen to any man who sows seeds of defection. Don't give anyone a reason to awaken old scandals. Your reputation must be whiter than the feathers on a dove's breast.'

Her reference was clear enough.

'I know,' I said, looking away to hide the sadness that those probing eyes might detect. 'I miss Dame Katherine.'

'So do I. Witch she might be, to seduce Lancaster—though I doubt he needed much seducing—but she has always struck me as a woman of uncommonly good sense. And without doubt Lancaster loved her.' The Princess finished the wine, her homily at an end. 'And now we've covered all the political goings-on at my son's court, it's time I met the bride. Braid my hair, Elizabeth.'

Standing, I applied the comb to hair now almost entirely grey but which once must have added to her considerable beauty. Once more in its confining roll, she inspected the effect in her looking glass, grimaced, but nodded.

'It's the best that can be done. In my time I had every man at court at my feet, but now…' She struggled with my help to stand. 'Take me to her and I'll see what I make of this Anne of Bohemia. Will I like her?'

'Yes, my lady.' I let her rest her hand on my arm as we walked slowly through the audience chambers.

'Will she prove to be a solid influence on my son?'

'I think she will.' I wondered if her suspicions of Richard's waywardness were as lively as mine, but could not ask. 'He has great affection for her,' I said.

'Then let us give thanks to Our Lady. May be she can achieve where we cannot.'

How I admired this woman who walked haltingly at my side, her fingers digging into my arm. So deeply in touch with events and movements she was, despite living in some seclusion at Wallingford. Princess Joan might appear indolent and pleasure-loving, but she was impressively well informed. Her discourse had appealed to my intellect as well as my pride. I would never allow myself to be ignorant again of matters that might harm the Lancaster household. I was grateful to her.

'Thank you, my lady,' I said.

'There!' she replied with a malicious little glint in her eye. 'I knew you would be useful to me. I have a high regard for your father. You can be my eyes and ears. Mine are beginning to suffer from advanced age.'

Taken aback, I slid a glance.

'When I am gone, who will put their strength behind your father? And when your brother becomes Duke in the fullness of time, who will stand beside him? I see dark clouds looming, storms and tempests the like of which we have never seen before. We women have a role to play. Family loyalty must not be taken for granted. A woman must foster it as she raises her children and stitches her altar cloths. *You* must foster it, Elizabeth, for my days are numbered. Men wield their swords, but women have the gift of careful listening at keyholes. And of persuasion when brute force fails.' Upon which she halted, clamping a hand in my sleeve, and regarded me even more sternly. 'I put this burden on you. Are you listening?'

'Yes, my lady.'

A frisson of interest, or was it disbelief, gripped me. What was she asking? Never had I been called upon to shoulder so weighty a mission, but of course I would obey. Was not my family the most important part of my life? Without question I would be Princess Joan's eyes and ears, open to any whisper of danger or attack against Lancaster. I would remain constant and steadfast all my days. And then, on a thought:

'Why did you not ask my sister?'

'Your sister will believe the best of everyone. She's no use to me. Now you, Elizabeth, are cut from quite a different bolt of cloth.'

Which made me laugh. 'I hope I am able to live up to your expectations, my lady. But I will certainly pray for this new marriage.'

'I know you will. And I know that you will prove yourself a magnificent supporter of Lancaster.' We began to move again, the Princess labouring a little but still as incisive as ever. 'But remember what I say. Don't smile too overtly or too kindly on my son.'

'No, my lady. I will not.'

'I wish I could believe you,' she remarked with dry appreciation as we at last entered the royal presence. 'I have my doubts. My son has proved himself a man who makes women forget their promises.'

I smiled. I would never again be ignorant, but indeed I could not promise. Nor was I worried about future storms and tempests for my anticipation of my next meeting with Sir John Holland was too keen. But I would, of course, be careful. My reputation, as the Princess had put it, would suffer no reverses. Could I ever be so well tuned to the political nuances of Richard's court as she? I could not, in my frivolous mind, imagine it. But I would never neglect my Lancaster blood. No member of my family would ever suffer because of some lack in me.

But first there was the tournament. My heart was light, my spirits overflowing.

★

The weather was a perfect January afternoon for Richard's festivities: cold and crisp and clear. Muffled in furs from chin to floor, the women of the court took their places in the new pavilion hung with bright tapestry enhanced with swags and gilding, Queen Anne in pride of place as Lady of the Lists, with me at her side, honoured, as was fitting, as her chief lady-in-waiting and cousin by marriage.

It was the simplest of matters for me to push aside Princess Joan's advice, her warnings that I should be aware of threat and danger at every turn. Of course she would see the dark side of every glance, slide and movement around the King, and, given her history, the insidious menace of scandal. Was it not the role of a lioness to fear for her cub? But I was young and beautiful and need have no fears. With my father once more counsellor at the King's side, why did I need to worry my mind with court politics? Was I not too young to carry such a burden? And I was wearing a gown so heavy in gold thread that it turned every head.

Above my head, pennons snapped in the breeze to display Anne's heraldic motifs quartered with Richard's. It was a fine display. Richard was very keen on display.

Across the field of battle we could make out the two

teams of combatants. My father was jousting today. There was Henry. And Sir John Holland in the Lancaster contingent. There was my husband, Earl of Pembroke, astride a lively gelding, proudly bearing a Lancaster banner as page to my father.

The opposition was led, reluctantly, by my uncle of York, but there would be no danger. Lances capped, it would be a tournament *à plaisance*.

Would we prove to be invincible?

Richard did not fight. Richard had no interest in fighting. The only time I recalled Richard being part of such a glorious event was in the Great Hall as a child, receiving a mock challenge from a squire tricked out in skirts and false hair as a young virgin. Was he the only Plantagenet not to enjoy bearing arms? Gloriously clad in silk damask and crown, he sat at his wife's side to enjoy the spectacle.

Excitement built within me like a hunger. I could no more have absented myself from this event than from the wedding ceremony. Anne might be Lady of the Lists but I knew who would be the chosen lady for John Holland. And there he was, his horse on a tight curb yet eating up the distance between us, the three golden Holland lions snarling across his chest. Jousting helm still in possession of his squire, my chivalrous knight bowed to me. Today there was no subtle perfume: the aroma of horse and leather and rank sweat was exhilarating.

'My lady.' His expression was as smooth as wax, as if there were nothing untoward in his request. And indeed his words confirmed his clever ploy. 'As a representative of Lancaster

on this auspicious day, and in the absence of your illustrious
husband from the field of battle, it would be an honour if
you would allow me, and my poor skills, to be your champion.'

How clever. How damnably clever. How could I refuse
so innocuous an offer?

'Why do you hesitate?' the Queen whispered in my ear.
'If you do not take him, I will!'

And I laughed at how easy it was to enjoy the attentions
of so talented a jouster. My mind was made up, if it had not
been already. Sir John would not wear the Queen's favours
this day.

'Give him something!' the Queen urged. 'Let's get on
with it. It's as cold as charity, sitting here.'

I thought of giving him my glove as a guerdon, but it was
too cold for that. I would be no martyr to John Holland.
The ring? No, I did not think so. It would draw too much
attention. Instead I burrowed under my furs and unpinned
a knot of ribbon from my bodice, handing it to one of the
Queen's pages with a gesture for him to give it to my chosen
knight.

'My thanks, sir. I trust you will carry it to victory.'

'Your beauty is only outshone by that of our Queen.
I pledge you my victory.'

Which went down very well, all in all.

★

It was a true conflict of knight riding against knight, each
pitting his skill with lance and horse against his opponent.
The Duke was superb. One day Henry would excel. But in

the middle of it all I watched John Holland perform with every brilliant feat of arms I knew he would exhibit to unhorse any man who rode against him. It was a *tour de force*. My father's knights emerged victorious.

It might have been an anticlimax that it was Queen Anne who awarded the victory garlands, but Sir John's words were for me.

'My lady. Your beauty spurred me on to victory.'

Tomorrow, I would be the one to crown him with glory.

After supper, he invited me to dance and I accepted, so that we wound round the great dancing chamber, my hand in his. At the end of which stately performance, he took the opportunity to re-pin the ribbon to my bodice.

'You are a brave woman, Elizabeth.'

'Why is that? It was you who exhibited bravery today, sir.'

Sir John kissed my fingers, fleetingly but with heat. My heart fluttered.

'Not all bravery is in wielding a sword or a lance. If you look round this hall, at this precise moment I think there are at least a dozen pairs of eyes fixed on you.'

'Because I dance so well.'

'If that is what you wish to believe. But I know better. And so do you, Countess.' His parting shot, before he strolled away to engage the Queen in some light conversation.

I knew what he meant. I was not naïve in the ways of the court, or in John Holland's unpredictable character. I was aware of Philippa's warning glance, of Henry frowning in my direction. What of it? Turning my back on them I set myself to dance every dance, foiling any attempt my brother might make to put his frowns into words. I had a suspicion of what he would say, but he was only my brother, and younger than I. There was no necessity for me to listen to him, was there? My public demeanour had crossed no line; there was no cause for me to acknowledge any social impropriety.

★

The second day of the tournament dawned, brother Henry taking the crowd by storm. Truly dazzling, the silver spangles on his armour, fashioned into the form of unfolding roses, elicited a cheer from the spectators.

I spent a moment in admiration. But only a moment for I was not here to admire Henry. Today, in the new Queen's gift I would be Lady of the Lists with the seat of honour. I would cheer Lancaster on to victory and I would be the one to crown Sir John Holland with laurels.

Much like my brother, I had dressed to take every eye at the tournament, a cloak of magnificent sables and a jewelled coif gleaming in the winter sun as I made my way to the steps where I would climb to the front of the pavilion, smiling at those I knew, exchanging words of welcome. Anticipation of what was to come was a fine thing that made me want to laugh aloud. The sharp sunshine set the armour and weapons glittering so that everything in my sight was hard edges, as if rimmed with a keen frost. I would enjoy this day like no other.

But was there something amiss? A watchfulness perhaps.

A standing on tiptoe tension. Yet how could there be? The jousting had yet to begin. As with all tournaments in my experience, the knights were yawningly tardy in making their preparations, the heralds were still deep in conversation, trumpets tucked beneath their arms.

No, the whole event was simply waiting on my appearance. As I lifted my furs to take that first step, I smiled with a comment to my aunt of Gloucester, who replied with a slide of eye towards the principal seats.

And I saw what it was.

The principal seat with its cushions and fringed awning—the one promised to me—was occupied by a diminutive lady that was not the Queen. Beautifully clad, the net that covered her hair thick with gems that caused her dark curls to glitter as if covered with rain drops, the Lady of the Lists held court, laughing with her ladies who had commandeered the seats beside her.

Isabella, Duchess of York, my aunt by marriage. Constanza's Castilian sister.

I hesitated, knowing that in this moment of my discomfiture I was on display, and would look callow and foolish if I hesitated here much longer. I was not the only one to know that the Queen had promised me this honour. Perhaps I had been unwise to broadcast my delight so freely. Now I could sense the faces turning in my direction, in amusement, or gentle mockery, or perhaps even malice from those who would gladly deflate the pride of Lancaster.

Where to sit? How to practice nonchalance with my aunt Gloucester smirking at my rigid shoulder blade.

Rescue was to hand; Queen Anne, taking a handful of my sables and pulling me to the seat next to her, where I subsided with much relief, well camouflaged as I twitched my furs into order. All smoothly accomplished as if this had been my intent all along.

'Are you disappointed?' she asked quietly beneath the increased bustle as the combatants rallied.

'Oh, no.' My smile was brilliant. I would never admit to so shallow an emotion.

'Richard changed his mind. He wished to honour the Duchess of York.'

And probably put me in my place, I thought. 'Richard often changes his mind,' I said. 'It is of no importance.'

I was too well mannered to make a scene, too conscious of my own dignity to draw attention to the dismay that hung heavy as a stone in my chest. It would make no difference, of course. Sir John would still be my champion. Or even the Queen's, which I could accept.

The knights approached, the Duke of York even more lugubrious than on the previous day. Here was glorious Henry. And Jonty, bearing my father's helm with great care, grinned at me, managing not to wave in recognition. And here, at last, magnificently mounted, all dark glamour from his ordered hair to the light glancing off his armour, was John Holland, who rode past me as if I did not exist.

My smile had the quality of a bizarre death rictus when my chivalric knight betrayed me to bow before Isabella, Lady of the Lists, who stood as she untied the obligatory knot of ribbons from her sleeve. Leaning forward, she presented them to her champion who tucked them beneath his breastplate. And before she released them, she had the temerity to press them to her painted lips.

It pained me to watch, but watch I did. How could jealousy be so painful? To have the Duchess of York preening as Lady of the Lists was one thing. To have John Holland fight for her was quite another—and her saluting him in this manner, giving credence to all the salacious detail of common gossip about the pair of them.

Was rumour true? It undoubtedly was. No one with any sense could deny it after this little show of intimacy.

'I will fight as your champion today, Lady.' Hand on heart Sir John bowed his head.

'I am honoured, Sir John.' Isabella's reply, coloured seductively by Castile and her own intent, slid smoothly on the air. 'I wait to reward you for your success.'

Her smile had a knowing edge. His was bright with mischief.

Suddenly I could not bear to look. Such treachery stoked my fury. Had he not promised me that he would once again wear my guerdon? And here he publically rode past me to dally with the woman whose name, coupled with his, had been the subject of discussion in every solar from Windsor to Edinburgh and back again. I might have claimed I did not believe all that had been said of his want of morality. I might have given him the benefit of the doubt.

There was no doubt at all!

It was as if he had blasted the scurrilous details of their affair for all to see and hear. And he had ignored me, leaving me to taste the ignominy of having no champion. Henry was encouraging his child wife to tie one of her scarves around his arm, while the Duke honoured Constanza. I, my Father's daughter, was ostracised with the less favoured, despite my magnificent furs and my equally magnificently plaited hair.

I gathered together all my pride and firmed my spine. No one—*no one*—would know my sense of rejection.

The Queen, taking in every nuance of the scene, was nudging my arm.

'There's your champion,' she murmured.

And there was Jonty, bursting with pride. Why had I not seen it for myself?

Because you are entirely too selfish, Elizabeth! Jonty would revel in such an honour! Dame Katherine again taking me to task, and with asperity.

Raising my hand I beckoned to my husband, and seeing, my father took the helm from him so that Jonty could approach with hard-held delight. Oh, it was a perfect remedy. The Earl of Pembroke, although only a page and so consigned to the sidelines, even if he did have a sword in his hand, wore my glove pinned to his slight chest that day with great pride. In a fit of guilt I even willingly tolerated cold fingers. I found no pleasure at all in the proceedings.

When John Holland won, as he did, it was the Duchess of York who crowned him, presenting to him the superb jousting helm, during which little ceremony I brought to mind every scandalous detail I knew about the torrid affair between the Duchess of York and Sir John Holland: the rumours of secret meetings and carnal knowledge between the pair, the acceptance of the Duke of York who could not control his wife. Although lacking inches, Isabella had a presence and an appetite, and one that John Holland was perfectly content to satisfy. Isabella had a lascivious eye. But then so did Sir John.

Unable to resist, I watched the Duchess as she sparkled and flounced, as was her wont. Isabella of Castile, older than I by almost a decade, with all the glamour of experience and foreign royal blood in her dark hair and dark eyes. A woman who intrigued me, even demanded admiration for her survival through the vicissitudes of her early life, when she was forced to exist with her sister in a hovel in Bayonne, before coming to England to make a diplomatic match with my uncle Edmund of Langley, Duke of York—this second Castilian marriage following rapidly after my father's to Constanza. Neither marriage was happy to any degree, my father continuing to consort with Dame Katherine, but Isabella casting her net wider.

At that moment my hatred for her knew no bounds. My face felt rigid with my effort to smile.

'I see your knight errant has turned his attention elsewhere, Elizabeth.' The voice made no attempt to moderate its tone. 'How infuriating for you when you had hoped to have him kneeling at your pretty feet!'

Did she have to announce my affairs to the whole pavilion? Princess Joan, with a nod of her head, encouraged the lady on my left to give up her seat, and gave me no choice but to collect my wits and reply with what I hoped was amused directness.

'He has, my lady.'

I had not known the Princess had honoured us with her presence on this second day of jousting, but here she was, large and sumptuous in a swathe of velvet and fur, missing nothing of the proceedings.

'A salutary lesson there, I think. Who would have thought to find such enjoyment from a tournament?'

I allowed my brows to arch. 'And I have learnt the lesson well. One can never rely on an arrogant man.'

'A promise given one day is broken the next,' added the Queen, joining in from my right. 'Even my lord the King is not immune.'

'None of my husbands were good on promises,' the Princess observed, spreading dry humour with superb confidence. 'My first husband, Holland, even forgot for a time that he had wed me, when the need to wield a sword overseas overcame his lust.'

'And I don't even expect promises from the Earl of Pembroke,' I agreed. 'He forgets them between Matins and Prime.'

There was a ripple of laughter around us, as the women of the court began to exchange their own experiences.

Beautifully done.

'There!' Princess Joan leaned close. 'Admit I have rescued you from too much unpleasant attention. Some maturity would become you. It is not wise to wear either your heart or your expectations on your sleeve, like that jewelled pin, for all to gawp at.' And fortunately not waiting for a reply, when a sharp one rose in my throat, added: 'Will you accept some advice?'

'Of course, my lady.' I was frosty, resenting any advice.

'My youngest son is not for such as you, even if you were not wed to that child.' The Princess nodded to where Jonty was helping Henry remove the pieces of spangled armour. 'My son has a temper and a questionable loyalty. He has an arrogance that is not to be trusted.' Her glance was quizzical. 'You look surprised.'

'I am, my lady. That any woman would hold her son up to such dismantling of his character.'

'I know rabid scandal when I hear it. It follows Isabella around. There is something about a woman with small, sharp teeth. As if she would strip the flesh from the bones of the man she covets—covets, my dear, not loves. I doubt she has the capacity to love any man. She has the morals of a cat on heat.'

Which seemed an indelicate observation since much the same had been said of the Princess herself in her lifetime.

'And if that second son of hers was fathered by York, I'll toss my coral rosary beads to the beggars outside our gates,' the Princess continued, her fingers clenching on the gold mounted beads that were strung across her formidable bosom. 'You know what's said of Isabella and my son?' She raised her brows 'Of course you do. Is it hard to see?' She turned to look along the row, making no pretence about it, to where Isabella sat, leaning forward, his eyes fixed on the figure of Sir John. Even when the Duchess returned the gaze, her expression one of hauteur, the Princess did not look away, and I knew full well Princess Joan's reference. There were many tongues to clap the rumour that the Duchess's second son Richard was also son of John Holland.

No, it was not hard at all.

'Do you see?'

'Yes.'

Now that percipient gaze slid to me. 'You should consider *thinking*, Elizabeth, before you draw the eyes and tongues of the chattering court in your direction. Do you want Isabella to see you as a rival for my son's dubious but entirely charming attentions? As for what that delightful boy will think when he discovers his wife to be treating her marriage vows with frivolity...' She nodded towards the glowing Earl of Pembroke. 'You should not demean yourself.'

'I would do no such thing, madam!'

'Perhaps not. But how pleasant for the court to wager on the consanguinity of smoke and fire!' she said dryly. And without waiting for a reply, the Princess changed her seat, to take up a position nearer a brazier for her comfort.

It had put me entirely in my place, a dagger thrust to bring an unpleasant day to a painful end. I was not frivolous with my vows. I had no intention of being so. Silently I nursed my vexation through the dying minutes of the tournament, praying for a quick end and escape. Only to be further accosted when the Duchess of York, brushing past me, lured by the pleasures of warmth and food, turned the blade. Unwittingly? I did not think so.

'What was disturbing the Princess?' she asked. 'She seemed very interested in me.'

'Only in Sir John,' I said. 'She was keen for us all to admire her son's skills.'

'We all admire him, do we not?' Isabella smiled at me as she collected her women and followed the Queen.

She was so very beautiful even if she lacked inches. It made a man protective of her, I supposed. If that was so, no man would be protective of me. I had inherited my father's generous height.

I hated that Isabella thought I was a rival for John Holland's attention. But after today I was not. He had shown me that I was of no value to him. What had made me think otherwise? As Princess Joan had observed, I would benefit from some maturity.

★

'Will you dance with me, Countess?'

His lips curved confidently. His hand, extended, had an element of command about it, as if it would be impossible for me to refuse an invitation from the victor of the joust. I looked at him, at the hand, finely boned, the fingers that had today gripped a lance with intent now heavy with gems. I looked at his face, the saturnine lines that spoke of temper and passion. At the knowing gleam in his eye, dark as a kestrel's.

Infinitesimally I tilted my head.

The insufferable arrogance of the man. Don't trust a man who is arrogant. My father was a man of arrogance, but that was an entirely different matter. I would not trust John Holland ever again. Had I not known that he would make this invitation, as if he had not spent the afternoon as the prime object of Duchess Isabella's lust?

I smiled.

I curtsied to John Holland, more deeply than was entirely necessary from one of my rank.

'It would be my pleasure to dance, Sir John.' It was in my mind to turn a chilly shoulder but that would put me too

much into his power. I knew he would make much of the
slightest indication that I knew full well that today he had
slighted me, after seeking me out yesterday. Ignore a woman
and she will come to your hand out of pique, as a lonely
lapdog will come to be petted. I recognised the game and I
would not play it.

'The music has begun,' he remarked, his smile quizzical
as I lingered. 'We will miss it unless you step smartly.'

'I am honoured. Thank you, sir,' I said. Then seeing a
perfect alternative presented to me. 'But I will dance with
my husband.'

'Does he know?' The eloquent brows rose.

'Of course. Here he is, come to claim my hand.'

'My lady!' Jonty, approaching at a fast lope, was deliciously decorous. 'Will you partner me?'

With a gracious smile I inclined my head and joined my
hand with Jonty's, who led me through the steps with lively
skill and some well-practised exactitude, during which I did
not once glance in John Holland's direction.

'Am I getting better?' Jonty asked at the end, only a little
breathless. His energy was prodigious.

'Marginally. You only trod once on my foot.'

Jonty grinned. 'I must leave you now, madam.'

'And why is that?'

'My lord the Duke has need of me to take a message.'

'Then you must go.' I straightened the fur at the neckline
of his expensive tunic. 'It would not do to keep the Duke
waiting.'

'No, madam.'

I watched him go, darting between the crowds, not so much to take a message, I decided with a wry smile, but to join a group of equally furtive pages up to no good. Wives did not figure highly in the Earl of Pembroke's plans. I wondered who had sent him to dance with me. I knew enough about Jonty to doubt it was of his own initiative.

For a moment I stood alone, conscious of my aloneness, which was ridiculous since I knew every face at the gathering. And yet in that moment I felt isolated, a little sad, as if I had lost my secure footing on the path to my future. Yet why should I not be secure? I was Countess of Pembroke with an income to fit my status. Soon I would have my own household. Until that time I could enjoy my days at Richard's court. By what right was I forlorn?

Because, I acknowledged, I needed someone who could stir my blood with passion. A man who could make my heart sing. Jonty would never do that for me, so I was destined to live a half-life, without passion, without knowing the hot desires of love.

And I was forlorn because the man I had painted as my hero had feet of clay and a place in another woman's bed.

My heart sank even lower.

And there was John Holland with malice in his twisted smile.

'Will you dance with me, Countess?'

Having no excuse this time, and because that smile made my heart jolt just a little, I curtsied and complied with impressive serenity.

'It would be my pleasure.'

The glint in his eye told me that he had acknowledged

the repetition of our courtly exchange, but he made no comment as we joined the circle and began the slow movement to right and left. No one had sent John Holland to dance with me. He had done it of his own free will, and probably, if I read him aright, to make mischief.

Yet my spirits lifted and danced with the music.

'Was the Princess warning you to keep your distance from me?' he asked.

'How should she? There is no need to so warn a wedded woman.' I moved away in the pattern of the dance, to return with neat steps to hear his reply.

'How true. You are the perfect married couple. Your eye will never stray.'

His sardonic expression disturbed me. How well he read my situation. How well he read my mind. For a moment I was struck by the thought that we were kindred spirits, both moved by impulses, both driven by strong emotions.

Which was of course nonsense. I was nothing like John Holland.

'Unlike your own eye, Sir John,' I observed.

'Unlike mine. But I have no wife to keep my eye secure on its prime objective.'

I moved beneath his arm, lifting my skirts so that the silk damask slid and gleamed, close enough to my partner for me to remark, 'no, but the lady who took your eye today has a husband.'

'Ha! The Duke of York is nothing but a bag of wind!' His scorn coated us both. 'Of course she is bored, looking for entertainment.'

'Which you provide, Sir John? I'm told you have intimate knowledge of her.'

'Passing intimate. Enough to know she has a voracious desire for entertainment.'

Again we parted, giving me time to replenish my armoury, as I was led on from hand to hand, to return to accuse: 'So it is the Duchess's fault that you are lured into an affair of the heart with her?'

'I doubt her heart's involved. Are we speaking of blame?'

'Certainly not.'

'Are you jealous, Countess?'

'Not I. I have a care for my reputation.'

'And you would never contemplate endangering the purity of that reputation by embarking on an intimate affair with a man who took your interest.'

'Certainly not,' I repeated, meeting his eye with what I hoped he read as indifference.

With warmth rising to colour my cheeks, I was not as certain as once I had been.

Sir John raised his hand to lead me round, stealing a quick kiss against my wrist as our bodies came close.

'I can feel your blood running hot,' he whispered.

'Because I am dancing, perhaps?'

'I wager it did not do so when your husband danced with you.'

Our parting in the dance meant that I need not reply.

And when we were together again. 'My liaison with the Duchess is at an end.'

An assertion so bluntly made. Did I believe him? Not for a moment.

But my blood was running hot.

★

I knew I would pay for that exhibition of outrageous courtesy by my partner. I could not hope that it had gone unnoticed, and there was Henry stalking across the chamber with a darkening brow, my cousin Edward of York following in his footsteps. No time for me to take refuge with Philippa, or even the Princess who sat in state with a cup of wine and a dish of honeyed nuts to sustain her through the hours. All I had time to do was take a breath and hope my heightened colour had paled, at the same time as I ordered my response to the inevitable attack. Henry had no reason to call my behaviour into question. The unfortunate flamboyance in that kiss had been John Holland's. Not mine. Better to challenge Henry now with a good strong denial of any wish of mine to draw attention to myself, before my brother's ire became too well-lodged to dissipate.

'You'd do well to avoid Holland, Elizabeth, if you can't behave with more perspicacity.'

Not a propitious start. Marriage had given Henry a degree of solemnity that was sometimes not short of pompous. I abandoned any thought of a greeting.

'Avoid him?' I said. 'How would I avoid the King's brother without discourtesy? Have you some advice for me, little brother?' I made it just a little patronising. I was still taller than he and could make use of my height.

Henry was unmoved. 'It looked like a flirtation to me.'

'You are wrong. It was not.'

Edward was hovering. Edward always hovered. Now

almost into his tenth year, he was a slight child who promised uncommonly good looks but I disliked his air of smug
superiority even more than the sly gleam in his eyes.

'Go away, Edward!' I said.

'I'm only—'

'You're only listening to what does not concern you.' And
I waited until he sulked into the crowd.

'He's a nuisance,' Henry observed, watching him retreat,
'with a bad case of hero-worship. I think it's the gilded
armour. Every time I turn round…' His gaze sharpened,
fixed mine again. 'About Holland. The Duke would not
like it.' He glanced over towards the far end of the chamber where our father conversed with the Earl of Warwick.
I doubted that he had even noticed. 'Nor would the Pembroke connection approve of your lack of discretion in
cavorting with the man who is known to spend more time
in the bed of the Duchess of York than the Duke does!'

'I care not what the Pembroke connection thinks or
does.' So Henry was well aware of the rumours, too. 'There's
nothing not to like in my dancing with Sir John. I am not
the only woman he has partnered.'

'You are the only woman whose wrist he saluted in the
middle of a dance, I warrant.'

'Were you spying on me, Henry?'

'Yes. Every time I set eyes on you, you are in his company.
He's not a suitable companion for you. Apart from anything
else, his allegiances are not trustworthy. He might accept a
Lancaster annuity today, but who knows where he will look
tomorrow.'

Anger had begun to bubble under my skin, alongside the

dismay. I would not be judged, I would not be watched. What right had my younger brother, however impressive in the lists, to be critical of me? I had done no wrong. As for John Holland's political inclinations, I could see no relevance.

'I'll dance with whomsoever I wish,' I said. 'How dare you speak to me of decorum? And how dare you blacken the name of the King's brother? A kiss on my wrist is hardly a matter to ruffle the sensibilities of the royal court.' I had worked myself up into a fine show of temper, at the same time as I refused to consider why I felt the need to do so.

'As long as it goes no further than that.'

'How dare you!'

'And keep your voice down. I know exactly the reputation of the King's brother! I'd make sure he did not dance with Mary.'

'I doubt he would wish to. She's little more than a child.'

'What do you mean by that?'

'That John Holland appreciates a woman with some degree of experience.'

'Like yourself.'

'If you wish! By the Rood, Henry.' This was getting out of hand. 'I only danced with the man. Is that so reprehensible?'

'You think you are so clever, so beyond criticism. Why will you not listen to good advice?'

No! No more advice!

'I will take advice. But not from you, little brother...' And having a weapon I could use against him, I did so, careless in my anger. 'Who are you to admonish me for my behaviour? You were told to keep your distance from Mary. But you couldn't, could you? And now she's carrying your child, and she not yet fourteen years.'

And immediately wished the words unsaid as high colour washed over Henry's cheekbones and a keen anxiety sparked in his eyes.

'I did not molest her!'

'I did not say you did!'

'Mary is my wife and I love her. There was no indiscretion. You do not know the meaning of the word discretion.'

Which fired my anger again. 'Discretion? You could not keep your hands off Mary, when everyone knew it would be better if you did! You have no right to take me to task.'

'I am wasting my breath.' Henry marched off, collecting his shadow Edward before he had gone more than a dozen strides.

So many warnings. Was I so much at fault? And now I had crossed swords with Henry and instantly regretted it. Mary had desired the union as much as Henry and was perfectly content in her pregnancy. It was ill-done of me to beat my brother about the head with it when they obviously enjoyed the deepest of affection. Unsettled, regretful, I had to watch the departure of Henry's rigid back and then Sir John leading Isabella into another dance. When I next looked, he had gone, abandoning Isabella too, who had enough court manners that she did not appear disconsolate.

Well, neither would I.

I joined hands in a circle with Philippa and Sir John's elder brother Thomas Holland, who was enjoying the status of his recent inheritance of the earldom of Kent.

'And are you going to douse me in reprimand and disfavour?' I asked Philippa when her lips remained firmly pinned together.

'No. I don't need to. You know you shouldn't encourage him. And you've upset Henry.'

'You don't like him,' I accused Philippa.

'I'm not sure. He's hard not to like. But I don't trust him.'

★

The final day of the tournament dawned as fair and crisp as all the rest. It was to be a day of miracles. I was Queen of the Lists, offering my glove—the partner of the one I had bestowed on Jonty—to John Holland who made me the object of his gallantry.

On that day he fought, demon-possessed. No one could defeat him. He was brave and bold and entirely admirable in his defeat of his opponents.

I crowned him with laurels: presented him with the purse of gold.

After supper I danced with him, conscious only of the clasp of his fingers around mine, the agile strength of his body. Never had I felt so full of life and joy. All sense of duty and discretion was set aside, all the warnings cast adrift. Henry and the Princess meant well, but I saw no dangers in my demeanour, even when Sir John stole another kiss on my wrist.

'You should not.'

'Would you rather I did not?'

'Would you desist if I did?'

'I would think about it…'

And he would do exactly as he pleased. And since John Holland loved no one but himself, he was no danger to me. And since my father did not see fit to reprimand me, then why should I not enjoy my knight's company?

Chapter Four

Well, I suppose I had expected this.

'Elizabeth.' My father had looked up from the document under his hand as I entered his private chamber, a room set aside for his exclusive use when he stayed at Westminster. The windows on one side looked out over towards the river, if the occupant could drag his eyes from the glory of the tapestries newly purchased by Richard in a bid to make his palaces the perfect setting for his magnificence as King. On this morning, from the expression on his face, the Duke was oblivious to the scenery and the surrounding grandeur.

I curtsied.

'My lord. You sent for me.' I waited until he had placed the pen beside the document with infinite care as if his mind were taken up with something entirely different from its contents. I had every premonition that this would not be a pleasant interview. There was a groove between his flat brows.

'I am gratified that you have enough energy after yesterday's exertions to present yourself at this early hour,' he said. 'I trust you are rested. Or do your feet ache?'

It might have suggested humour, but obviously not. I had been summoned by the Duke. It would not have crossed my mind to be tardy.

'No, sir,' I replied warily. His expression was particularly severe, but he rose from his chair where the window allowed what light there was to flood the room, bowed courteously, and came to lead me to a seat by the fireplace. Flames leapt to warm the room but I suddenly found myself shivering with tension and my belly was cold. The Duke's concern for my comfort was soothing, but my father was well-mannered even when furiously angry, and that is what I saw in the stark lines of his face. Here was to be no easy discussion of the state of the Pembroke inheritance.

'A cup of wine?' he asked.

'Thank you, sir.' Taking the cup, I remained wary. 'You wished to see me.'

'Indeed.' Unfailingly urbane, yet he looked weary to my critical eye. He was missing Katherine, I thought. It had been a difficult year, with an unmendable rift between them of my father's making. Yet what choice had he, when Walsingham heaped England's ills on his shoulders? I regretted Dame Katherine's absence, and so did he. His temper was short.

'It is my opinion,' he pronounced, having poured wine for himself and taken the seat opposite me, 'that you have entertained the court sufficiently with your conduct in the company of John Holland. I think I have rarely seen you so lacking in dignity since you grew out of your childhood. I wish such behaviour to stop.'

Abruptly I stood, the wine splashing in the cup, unable to sit under such an unexpected attack in so harsh a tone.

'Sit down, Elizabeth.'

I sank back, my fists clenched around the stem of the cup. Had I expected this? Perhaps I had when the summons had been delivered. But had my behaviour been so very bad? I had laughed and danced, encouraged by John's charm. Had I abandoned dignity? I did not think so. I had merely thrown myself into the joyous celebration of the day.

Without doubt, I could find all manner of excuse.

But had I flirted? Undoubtedly I had. An honest assessment of my behaviour brought a flush to my cheeks as if I had already drunk the wine that had splattered the front panels of my gown. And now my father, witness to it all, would take me to task.

'I do not wish your name to be coupled with that of Holland,' he said, still pronouncing every word carefully as if I would wilfully misunderstand. 'You will not allow it. You will remember what you owe to your name. Your behaviour will never be less than unimpeachable.'

'Nor will it, sir.' I was not a little hurt.

'Don't be foolish.' There was no sympathy in my father's face. 'After Holland's close attention to you yesterday, and your willingness to be encouraged in all sorts of extravagance, I doubt there is anyone in this place who is not commenting on it this morning.'

I felt the flush in my cheeks deepen.

'Which I regret, sir.' For I did, in the cold light of day.

And in all honesty: 'You are not the first to point out the error or my ways, sir.'

My father's straight brows rose in query. 'Do I understand you have already been taken to task?'

'Henry has expressed his disapproval. He was very forthright.'

The Duke was lured into a dry smile, which did not fool me for an instant. I was still not forgiven. 'And do I imagine that you accepted his criticisms?'

'No, I did not,' I admitted. 'Henry informed me of Sir John's affair with Isabella. Which I already knew. I did not need reminding.'

'Did he? I am impressed.'

'Princess Joan also discovered a need to warn me.'

My father gave a harsh laugh. 'Did she now? The Princess is always full of surprises and has this family's welfare securely fixed in her heart. What a shame she was not born a man. Her nose for politics is superb.' He sobered, bending a forbidding eye on me again so that I shuffled in my chair, sipping the wine to moisten a suddenly dry throat. What penalty would he demand of me? Whatever it was, I would have to accept it.

'You should have listened to Henry,' the Duke observed. 'He has a mature head on his shoulders. But I don't suppose you did. Indeed I'm certain you didn't since you spent most of yesterday in Holland's company. And don't tell me that you were unaware of it, Elizabeth. It could hardly be missed when the Queen of the Lists lavished all her attention on the Champion at the banquet and the subsequent dancing. What were you thinking? I thought you had been raised to know how to conduct yourself, whether at court or in your own home. Your mother would be ashamed of you. And so would Dame Katherine. You do not bestow your favours on one man to the exclusion of all others unless you wish to be an item of salacious gossip. And certainly not if that man is John Holland. He has a reputation that would scorch the hide of a wild boar. You need a longer spoon than you possess, my daughter, to sup with the likes of John Holland.'

I bristled. 'Sir John says that his affair with Isabella is at an end.'

'So were you perhaps planning to replace that lady in his bed?'

Guilt spread beneath my skin when my father used that particular tone.

'No! I would not.'

Perhaps denial sprang to my lips more speedily than truth merited. I had thought about what a night in his arms would be like.

'You deny it, my daughter, but would you have refused him if he had offered? He is a man of enormous charm and eloquence. It would have been the worst move you could have made. You must know how dangerous it can be to put yourself into the hands of men such as Walsingham who would delight in finding ammunition against our family.' His lips were white with passion, one fist clenched on his knee as he loosed the reins of control a little to make his point. 'You know I speak from experience. I'd not have you make the mistakes that I made.'

Such an admonition astonished me, that he would acknowledge his affair with Katherine to be a mistake. And that he would use it to enlighten me, his errant daughter.

'Did you not love her?' I said without thinking.

'I loved her. I still love her. But I would not have you follow the path I took. The consequences can be painful beyond acceptance, and I'd not have that for you.' The timbre of his voice softened at last. 'You may resent my words, but I have your wellbeing in mind.'

I had the grace to hang my head and study the swirl of wine in my cup. 'I am sorry.' The words were stiff, difficult to say. I sighed. It was impossible not to read the pain.

'I understand his attraction, Elizabeth,' he said gently, encouraging me to look up into his face again.

'I like him.'

'I am sure you do.'

'He makes me feel like a woman who is beautiful and desired. For herself.'

'I imagine he does. I imagine he makes any number of women feel the same.'

'He seeks me out because he enjoys my company.'

'Do you think so? I think you are unaware of the turbulence in this particular stream.' He paused, chin raised, listening to an outburst of laughter from beyond the window that overlooked the inner courtyard. 'Come. Let me show you something.' He offered his hand, tucking mine through his arm, and led me to the window. 'I am not angry with you.' He smiled. 'I was, but I know this marriage has its difficulties for a high-spirited woman. But you are quite old enough—and intelligent enough if you will put your mind to it—to understand. Look down there. It is a lesson in alliance-making that you will not find in the books of your childhood. Who do you see?'

Obediently, intrigued, pleased to be forgiven, I looked down to the source of the laughter and raised voices. It was Richard surrounded by a group of courtiers. Some were standing, some sitting. A page was handing round drinking cups. A minstrel strummed on the strings of his lute, but no one was listening. All attention was centred on Richard.

'Who do you see?' the Duke repeated.

'My cousin the King. Dressed like a peacock for a feast. I swear he wears cloth of gold and rubies in bed...'

'Never mind that. And who is with him?'

Presented as I was with a strange foreshortened view, it was difficult to see. 'A group of courtiers. Richard's friends, I expect.'

'True. Then who is not there?'

I glanced up at him, sensing for the first time where this might be leading. My education was coming on in leaps and bounds.

'The Queen.'

'Exactly. And?'

'Apart from the Queen? I don't see any of his uncles. Not Gloucester, nor York—nor you of course. But then, they are all young men down there. More likely to be Richard's friends.'

'Well done. Look again, Elizabeth.'

I did , as well as I was able. 'His brothers are not there. The Hollands.'

'That is so.'

And then I realised. 'Nor Henry.'

'Excellent. Not Henry. This is a gathering of Richard's own choosing. And it's all a matter of political manoeuvrings, Elizabeth, of making alliances, of forming groups and interests at court with those of use to you. Richard, as he grows, is feeling his way to making connections that please him.' The Duke's voice acquired a brittle quality that had nothing to do with my sins. 'Nor is he keen to take advice over who might be the best men to choose to stand at his shoulder.'

I watched the group, the friendly intermingling. Richard was at ease, as he never was with my father. Laughter rang out. More wine was poured, the sun glinting on Richard's rings as he clipped one of the men on the shoulder in easy camaraderie.

I frowned a little at the scene.

'I see that it's Richard and the friends of his choosing, but I don't see what effect it has on me.'

'In a year,' my father said, 'Richard will achieve his majority and will take up the reins of power. He will insist on it, although some would say he is not yet strong enough or sufficiently wise to manage policy. But Richard will assume the mantle of kingship and make his own decisions, shrugging off his advisers who have led him so far. Including myself.' He turned from the window as if the scene pained him, returning to his seat by the fire. 'My own influence hangs by a thread, but I'll work hard to keep it from being completely severed. Richard, I hope, will still give me an ear, even though he resents my advice as interference. Certainly he has little time for his other uncles who would lecture him rather than persuade. My days are numbered but he values my diplomatic skills in making treaties with foreign powers if nothing else. I hope to hold his loyalty.'

Never had I been in receipt of such weighty matters. From the window where I remained, I studied my father's austere profile, at the lines that had crept there when I had not noticed.

'Would Richard cast you off?' I asked, aghast at the thought. Had my father not guided and protected my cousin since his father's death, the most loyal of uncles? Surely Richard would not be so ungrateful. And yet had not Princess Joan hinted at such an eventuality?

'One day he will. I see it on the near horizon, and then where will Richard look for his new counsellors? Where will he give promotion? To whom will he hand titles and gifts and royal preferment? To those young men you see around him, out there in the courtyard. It is youth that cleaves to youth. In the future there is no role for me. Nor for Sir John Holland who may not be of my generation, but is not young enough to appeal to our new King.'

I watched the little scene unfolding below, where Richard was laughing, accepting a hawk onto his fist— obviously a gift from one of his companions who leaned to whisper in the royal ear.

'Who is the dark-haired lad with the velvet tunic and the feathers?' Perhaps a few years older than I, his hair was iridescently black in the sun, his features, what I could see of them, vividly attractive. 'There.' I pointed as the Duke returned to my side.

'Robert De Vere.'

We watched them for a moment.

'He's trying hard to win Richard's attention.'

'And not without success,' the Duke agreed dryly.

'Henry is not one of them. That's important, isn't it?' I was beginning to see, all too clearly.

'Richard and Henry do not see eye to eye. They never have.'

'Will de Vere and the rest make good advisers?'

'Who's to say? I trust that the Queen might have enough influence to steer Richard onto a sensible path.' He shook his head, his shoulder lifting with unease. 'But as for Holland…Where does he see his future? He cannot stand alone. He would be the first to admit that he is a man of ambition, and without the King's patronage his hopes could well be destroyed. So if Richard will not help him to power as a royal counsellor, he needs to look for new allies. He looks to Lancaster. Do you understand?'

'Oh!…' I was beginning to see very well, but my father left nothing to chance.

'You have spent your whole life surrounded by treaties, alliances, affairs of state, Elizabeth. Have you remained ignorant of what goes on between the high-blooded families of the realm?'

'I am well aware. My own marriage was such an alliance.'

'But you did not see yourself as a means to an end in Holland's planning.'

'He would not be so unscrupulous!' Oh, but the doubts were already swarming.

'Why would he not? When are any man's motives innocent, in the friendships he makes, the connections he weaves together? A man of ambition will use every means he can to strengthen his position with one faction or another. If de Vere seduces Richard's affection, then Holland's days are numbered unless he has important friends. Do you see?'

'Yes I do.' I pursed my lips. I had always known that my marriage would be one of family alliances. What young woman of my situation did not? But to find myself singled out, wooed in fact, to further a man's career, because I was a daughter of Lancaster… all my joy of the previous day was suddenly buried under a blanket of dismay.

'Richard is thinking of sending him to Ireland, as Lord Lieutenant', the Duke explained. 'It may be that Holland has no wish to go, but would rather enhance his connection with the English court. With me. To be sent to Ireland could be death to a man who seeks power.'

Dismay was fast becoming transposed into horror.

'I have not been very wise, have I?'

Was that all there was in John Holland's fine words and finer gestures? Is that what it had all been about? The close attention, the playing fast and loose to lure me on, the flattering compliments, all to get a foothold in the Lancaster camp. Was I simply a means to an end, a step closer to the Lancastrian interest? Well, yes, it was entirely possible. He had gone with the Duke to St Malo, using his military skills to win grace and favour. With no war in the immediate planning, he needed another gambit. And I was it. The way to my father's side.

How could he be so devious and yet so attractive?

'You don't like him.' As I accused Philippa, so I asked my father.

'Liking him is an irrelevance. I see his good qualities. I am wary of his bad ones. He has a handsome face, a smooth tongue and an ease of manner. He is hard to withstand. But however hard it is, you have to accept that his interest is not so much in you, as in what you stand for. Being a friend of Elizabeth of Lancaster can do him no harm.' The Duke surprised me, lifting my chin so that he could peruse my face. 'To be her husband can only be better.'

It made no sense.

'But I am wed.'

'And young lives are cheap. Who knows what the future will bring.'

I saw the strain on his face. We knew the grief of young death. Sometimes I forgot, but the Duke and my mother had mourned the loss of four of their children. Death was no respecter of rank or age.

'So if Jonty were to die, Sir John would be ready to step into his shoes, and I, neatly, effectively seduced, would not be unwilling.'

'Yes. And even if there is no such eventuality, it could only be an advantage to have a daughter of Lancaster with more than a friendly ear.'

'It is heartless.'

'It is pragmatic. How often is politics lacking in sensitivity? And I doubt that you are the only fair carp in Holland's pond,' he warned. 'I'm certain he's a master-planner, like a juggler with clever sleight of hand and agile fingers.'

Still I sought to excuse him.

'Why not seek to engage Philippa's interest?'

'He knows my plans for Philippa. I would never allow her to wed Holland.' The Duke gripped my shoulders, turning me from the window. 'With or without marriage, you must distance yourself from him.'

How difficult it was to accept such a dictate. 'He makes me feel alive.'

'Pembroke will soon be old enough to be the husband you desire.'

'But he is a boy. And John is…a man.'

'I know. That is what I fear. And that is why I will send you back with Constanza to Hertford tomorrow.'

'No…'

'You will go. It is arranged.' There was no gainsaying him. 'I am not unsympathetic. But it's time you grew into your position. I suggest that you use the royal audience this morning to see which way the wind is blowing for Holland. I think it will persuade you, if I cannot. Women are used to make alliances. What does Sir John want from you? A voice raised in his favour? Whatever it is, beware. Will you promise me?'

How could I do other? Life at Hertford with Constanza stretched before me, week after tedious week. 'Yes, my lord. I promise.'

'And make your peace with your brother.'

'Well…' It was not a scene I looked forward to.

'You will do it, Elizabeth, and restore some vestige of serenity to our family.'

I read the implacable determination, the complete lack of tolerance for anything but my compliance. Family was power. Family was everything.

'Yes, sir. I will do it.'

★

I saw it for myself at the royal audience, Richard saying farewell to a handful of the Bohemian dignitaries who had come to wish the happy couple well while the most influential were invited to remain in England, and, unfortunately in the eye of my father, at English expense. It was another monumentally grandiose occasion, and once I would have enjoyed it for its own sake but now I was a different animal, my eyes and mind opened to the truth of what was obvious but not being spoken aloud. Whereas of late I had treated the warnings of Princess Joan as the worries of a mother for her children, and had been quick enough to reject them, my father's explanations, delivered with such cool conviction, had hit home. He had addressed me as a woman, as an equal almost. He deserved that I build on that crucial lesson.

So, while my hurt at John Holland's behaviour rumbled in the background, I watched the political manoeuvrings at Richard's royal audience. It was indeed an education in itself, now that I knew how to see the settings of the chess pieces on the board. Why had I never realised it before? I had been too taken up with the individual knights and pawns, the King and Queen. Too interested in their characters, their clothing, the rumours that knit them all together into a family, I supposed.

Be my eyes and ears, Princess Joan had instructed me, and I had agreed with no real understanding of what it would mean. But now I did. Now I separated myself from my family and watched them with a political eye. My father would have been proud of me. I saw their movements, like those same chessmen. I sensed the political cunning.

Some were moved and directed by Richard himself, those

set on the fringe of the gathering. The royal uncles. My father. Even Henry. Even the Queen who my father had thought might be a power to be reckoned with but still had to find her feet in this country alien to her. One day, perhaps. But for now Richard saw her as an acquisition who would enhance his own glory. When I caught her eye and smiled, I thought that she was watching and assessing as closely as I, even if for entirely different reasons.

For there also, not quite in the royal eye, were the two Holland brothers. How accurate my father's reading of their isolation. Although they conversed easily with Richard, there was a quickly veiled irritation on John's face when he observed, as I did, those who were fast becoming Richard's new court. The expensive coterie of flamboyant, fashionable courtiers. All young. None of the older generation who had nurtured Richard from child to man.

And at the centre, the vivacious Robert de Vere, well-born, well-blessed with looks and stature, son and heir of the Earl of Oxford. They were the group from the court-yard, well-mannered, courteous and dignified in this formal audience, and yet there was the same flattery in their glances. The same fawning as they hung on Richard's every word. And Richard loved it. Richard was in thrall. When they covered him with praise, he laughed. To one he handed a ring as if it were of no consequence, even if the stone glinted its value from across the chamber. To another he handed with casual brilliance a gilded Book of Hours worth more than my precious gold-stitched gown.

Whose was the master hand here, moving the King in his solitary steps? Was he his own man? And I knew that he was not. I could see it. It was Robert de Vere who smiled and spoke, soft-voiced, encouraging Richard in his extravagance. It was not John Holland. Richard's half-brothers received no gift on that day.

How important it was for ambition-ridden John Holland to build himself a new alliance—for he would get no promotion from Richard who had eyes for no one but de Vere. So John would make his fortune with my father. Was I then truly a part of the plan? To gain my sympathy, my compassion, my support? Was John placing stones one on another to build a formidable position of strength, with me as one of those blocks, smoothed and created by his own flattery? My father admired his talents if not his character. Henry owed a heavy debt to him, for the rescue from certain death in the Tower. As did I. Henry might scowl, but there was a powerful connection there that would never be truly severed. So what if Elizabeth was also a useful tool to weld the Hollands and the Lancasters into a formidable block of power? I could forgive him the torrid relationship with Isabella. Mostly. But to use me as a pawn in his political game I could not forgive.

And oh, I was awash with regrets, for physical desire had struck me down.

Foolish dreams indeed. The dreams of a young girl who was no longer a girl but a woman—who must accept the responsibilities demanded of her by her family, in which John Holland had no place. His seductive words, his smile, his touch—how they had roused in me a bright longing! Yet it had all been to gain my trust so that he might consolidate an alliance with my father, because Richard would give his gifts and titles and land grants elsewhere.

I spent a restless night in which all the foolishness of the tournament came to an end, leaving me to despise the exhibition I had made of my pleasure in his company. Hopefully the court would read it as mere high spirits. John Holland had no part in my future. I would go back to Hertford with Constanza and wait for Jonty to grow up.

Elizabeth of Lancaster did not wilfully satisfy her lust. The scandal of it would bring my world down upon my head, and I could not bear to see bitter condemnation in my father's face. But first…

★

I sighed, but grasped the nettle of my brother's displeasure. 'I have come to apologise.'

'And so you should.'

'I was ungracious.'

'You are always ungracious when you don't get your own way. I don't know why I expect any different. Why would you take any notice of me?'

At least Henry waved his squire out of earshot. Henry had not been difficult to find, in the stables where he was personally grooming his favourite horse, the roan stallion that had carried him to victory in the lists. Nor did he stop when I loomed at his shoulder and delivered my apology, for what it was.

'You might stop doing that, Henry.'

'I might.'

His back was discouragingly turned towards me as he wielded the brush with long sweeps over the animal's haunch. I glowered at his shoulders. Unfortunately the

fault was mine and I must make amends. I stood my
ground.

'I am trying to say I'm sorry. And I know you love Mary
more than anything in this world and would never say or do
anything to hurt her.'

A grunt.

I punched him on his shoulder, which had the desired
effect. At last he stopped wielding the brush, rubbing his
arm with a grimace.

'Yes, I do. And no I wouldn't.'

'And in three months you will have your son and heir.'

A smile transformed his face. 'Or a daughter…I pray she's
not like you!'

And I smiled back. 'Am I forgiven?'

'Perhaps…' And then when I opened my mouth to
argue: 'Yes. I forgive you.'

'Take my love to Mary.'

He cast aside the brush and enveloped me in his arms
in an enthusiastic hug, redolent of horse and smoke. I was
forgiven. I returned the embrace, briefly, then pushed him
away, brushing my hands down my bodice and skirts.

'Holy Virgin, Hal. You reek of the stables.'

'Of course I do. Is the Duke sending you home?'

'Yes.'

'You'll come to court again.'

'Perhaps. Will you be here?'

He shook his head, and I could see the exhilaration in
him. 'There are tournaments to be visited, where I can
joust. One in Hereford…'

All was right with Henry's world. If not with mine.

We left early next day, Constanza keen to set out with a strong escort and Jonty who was returning to Hertford with me. For once it was a relief to leave court with all its undercurrents and challenges. I had already made my farewells to Philippa. So now, mounted on my mare, engaged in arranging my skirts while awaiting the Pembroke escort to assemble and for Jonty to finish tightening his girth, it seemed uncomfortably as if I was running away. Or being dispatched in disgrace, which was even worse. I raised my head, fixed on presenting a picture of self-composed pride.

'Will you be ready this side of Compline, Jonty?' I asked.

'I doubt it.'

The voice, unmistakeable, smooth, honeyed, lethally attractive, pierced my composure. There he was, moving slowly to stand at my horse's shoulder, his eyes on my face as if absorbing every thought, every emotion.

Oh, I wished he had not come. To my shame, my discomfiture, I could not return the stare. Yesterday I would have. Before my father's clever lesson I certainly would have. Today I could not. Instead, with a bright smile, I looked over his head towards Jonty.

'I fear you are right, Sir John. But perhaps he is ready at last…'

Sir John laughed softly. 'Where has my sprightly Lady of the Lists vanished to?'

Now I had to look at him. 'I don't understand, Sir John.'

'No? Why can you not look at me?'

'I am looking at you.' But I looked away.

'You are very stern. I read unhappiness in your face. I see you have been warned off by a more powerful voice than that of my mother. I wonder what the Duke has said to you.'

How clever he was at reading court wiles and stratagems. I did not pretend to misunderstand. I had too much pride for that, and gathered it tight about me. Under such provocation my eyes flew to his, and stayed there.

'Yes. I have been warned.'

'Did my past dalliance with the lovely Isabella matter so much to you?'

'It was not your past mistress, sir. It was your present politics.'

'Ah! But I don't seek a political alliance with you, Elizabeth.'

His implied meaning shivered over me, but I would not be won round. 'No, but you do seek one with my father.'

'How should that be? I am in no need of Lancaster. I am the King's brother.'

He was almost persuasive, but I knew what I had seen. 'The court is splitting into factions. I have seen it. I know where your interests lie. I know that Richard intends to send you to Ireland, and you would rather not go.'

He allowed his hand to drop from my bridle, his voice suddenly severe and cold, yet no colder than his eyes.

'I did not dance with you for politics.'

'But you did to win Lancaster support, perhaps.'

A flash of anger was there, swift as a dragonfly. And then it was gone. 'It was not to encourage you to speak favourably of me that I fought for you and carried your guerdon.'

'But it would undoubtedly have been in your interests to do so, if you impressed the Duke.'

'I impressed him well enough at St Malo without your help. My skill with sword and lance would stand me in better stead than my ability to charm a woman.' I could see the sharp displeasure as he took a step back, away from me. 'I see that severe damage has been done and your mind twisted against me. By the Duke? Of course. I misjudged you, Elizabeth. I thought you had a mind to make your own decisions.'

'I do.' I leaned forward, keeping my voice low. This was not a conversation to make available to eavesdroppers. 'I see Richard with Robert de Vere. I see you clasping hands with my father and brother. I too am of use, as a pawn in your own particular game. Farewell, Sir John. It was a most enjoyable experience. You have extended my education in the value of a woman of my bloodline. And the heady delights of flirtation, of course, which I expect to find efficacious in the future. But not with you, Sir John.'

I gripped my reins, to urge my mare forward, dropping one of my gloves as she tossed her head, instantly furious with my clumsiness in doing so. Sir John retrieved it, brushing the dust from the embroidered gauntlet while I held out my hand imperiously, for fear he thought I had done it with purpose. Which I had not, although once it might have crossed my mind.

'I was maladroit.'

'I think I will keep it.' He did not seem to have much pleasure in the thought.

'What is the use of a single glove?'

'None at all. Give me the other.' He held out his hand.

'Not I!'

And then the smile had returned, that disarming gleam that swept away all his anger at the same time as it threatened to undermine my irritation with him.

'Perhaps one day you will. Or I will return this to you. For now I will keep it, in memory of a pleasant interlude. Brief but unforgettable.'

He tucked it into his belt.

'What is the point of that?'

'I don't know yet. But one day I will.'

'You will forget me as soon as I am out of sight, Sir John.'

'I will not forget you. Nor will you forget me.'

'I will try very hard.'

'I'll not allow it.' The gleam had vanished, the temper returned twofold. It was like conversing with the Roman two-faced Janus, lurching from one emotion to another.

'And how can you prevent it?'

'Elizabeth, you know as well as I that our thoughts are destined to run in tandem.'

'No, they are not!'

Hopelessly I kicked my mare to walk towards where Constanza was seated in her litter, yet could not resist looking back, and asking; 'Was I only a pleasant interlude?'

A show of puerile weakness I instantly regretted. Sir John applauded. I scowled.

'What is that?' I demanded, as cross as he, as the slap of palm against palm echoed off the walls.

'My congratulations. How well schooled you have been by the Duke to see only ill in me.'

'You misjudge me.'

'*You* misjudge *me*, madam. If you think that I courted you simply to pass the long hours at court, you might as well leave.'

'How would I know?'

'How would you not, if your emotions were truly engaged? You were the least compliant woman of my extensive acquaintance. It took me much time and effort to win your regard, and I thought it well spent. I see I wasted my time. Go then!' He bowed with exaggerated depth, the jaunty feather in his cap sweeping the dust in saturnine mockery. 'Good day to you, Countess. I wish you well in your chosen life.'

Which made me lift my head in hurt pride, presenting my back to him, furious with his rejection and with my weakness in stepping into the trap. And then behind me I could hear Jonty's voice raised in some exchange, followed by Sir John's replying to him, a reply that made Jonty guffaw with laughter. That was my future. Jonty. Not John Holland.

My heart sank along with my spirits.

I would see him again. Of course I would. Of necessity our paths would cross, but I would greet him as an acquaintance. The magic was gone. He would make his way in the world, one way or another, and I would have no part in it other than as a mildly interested member of the court. I had lost him. My floundering heart was sore indeed.

I looked around me at the Westminster scene I was leaving. What was there for me now? My father's words of disapproval, his sharp lesson in court politics, hammered into me and I knew I must concur. I would do what Philippa would do in my shoes. I would be what she would be. I would go with Constanza and Jonty and transform myself into an exemplary daughter, wife, sister. Until the day when I would fulfil my role and become an exemplary mother to the Pembroke heir.

Meanwhile I would rage against the unfairness of life, that the man who stirred my senses like the ingredients of a stock pot, had his eye set on some far distant goal that did not encompass me. And had reprimanded me for my lack of compliance.

Well, I would not comply.

And then Jonty was there, grinning, at my side.

'Are we ready?' he asked, manner disgustingly bright.

'For the past half hour.'

We rode out together.

'I like John Holland,' he said. 'Do you?'

'Once I did.'

'Oh. Have you quarrelled?'

'No. I don't quarrel.' I caught his stare. 'Well, sometimes.'

'You've lost a glove.'

'So I have.'

'I'll buy you another. It's the sort of thing a lord gives to his lady.'

'So it is.'

In the end, against my intentions, I looked back.

He was not there. Of course he was not. He would be gone to plot some other means to place himself at the centre of power. The quick blaze of his anger had surprised me, but did I not have more right to anger than he?

Chapter Five

Was there ever a man who kept his word? I did not think so.

I was settled at Hertford in stifling luxury, far from the glamour of Westminster and the questionable allure of John Holland's personality, and decidedly unhappy. Men, I decided, were the source of much heartache for women.

At court, John Holland had become a necessity for my happiness. Now that I had rejected him and his campaign for self-aggrandisement, there was no place for him in my existence. This was my life, Countess of Pembroke, waiting for her lord to reach maturity, while Jonty, running wild with the other lads of our household whenever the Master of Arms took his eye off him, showed little sign of arriving there.

I hoped the Duke was satisfied with the sacrifice I had made in the name of family alliances, for I was buried in impossible boredom and exasperation. Moreover I felt that

I had been dispatched here in disgrace, although my father had been more circumspect in his wording. Still it rankled.

John Holland had promised that he would never allow me to forget him. The silence from that quarter was shrieking in my head.

The Duke, as a placatory gesture, had offered to take me with him to Calais. I was not invited.

Jonty had promised me a pair of new gloves. I was still waiting, and would wait for ever. When he went north to Kenilworth, my husband sent a scribbled apology for his omission and information that he had a new hound. Not that I lacked such items or the wherewithal to purchase a pair with the finest leatherwork around the gauntlet, exactly like the one in John Holland's possession.

Why would he not return it?

How repetitious my life became in those months after my return. Early rising for Mass. Some reading, stitching, conversation with Constanza. Perhaps a little hunting or hawking, or walking in the gardens as the weather grew milder. The day-to-day affairs of Hertford ran as smooth as the length of silk of the altar cloth I was stitching. Our steward would have politely deflected any interest I might show. And rightly. I would have been dabbling for dabbling's sake. I had no interest in domestic affairs.

'Are you quite well?' Constanza asked, when I must have sighed inordinately over the gold thread that tangled itself into knots in my careless fingers. I cared not whether the panel was ever complete.

'I am in perfect health.'

I resisted casting it onto the floor. I must not sigh or draw attention to my restlessness.

'You are very self-absorbed. Which is unlike you.'

'I find the days heavy,' I said, as much as I was prepared to admit. 'The time hangs as if it were still.'

'Prayer would help.'

Prayer would *not* help. 'The fine weather will improve my mood.'

'Perhaps you feel for your brother's grief,' Constanza suggested, her own eyes moist.

'Yes.' And I bowed my head so that she could not see how deeply I grieved for him. And for Mary. The much desired child, a son, born at Rochford Hall, had lived no longer than four days. I had not seen Henry, and could only imagine his distress, but I mourned for him, recalling our quarrel at Westminster, which might be healed but still hovered over me. The sad loss and Mary's devastation, even though I had no experience of such grief, merely added to the weight of those days.

'I would still recommend prayer. We will pray together after supper.'

I sighed.

How lacking in excitement, in flavour, my life had become, like a winter repast, stripped of spice and herbs. Like a constant diet of salt fish and pottage. Even our visitors were dull, with nothing to say for themselves.

And still John Holland haunted me.

And what was he doing? John Holland was far too busy to have any thought of me, honing his diplomatic skills in embassies with the Duke in Calais. He was in good favour with my father. Obviously my support for his cause was an irrelevance.

As his presence was to me.

I set another row of stitches with consummate concentration before abandoning it, informing Constanza that she would find me in my own chamber. I did not know what to do with my thoughts or my restless feet and fingers, but at least I could pace there without drawing attention.

'Don't forget to meet for prayers, Elizabeth.'

'Nothing would please me more, madam.'

*

And then it began, with a Lancaster courier bringing letters and news to Constanza, as they frequently did, passing over a little package with what could only be described as a sly grimace and well-practised guile, as if he often delivered packages which should not be delivered. I received it with equal sleight of hand, hiding it in my oversleeve. And when I unwrapped it, it was to find a silver pin in the shape of a heart, quite plain without gems, but snapped in two. Wrapped around the damaged silver was a twist of parchment and a note in a hand I did not know.

A trifle, broken asunder, as my heart is damaged.

It gave me much food for thought, wagering an emerald pin on the author of that sentiment. It was not Jonty, for whom poetic chivalry was still buried deep beneath the urgent training of hawks and hounds.

Who would single me out for a gift worthy of a chivalric troubadour?

Ha!

And with the passage of days and weeks the gifts continued, all under cover, all small enough to be hidden away from prying eyes in my elm coffer. In some weeks not one courier set foot in Hertford without some item accompanying him, cleverly wrapped in leather or a screw of paper, and the note that accompanied each was brief, enigmatic and unsigned. There was no clue here to the author of the gifts. But for me, there was no riddle to solve.

A pilgrim's token from the shrine at Walsingham, the cheap pewter dull with the damp of travel.

May the face of the Blessed Virgin smile on you, when you do not allow me the privilege.

A mirror case carved in ivory showing a lady crowning her chosen knight with a garland.

I cannot see my true love, but you can see the face that stops my heart.

A pair of candle trimmers. Very practical!

As you douse your candle, imagine my arms enfolding you in the dark of your bed.

A feathered mask, its edges frayed with age, reminiscent of some past Twelfth Night masque.

Would you hide your true emotions from me?

A ribboned lover's knot, nothing more than a fairing.

What value my love for you, Lady of Lancaster?

A pair of finches in a wicker cage, which arrived in the full light of day, singing cheerfully.

They will sing my petition for your true regard, whereas I cannot sing at all.

Which was true enough. John Holland might have no voice but he was not without low cunning. Had he also lost

his wits to send me so winsome an offering, but something
so obvious and impossible to accept discreetly?

'Who are the birds from?' Philippa asked when I had
hung them in my chamber and they began to trill in the
sunshine. Philippa had returned to Hertford for which I was
inexpressibly grateful.

'Jonty,' I replied. 'In recompense for forgetting the
gloves.'

Whether my sister believed me or not I had no idea, but
I found myself waiting, day after day, for the next offering,
disappointed when none materialised, setting up a dialogue
that part infuriated me, part intrigued.

He will grow tired of it.

He will not. He is trying to wear down my resistance to
him.

He will grow weary if you do not reply.

But I will not reply. To reply will put me in his power. To
show any interest whatsoever will tell him that he is in my
thoughts.

Some of them are charmingly subtle.

And some are particularly crude!

Some are romantic.

Wait until he sends me a dose of agrimony to move the
bowels…

*What does he intend, with a wooing of such charming foolish-
nesses?*

I knew exactly what he intended. He had great practice
in seduction. Did Isabella not have a coffer full of such offer-
ings?

Do you care what Isabella has?

No. And I wish he would stop!

But he did not, and the gifts, trivial as they were, warmed my heart's blood. But I was not seduced. I would not be. My feet could never walk in unison with those of John Holland.

And then. A single glove, which I recognised full well. My own. Was he returning it to signal he no longer had a care to keep it? Perhaps he would at last allow me to forget him, for my mind and my senses to live at ease.

My heart leapt, dismay a chill coating in my belly. I did not want that. I tore at the wrapping, dropping it to the floor. 'It's just the glove I lost.' Philippa was keeping a closer eye on my gifts. I busied myself discovering its mate in my coffer to hide any heat in my cheeks

'No need for Jonty to buy you new ones then!' she remarked dryly. 'You seem to be in receipt of many packages.'

I crunched the message in the palm of my hand, smoothing it out as soon as I could, and exhaled with relief.

To restore the lost glove to its partner. They were not made to exist apart. As you were not made to live apart from me…

Slowly I pulled on the reunited pair, smoothing the soft leather over my fingers. No, they were not made to exist apart. This was right that they should be together. But was I prepared to acknowledge my own need? He was not allowing me to forget him. It exercised all my will to struggle to banish him from my memory. I was burning with loss and longing. And would have continued to do so until another torn piece of parchment, finely folded, made its way to me. As I opened it, suitably intrigued at the blank sheet with no message, a smattering of coarse dust fell to the floor. I knelt. Not dust but tiny pieces of dried leaves. Rescuing some of them, I placed them in my palm and sniffed. The aroma was very faint.

'What's this?' I asked Philippa, holding out my hand.

She too sniffed. 'An herb. Is it rue?'

It could be. So what was this? A pinch of rue and no words of love or seduction. I knew its uses, but not its meaning. As it crossed my mind to wonder which of his female acquaintances had supplied him with this, I headed to the kitchens for a discussion with Constanza's cook, to ask the question: 'If a woman receives a gift of rue, what should she understand by it?'

★

John Holland intrigued me, fascinated me, repelled me. I despised the artifice he employed to woo my senses, for rue implied regret. It implied grief and farewell.

He had given up on me at last.

Or had he? Was this merely another ploy to whet my appetite, enticing me with sentimental humours, only to cast me adrift with a clever pinch of crushed leaves that I had dusted from my hands to the floor?

I cared not.

Oh, but I wished…But then, I did not know what it was that I truly wished for. All I heard was the echo of John's voice in my mind, in my ear, whispering inducements with all the subtlety of the snake in the Garden of Eden. It was dangerous, but I enjoyed the danger. What woman would not?

★

One of Philippa's women fetched me, with a warning that set my heart racing. My sister was unwell. When I came into her bedchamber, it was to find her weeping without restraint, her ladies fluttering round her.

'Philippa!'

I was across the space from door to bed in an instant, taking her in my arms.

'Don't mind me.' Her reply was muffled against my shoulder. 'It's nothing.'

My sister did not weep for nothing. My sister rarely wept. I cast about in my mind for a reason that would reduce her to such misery.

'Is it Henry?'

'No.'

'Mary, then…' Had she not recovered from the tragic birth of their little son?

'No. They're happy enough. They've agreed to wait before Mary invites him to her bed again.'

And Philippa wept even harder.

'Tell me.' Waving her women away, I shook her gently. 'I'll hang the finches in your room if you don't.' Their shrill singing wearied after a while.

'What will become of me?'

'I can't imagine. Are we talking about the next hour or the next three years?'

She did not smile, but at least she told me.

'I am twenty-two years old. Where is the marriage plan for me? What if there never is?'

'But there will be.'

'Don't tell me there is a foreign prince just waiting for

me to land in his lap. Sometimes I have a terrible conviction that I will end my days in a convent.'

I smoothed her hair, wiped her cheeks. Philippa was softer than I, gentler, far kinder. What a waste it would be if she did not have her own family to love and cherish.

'It will happen. You know that the Duke will…'

'I have no one—and you are so ungrateful,' she interrupted on a wail of misery. 'You have a husband. You have a man who flirts with you disgracefully. And you don't want either of them…' She covered her mouth with her hands looking at me in utter dismay, eyes blind with tears. 'I never meant to say that.'

I grew still under the bitter lash. Was it not true? I was wrapped about in my own desires, with no thought for Philippa's lack. How hard she must find it, with both Henry and I wed, and there was nothing I could say to remedy her grief. Except that I could be more understanding, less heedless of everything that did not touch my own life. I promised myself that I would try. But for now…

'I'll let you have John Holland,' I said.

'I don't want him,' she sniffed. 'He's a born troublemaker.'

'Then you can share Jonty.' Philippa sniffed again, but her tears were ending. 'A new audience for his enthusiasms is just what he wants. If you talk to him about anything that yaps or cheeps he will love you more than he loves me.'

At last she smiled, but it had put my faults into stark relief. I was too self-absorbed. I always had been. Maturity demanded that I make amends. In the following days, I devoted myself to her entertainment, until Philippa smiled and played her lute again without descending into lachrymose melodies, and I did not mention Jonty or John Holland even once.

The news of the cataclysm, the whole unbelievable order of events, kept company with us, dominating our thoughts, throughout every mile of that endless journey from Hertford. In the heat of the summer of 1384 Philippa and I were riding for Richard's court at Sheen on the Thames, as if a storm wind harried our heels. Not Constanza—it would take a major tremor of the earth to move Constanza from Hertford—but Philippa and I discovered a need to be where events were unfolding.

Or at least I did, and persuaded my sister who was not averse to accompanying me, even if we were silent for most of the journey, the potential horror of what might have occurred cramming our thoughts without mercy. Philippa had the angel of death riding beside her to expel her anxiety over her unmarried state.

It had all begun at Salisbury where Richard, summoning a meeting of parliament, was staying at a house belonging to Robert de Vere. Was Richard ever so uncontrolled, so lacking in good common sense? Richard's political acumen barely matched that of a tadpole. After an early Mass, a Carmelite friar had found his way to whisper in the ear of our puissant King that our father, the Duke of Lancaster, was knee deep in a plot against Richard's life. The Duke, the friar said with monastic certainty, had the death of Richard in mind. On what evidence? The friar did not know, but he had been told. No, he could not recall who had told him...

What would I have done in the circumstances? The question beat at my mind in time with my mare's hooves.

Thrown the accusation out, along with the mischief-making friar.

What did Richard do?

I hissed a breath as my mare, under pressure, stumbled.

Richard flew into a fury, ordering that the Duke be put to death for so foul a treason.

'Why would Richard do so ill-considered a thing?' I demanded of Philippa. 'To execute our father without trial. To even believe it in the first place.'

'Because he is afraid.' All Philippa's anxiety over her virginal state had vanished under her disgust. 'Richard is afraid of any man with royal blood who wields power more adeptly than he can.'

'Surely he cannot believe the Duke's guilt. I would not.'

'Richard does not have your confidence, Elizabeth. Or your loyalty to family.'

No, he did not. Fortunately the more reasoning of the lords around him persuaded our King of the unwisdom of so precipitate a reaction. So the Duke was safe, that much we knew, but in the brooding atmosphere at court, who knew what might transpire? We needed to be there to see for ourselves. Nothing would have kept me at Hertford.

Yet for me there was another gnawing anxiety, far more urgent now that the Duke was safe.

What was John Holland's role in this? I was unsure, and I disliked what I had heard. The friar, taken into custody for his lies, had been seized by men who proceeded to apply unmentionable torture to extract information over the origins of the plot, until the friar died a horrific death. Which might, as I was forced to admit, have passed my attention except for the name of one of the royal household involved. The hands of John Holland, the same hands that chose and sent me gifts and fairings, were now coated in blood in this unpleasant episode.

Why was the friar dead? To close his mouth for ever, stopping any incriminating evidence against those who paid him to perjure the Duke, the court gossips opined. For who was to blame? The men who had done him to death, perhaps?

I needed to see John Holland. This man who touched my heart in some manner, had by this unsavoury incident shattered my confidence in my own judgement.

Before we left Hertford, I handed a bound coffer to one of our escort to strap to his saddle.

'Come on, Elizabeth! Do we need the extra burden?'

'Yes,' I replied to Philippa who was hovering.

'What is that?'

'Don't ask.'

When I handed the little wicker cage containing two singing finches to one of my women, Philippa made no attempt to disguise her impatience.

'Do you really need to take those? You can buy them two a penny in the street in London.'

'They travel with me,' I said.

'If you want to be rid of them, why not just open the cage door?' My sister had the uncomfortable ability to read my mind.

'That would rob me of a chance to drive my opinion home,' I replied.

'I'll remind you of that when the birds drive you demented by their tweeting.'

But I was already mounted, my mind already in London. What would I say to him when I met him again? Was ever a woman thrown into disarray by the actions of a man who should have meant nothing to her?

You love him, don't you?

I was not entirely certain that I knew what love was. And how could I love a man who might be embroiled in foul murder?

*

'What do you think?' Philippa asked as we approached the gateway to the royal palace at Sheen, and were forced by untoward circumstances to draw rein.

I looked aghast at what we saw. As did my sister.

'I think there's a storm about to break on our heads,' I replied. 'I don't like it. And I don't understand why our own Sergeant at Arms looks as if he would turn us away.'

There were guards at the gate, forbidding us entry, and the guards were in Lancaster colours. I recognised the Sergeant at Arms; I could even name him. I could not imagine what was afoot. All the personal anxieties, the difficulties of choices when violent death had taken a role, were swept aside by the sight of the Lancaster retinue equipped for war.

'Has something happened we don't know of?' I asked.

Philippa merely shook her head.

All was not right with Richard, that much we knew. For the past months his court had exuded the noxious stench of a festering sore, the atmosphere tense, strained with rifts within and without. Dangers had rumbled, from a Scottish invasion of Northumberland, to Richard's unpopular policy of negotiating a peace with France. As for the cost of Richard's household and entertainments, parliamentary voices were raised in dismay, and aimed at the royal favourites of Burley, de la Pole and de Vere. Over it all had hung the uncompromising heat with no rain to assuage heated tempers. Drought had threatened. Famine and death.

But this was quite different, enough to touch my nape with fear. Lancaster guards on the gates of Sheen?

At least they recognised us, the Sergeant at Arms offering a smart salute.

'What's going on, Master Selby?'

'Some trouble, my lady.' A laconic enough reply but his face was set in grim lines.

'Is the Duke here?' Philippa asked.

'He is, mistress.' He helped me to dismount. 'If you go in, you'll hear his voice. He's not best pleased—and who can blame him, I'd say.'

'Is Sir John Holland here?' I asked.

'He is. And doubtless deciding which way to hop.' And when I looked puzzled, he added: 'Which side of the fire will scorch him least, if you take my meaning.'

Which made not much sense, until we stepped into the Great Hall which was awash with uncontrolled emotion. It all but blistered us so that we halted in the doorway.

'Your father would call down shame on your head if he saw the counsellors you choose to give ear to.' The Duke, in the centre of the chamber, raised his voice well above normal pitch as he addressed Richard.

'I am King. I choose my own counsellors.' Supreme on his dais was the King, his pointed nose quivering with fury, fists clenched.

The heated heart of a conflagration the like of which I had never seen. And there were Richard's courtiers, including John Holland, awaiting the outcome.

'And bad counsellors at that.' The Duke was in no mood to retreat. He might not name de Vere, but there was no doubting the sleek object of the Duke's disgust.

'I do not have to answer to you, Uncle. By what right do you take me to task?'

'As for shame…' My father continued, jaw rigid with a pure reflection of the royal fury. 'How shameful is it for a King to stoop to murder one of his own family? His own blood. You would have me done to death?'

Was this some monstrous joke? Some ill thought out masque?

It was beyond belief, but my heart began to throb with a heavy beat as I allowed myself to observe the faces of those present. There was no laughter. Nor was there shock. No one questioned the accusation, despite Richard's face becoming perfectly white. The Duke was fearless in his attack, but I could see the lines of a breastplate beneath his robe. He had come here in fear of his life. John Holland, eyes alert, lips close set, standing a little apart from both, kept his gaze close-trained on his brother. What he was thinking I could not imagine. If he saw my entrance, he gave no reaction. Nor would he, for all was balanced on a dagger edge and any dalliance would be far from his mind. This was a catastrophic expression of power with the outcome undecided, and with a crucial decision for John Holland to make. Lancaster or King? How mask-like his face, a face I had come to know with its range of vivid expression. John Holland's decision today might deny any need for me to be here, effectively ending any future communication between us.

This was politics in the raw and my stomach lurched.

'Why would you see a need for revenge on me, sire?' the Duke demanded. 'I am your man. I have always been your man.'

'You humiliate me by your lectures, sir.'

'So you would plot my murder with the likes of de Vere?'

The gathering was still, motionless in anticipation, de Vere as frozen in time as the carved doorpost on my left. John Holland took one step forward.

'Sire…'

But Richard commanded his brother's silence with a crude gesture. 'How dare you so accuse me?' Richard said to the Duke.

'Because it is the truth. I will no longer attend you at court. I fear for my life at your hands. Should a man have to wear armour in the presence of his nephew? By God, he should not.'

And on that, the Duke bowed and stalked out, brushing past Philippa and me without any sign of recognition. The expression on his face smote at my heart.

'You will not walk away from me!' Richard's words exploded, high-pitched, his hand clenched on the sword at his side, and he would have leapt from the dais if John Holland had not stepped forward.

'No, sire.' His hand closed on Richard's sleeve. 'Would you strike your uncle?'

'Don't touch me!'

'Richard!' I saw it, the tightening hand of a brother on the King's sword-arm as Sir John strove to draw the poison from the deadly situation. I took note as Sir John's hand moved to close round the King's wrist. And Richard paused. 'You need to consider, sire.'

'Why would I need to consider?' Still Richard's features were livid. 'I am King here and I demand honour, even from my uncle.'

'Lancaster does indeed honour you. Has he not always been the most loyal of your subjects?'

He might release the sword, but Richard wrenched his arm away and stormed from the room. With a shrug and a glance at his brother Thomas, John Holland followed the King.

Thus the audience stuttered into an uneasy end.

Oh, I admired the stance John Holland had taken, his calming words, his attempt to deflect Richard's wrath. Here was a man who was more than a skilled courtier, all outward glamour with sword and tongue. Here was a depth of understanding that surprised me, a skill to diffuse a potentially unpleasant situation, and a concern for my father that touched my senses.

But in pursuing Richard, to whose side had John Holland, as Master Selby had so aptly put it, ultimately hopped?

★

I sat on the edge of my bed, hands clasped tightly in my lap, and thought through the mass of uncontrolled passion and dark threats I had just witnessed. So much anger. So much potential violence. And then, because it was not in my nature to sit, I prowled round the room. A royal plot to murder my father? How could I believe that? Yet there had been no hiss of disbelief, no intake of breath. Richard had denied so heinous a crime, but he would hardly admit to it in public.

And where was John Holland now?

He had followed Richard. If he had given his loyalty to his brother, what need for me to be here? Suddenly the death of the Carmelite friar was shadowed into insignificance, the events of the past hour stirring my thoughts into a new pattern, but one equally disquieting. The choice I had come to Sheen to make might not be mine to make after all. Richard's perfidy might have driven a sword into the very heart of his family, creating new alliances, dividing irrevocably friend from foe.

If I was of a cynical mind, this was a ploy in the game John Holland had instigated, bringing me back to court, where his influence could once more hold sway. But this was no game. This was a royal challenge for power, Richard throwing down his gage. The whole affair stank of blood and betrayal.

'Stop it!' Philippa said at last after another track across the room.

'I can't.'

'Is this the man you have a…' she struggled for words— '…an *affection* for? For shame. Do you not see what sort of man he is?'

Affection? It was no light affection. I wanted him.

I formed the words in my head. Then out loud. 'I want him.'

'Then that is the sin of lust!'

I pondered. No—I did not think it was. There was something deeper in the way this man encroached on my thoughts as well as my emotions. But my sister was right, I was in need of some answers.

'If you want my advice,' she chivvied, 'go and return all those silly trinkets to him and make an end to it.'

I stopped mid prowl, my gaze finding hers.

'Go and see him,' she urged. 'Whatever it is between you, end it. Tell him not to send any more. No good will come of it, and you're a fool if you persist in a flirtation that will end in nothing but shame and scandal—for you if not for him.'

Of course she had noticed the gifts and deduced the giver, adding two and two to make enough white doves to fill a dovecote. How could I have thought that she would not? Philippa, leaving me in no doubt of her opinion, was rarely so acrimonious in her choice of words.

'I doubt he is in the mood to send more gifts.' I worried at the border of my flowing oversleeves, teasing the delicate stitching without mercy.

'No one is. It seems to me that no man at court is in a mood to do anything other than drive a dagger between the shoulder blades of his nearest opponent.'

'I doubt he is in the mood to see me,' I continued, realising how trivial my own concerns were in comparison. And yet this was a matter of my own flesh and blood. And, for me, of the heart. 'I don't even know if he has turned his back on Lancaster and is even now bolstering cousin Richard in his plots to have us all murdered in our beds.'

'You won't know until you talk to him. Do you think he was involved in the plot against the Duke?'

'How can I possibly know? My heart says no, but it seemed to be that every man in that room looked guilty of something!' It took me the length of a breath to decide. 'I'll go.'

'What will you do?' she asked as my hand raised the latch.

I paused, looked back. 'I don't know yet.'

Nor did I. All I knew was that I must hear from his own mouth that he was innocent.

'Just don't forget that you are a married woman, Elizabeth. And he is a man who is not averse to taking advantage of you.'

'How can I forget?'

★

While Philippa took her sharp eyes and even sharper tongue off to find the Queen, to discover the present situation between Anne and her husband, I organised one of my waiting women for appearance's sake and, carrying my birdcage, marched the chilly journey to where the King's brothers were housed in the rambling palace. I met no one, heard nothing but the occasional cheep from under the cover. I stopped outside the door, which opened as I raised my hand to knock, and Thomas Holland strode out, coming to a halt.

'Elizabeth.'

'Thomas.'

Neither was pleased to see the other.

'Not a propitious time for one of your family to be here,' he said, mildly given the circumstances, with the King fuelled with blood-lust. He eyed the birdcage. 'At least Henry's had the sense to make himself scarce.'

'Is your brother in?' I asked, ignoring the warning.

'Yes. I'd come back later if I were you. Or not at all. We've enough to worry about without you adding to the mix.'

I stood my ground. There was too much I needed to know, to say.

When Thomas shrugged and marched off, I knocked and, giving no time for the occupant to refuse or procrastinate, entered into a chamber that was stark and tidy, everything in its place. It was the chamber of a soldier used to campaigning, rather than the flamboyance of one of Richard's courtiers, but I had no time to dissect my quarry's taste in decoration. John Holland was standing by the window, a cup of ale in his hand. Hearing the latch, he spun round.

'What in God's name do you want now?' Fury was vivid in every line of his face. So strong was it that I had to resist taking a step back. Nor did it dissipate when he recognised me. 'Go away, Elizabeth.'

I would not. Instead I smiled at my waiting woman as if there were nothing amiss. 'Leave those. You may wait outside for me.'

A curtsy and the travelling chest was placed on a coffer, next to which I added the cage of singing finches, who instantly fell silent. The sneer on John's face made me flinch.

'Don't tell me. You're returning them all.' He strode to

the far side of the chamber as if he would put distance between himself and my female stupidity. 'In God's name, girl! I've no time for trifles.'

'Is that what they are?' The answer to my question was vitally important.

'Of what importance is a handful of silly, worthless fairings compared with Richard's stupidity and betrayal of Lancaster on one side, and the Duke's intemperance on the other?'

'None, of course.' So that was all they were to him. 'You followed Richard. Have you sworn your support to him? Have you abandoned service to Lancaster?'

'I have not. I delivered my brother into the hands of the Queen and wished her well of him. I don't hold out much hope. Only the Princess has the power to offset de Vere's present influence over Richard. Do you know what my brother's done? Only given the town and castle of Queenborough to de Vere as a symbol of his affection. A royal possession, handed over like a piece of marchpane. And then Richard explodes with fury when Lancaster and others take him to task for poor government. But I don't expect you to see what's going on under your nose, any more than those damned birds.'

'I do see.' The finches were singing endlessly again in incongruous backdrop to the emotion in the room. My heart might have sunk to the soles of my feet under his crude animadversion on my frivolity, but indeed it leapt a little. 'Do I understand that you have not withdrawn your allegiance from the Duke?'

He did not hear me, anger roiling through him so that

the air all but shimmered. 'The Duke had every justification in his attack, even if more forthright than usual—which is never good policy with Richard who is congenitally incapable of accepting criticism. De Vere and Mowbray are a bad influence and Richard hasn't the sense of an earwig to see it. So here's the King digging a hole at his feet, into which he'll assuredly fall if he allows his passions to rule his wits. What is he thinking? Antagonising Lancaster. Plotting bloody murder. Has he no sense? God keep us from idiot kings. And there's nothing we can do about it.'

Put so brutally, I realised anew the conflict that threatened to rend my kindred apart. Meanwhile, John drained the cup, looking as if he might toss it against the wall, but placed it carefully on the hearth at his feet. His temper might be up, but he still had it in hand as he took a breath and looked at me. Perhaps the fire in his eye had died a little. He sighed as if he realised the futility of trying to reason with Richard. Or indeed with me.

'What are you doing here?' he asked.

'I came to see you.'

'I thought you had rejected me as an ambitious upstart, intent on furthering my career at the expense of the Lancaster connection. Using you as a pawn in my own particularly nasty game, I think you said.'

'That was before your gifts.' I ran my finger along the bars of the cage, making the little birds chirrup even louder. 'I came here to ask you if what I had heard was true. That you had been party to the torture and murder of the friar. Is it true?'

'Yes. Does it trouble you?'

He was brutally frank. 'I'm not sure. And my next question; are you a man of crooked loyalties?'

He grimaced. 'Crooked loyalties?' Then suddenly he smiled, a curve of his mouth that, unpleasantly, was almost a leer as he leaned his shoulder and elbow against the window surround, blatantly disrespectful of my presence. No, he was not in the best of moods. 'So you don't like the thought of a lover with blood on his hands.'

'You are not my lover. But if you were—what woman would?'

'Have sense! How can it disturb you to any degree, after what we have seen today, when it's clear that Richard has no thought for your father's safety? Of course I was involved. What do you do with a priest who claims to have evidence of so vile a plot at Lancaster's hands that you know it cannot be true? You discover the source of the slander.'

'I understand that.'

'If you are asking if it was my hand that took his life, it was not. If I was cognisant of what went on and gave sanction, yes. It's not important. Not after today's episode.'

'What if there were more evidence?'

'There was no more.' The quality of his voice was chilling in its lack of tolerance. 'Or do you think we closed his mouth for good to stop him pointing an incriminating finger? And if you think that, where would that finger point, Madam Elizabeth? Would it perhaps point at me? Do you suspect me of plotting to rid England of Lancaster's influence?'

The fury was truly alight again.

'That's not what I thought.'

But it had stepped into my mind. It was not impossible. For the guilty to destroy the one witness who claimed knowledge of the evidence, evidence that would drench them all in treason. How many at court would willingly destroy the Duke? But would John Holland put his hand to such a betrayal? It was exactly the dilemma that had kept me vicious company since the rumours began.

'Would you think that of me?' he demanded.

'No.'

'Thank God for that.' The leer hardened into cynical, but in an instant he swooped, crossing the room to seize my hands in his before I could stop him. 'I did it *propter amorem ducis*, Elizabeth, for love of the Duke. Just as I tried to remonstrate with Richard today. Since Richard is become unreliable and uncontrolled, the Duke needs friends at court. I am honoured to be called one of them. Does that set your mind at rest? Is the lesson in politics over?'

'I needed to know that you were still a friend of the Duke, not his enemy.'

He released me as if my hands burned, and I realised that, by questioning his loyalties, I had hurt him. How much hurt was there in the palace of Sheen on this day. He prowled the room, much like a wolf before the hounds that would bring it down. Striding to where the chest and birdcage sat, he placed one on the floor and held the other out to me, then delved into the coffer beneath. From it he took a silver collar that glittered in the light as he held it up.

'Do you recognise this?'

Yes.' Of course I did. I had probably seen one such every day of my life.

He cast it over his own head so that it lay flat on his shoulders, the joined 'S' shapes neatly fitting together with serpentine splendour. A Lancaster livery collar, a symbol of loyalty and maintenance, much prized by those in service to the Duke.

'This is mine, given to me by your father in recognition of my support in times of war and peace. As well as in gratitude for preserving the life of his son and daughter when the rebels would have shed their blood. I wear it with honour. I will continue to wear it with honour towards you and your family until the day of my death.'

It could not have been stated more succinctly, even though his voice was rough-edged as he came to stand before me.

'Does that satisfy you?'

'Yes.'

Lightly I ran my fingers over the gleaming links, but, still in the grip of emotion, he pulled away to stride to the empty hearth.

'So. To return to your presence here. Are you returning those?' he asked over his shoulder as he retrieved his cup and refilled it, then emptying it in one long swallow, wiping his mouth with his hand. 'If so, you've done it, so go away and leave me in peace.'

And this time he tossed the empty cup on the hearth where it shattered, shards of the glazed pottery spread wide. It could all end here, all the tantalising dreams demolished. Is that what I wanted? Would that not be the best outcome after all?

Go. Go back to Hertford.

There was not one of my family that would advise me otherwise.

'I was going to return the gifts,' I stated carefully, still holding the infuriating birds. 'I thought it was a complication I did not need in my life. But I need to know.'

'What do you need to know, apart from whether I murdered the hapless friar?'

'If you meant what you wrote with the worthless trifles.'

'Yes. Why else would I write them?'

'Were they worthless?' Abandoning the finches, walking forward to stand in front of him again, I looked up into his face. Our eyes were not quite on a level. I had forgotten how tall he was, how effortlessly he could dominate a room, a conversation. But I did not want flippancy. I wanted honesty.

'Were they worthless to you?' John Holland looked at me, questioning me, the careless violence now in check, the anger gradually draining, so that I could see the tension in his body relax, the tempestuous passions gone at last. 'What do you want from me, Elizabeth?

'I am not entirely sure. But I thought I should put you right on one matter.' He tilted his chin as I drew from my sleeve a bunch of rue that I tucked into the links of the livery chain. 'You were wrong to send me rue with no inscription. Rue is not only an expression of regret and goodbye. It is powerful protection.' I had used my time well amongst the ancient works in my father's library at Hertford. 'It claims a healing power against all manner of poison and the evil eye. I think you might need it, as matters stand at court.'

He laughed softly.

'So you came to put me right, Madam Elizabeth.'

'I thought I should.'

I was trembling at what I had done, at what I was hoping for.

'You might not know your own mind, but I know what I want.' His voice had become as gentle as the soft paw of a kitten. How silver-tongued he could be when he chose. 'There is no ending, no regret between us. There is only what we choose to make of the future.'

'I think I am afraid,' I admitted.

'What need? Our future is ours for the making.' My hands were back in his, held firmly. 'Get an annulment and let us join hands. Enough of wooing. Let me show you our future unwinding before us.'

Drawing me forward he bent his head and touched his lips to mine, a momentary brush of mouth against mouth, when I had expected something of an onslaught.

'I have discovered a desire in me, a desire far too strong for my own good, I expect,' he said. 'I would sweep you up, but must remind myself of your inexperience.'

Never had I expected him to offer such a declaration. 'Do you desire me?' I asked, startled into so clumsy a question.

He kissed me again, lingeringly this time, invitingly, and I allowed it with warmth spreading down to my feet, until he raised his head, and waited.

'*You* have to reply in kind,' he advised when I remained mute, conscious only of the jolt of pure desire. 'Have the troubadours taught you nothing?'

I struggled to explain, helplessly. 'I think that I have…that I have a desire for you too.'

Which made him laugh. 'Well, that will not move the earth as a declaration. Another kiss perhaps.' Which he applied with some fervour. And another until all thoughts were driven from my head. Then: 'What made you change your mind?'

'I didn't. I haven't.' How foolish such a denial when my lips were warm, my blood a drum-beat in my ears. 'Even at the last moment, as I stood outside your door, I came to say it must stop.'

'How you compromise the truth, Countess! I don't believe you. Why not just kept the fairings without any commitment, or send your serving woman to deliver them and leave them outside my door?'

His smile was like a blessing, the return of his seductive tone a joy to me.

'I always tell the truth.' I smiled.

'Then you are unlike any other woman I know.'

'Well, I'll tell you. The finches are a nuisance. I had to return them.'

'You could have given them to Constanza rather than bring them all the way to Sheen.' He kissed me again, tempting me to kiss him back, which I did. My education in the arts of love was being extended by the minute.

'What made you change your mind, my wanton love?' he asked, placing me a little distance away from him.

So in the end I told him as much as I was prepared to say, only a portion of the truth, but all I would admit to him.

'It was the glove. You returned it, to restore the pair, two halves of a whole.' It seemed to me a reasonable argument that he might accept.

'Is that what we are?' The tilt of his head was encouraging.

'So I think. I might be certain if you kissed me again.'

I did not tell him the full truth of it, as he was pleased to humour me with a succession of kisses. I would not. As I knew full well, there was the threat of too much pain in this relationship, for both of us, and yet I was drawn into it beyond all the teachings of my young years. All my good intentions had been cast aside.

What was it that I had seen that day at Sheen that had shaken my determination to reject John Holland's gifts and his professed desire to know me more intimately? Standing in the doorway of Richard's audience chamber, I had become aware of such bitterness, such strife that would destroy the unity of those I loved. Henry deliberately absent. Constanza lonely, succoured only by prayer and futile ambition at Hertford. Richard and the Duke at lethal odds. Philippa unhappy in her unwedded state. Dame Katherine rejected and isolated in Lincoln. And I in the grip of a loveless and hopeless marriage.

Was happiness to be discovered anywhere, for any of us? What an untrustworthy emotion it was. And how ephemeral in its power. In the face of such a vast well of despair, how could I not decide to seize the chance of happiness with a man I believed had more than an affection for me? A man who might just touch my soul?

And so my father's warnings were swept aside along with my brother's disapproval, my new political awareness tucked away in a coffer like an unwanted gift of a bodice that did not become me. Yes, it was wrong. Yes, it would bring down a maelstrom of horrified accusations upon us if we were anything less than discreet. And yes, there were clear bounds to this relationship beyond which I would not yet go. But the delight when John Holland kissed me erased all sense of duty and honour and loyalty. All I had been raised to believe to be acceptable for a daughter of the Duke of Lancaster was scattered like blossoms in a high gale, and all for the sake of John Holland. As our families strained under increasing acrimony, we would acknowledge our attraction to each other.

And here was the true reason for my present embrace within the confines of John Holland's arms. The Duke would be appalled if he knew the exact moment when this change of heart had been born. He would condemn me utterly, but there he himself stood at the very centre of my decision, for I had seen the pain on my father's face as he had walked from that audience chamber. A proud man, a clever man, a man who wielded authority with all the confidence of his royal blood, never had I seen the Duke wear his years with such anguish as when his life's work to guide Richard seemed to be over with such a brutal exchange of accusation and counter accusation. I had seen how alone and isolated he was in that Great Hall at Sheen, ripped apart from his royal duty on one side, and from the woman he loved on the other.

How important was Dame Katherine to my father?

She was the reason he lived and breathed, and how ardently he mourned her loss. It was written in the grooves that marked his brow and indented his lips. And now, searching John Holland's saturnine expression, I let my thoughts settle, fitting together into a plain pattern. How important was this enchantment that called to my heart? If I was fortunate to discover it I must not let it go. I would never find it with Jonty. But it seemed that I had found it, even in the few hours we had spent together, with John Holland.

Oh, I was not blind. John Holland had a temper that could gallop like a frenzied horse, coupled with an ungovernable restlessness more powerful than mine. He was a law unto none but his own ambitions. He could use words to flatter or destroy. Could I love a man such as this? Could I ever, with a whole heart, trust him?

But there was also, I believed, an unquestionable streak of loyalty in him. In receipt of my father's annuity, he had stood for him against his own brother. How hard must that have been? Here was a man of some tenacity of mind, a man I could admire.

Then again—did I want a man to woo me who had blood on his hands, by his own admission?

'One thing…' I said, closing my fingers around his wrist as he finally led me to the door.

'Another question?'

There had to be, a final laying to rest of the events of that day, but I hoped I could read John Holland accurately enough to anticipate his reply. If I could not, then all my decision making was in vain 'Was there any evidence at all that the friar's tale was true? That my father was involved in a plot against Richard? Was the friar's death worth the doing?'

'None.' His eyes were without shadow, without deceit. 'There was none at all. It was a plot against the Duke by his enemies. Your father is without blame.' A final kiss, still beautifully controlled but with the promise of more. 'Now go, before we compromise your sparkling reputation further.'

He filled my youthful heart with joy. It was as if a candle had been lit to illuminate every vista as I walked back to my own rooms, my waiting woman carrying the coffer and the finches, to hang them once again in the window, their twittering a symbol of my choice.

'I see we are still saddled with those creatures,' Philippa observed. 'Does that mean that your meeting with Sir John was to your liking rather than mine?'

'Perhaps.'

I would tell no one. Not yet. Not while it was still so new and bright and yet so dangerous.

'I will pray that the Blessed Virgin protect you.'

But from what I was entirely uncertain.

I fell into pensive mood. Why this man? Why was John Holland, of all the courtiers I knew, able to demand my attention? Even to lure me into impropriety?

Was it his unquestionably handsome features? I did not think so. There were many pretty creatures at Richard's court who stirred no emotion within me unless it was envy of the gleam of their hair or the length of their eyelashes.

Perhaps, then, it was his presence, the impact of his will, even when unspoken. But I had been used to that all my life. No one could compare with my father for making an entrance, and Henry bode fair to match him. Why should I be drawn to John Holland's bold demeanour?

His skills in the jousting were incomparable. The lithe,

muscular strength, the practised agility, the flamboyant display of pure talent all made other women sigh too, but that was no reason for me to abandon all I knew of behaviour suitable for a Plantagenet daughter. Why not just sit and admire? No need to endanger my reputation for kisses with a tournament champion who had a host of women willing to humour him.

A reputation for wild intransigence, was, of course, always attractive in a handsome man, but was that enough?

John Holland was beautiful, intemperate and self-aware. He was clever and headstrong and mercurial and…

And it came to me, so that I laughed a little. He was very like me. Was I not the same wilful creature? Was this, then, a simple matter of like attracting like?

I gave up on my tortuous thoughts. Whatever the cause, when John Holland entered a room I was aware of no one else.

*

Meanwhile, in the environs of the court, it was like walking on icy pathways, a fatal slide and slip possible at any moment to cast us all into a welter of blood and treason. But, in the usual manner of courtly circumspection, when the alternative was too dangerous to contemplate, relations were patched and mended when we left Sheen to take up residence within the stark walls of Westminster Palace. The chill formality of the rooms might match the general mood, but Princess Joan, descending in a glory of green silk, heaved herself from her litter and took her royal son to task, not mincing her words. Of necessity the Duke swallowed his pride to meet the King in a sour spirit of reconciliation.

No one believed it would last beyond the length of the Princess's sojourn with the aggrieved parties, even though hands were briefly clasped between uncle and nephew and smiles forced.

'Like new cloth stitched to an old gambeson, that will rip apart the first time you raise your arm to draw a sword,' John Holland grimaced. 'Which Richard is more than capable of doing, by God.'

In blind rage, Richard had drawn cold steel against the Archbishop of Canterbury.

Never again would I close my eyes to what was happening to the disparate strands of our family. Yet, anxious as I was, I snatched at happiness and clung with a bold tenacity. Why would I not? I had learnt the frailty of life, the chancy basis of power, when faced with the King's intolerance. I had no influence to bear on the rift between King and Duke, all I could do was watch and worry, and I did.

My education in the art of giving and receiving kisses was thorough. And highly enjoyable.

Chapter Six

1385, Windsor Castle

It was not a gentle courtship, for what we were intent on was forbidden and perilous. How to conduct a dangerous intimacy in the public eye, with absolutely no privacy to be had within the royal court in those days when we were swamped with preparations for Richard's Scottish war? Not a love affair on my part, I argued, but an increasing fascination, an entrancement, a fiery passion that heated my blood and drenched my dreams in longing. But what of John Holland? He was hunting impatiently and in earnest, and left me in no doubt of it.

'An annulment!' he breathed sacrilegiously at High Mass under the soaring roof of St George's Chapel, as the host was raised. 'Get an annulment and wed me.'

My silence was my refusal. Too far. Too fast. I might yearn to know more than chaste kisses with this man, but annulment was impossible. The Duke would never agree. As for committing the great sin of carnal knowledge in the Holland bed, the imagining was one thing, the doing of it quite another.

'I'll be the husband you need, a man who will treasure you, revere you. Not a boy who sees you as sister rather than wife.'

How alike his voice was to that of Princess Joan when intent on persuasion. Smooth and melodious, impossible to withstand. How many times did he urge me to seek an audience with the Duke, a request with which I could not comply? I would not present my father with yet another burden. There must be no further scandals to stir the witches' broth of court intrigue. For the Duke's daughter to become embroiled in lascivious marital complications would be selfish indeed.

'You're not afraid of my temper, are you?' he demanded with more than a hint of it.

'Certainly not!'

'I'll never let it harm you. And I won't give up. I'll hound you until you give in.'

'I know you will.'

'I'll tumble you into my bed before you can blink.'

'But not today.'

'What do you want from me, Elizabeth?' How many times did he pose that question, sometimes with a smile, sometimes with an edge of impatience. More than once in anger.

'I don't know.'

How many times did I reply in kind, my future being a

swirl of grey mist where nothing was certain. All I knew was that I wanted what we had at that moment.

'Let me show you how much I love you.'

I could not take that final step.

'Then do I let you go?'

'No.'

I could neither live with him nor without him. So this half-life was all I had.

'Will I still be sneaking into corners to meet you when I am too old to climb onto my horse?' he asked, not entirely in jest. I felt his desire in his hands, his mouth, and the quizzical expression as he gripped my shoulders and dragged me close. 'Why do I love you when you are so intransigent? Could I not find an easier woman to love?'

'Perhaps you could,' I challenged, a little disconcerted, turning my face away. 'I'm certain you would entrap a goodly number of handsome women who would fly to your lure. Perhaps you should go and do it now, before you march north. I will not hinder you, but accept our light liaison as a mere pleasant experience.'

Which made him grin, all irritation vanished in a blink of an eye. 'You wouldn't like that at all if I did, Countess. Nor would I, God help me. I am forced to admit that for reasons I cannot comprehend, you are the one woman I love. I might wish it otherwise but you are lodged in my heart.' He turned my chin with his hand and planted a final kiss on my lips. 'And you'll regret spurning me if I meet my death on a Scottish battlefield.'

'You wouldn't have the temerity to die in battle!' I replied smartly.

Yet it was a worry that wriggled under my skin, for unseeing though I was of the future, I was helplessly trapped in the net of his deliberate campaign. And what an adventurous campaign it was, unfolding day after day through the endless banquets hosted by Richard, when my importunate lover and I were seated under the canopy of state on the dais as royal family, and I, forsooth, did nothing to spurn him.

What could not be achieved under the auspices of a formal banquet?

It astonished me, and I participated with relish.

The words we exchanged between this and that interminable course might be innocent, but our gestures were heavy with meaning. My appetite for food fled; for the company of John Holland it burgeoned, as in the days after a Lenten fast when the tongue craves rich sweetness. We might indeed fast from physical touch, but his wooing of my senses wound them tight, like a thread on a distaff, so that all I desired was to be in his company. I was lured to him with every breath, every clever ruse employed by John Holland to weaken my resolve not to cast myself entirely into his power.

'May I tempt you, my lady?'

A gobbet of delicate roast heron presented to me on the point of a knife. A spoonful of spiced quince dumpling handed to me—who was to know the spoon, the silver prettily chased with an E, was a gift from him to me? It made me laugh, although I would not explain. Would this spoon be long enough for my supping? Oh, I prayed that it was. And then there was the stare that caught mine and would not release me, shielded by the magnificent tail of Richard's stuffed peacock.

'You are the most beautiful creature here today. Except for this poor bird before us, stripped and stuffed back into its skin.'

Which made me laugh. And if that were not enough, it was the comfits and hippocras of the *voidee*, served only to the pre-eminent guests, that heated my limbs with an inappropriate stroke of lust. And the wordless toast in the spiced wine.

I was truly enamoured.

And finally: 'God keep you safe, Elizabeth, when I cannot.' A mark of possession, uttered as the chaplain brought the feast to an end with fulsome prayers. The solemn pronouncement stirred my senses as the chaplain's did not.

'May the Blessed Virgin keep you in her heart and smile on you,' I replied in a furtive whisper, when I would rather be kissing him and he kissing me. 'May she bring you back safe from war, without harm.'

And then innocence was abandoned, along with the bones thrown to the dogs, for Richard's march to intimidate and harry the Scots was imminent.

'And if I'm so preserved, perhaps you might consider celebrating with me between my sheets,' he murmured *sotto voce*, under a swell of minstrel enthusiasm from the gallery above our heads.

'I am a respectable wife,' I mouthed back.

'Sadly not mine.'

Thus the tenor of what was for me an illumination, like entering a light-filled room from dark antechamber, into how physical desire could colour every action, every sentiment uttered; and what for John Holland was a determined seduction.

'You are my Holy Grail.'

'I am no such thing!'

'I am embarked on my life's quest to win you. No castle will be impregnable to my assault.'

My cheeks were on fire. I could find no denial. Silently I wished him every success in storming his castle walls.

Ultimately, lingeringly, forlornly, clinging to what solace I could, I kissed John Holland, safe from prying eyes at the foot of the outer staircase to his room. In public I made a decorous farewell to the King, my father and brother and my would-be lover as they rode out to war. Generations of Lancaster women had been waving their menfolk off to war, as did I, with a bright smile and dread in my belly. I forgave John his preoccupations.

Philippa kept her own council other than to remark at regular intervals: 'I don't know what he means to you, but why will you still play with fire? I pray that you will not be singed beyond bearing.'

'And I pray for you a husband, as soon as the Duke returns,' I replied, my own temper short in those days when we received no news. 'Then you will know that sometimes playing with fire is as essential as breathing.'

I was already mightily singed. Jonty, far to the north in Kenilworth, retired into the shadows. John Holland, even further away in Scotland under the royal banner, stood in my mind in the full rays of the noon-day sun.

★

Our military force finally departing to the north, I prayed daily for their deliverance from our enemy the Scots. Not that I needed to wear out my petitions on my knees, when the proud advance fast deteriorated into a humiliating retreat, Richard being the first to return to London. Relief laid its hand on me. The rest of our men would follow and soon I would see John again.

Perhaps we would do more than mime across the expanse of a fair cloth.

Then the news trickled through, the deadliest of poison.

'Ralph Stafford is dead.'

At first it was whispered, for was not Ralph Stafford, a young courtier with dash and style and a powerful family behind him, particularly loved by Richard? How long could the news be kept from him that one of his best-beloved friends was dead? And when Richard discovered it, what fit of temper or utter remorse would take hold of him?

'Struck down in cold blood.'

Pray God that Queen Anne could soothe him with her calm good sense and soft words.

And then the details unfolded, like a stream gathering momentum in a summer flood. And one particular detail. That one inexplicable detail that stirred the whispers to a deluge of gossip and reduced me to a mass of shivering fear.

Ralph Stafford was cut down, in a despicable, unprovoked blow, by John Holland.

The whole court talked of nothing else. Those who had no love for John Holland and his aspirations to power rubbed their hands with glee for surely there was no redemption for him here. And those who saw behind John's

ambitions to the brilliant skill, men such as my father, failed
to hide their dismay. How could this cold-blooded murder be excused? The death of the friar under questioning
could be overlooked as a necessity in the face of treason,
but this victim of John Holland's outrageous temper was a
young man, son and heir of Earl of Stafford, with many
friends.

John, it became clear, had few friends to leap to his
defence.

As the tale grew in gore and viciousness, I tried to preserve a dispassionate face, even joining in the speculation of
how Richard would react to his brother's crime, while my
heart became a thing of ice and my spirits in tatters. If the
telling of the deed was true, not even I could vindicate John
from the foul deed.

How could I justify this? I knew John's temper. I knew it
could rage on the very borders of control. Far to the north
in York, one of John's squires had been killed in a drunken
brawl by an archer in the retinue of Ralph Stafford. An
unfortunate killing in the heat of ale, but John, full of ire,
went hunting for the perpetrator, and when, riding through
the night, he came across a Stafford retinue, John drew his
sword and killed the leader, without waiting to discover that
it was the Stafford heir. Or perhaps he did know, some muttered, but the violence of his temper drove him on to avenge
his dead squire.

No matter the detail, John Holland had run Ralph Stafford through with his sword, leaving his dead body on the
road.

The news could not be kept from Richard who was

gripped by a silent rage, seated immobile on the throne in his audience chamber, tears fresh on his cheeks, unresponsive to Queen Anne who left him with a lift of her shoulders.

So what now? the court mused. And so did I with a dread that kept me awake through the early hours when fears leapt from every shadow. Stafford was demanding vengeance. John had taken refuge in Beverley Minster, surely evidence of his guilt. But what would Richard do?

As I considered the possible scale of Richard's revenge, an undercurrent of pure rage rumbled beneath my speculations, aimed at both men. Richard might well dole out the ultimate penalty for murder, so that the royal brother would face the axe. Or be banished from the kingdom to seek his turbulent fortune elsewhere. I had no faith in Richard's compassion.

As for John Holland, how could he have been so intemperate?

And then the undercurrent became a raging fire that swept through me as I put the blame where it lay. John was everything to me, and I to him. How could he risk all that we were to each other by a blow of a sword on a dark road? I could not justify his lack of humanity, of morality, his lack of foresight in bringing about an innocent death.

Had he not promised never to allow his temper to harm me? But he had. Oh, he had. His life might be forfeit and I left to mourn a love that shook me with its power.

The fault was all John Holland's, and Richard's grief erupted into an outpouring of rage against his absent brother. Fraternal affection held far less weight than the loss of Ralph Stafford. John Holland, Richard swore, would answer for his crime, while I was cast into a desperate fore-boding. I was helpless.

But was I? Laying my anger aside, I gave my mind to plan, to plot—for was not Richard my cousin who might be open to persuasion? Richard would never condemn his own brother to death or even banish him from his pres-ence. Richard had a brother's love for John Holland. What if I appealed to him for clemency? Would he listen as he had listened to me—and obeyed me—in our childhood games? But those days were long gone, Richard now eight-een years and a man grown, a man driven by extreme pas-sions when his will was crossed. If he could conspire in the death of a once loved uncle, Richard was not the cousin I remembered. And how could I confess my interest in John Holland, in full public gaze, when as a married woman I was not free to do so?

But I could not sit and allow John Holland to come under royal vengeance.

Who could help me?

I considered petitioning the Queen, but her eyes were strained with sadnesses I could only guess at. Not de Vere and the courtiers of Richard's charmed inner circle. Never them. Would they not rejoice in John's fall from grace? Princess Joan was not in health, residing with her own household at Wallingford Castle. I could think of only one voice that might, in spite of everything, still have Richard's ear and the authority of royal blood.

I attended Mass, from which Richard was noticeably absent, even though it would have been good for his inner peace, then went in search of my father in his accommodations.

'Elizabeth.' He looked up as I entered. 'What brings you from your bed betimes? It must be urgent.'

He was, as usual, in the depths of state business, the table before him covered with lists and correspondence. It would fall to him to secure the Scottish border against reprisals after Richard's abortive campaign. His eyes were tired. I noticed the grey in his hair and felt the weight of his responsibilities. Would it be thoughtless for me to add to his burdens?

'Are you too busy?'

'Yes. But since you think it's important enough to come and see me, you'd better tell me. What is it you want me to do for you this time?'

I felt my face flush, but returned his kiss and allowed him to lead me to a seat in the window. I knew I was taking a risk in broaching this matter, but I could not reconcile myself to letting events take their course.

'Well?'

'I want you to put Sir John Holland's case before the King.'

The Duke's expression did not change. 'And why would you wish me to do that?'

I folded my hands neatly in my lap. 'Because he does not deserve Richard's wrath. There is talk that Richard will bring the weight of the law down upon his head.'

The Duke inhaled sharply, but at least honoured me with his reasoned thoughts. 'Holland is his own worst enemy. He killed Ralph Stafford. He has not denied it—his flight to seize sanctuary is proof enough. If he had bothered to think before drawing his sword…I understand his displeasure over the loss of his squire, but his response was reprehensible. If he were a dozen years younger, with adolescent lack of control, I might excuse him, but he is thirty-three years old. There is no excuse.' He looked at me, brows flat, mouth unsmiling. 'And why are you so concerned? I thought I had made it plain that it was not wise for you to give any level of thought to John Holland.'

'I do not think of him,' I responded gravely as I marshalled the line of reasoning I had constructed during the night hours. 'But I think he deserves that we take an interest in his preservation. He has not been backward in supporting our interests.' I would not mention the friar—it would not enhance my argument—but moved on into less troubled waters. 'He rescued me, if you had forgotten. He saved me, and Henry and Princess Joan, from certain death in the Tower. Can we allow him to fall victim to Richard's temper? The Princess is your friend. Can you turn your back on her? She pleaded for you when Richard was crying foul over your attack on de Vere. She persuaded Richard to come and meet with you.'

Here was the argument that might do the trick. I waited, wondering if my ploy would work. My father had a debt to pay to the Princess. If he could see the need to pay it on this occasion, he might be willing to stand between her two sons and beg for mercy for one of them.

'Does Sir John not wear your livery?' I added, innocent enough, when the Duke's thoughts engendered nothing but a heavy frown.

'Very true.' The driest of comments with no inflection.

'So will you?'

'I think Princess Joan will make her own powerful arguments without my intervention. I am barely reconciled with the King.'

'Princess Joan is not fit to travel. She might hope to rely on you.'

As my father studied my face, I tried to breathe evenly despite the leaping anxieties.

'You are very importunate.'

I was very afraid. I tried a lift of my chin, a calm smile. 'I would see justice done.'

'For John Holland rather than Ralph Stafford.'

'For both. I don't ask that Sir John go unpunished. Merely that Richard does not order the executioner to sharpen his axe. If it were not for Sir John my neck would have felt its kiss on Tower Green. And Henry's.'

I drove the nail home with little subtlety. It was the strongest point I could envisage.

'I will think of it.'

No promises. I had to cling to hope. I had done what I could.

Why did you have to do it, John? You promised me that your temper would never harm me. It could destroy our love—so young, so new and untried—for ever.

★

We were announced into the audience chamber at Windsor as if we were a foreign delegation, to be received by Richard seated in state, the royal crown on his brow. Gone were the tears, the pale cheeks of past days. Now his face burned with fury. My pleas to the Duke had held weight, but I had no anticipation that Richard would hear. Beside him sat Queen Anne, straight-backed, watchful, equally resplendent in royal robes and coronet. The Duke and I had clothed ourselves in silk and damask as if for a formal audience rather than a family petition. I was relieved that we were alone, without the keen-eyed, long-eared courtiers primed for further gossip about royal disputes.

The Duke bowed. I curtsied. Richard gave no sign of recognition. The Queen leaned across and touched his arm.

'Have you a request for me, Uncle?' Richard blinked, as if suddenly awakening. 'I did not think we had business to attend to.'

'No, my lord.' The Duke wasted no time. 'I am here on family matters. To ask your royal pardon for your brother, John Holland.'

'What is it to you how I deal with Holland?' Richard all but spat the name.

'He is a useful man for you to have on your side, sire. A gifted man.'

'At the tournament.' Richard surged to his feet. 'I see no other gifts!'

The Duke was patient. 'He has excellent judgement as a soldier, a leader of men. It would not be politic to alienate him from your side. His loyalty to the Crown—to you—is without question.'

'Politic?' Richard snarled. 'Holland murdered my friend!'

'A sad misjudgement, sire.'

'A symptom of his vicious temper!'

The Duke inclined his head. 'If you could find it in your way to be magnanimous.'

'I could not.' Richard turned his face away.

All of which I could only absorb with increasing anxiety. If my father could not sway Richard, who could?

The Duke glanced at me, then back to the King. 'Sire...'

'You have our answer. Leave us.' His fair face was dark with an intensity of hatred. 'I will not receive into my presence those who would support a murderer.'

I looked towards the Queen. So did my father, but she merely shook her head. My father bowed, I curtsied. What a brief, disastrously unsuccessful audience it had proved to be. But as we turned to go, the door was opened, with a disturbance outside.

'Now who dares to disturb my peace...?'

Richard strode forward, leaping from the dais, as if to slam the doors shut with his own hands, but stumbled to a halt.

'Madam!'

In the doorway, aided by one of her serving women who held her arm firmly to guide her faltering steps, was Princess Joan. Burdened by rich cloth that did nothing to disguise her swollen flesh, Joan struggled forward with agonising slowness. How she had aged in those few short weeks since she had argued my father's cause with such skill. I now understood why she lived in seclusion at Wallingford. Every step was for her an agony.

And yet here might be the one voice to persuade Richard to show mercy.

'What brings you here, madam?' A belligerence but a

wary one, as if Richard might still heed his mother's words. I prayed that he would. There was only one possible reason for Joan to be here at this crucial hour. 'Can I guess? You have wasted your time.' Richard, who usually spoke to his mother with tenderness, was brutally intolerant.

'You might well guess.' The flesh of her once beautiful face was drawn with effort and a quality of grief I had never experienced from this redoubtable woman. How she must have suffered on her journey here, in mind and in spirit. 'I am here to see you, my son.'

'To see your King.' Richard's chiding was remorseless.

'As you say. You must excuse the frailty of my flesh, that I cannot perform the obeisance you clearly hope for. I must assure you that you have my regard and my loyalty as my lord and King. As you have my love as my son.'

Her flesh might be weak but her voice was as strong and assured as it had ever been. Princess Joan raised her chin with a direct stare.

'There's no need to say more. I know why you are here. And I won't do it.'

'Then I ask pardon for importuning you.' The Princess glanced at us, her eyes keen even as her body trembled, betraying her. 'I see I am not the first, if I read this right.' Then she fixed Richard once more with the flat regard of a woman who had survived more scandals than anyone I knew. 'It is not fitting, Richard, that one brother should seek the life of another.'

'He has committed bloody murder,' Richard roared.

Joan raised one hand. 'He has killed. I know not his justification. Or even if he had any. Have mercy, Richard.'

'I will have no mercy.'

'Help me!'

The command, addressed to her woman, was harsh, as with greatest difficulty and a groan of anguish, the Princess fell to her knees. And before my father could move, I was at her side, kneeling with her—some would say driven by my own selfish desires, but how could I not be moved by compassion for this courageous, suffering woman?

'I beg of you, sire,' I pleaded as I had never pleaded with Richard before. 'Have pity on this lady whose health cannot withstand the loss of one son at the hand of the other.'

The Princess grasped my arm hard, but there we knelt. What an image we made, two nobly-born but impotent women, like the sea washing up against the impregnable rock of Richard's intransigence.

'Go back to Wallingford, madam,' Richard said in cold judgement. 'And you, Countess of Pembroke, should return to your husband. What is it to you how I deal with those who commit crimes in my realm and disturb my peace?' Richard's eyes were as killingly bleak as those of his favourite raptor. 'You do no good here. Neither of you. I will not be swayed by the whining of women over matters beyond their comprehension.'

Joan held on to me, pulling her spine erect. 'I will not go, my son, until I have your answer.'

'Then here it is, since your understanding seems to be lacking. John Holland, whom I will no longer call brother, will face the demands of the English law. Coward that he is, he lurks in some northern sanctuary. If he dares to show his face before me, he'll suffer the blow of the axe to his arrogant neck.' He addressed Joan's woman. 'Arrange for this lady's return to her home. She has made her petition and I have answered it.'

With a silken swish of the folds of his houppelande, Richard swept past us, leaving the Duke and me to raise and shepherd a tearful princess to her waiting litter. The fact that she wept was more shocking than all the rest.

'I doubt she's fit to travel,' my father observed as the Princess insisted, all traces of tears dashed away, but her hands shaking as she drew the covers over her legs. 'I think today we have seen Richard sign her death warrant. He has broken her heart.'

I thought he might have broken mine too.

'Did we achieve anything?' I asked, even as I knew we had not, but all I could do was cling to a last hope. 'Will he at least consider compassion as his anger fades?'

'No. Not in his present mood.' The Duke pressed his lips to my forehead. 'Go with her, Elizabeth, and do what you can. She has an affection for you and she is a broken woman.'

I went to Wallingford Castle, unable to soothe the distraught lady whose breathing worsened and whose pallor frightened me. She would neither eat nor drink. When we arrived at her refuge the shadows beneath her eyes were as livid as bruises.

'Speak for him, Elizabeth. Speak for John. I know you have a softness for him.'

I did not deny it. How could I? My heart was as heavy as Joan's with the certainty of failure.

Richard has broken her heart, my father had observed. But so had John Holland. How could I argue against that? Were they not both to blame, one for vile murder, the other blind intolerance? It was as if all the life had been sucked out of the very stones of the castle at Wallingford, and out of Joan too as she sank into a torpor. The fear of one son being responsible for the death of another was too much for her strained heart to bear. Refusing all food and drink, the once valiant lady seemed to be sliding slowly but inexorably into the arms of death, and I was helpless to prevent it.

'You must live. You must live to petition for your son,' I urged, trying to help her sip from a cup of wine.

'I have petitioned,' the Princess whispered, pushing the wine aside. 'Richard will not hear me.'

'He will. He will regret what he has done to you. How he has reduced you to this. Let me send for him.'

'There was no regret in his eyes.'

She turned her face from me, and death came swiftly then as if she had willed herself out of this world that promised so much pain. The Princess abandoned the struggle without another word being spoken, other than to me and her confessor. The words the Princess whispered to me held the weight of a confession, indeed of a binding oath, and put a burden of conscience on my soul. Meanwhile Wallingford stood stock-still in shock at this long and eventful life coming to so puny an end. Had we not expected a shower of stars in the heavens or the raging torrents of a storm? Princess Joan slipped, unrecorded by any of her own family, into death.

And then the aftermath, which fell to my hand. Servants whispered in corners as Joan's women packed her garments into coffers, uncertain of their future as the whole household was put into a state of mourning and I ordered the black robes last worn for old King Edward to be brushed and aired. Musty and creased they might be, but we would show appropriate solemnity.

Her chaplain, William de Fulburn, looked to me for direction.

'You must inform her sons.'

'Yes, my lady.' The priest looked uncertain. 'And arrangements for my lady's burial?'

'I can't advise.' I rubbed my hands over my face. How wearing it was to bring to order a grief-stricken household where the women were wont to dissolve into tearful reminiscences whenever a bright memory struck home. 'What did she wish?'

'The Princess did not say. I must inform the King.'

Sorrow gave way to anger. 'Tell the King that grief killed her! That his cruelty brought her to death's door and beyond!' He looked askance, and I sighed. 'No, of course you cannot.'

He swallowed painfully. 'I'll send a courier to the Earl of Kent. Where is Sir John?'

'In sanctuary in Beverley Minster, when I last heard. He will be a sensible man if he stays there.' I smiled briefly without humour. 'Do what you can.'

We washed and clothed the Princess, placing her body on a bier before the altar in the chapel, as befitted the King's Mother, covered with a cloth bearing the arms of her husband the Prince of Wales, and awaited instructions. I would return to court. I could do no more here. Meanwhile, before I left, I would keep vigil. Princess Joan had shown me kindness and I knew the Duke would want me to take command in a house that had no mistress. We would honour her as the King her son had not honoured her at the end. And if my thoughts were more closely entwined with her son in sanctuary, a foresworn murderer, I did not think that Joan would find me in any way lacking.

'Where is he? Why is he not here to mourn the woman he helped to drive to her death?' I prayed aloud, kneeling beside her earthly remains, my voice echoing strangely in this space that contained only me and the dead.

Yet how could he be? Sanctuary or flight was the only hope for him.

'But I am here.'

Hands loosely at his side, the culprit stepped into my line of sight and bowed, whether to me or to his late mother I was unsure.

'And what is the Countess of Pembroke doing here?' The voice was smoothly scathing, the eyes, now that the man stepped full into the candlelight, hard and lightless. 'You were the last woman I expected to see at Wallingford. And, if I'm honest, the last woman I could have wished to see.'

It was like an open-handed slap, taking me by surprise, so that I had no time to marshal my reaction to him. All I could do was stare, shocked by the overt belligerence, impressed against my will by his appearance. He might have travelled far but the leather and damask of his clothing was immaculate, his hair combed into ordered waves, as if he had prepared for this meeting.

I was not prepared. Outrage made me brusque. 'Far more to the point, Sir John, what are you doing here? For you, being caught out of sanctuary, could be certain death.'

'I am aware.'

'Then why…?' No longer kneeling, I waved away the chaplain who had appeared in the doorway behind him. 'Not a word of this to anyone!'

And as the cleric retreated, my displeasure, so close to the surface in those days, flared without control, spilling over into raw anger at John Holland, at what he had done in shedding innocent blood. Very few had a good word to offer on his behalf and here he was, rejecting sanctuary, with death or banishment hanging over him. Was he a fool? How could he be so careless of his safety, of the burden he had placed on Princess Joan? In that moment I could find no sympathy in my heart for him.

He was responsible for the pain in this house. How could I trust him ever again? In that moment I wished I our paths had never crossed.

'You should not be here,' I stated flatly.

'How could I not come? I heard the Princess was…unwell.' I saw understanding darken his eyes to lakes of basalt. 'I see that I am too late. What are you doing here at Wallingford?'

'I escorted your mother from London when she was beyond consolation. Did your sources tell you that? She had travelled to court even though her health was failing. Did they tell you that she fell on her knees before Richard to beg

for your sorry life? Without effect, I might add, other than
to cast her into utter despair when Richard mocked her and
dispatched her without mercy.'

'Then I must thank you for being with her.'

'Thank my father. He thought she should not be alone in
her extremity.'

But of course, it would be unfair to blame him for that.
He had not known. It was the only sin from which I could
give him absolution.

'When?' The timbre of his voice had lost all its liveliness.

'The Princess died yesterday morning at the hour of
Prime.'

'So I could not have got here in time.'

'Did you try?' I had no patience, not while the wrath
raged white-hot within me. 'Your garments are more suitable for a banquet than a mourning feast.'

His tunic was magnificently crimson, the cuffs and edges
dagged in blue and gold.

He did not reply, but walked around me to the draped
figure, the lions of England disguising the bulk of Joan's figure, and there I remained when, continuing, John walked
to the head of the bier, to look down into her face that was
uncovered, the silk cloth that would finally hide her features
still lying folded on her breast. Her once fine features could
be detected beneath the gross flesh, like the familiar outlines
of a finely constructed garden beneath a fall of snow.

Sir John bowed, one hand on his breast, then leaned to
kiss her cheek.

'She was a courageous woman. She knew what she
wanted in her life and, once she was of age, refused to let any

man stand in her way.' He smiled briefly, the grief he might be feeling, if any, well hidden. 'I have never met any woman as unwilling to be guided, if the advice did not marry with her wishes. Unless it is yourself, Countess.' How formal he was, as if I were no more than an acquaintance. 'She was wilful and headstrong. But she had an enormous capacity for affection,' he continued. 'Her family meant much to her and she would fight for any cause that would bring them advantage.' He paused, touching her cheek with gentle fingers. 'She did not deserve the cruel scandals of her youth.'

How could he not even give a passing nod to his own part in the lady's death? Not one word of explanation or justification for the vicious deed. Which drove me to say:

'Your scandals, of course, have cast hers utterly into the shade.'

His brows rose, his features sharpened as his hand fell away.

'You are astonishingly vindictive in the face of death, Countess.'

'You must forgive me if I come too close to the bone. The last days have not been easy ones. Of which you seem entirely insensible.'

He opened his mouth as if to reply, then shut it like a trap.

'And don't tell me it was worse for you.'

'I wouldn't dare.'

'You brought it on your own head.'

'Indubitably.'

'Your behaviour has been…' I sought for an appropriate word. 'Dishonourable!'

'I have no honour.'

My heart seemed to be nothing more than an insensible rock. I had imagined my reconciliation with John Holland on his return from Scotland in many circumstances, but never over Princess Joan's corpse, with Sir John as biting as a winter frost and with not one word in his own defence. Presumably there were none to be had.

Treading lightly round the bier, relighting some of the candles that had died, guttering in their wax, he murmured as if speaking to Joan herself. 'Perhaps you loved Richard the best of all. To be expected, I suppose…' He touched her hands, still jewelled with priceless rings that all but cut into her flesh, then straightened the fold of her gown, then his stare was holding me. 'How did she die?'

'In silence. In despair.'

The flesh on his cheekbones flattened. 'Don't spare me.'

'I won't. She died in anguish when grief overcame her. Her heart was not strong and she could not bear the burden of what was placed on her.'

'Who did she blame?' His tone was viciously cold.

I thought about this, because honesty mattered. 'She blamed you for the act. But it was Richard's refusal to be merciful that killed her.'

With which the glance slid from glacial to saturnine. 'And in your informed opinion, Countess, who is to blame for this sad event? Richard or me?'

'Does it matter? And do you have to address me as if I were one of my Father's men of law?'

'Yes. Today, I do.'

'And tomorrow?' I took a breath, refusing to be lured

into any personal quagmire that might pull us both under. I was wallowing in uncertainty as it was. 'What in God's name did you think you were doing, killing Stafford? Or perhaps you did not think at all.'

'I will not justify myself to you.'

'No. Save your breath, for when you're hauled in front of Richard to answer for your sins. And you won't have your breath for long. Unless we pray for a divine intervention, he will call for your death.'

Turning on my heel, I left him there. I could not bear to stay with him, to hear any empty excuses, a man standing beside his mother's body with blood on his hands and in his heart. To be addressed as Countess as if I were nothing to him. I could not understand what made him rebuff me in such a fashion. There was suddenly a chasm between us as wide as the sea between England and France.

I looked back.

He still stood, immobile. Did he not care? Could he not even kneel in contrition and respect?

★

Next morning, rising early, donning the black of mourning and intending to take him to task, I could not find him. Had he left at dawn to find some new sanctuary where he could live out his days, secure from Richard's judgement? After our exchange of the previous night, I thought he would be in no hurry to remain in my company. For the briefest of moments I gave heartfelt thanks, then was sorry. I realised I needed to see him, if only to heap my fury on his head once more.

Or discover the reason for his antagonism.

Or plead with him…

My emotions were all awry.

'Where is he?' I demanded from Master Worthe, the Prince's steward.

'In the muniment room, my lady. He's been there since dawn.' The steward sniffed his approbation. 'He shut the door on me.'

I made soothing noises. So what would he want there? If it were privacy, he would not get it. I opened the door without compunction. The errant son had taken a jug of ale, a pottery cup and a platter of bread and meat from the kitchen, and there he was, sitting at the table where the steward usually dealt with the demands of the day. The cup was empty beside him, the wood covered with crumbs, the movement of his hands over the documents before him purposeful. There was still no grief evident either in his demeanour or in the brightly hued tunic.

'What are you doing?' I said without introduction.

For a moment his hands stilled, but he did not look up.

'I am looking for the Princess's will.'

'Are you so greatly in need of her wealth?'

Now he looked at me, eying me beneath lowered brows.

'Of course. What else would I be looking for?'

'And the Princess not yet buried.'

'But she has no need for her wealth, and I have.'

Was he ever so callous? I had learned much of this man within the hours of the last day.

'Are you planning to leave the country before Richard

can set his teeth into you? Were you planning to tell me before you left? And a will is no use to you. You need hard coin.' Still he turned one sealed page after another. 'Perhaps you have not been told that the King has confiscated all your property. You are no better than a penniless beggar.'

'Am I now?' At last his hands paused in their search, arrested at the news. 'No matter—or not yet. Ah! Well this is interesting.'

'What?'

'This, my singularly sharp Elizabeth, is where the Princess wished to be buried.'

Well, at least he had not addressed me as Countess.

'Her chaplain did not know.'

'Her chaplain did not search diligently enough.' He smoothed the parchment beneath his palm, before turning it for me to read in the clerkly hand that had written to her dictation. 'Now, that does astonish me. She requests that she be buried beside my father.'

'In Stamford?' An unexpected choice. I took the time to study his face as he folded the document and tucked it in the breast of his tunic. He was calmer, rested, with an air of resolution, but still a need to keep me at bay. So I would allow it. 'I suppose it is important to you,' I said. Then with a little brush of intuition, light as a butterfly's wing. 'You thought she would choose the Prince, in Canterbury, didn't you.'

'Perhaps.' He was brisk again, giving nothing away, all emotions if he had any, subsumed in practicality as he shuffled the rest of Joan's documents into a neat pile. 'I was wrong. I will arrange it in Stamford, next to my father's monument, as she asks.'

'Then arrange it fast before you are taken into custody. Richard would as soon drop you down a well as share a cup of water with you.'

Even teeth bared in a grin. 'Are you thinking of informing against me, dearest Elizabeth?'

'Not at the moment, but who's to say tomorrow?' I sat down opposite, on a clerk's stool, on a whim. 'What next, Sir?' I could be annoyingly formal too, and also provocative. 'Do you make a run for France?'

'No. And it's nothing for you to concern yourself with. I'm going to Windsor.'

'Are you a fool?'

'I cannot run for the rest of my life. My lady mother has left me her third best bed. I intend to live to use it.'

'Then I'll go with you.'

'I've no wish to ride for London with an ill-tempered witch as companion.'

'I am neither ill-tempered nor a witch.'

'But you're not good company.'

'You are a forsworn murderer. If I can tolerate that, you can put up with me.'

The previous amusement slowly faded, for his mind was already far away, considering his future. 'I can't deny it. Then we will deal well together. We will go to Windsor.' On his feet, he strode to the door, opening it and standing back for me to pass before him. 'Get ready or I'll leave you behind.'

'Oh, no. I'll be there at your side when you are on

your knees before the King.' He became very still. When I too stopped, surveying his face, it was to see every feature engraved in stone. 'What is it?'

'No, Elizabeth. You will not be there.' His fingers, still grasping the latch, whitened.

'No?'

'You will not. I'll not have it so.'

Barely a whisper but indisputably threatening, but I would do as I pleased, and was in no mood to take orders. I would see this out to the bitter end.

Taking note of the lift of my chin, his mouth acquired a sardonic twist: 'Why would you wish to associate yourself with such as me?'

'I don't know. I know even less after witnessing your lack of finer feelings towards you mother.'

'I have no finer feelings. Did you not realise that?'

Which summed it all up for me. Why had I gone to such trouble for him? He was a murderer, his immortal soul in jeopardy, without remorse, without pity for his mother. How could I have wanted a man like that? But I could. And yet I could not see the direction of his mind. He had not touched me. Not once. Any heat that had existed between us in those heady days at court had been obliterated, deliberately, by this man who was as unyielding as a frozen carp pond.

I prepared for my departure in despair, meeting up with the Princess's steward one final time in the pervading bustle of the entrance hall.

'We are leaving, Master Worthe.'

'Certainly, my lady.' He looked relieved that the organisation of the Princess's burial had been removed from his shoulder. 'I did not think Sir John would wish to travel on today.'

'Why not?' I was already walking to the door, arranging my hood, pulling on my gloves. I dare not be late. The man was quite capable of leaving me in a cloud of dust.

'Sir John did not sleep last night.'

Which made me stop and look back over my shoulder. 'Tell me.'

'Sir John spent the night in the chapel, my lady.'

So he has spent the night beside her body, and then sought her will, to arrange, if I believed him, for her final resting place.

'He mourned the lady well,' Master Worthe was saying. 'He left monies with me for payers for her soul.'

So John Holland was not immune to pain after all. He had hidden it well. He had certainly hidden it from me. But I could not think of that. He would suffer far greater agony at Richard's hands unless we could work a miracle, and I was duty bound to stand at his side, whether he wished it or not.

★

It was a particularly silent ride, much as the one I had shared with the suffering Joan, but for entirely different reasons. Her son was in no mood for conversation, trivial or otherwise. Brows drawn into an uncompromising line, his eyes remained fixed on the road before him as it unwound towards an uncertain future. These might be his final hours of freedom if Richard proved to be as intransigent as I feared. Whatever John thought about it he was not saying. I thought he might try to win me round to his way of thinking, with charm and clever use of words. I thought he would justify his actions, practising arguments that might appeal to his brother. Or try to explain to me. He might even try to explain the vast space he had allowed to yawn between us.

He did not.

Curt, introspective, heavy-browed, John Holland rode on to his fate while, unbeknowing to him, I trembled at his side. He might appear sanguine but I could not be. I had experienced Richard's temper. But surely he had too.

Sympathetic to his mood, I rode in silence beside him, only exchanging a word with my women when I felt a need to speak about something, anything. Perhaps it would even entice my companion from his preoccupations. But when the female gossip, rejoicing over the fall from fashion of the wimple—and the Virgin be praised for that—grew too much for him, he spurred his horse on ahead, leaving me to sigh with a strange depth of disappointment.

Murder and sanctuary seemed to have cured him of his infatuation for me. So much for kisses and silver spoons. I had been abandoned. Perhaps I had been too cold in my refusal, too sure, too wilful. Whatever the reason, the days of our courtship were long gone. But then I should be glad, should I not, for would not murder cure me of my own intemperate longings? Sudden, bloody death was not unknown to me. Which man of my family did not have blood on his sword? But not with deliberate vile intent.

I was no surer of my emotions than on the day I had heard of what he was capable. I did not even know why I was following him to Windsor.

★

We were within an hour of Windsor when my morose companion ranged alongside me.

'So you will deign to speak with me.'

'Yes.' His grin, entirely lacking of late, was all I recalled from the days of his pursuit of me. Sharp and bright and seductively attractive. All the earlier melancholy and ill-manners had been cast aside. Did this mercurial man ever apologise? 'This, madam Elizabeth, might be the final time that we have freedom to talk.'

It made my breath catch but I kept the mood. 'So you are confessing your sins to the friends you have left. Better that you confess them to your enemies, I think.'

'And which are you?' He stretched out his hand to touch mine where it gripped my reins.

I snatched my hand away. 'You must not.'

'Why not?'

The reasons tripped over each other. Because it is very particular, and such particularity brought enough trouble to the Duke and Dame Katherine. It draws attention to us, and you must not. Your touch makes me far too aware of you. That is the first time you have touched me since you returned, and it burns like a brand. I don't want it. I don't want my emotions to rule my response to a man capable of such uncontrolled violence…

But I did not explain any of it. Rather, coldly impersonal, I forced him to look ahead.

'What will you do when you get there, to Windsor? You have few friends at court. Ralph Stafford had many.'

His smile remained intact. 'I note you did not allow me access to your own inclination, but no matter. Here's what I'll do. I'll bow the knee before Richard and hope that my honeyed words and our mother's sad death will wear him down and wash away his need for my blood in recompense for that of his friend.'

'You are glib, Sir John. It astonishes me that you will risk it.'

'I can't live my life on the run from my brother. Nor do I wish to spend it in exile. I want to live here, to take my rightful place at the King's side as a valued counsellor, and so I will plead my case. Richard will listen. Never doubt it.'

How arrogant he was. How confident. The light was back in his eye, the smile indenting the corners of his mouth. He sat his horse with ease, the wind lifting his hair, and I noted that he had taken care with his appearance even though in sombre hue, dressing to make an impression from the folds of the velvet chaperon to the soft leather of his calf-length boots and all in between, every inch the King's brother. He had no intention of scuttling into Windsor, attempting not to draw the eye, but would challenge any who felt an urge to manhandle him. No decision had been made about his future. He was innocent still, until Richard pronounced.

Suddenly his eyes snapped to mine, catching my assessment of his figured houppelande in forest green and black falling in heavy folds over his thighs, making me flush, but he made no comment. 'Will the Duke speak for me?' he asked.

So perhaps the confidence was a façade after all. Who was ever to know?

'Do you wish me to ask him?'

His reply was dry, confirming my suspicions. 'It all depends on the welcome I receive when I ride into Windsor. I might not get the opportunity if I'm hustled off into some place of confinement at Richard's pleasure. So talk to the Duke for me, Countess, out of the goodness of your wayward heart.'

Undoubtedly a command. 'I might.'

Before I could react, he had seized my hand, stripped off my glove and kissed my fingers. 'Do you want persuasion? I would be everlastingly grateful. I would fall on my knees at your feet to urge you. What else can I say to encourage you? I could woo you all over again, of course, since you've clearly fallen out of love with me. Get the Duke to speak for me and I will declare my undying love for you.'

'And would I believe you? I don't think so.' Flustered, aware of the presence of my women, I tugged hard to recover possession of my hand, to no avail.

'Why not? You are very difficult this morning!'

'You don't have to ride with me.' Oh, I would punish him.

'Of course I don't. But I wish to. So what shall we talk of, Countess? I think I might woo you again, just to pass the time.'

Woo me? As familiar anger rose to grip my throat, and

I turned to stare at him, he kissed my fingers again, his lips warm against my skin, his grasp firm so I could not pull away.

'Woo me,' I repeated. 'You have no shame.'

'No. I don't expect I have.'

'Are you never discomfited?'

'No.'

'I don't know you at all, do I?'

'What's to know?'

All my doubts, all the accusations bubbled up to spill out.

'You killed a man. You cut him down on the road. He was innocent and yet you drove a sword through his heart. What sort of man does that?'

'And you are so sure of my guilt.'

'You have not denied it. And I suppose you will argue your innocence before the King as well.'

'How can I? I am as guilty as hell.'

I stared aghast. Had I not hoped against hope that it was all a mistake?

'Can you love a guilty man, Elizabeth?'

'Before God, I do not know.'

And he promptly returned my hand to my bridle, so that I was the silent one for the rest of the journey. Could I love a man guilty, by his own admission, of the unwarranted death of a young man whose character was without stain? I could not. I should not. And yet I could not let him go. Nor was it just the binding quality of Joan's final instructions to me. Deep within me there was a belief that beneath the temper and ambition, beneath the pride that equalled that of my father, there was a man who was worthy of my love. He was honest to a fault. I thought I could trust him, and that he would never wittingly do me harm. He would never be a good man, but he would be a loyal one. And a man whose smile weakened all my resolve to cast him off.

And then we were riding into the castle courtyard, and there was the Constable, indicating that John should dismount and follow him. No force was used, none of my feared manhandling, but the implication was there in the armed soldiers and the Constable's set face. John turned once to look at me. His gaze was long and grave, his command cut me to the quick.

'Go home, Countess. Go back to Hertford.'

Chapter Seven

Not even waiting until the following day, Richard sat enthroned. The Earl of Stafford stood at his side, the epitome of belligerence, his hands fisted on his belt as if to curb their desire to strike out at the man who had done his son to death.

It had not been difficult to discover when Richard would give audience to, or pass judgement on, his brother. It was the talk of the Castle. It was not difficult to find my father and apprise him of what was afoot. It did not need me to tell the Duke that without his support, John Holland would have no voice raised for him. We did not bother with arguments. We had been over this ground before, without the culprit in our midst to stir the ashes to flame if he was of a mind to.

'Is he repentant?' the Duke asked.

'Not that you would notice. And I will accompany you.'

'Why?'

'This is a family matter.'

I would not be swayed. If John Holland would tell Richard the truth, I needed to hear it. I needed to see and hear if there was any mark of grace on the soul of this man who, for reasons I could not determine, held my heart in his hands.

The Duke raised his brows but let it lie.

★

'Well, my lord uncle. Back again to plead for the black sheep who wishes to return to the fold?'

'If need be, sire,' my father replied. 'Or to remind you of the value of compassion at the hands of a powerful king.'

Or more like to prevent him from waging war against his own family.

John was escorted in, the armed escort far more obvious now in its close formation around him. Groomed, cleansed of the dust of the journey, superbly composed, John Holland made his entry, his face governed into stern lines that could not be suspected of flippancy. I watched him approach, taking in the elegance of his movements, even though he must feel the ignominy of having his sword removed from his side. I saw him take in Stafford's scowl.

And then all was drama.

John halted before Richard, where of his own will he knelt, straight-backed, head bowed, hands overlapping on his breast where the royal livery chain with its white hart glittered. A supplicant, but a clever supplicant to promote his allegiance to the King, and one with pride. He had not been beaten to his knees. The choice was his.

'Well?' Richard glowered.

'I am here, sire, to beg your forgiveness for my heinous crime.' His glance moved over those present then returned to the King. 'I would ask your compassion to allow me to speak with you in private.'

For a moment, the length of a breath, entirely dead of feeling, John Holland's regard rested on me, then moved on to return to the King, but not before I had read in it a cold alienation from what was about to come. It struck at my heart, but there was no time for that. Richard was spitting in red-hot ire.

'You will answer me at my behest, not at yours. What have you to say of this crime of which you are accused by my Lord of Stafford?'

'Might I rise, sire?'

'No. Answer on your knees.'

John bent his head. 'The Princess Joan, your lady mother, sire, is dead.'

'As I know.' There was no diverting Richard here. 'Any man with two thoughts in his head would say it was your behaviour that killed her.'

'The Princess remembered you kindly in her will, sire. She left you her best bed.'

Which took the breath from Richard, even as he continued to glower.

'Her death has touched me. I will always remember her with affection.' His eyes sharpened. 'How will you justify what is murder?' Richard flung out his arm to encompass

Stafford. 'How will you answer this man's desire for your death in payment for his son's?'

'I cannot. I am guilty as charged. I cut him down in the dark, thinking we were under attack. I gave the command, knowing it was a Stafford. I reacted. It was a terrible mis-judgement, because I was driven by anger at the loss of my squire. I deserve punishment, but I throw myself on your ineffable mercy, sire. I ask pardon.'

'There, sire. There is his guilt, expressed for all to hear. What more do we need to know…' Stafford urged.

But Richard lifted his hand to silence Stafford.

'I have sworn to have your life for this, Holland.'

'I beg that you will reconsider.'

'Kings do not reconsider. It's a weak king who changes his mind.'

Taking all by surprise, Richard thrust himself to his feet, striding across the chamber to a window embrasure where a chess set had been positioned on a low table, the chessmen in process of someone's game. Seizing one of the figures, Richard hurled it the length of the room so that it clattered on the tiles. But which figure had he selected?

'What do you think, Holland? Knight or King? Who has the pre-eminence here?'

Oh, Richard!

Inwardly I raged against his uselessly dramatic gesture, at his need to be at the centre of every stage. Of course he was at the centre. Was he not King? But his love of display made him draw all eyes to his person. How would he decide? What would bring him ultimate glory, to summon the axe or wield magnanimity? The odds were, I feared, stacked against John. He could be disposed of as quickly as Richard had rid himself of the little knight that lay in two pieces of carved ivory against the far wall.

I realised that I was holding my breath.

A movement at my side as my father stepped forward.

'Sire. A wise king can be persuaded to change his mind. If there is doubt over the crime.'

'God's Blood! There is no doubt. He admits it himself…'

'Or if he confesses his misjudgement.'

'Misjudgement!' Stafford exploded.

'Or if the man is one of great gifts.'

'Not if he is a man of vicious humour,' Stafford growled.

'I ask you to reconsider, sire.' Still the Duke pressed on. 'It is my belief that Holland is repentant.'

'Well?' Richard returned to loom over his still-kneeling brother. 'You have my uncle to speak for you. What do you say?'

'That I am full of regret, sire. I will accept any punishment that allows me to continue to serve you.'

The King pondered. Stafford's hand tightened on his sword. John was motionless, so still that not a hair of his head moved, the light gilding his hair and shoulders, adding patches of red and blue from the stained glass. The Duke shifted softly from one foot to the other.

And I?

Since I had come here, I must make my case. I stepped to my father's side. My voice was clear and carried well, so strong it all but overpowered me, but I did not hesitate.

Princess Joan had demanded my oath and I was the only one here who could speak for her. My father frowned at my forwardness. Richard scowled. Stafford turned his back. As for John Holland, he did not want me here. Had he not commanded me to keep away? His motionless posture said it all, his eyes remaining resolutely on the wall behind Richard's shoulder. And did I wish to be here, forced to acknowledge the ignominy of a man I had thought I might love? No, I did not. But Princess Joan had passed this burden to me and I would not falter, even in the face of such concerted opposition and rank disapproval.

'Will you hear me, sire?'

Flinging himself back on his great chair, Richard did not even look in my direction. 'If I must.'

'In her dying words before her confessor, Princess Joan asked that I plead for her son John Holland. As she lay dying, she still had hopes that you would be satisfied with less than his death.'

'I will consider.'

'The Princess expressed her love for you. She prayed that you would show the same greatness of character as your heroic father, the Prince of Wales.' I took a breath. I would risk all. 'She believed that her own blood was strong enough in you to melt your stony heart and allow you to heal the wounds in your family. The Princess vowed that she would only rest in peace when you were reconciled with Sir John Holland. She begged that you listen and give good judgement, tempered with affection, for her and for your brother.'

'A reasoned argument, by God!' Richard's eyes widened

on me, but he was still surly, turning on his brother, fists clenched. 'Why did you have to do this? I detest that you gave no thought to my situation. I loved you, and this is how you repay me. I see no way of pardoning you. It is all your fault…'

My heart was thudding loudly in my ears. The only man present who seemed to be unmoved was John Holland, his back as rigid as a pike, but by now I knew well his ability to dissemble. His fate lay balanced on Richard's chancy judgement.

My father, mightily controlled, bowed. 'Might I suggest, sire, that with a pardon from the King, Sir John might work for his reinstatement in your eyes by joining my expedition to Castile in the Spring of next year.'

Well now! I slid a glance towards the Duke, whose expression was one of mild interest, his offer so smoothly delivered that it came to me that I was not the only one to have an interest in this outcome. Here the Duke saw an opportunity to bring Sir John into the Lancaster fold, and keep him there through saving his life. Sir John would be a redoubtable asset in the foreign expedition. Was every man in this room driven by intrigues and stratagems? But then, so was I. And I cared not as long as John Holland's life was saved.

'I have use of a man of such talents as his with my army,' the Duke continued. 'He will be able to prove the worth of his repentance on the field of battle. Would you join me in Castile, Sir John?'

The room hung on the little pause. So John Holland too saw the tightening of shackles around his wrists. Either he bared his neck before Richard's verdict, or committed himself to a campaign of uncertain length and outcome in Castile. But of course there was really no choice for him to make.

'I would accept.' John Holland's voice was as uninflected as my father's.

'Would you consider such a request, sire?' the Duke was asking. 'It could only be to England's advantage.'

Once again I was holding my breath as Richard stood, to walk slowly forward to his brother, walking round him, his robes brushing against John's boots. A smile touched his lips. Widened to become a gleam of delight, although not one I would trust. I had seen the same smile when Richard had got his own way as a thwarted child.

'It seems eminently suitable,' he murmured.

'But sire...' Stafford' s fingers visibly gripped his sword belt.

'Princess Joan would lie at rest, sire,' I interrupted. 'She was greatly troubled and this would give her soul peace.'

'Good, good.' And there was Richard in our midst, all graciousness, as if there had been nothing to disturb his untrammelled existence. 'I will order a Mass to be said in her name. As for you, brother... You must make recompense. You must establish three chaplains to pray for Ralph Stafford's soul in perpetuity.'

'Gladly, sire.'

'Will that satisfy you, Stafford?' I knew it did not but it would be an unwise man to gainsay his King. 'Stand up,' Richard commanded his brother.

John stood.

'I will restore your property to you, of course. I can't have my brother living on my generosity, can I?' He enfolded John Holland's stiff shoulders in an embrace. 'You should not do this, John. It unsettles me. You should curb your temper. I don't wish to be at odds with you.' All his ill-temper blown away, Richard was unnervingly friendly. 'I need to know that I can rely on you.'

John returned the embrace. 'I am your man. Now and forever.'

The relief in the room was tangible, except for Stafford whose stare at John held a quality of hatred.

'I will hold the pardon over your head, you know.'

'My future behaviour will be without stain, sire.'

'Then come, John, and drink a cup of wine with me.'

He was swept off by the King, Richard's arm looped through his as if nothing had ever occurred to undermine their closeness, leaving the Duke and me to watch them go. At the last John turned and his eyes, wide and dispassionate, met mine, reminding me of the venom of his arrival at Wallingford. Then he smiled at the King at his side, and was gone.

'He looks at me as if he despises me,' I spoke without thinking.

'Are you surprised? What did you want?' The Duke was already following Stafford and the Queen from the room. 'A herald's fanfare for coming to his defence? What man of pride wants an audience for his annihilation?'

'I did not think.'

'Then perhaps in future you will.'

Of course I remembered, the moment he had registered my presence beside the Duke. He had not liked it. He had

not expected this very public audience. He had indeed despised my seeing him on his knees, witnessing the outcome,
witnessing his downfall and his humiliation. How much he
would detest that I had pleaded for him with Joan's final
words. He did not want me there. Go home to Hertford,
he had said. A man of pride, he did not wish to be humbled
before me.

'You don't understand a man like John Holland.'

Was that it? Did I not understand him? But I thought I
did. Pride. That was all it was. But what value pride when
a man was fighting for his life?

I exhaled slowly, but the Duke, waiting for me, continued
to watch them go.

'They are both dangerous men, Richard and Holland, in
their own way,' he observed, as well he might.

'Will you take him to Castile?'

'Of course. If nothing else he is a brave man and a good
one to have at your side. He can mend his reputation with
his sword in my service.' He turned to me. 'And you, I
think, should return to Kenilworth. It's time you saw that
young husband of yours.'

'Do you think I'll forget him?'

'More like he'll forget you. I'm travelling there in two
days. Accompany me. You should see him. He'll soon be of
an age to be a husband to you.'

Or more like Sir John's charm would tempt me into sin.

But in that charged interlude all intimacy had been swept
away.

Forget it. Forget him. The Duke was right. I did not
understand him at all.

Oh, but I wanted to. On that day I had watched a man sink his pride and beg for his life. I could not abandon the flame he had lit in my heart because it still lived, faint and flickering under his rejection, but not dead.

I feared that it would never die. I would live with the joy and sorrow of it until my own death when my last breath doused the flame.

★

Richard kept his brother close, as if to let him out of the royal sight would give him leave to commit some new, monstrous crime. I saw him, as I must, but at a distance, wrapped around by royal favour. No more outrageous communication as the sumptuous dishes of Richard's cooks passed before us. John Holland sat at his brother's right hand, his attention demanded wholly by Richard. When we rode to the hunt, John Holland, firmly ensconced in Richard's intimate coterie, even ousted de Vere from the royal side. It would have been entertaining to watch the favourite's ire, if it had not been so infuriating.

Meanwhile, throughout the whole, John Holland's face remained as expressionless as a Twelfth Night mask. If he was playing a role of the regretful penitent, he was doing it with a flourish, while Richard smiled on him. Richard smiled on all of us. It was like the smile of a raptor seeing its prey in the long grass.

John Holland did not come near me, not one step closer than he had to through necessity, and with my new knowledge of him, I understood why. He was too proud. He had been forced to cast himself on his brother's mercy and bear

Richard's patronising tolerance. John Holland was undoubtedly nursing his wounds.

Preparations went ahead for me to travel north with the Duke whose directive in the months before he embarked for Castile was to personally secure the border against Scottish inundations.

I fidgeted and snapped. I could not leave things like this, even if John Holland could. Had I not risked Richard's displeasure to plead for him? Following the distant pattern of his thoughts as he bowed with exquisite grace in my direction, accompanied by a fierce smile that had all the charm of a rat, was like trying to follow the path to the centre of a labyrinth. I could not reach him, and in two days I would have retired to the wilds of Kenilworth, to be reunited with Jonty, who was fast growing up. I would no longer be a virgin bride.

I slammed the lid of a coffer in despair.

How could I love a man who holds life so cheap? But I did.

'I should not even think of him, but there he is, in all the spaces of my mind. It's a hopeless case, isn't it? I am caged, just like you,' I lectured my finches.

They twittered mindlessly.

'Then I must go to him. If I can find him without the circle of his new friends,' I remarked sourly. Unless I could fling a bridge across this raging torrent, then we would be apart for ever. Unfortunately that might be exactly what he wanted.

★

'Well, if it's not the little flower of Lancaster!'

This did not bode well.

'You have been avoiding me.'

Once more I had hammered on the door of John Holland's chambers and thrust open the door before anyone could prevent me. I did not have one of my women to dance attendance. I had come here as Elizabeth of Lancaster, royalty in every drop of my blood, and I would not be gainsaid by anyone. There might have been an air of desperation in this last resort, but I hid it beautifully behind accusation.

Royally housed though he might be, my quarry did not stir from where he was sitting on the floor—which in itself almost shook my nerve—beneath the oriel window, light flooding down on him as he lounged, one knee drawn up by linked fingers. By his thigh was a cup of wine. There was no temper in his wide-eyed stare today.

'And very successfully,' he observed in a chatty tone. 'I would wish to continue to do so. Perhaps you would close the door as you leave.'

'I know why you're doing it.'

He tilted his chin, assessing me lightly from head to toe. 'Do you? It's more than I do.'

So he thought he would undermine my confidence. He would not. Should I go and sit with him in the dust? Instead I walked to the single armed chair in the room and sat, my feet on a little stool, as if I would receive an audience. Folding my hands in my lap, I linked my fingers. Sir John watched me with mild interest. Only when I was settled, my skirts falling in elegant folds, did I reply.

'You know very well why. The Duke asked if I expected a victor's garland for leaping to your aid.'

'Did he now?' All languor, he brushed his hair from his eyes. 'It always astonishes me, the perspicacity of the Duke. And did you expect it? The victory garland?'

'I expected nothing.'

'Then that's what you'll get. Will you take a cup of wine with me?'

An insult in the way he cocked his head, he made no effort to pour me one.

'No. I am not here to celebrate with you. I'm here to apologise.'

'Then since you have, this interview is at an end. Perhaps you would pour me another cup on your way out.'

This was hopeless. I knew a lost cause when I saw one. All my attempts at constructing bridges were being expertly demolished and thrown into the foaming water below, but I preserved my composure. Was he worth fighting for? At that moment I would have said no. Magnificent his garments might be, embroidered and jewelled, but there was a dishevelled loucheness about him.

'The wine is on your right,' he observed.

'I'll not pour it for you. If you need more to drown your sins, get it yourself.'

I would find out if he was worthy of my efforts before the end of this exchange, but not in the dregs of a cup of wine.

'I have come to make my farewell,' I said.

'Abandoning our happy family gathering at Windsor, are you, little flower of Lancaster?' He repeated the phrase as if he enjoyed it. I did not. I gritted my teeth.

'I am going to Kenilworth.'

'And the fortunate Earl of Pembroke will be there to enjoy your return, Countess. Are you come to wish the black sheep good fortune on his way to redemption under Richard's brotherly love? I am for Castile where I'll either make recompense for my sins or die in the attempt. Will you miss me if I shed my blood on foreign soil, Countess?'

So we were back to formality, and a raw cynicism that hurt with every syllable. There was no reply I could make.

'And where is Henry? And your beautiful sister? Do they leave, too? But of course Henry is keeping his distance—he has no love for cousin Richard, does he?' He smiled confidentially. 'It is truly a wonder and marvel that I am reinstated, and how wrong you were. You would have advised me to run for my life.' He gestured widely with one hand. 'And here you see me, in favour with every man at court.'

'Except Stafford.'

'To the devil with Stafford.' He snapped his fingers. 'So you have you come to kiss me farewell, dear girl.'

As he moved his arm, the light hit on the chain hanging negligently around his shoulders, enough to catch my attention. It was Richard's livery, the white hart gleaming against the dusty damask of his tunic. The livery he had cunningly worn the day of the charged interview with his furious brother. And then my eye moved to a similar gleam on the floor beside the cup. The chain of 'S's that marked my father's livery, the links abandoned in a little heap of silver.

I found it hard not to sneer.

'And which of those will you wear today, Sir John?' Was he ever to be trusted? 'To whom will you give you allegiance this morning?'

'Which will I wear?' He picked up the Lancaster collar, squinting at it as it swung in a glittering serpent-like string. 'To whomever I consider will further my ambitions most,' he said. 'And today it is our superlative King. But who's to say what I might do tomorrow.'

The bright glitter of his eyes, the supremely careful enunciation, the repetitions. My suspicions were becoming confirmed with every moment.

'You disgust me.' *And my heart is breaking. This is not love…*

'But will you still be disgusted tomorrow, fair lady?' And then, as I stood to leave: 'Will you dance with me? If I can struggle to my feet. It may be the last time we will tread these steps.'

He made no effort to stir. His eyes touched on mine, then slid away.

'We have no music.'

'Do we need music? You can sing if necessary.'

In one movement, fluid and graceful, that denied all my suspicions, he leapt to his feet, seized my hand and pulled me into a few ragged steps. Which once again confirmed everything.

Forcing him to come to a standstill in the middle of the room, I faced him.

'How long have you been celebrating?'

'I have been celebrating—endlessly, my peerless maiden come to rescue her knight whose armour is definitely in want of shining—my return to royal favour. Richard is keen to show his love for me. By God, de Vere can drink!'

'And you have joined the inner circle.'

'What else?' he leered. 'Don't tell me you disapprove.'

I released my hands from his now lax hold. 'I'll tell you no such thing.' I could either leave him to wallow in his own self-imposed misery, or try to steer the conversation into more sensible channels. 'Will you go with my father to Castile?'

'It will be my joy and my delight. But then, have I a choice? It's the only reason Richard saved my worthless neck. As he informed me. And he will keep his jaundiced eye on me until I am launched with the fleet. I go to fair Castile to reinstate my reputation. He'll be pleased to see the back of me and the Duke. How much more comfortable life will be for him.' He turned on me, a bright flare of anger no longer hidden. 'You should not have been there, Countess.'

'I had to speak for you. I had promised your mother. Would you wish me to break my promise to her, on her deathbed?'

'I care not what she wanted.'

But now I knew enough about this difficult man to deny him. 'You cared enough to spend the night beside your mother's bier.'

For a moment he froze, lips tight pressed. Then: 'So her busy steward found it necessary to gossip to you. I should have known.'

'And I know why it was important for Joan to be buried next to your father. How old were you when your father died? I'll tell you. I've been doing my own gossiping.'

It was as if a pail of cold water had been emptied over his head.

'That is all in the past. Why would it concern me? You take too much on yourself…'

'You were a seven-year-old boy,' I continued, despite the ice that now coated his every word. 'I know about the gossip and the scandal that coloured the Princess's years with your father. It would have mattered to you. It would have mattered to anyone with even a speck of sensitivity on their soul, that she truly loved your father.'

He flung away from me. 'This is some myth that you are concocting…'

'Then why,' I addressed his damask-clad back, 'did you let me think that you were rustling through her papers because all you cared about was her money?'

I saw rather than heard the sigh. 'Leave it, Elizabeth.'

'I will, but this I will say.' I followed him, took hold of his sleeve, gripping it tight. 'Go to Castile with my father. You can rebuild your ruined reputation…'

'Or die in the attempt. Oh, I will go. Never fear.' He wrenched his sleeve out of my hand, strode back to the oriel where he picked up the cup and drained it dry. Only then did he turn his head to look at me over his shoulder, all the pent-up emotion clear in his measured tones. What must it have cost him?

'Do you think I enjoyed it? To beg from a King who sways like a reed in storm at the whim of de Vere and Mowbray and every other toadying sycophant? Do you think I felt no disgust, confessing my sins in full public eye, with you and the Duke as an interested audience? Yes, I killed Ralph Stafford, but it was not murder, I swear. It was a careless blow, full of passion, on a dark road.' He drew in a breath, but his attack was not mellowed. 'Should I thank you for your clever words of wisdom on my behalf, your heartfelt plea for clemency? I haven't thanked you, have it? So if it matters to you, you have my undying gratitude. And I am committed to a foreign campaign, whether I wish it or not.'

It hurt, how it hurt, but I would not show it. 'It is only pride that makes you seek to wound me,' I observed as dispassionately as I was able. 'Why should the opinion of de Vere matter to you? Why would you not wish to go to Castile and win military glory?'

'Yes. Pride is all I have,' he retaliated smartly. 'Before God, Elizabeth, it's not the sneers of de Vere and Mowbray that get under my skin. What man wishes to be seen on his knees, begging for his life, by the woman he adores and wants more than life itself? How is it possible for him to put himself right in her eyes, when she has been privy to his degradation? I love you, Elizabeth Plantagenet. Don't you realise that yet?'

It was as if the words slammed me back against the stone wall, robbing me of the power to reply. Not lust, not desire. He had said he loved me. How he must have felt the shame of it.

'I did not know,' I said.

'Well you do now! I think, God help me, I loved you from the moment you turned on me, all filth and fury and ravaged clothes and ordered me to take my hands off you for you would bow to no lawless rabble.' He stopped abruptly. 'And by God, my head throbs like a blacksmith's anvil!'

In a fast, controlled movement he flung over to embrasure set in the wall, where stood a silver pitcher and basin, a soft length of linen at the side. He poured water, then hands cupped, splashed it liberally over his face, his hair.

'God's Blood!'

With the linen he scrubbed his face dry, running his fingers through his hair, scattering droplets.

'That should make me see the future more clearly, although I might regret it.'

Before I could think of a biting reply—that it was a pity he hadn't seen the future clearly from the beginning of our conversation—he was there, and in what could only be described as a pounce, gripping my shoulders with a little shake.

'Look at me. I did not intend to say that. See how you have the power to undermine all my good intentions and destroy my self-control. I want you, Elizabeth. I have always wanted you. And now that death has come close to me, I'm in a mood to take what I want. *In vino veritas* indeed, and since you are foolishly here without a chaperone...'

So the cold water had not remedied the wine swimming in his brain. Was this what I wanted? My heart leapt into my throat at the image his few words had painted for me. His kisses I knew. The touch of his hands, the power of his arms around me. The strength of his shoulder where I might rest my head. But here he was in a mood to take more, much more.

'I thought the water would have brought you to your senses.'

'It will take more than that! I want you, drunk or sober!'

His mouth on mine, neither gentle nor seductive, tasted of wine and despair.

'I cannot…' All my confidence was subverted by the hunger in those expressive eyes.

'Cannot what? Take a lover? Of course you can. I'm in no mood to be tolerant. We should celebrate my escape from Richard's revenge. I am in a mood to celebrate.' Another kiss, his mouth hard against mine. 'Don't tell me that you don't want me as much as I want you.'

'Not like this…! I won't be party to a drunken display of self-pity!' And, a little panic fluttering around the edges of my reason, I was pushing against his shoulders, uncertain that he would comply. But he set me aside, with a sigh that seemed to come from his soul. It was he who stepped back.

'Forgive me. Forgive me. Self-pity is a despicable thing. I have not drunk so much that I cannot treat a woman with courtesy.' His voice had softened as he held out his hand for me to take if I wished to. And I did, knowing instinctively that the exhibition of uncontrolled force was over, even when he held them, palm to palm, between his own.

'My dear love. Here's my declaration and my apology, if you will hear it…'

I nodded.

'I am not worthy of you but I cannot let you go. My life is tied up with yours. I love you inordinately. But I should warn you: it is no mild affection. This is nothing selfless, where the knight gives all and expects nothing but the right to adore at the feet of his mistress. My desire for you is sensual and passionate and possessive. It is love of the heart and mind and body. I want everything from you. And I won't let you refuse me.' The chain on his breast glimmered as he took a breath, and his grasp of my hands tightened. 'Unless you cannot, in your heart, love me in the same way. You must say so now, before it is too late for us both to step back from the brink.'

The power of his words struck hard. A choice for me to make. A denigration of his own powerful feelings. All creating a deliberate clarity of what it would mean if I gave my consent to what he wanted from me.

'I'll never be your perfect, gentle knight. But I'll be more. I'll protect you. I'll never desert you. I'll worship at your feet for ever. Flawed and mired in sin I might be, but I will be your knight, Elizabeth of Lancaster.' He pressed his mouth to my fingers, as gallant as any chivalrous knightly lover. 'Will you give yourself to me. Knowing what you do of me?'

It was as if he had written the words in gold, offering me a choice to make of my own free will, with no attempt, finally, to force my steps. And what a simple choice it was. A beat of my heart, deep and sure, carried me forward, over the dangerous boundary from immature attraction and infatuation into a physical longing so strong it shook me. This was love as I had never known it. No it was not selfless. It was potent, all-controlling. Every admission he had made to me I could recognise within my own response to him. How had I ever thought my romantic notions of him were real love? Now I knew the power of my acceptance of him, with all his charm and all his complexity. In that moment I knew it: this love would never let me go. Any step I took now would, I accepted in the recesses of my heart, be absolute.

'Will you, Elizabeth?' he asked. 'I'll not plague you if you decide on a fast retreat.'

But I had seen the glitter of provocation in his eyes behind the courteous approach. And of desire. John Holland would not only plague me, he would hound me unmercifully.

I breathed in. And out.

'Yes. Yes, I will.'

And I took the words deep into my own heart as I spoke them.

It was such an incontrovertible response to make, that answered every question I had ever asked of myself. Would it make me as wilfully lustful as Isabelle? Would I be as shockingly immoral as Dame Katherine? In all honestly there would be those who would so condemn me, but there were no such fears in my mind. My only thought was how I could have held back from him for so long. And that being said, John did not disparage me by asking if I were sure. Time for words was long gone as, my hand in his, we took occupation of his bedchamber in mutual agreement, where he managed the layers of my outer and undergarments with a not unexpected depth of skill and formidable alacrity. Even so, despite his expertise with buttons, he found room to complain.

'Could you not have dressed more simply?'

'I could, of course. But I did not expect to be disrobed by a lover.'

'Always be prepared, Madam Elizabeth.'

'Do you mean that this will occur with some frequency?' I risked a glance at his frowning concentration.

'As often as I can arrange it.'

I did not need to tell him that this was all new to me. Was that not the reason he talked throughout the whole of my disrobing, when I was unable to prevent my nerves from shivering over my skin? Who would have thought that he could be so very kind?

'What do I do with all these pins?' he asked as my hair unfurled like a banner in his hands to cover my shoulders.

'Throw them on the floor,' I replied, breathless.

Then there was no talk. And no more kindness. How simple an emotion kindness was, whereas there was nothing simple in what passed between John Holland and me. In that hour—or was it longer? —I received the first steps in a thorough education unlike any I had imagined when my dreams had stretched no further than the pages of the books in my father's library where knights were courteous and never unclothed. Where love was expressed in gifts and words and chaste kisses.

Here was a new and entirely physical world, spread out for my delectation.

I learned the delights of a man's body beneath my hands, where muscles were tense with smooth power, well harnessed until need took over. And then it was as if I was tossed into the waters of a mill race, all turbulence and mastery which I was in no mood to resist.

I learned about sleek arms that held me tight, and thighs hard with sinew and some abrasions. What a work of art a man's body could be, even with evidence of battle. Here there was no conflict, only heat and desire.

I learned about my own response to a well-placed kiss or a trail of fingertips that made me shudder and gasp with astonishment. Just as I learnt about the hiss of pain, and about its transmutation into breathless pleasure. And then I learned about my own skill in initiating the slightest movement to make a man draw in his breath. And groan when I repeated the caress.

I learned about tenderness too. The magic world of words to enhance caresses.

'You are the brightest jewel I have ever owned.' His hands framed my face.

'You are the lover I have always desired,' I replied, for I could see myself reflected in the brightness of his gaze.

And then there was laughter.

'Don't hold your breath!'

'I wasn't!' Oh, but I was, for his touch drove me where I could never have imagined.

And in the end I learned about love.

'I love you.'

I would never be given poetry by John Holland.

'I love you, too.'

Did it need us to say more, when we had made such a statement of our love? I did not think so, and applied my new knowledge of the seductive power of kisses until his ability to speak was destroyed, and my mind was unfit to learn any more, aware only of the thud of his heartbeat with my own sighs in contrapuntal unity. I had not sought such a depth of love, but it had surely found me.

I gave no thought at all to the enormity of the sin I had so happily committed.

And I was quite sure that John Holland did not.

★

'I must leave Windsor. I must leave you', I said, sharp dismay fast surfacing.

'And I must return to dancing attendance on my brother.' John was replacing the garments he had stripped off so rapidly. Hose, tunic, boots, in quick succession. 'But I have every excuse to travel to Kenilworth between now and our embarking. I'll need to discuss transportation of troops and equipment with the Duke.'

Doubt suddenly struck home.

'And will you discuss your inordinate love for his daughter?'

His hands stilled on the buckle of his belt. 'I will if you give me leave. Get an annulment and I'll wed you tomorrow.'

But still I stepped back, baffled by my own unwillingness to admit my love for him so openly. Or was it shame in the confession of so blatant a sin? As I watched him, there was not one single regret in my mind. Perhaps it was simply a fear that the Duke would refuse the annulment. If he did, he might force my intimacy with John Holland to come to an end, as it would anyway with his embarkation for the Castilian enterprise. This was all so impermanent, uncertain. As it was, John's reputation had been discredited. To reveal an inappropriate relationship with me would stand him in no good stead.

I smiled a little. How selfless I had become now that love had touched me. Why ruffle the waters further to create a great storm that might overwhelm us both? Better to enjoy what we had until our future was clearer. Perhaps when John returned from Castile, shining brightly with royal favour…

'Not yet,' I said, intent on pushing the problem aside without further discussion as I pulled my shift over my head, fussing over my hair that he had unbound. 'It's too difficult.'

'I don't see why.' Buckle secured, he swooped to plant a kiss on my brow. 'But I'll do as you wish. For now. I'm gone from here.'

And I was alone in his room, all the passion and heat gone with him, but not from my heart. I might not see the future with any clarity, but the present was as precious as the finest jewel in Richard's treasury. Slowly I dressed. And then as any woman in a new intimacy might, I investigated the items of John's property, touching, arranging, to get a sense of my new lover from his possessions. All was neat. Everything in its place as I had once noted before. Clothing folded in coffers. No books, as my brother would undoubtedly have had around him. John was no reader. No jewels or valuable hanaps as my father might have to display wealth, the gifts from friends. Nothing to give me an insight into the man who had filled my whole body with light. I lifted the livery chain that he had left on the coffer lid…

And smiled.

It was a fine gesture, strangely honourable in its execution from a man who in a blast of despair had claimed he had no honour. It caused a warmth to spread through me, rivalling the heat of the sun that had moved across the floor and now touched my hair, my shoulders. What a spectacular choice he had made. My lover might be bowing in contrition before his brother but here in my hand was the chain with the white hart. Today he wore Lancaster livery. Seeing no need to boast of it, or winning my favour by ensuring that I knew of his choice, he had done it without explanation, a silent mark of honour. Today he was mine.

My love for him knew no bounds. I had built a bridge and he had crossed it. Or we had crossed it together. I lived for the days when he would come to Kenilworth.

Chapter Eight

June 1386, Kenilworth Castle

'I cannot take every shift, gown and pair of shoes I possess. What do they wear in Portugal, anyway?'

Philippa stood in the centre of her chamber, rather crossly, surrounded by travelling coffers and drifts of costly material and her busy women.

'Why worry? Set your own fashion.' I sat on her bed, not helping. Then on a thought: 'You could give me that blue damask. I've always coveted it.'

'And you've enough gowns of your own to clothe Richard's spendthrift court from head to foot.' She smiled but her eyes were wide and I thought I saw trepidation there, even though she had dreamed of marriage for so long. This would be the fulfilment of her dream, the end of all her fears that she would never have a husband and children of her own. But a marriage far from home and those she held dear would have its own heart-break.

I would not speak of my own sense of loss.

'Do I take my lute?' she fretted, her fingers dragging unmusically over the strings. She hugged it to her breast.

'Your new husband will give you a dozen. You will be Queen of Portugal, commanding all you desire.'

'And, oh I shall miss you.' The sudden gleam of tears in her eyes shocked me, but I forced myself to laugh as if I had not noticed. The last thing we needed was for us both to become lachrymose.

'When you decide that you are missing me, just recall all the times I annoyed you and you wished me wed to a man in Cathay,' I said instead.

'True. I remember now.' She wiped the tears away with her fingertips, then touching my shoulder in acknowledgement of what I had done before rolling a jewelled bodice in a length of linen.

It was a time of melancholy for both of us with the prospect of much parting and some tears. This was a loss I had experienced before and anticipated the long months with a mix of fear and heartache. Plantagenet men went to war. Had not my grandmother, Queen Philippa, experienced the same when King Edward had led his knights and archers to Crécy, the great victory that was still talked of, even by those who had no memory of it. When Richard's father, the Prince, had taken the mantle of leadership and raised his standard at Poitiers, Princess Joan had been with him in Aquitaine, but her anguish would not have been any the less. Would our father fight a battle as dangerous as these that lived on in the memory of our knights? Minor skirmishes were just as lethal. And the ambushes. And dysentery. The cold of winter, the arid heat of summer in these southern climes.

I could not think of it.

For my father was intent on war, leading the expedition to Castile that was now imminent. Travelling with him was Constanza who hoped never to return to England but to win the crown from her cousin who had usurped her rightful claim. And if my father was successful, would he ever return, or would he remain to rule Castile as king?

It was possible. It was entirely possible for an ambitious and able man who saw no future for his ambitions at Richard's unpredictable side. That I could accept. But with my father, as Constable of the Army, went Sir John Holland.

We had met, in bed and mostly out, when Sir John found it necessary to discuss affairs of soldiery and equipment with the Duke. Far easier for us to achieve heated moments at Kenilworth in the middle of war preparations than in gossip-ridden Windsor.

And now, even though it had always been hovering on my horizon, my heart lurched, that he too would be leaving me. I could imagine his swagger as he landed in Corunna, the search for wealth and reputation and fame that would drive him to brave deeds and perhaps foolish ones. Sometimes a dark mood settled on me. Would he discover some black-haired Castilian lady who would not refuse him every time he offered marriage, as I did? I could not imagine John following a life of noble chastity. He might think of me between breaking his fast and leading a sortie against the enemy, or between kissing some pretty girl's lips and disrobing her.

I realised I was scowling, and stopped. Would he miss me at all? He said he would, but with the distance of time and vast swatches of land and sea between us, how could I know? How ephemeral our love with no anchor, no firm footing—mere snatched moments because that is all we could allow.

'Wed me.' His final exhortation, his mouth powerfully possessive against mine in a snatched embrace within the old keep, before he had left Kenilworth at the Duke's behest with a troop of soldiery, bound for Plymouth.

'You know I cannot.'

'I know you can. Will you allow yourself to be tied to this boy when it is a man who has your heart? Repudiate this false marriage to Pembroke.'

'It is not false, merely a marriage in waiting.'

'You are a grown woman. You can wait no longer. I would make you as prestigious a husband as young Pembroke. When Richard decides to forgive me utterly, he will reward me and restore my lands to me.' All his old confidence, and more, had been restored with the prospect of action. 'I am a man on the cusp of power and influence. Lancaster will not cavil at me as son-in-law.'

'He would at having to break an alliance made in good faith. My father has strong principles.'

'Not so strong that he has been able to live with a mistress in the eye of his wife for the past fifteen years! It is no marriage for you, Elizabeth. You cannot wait. Desire burns in you.'

'I may not have to wait,' I admitted, allowing a little fear to shimmer to the surface.

It had come to me that my father might give Jonty permission to claim his marital rights before he sailed. It had crossed Jonty's mind too. I saw him watching me. He was no longer the young lad I had wed but a squire who sneaked kisses from the serving girls in the buttery.

'I won't have you in any man's bed but mine. Certainly not that of a barely-grown boy with no knowledge but of clumsy fumbling.'

I could do nothing to assuage John's irritation.

'And you won't take a Castilian paramour on your travels, I suppose.'

'I might have to if you don't put me out of my misery. There must be some girl of birth and fortune, waiting for me in Portugal. What would you say if I brought a Portuguese princess home with me?'

'I would put poison in her soup.'

'Why, Elizabeth!' His brows had risen. 'Do you love me after all?'

My elbow found a tender spot against his naked ribs. We laughed and loved, holding the brief moment to ourselves, despite the discomfort of his squire's room that we had commandeered. And then he had left me, our future as hazy as ever it was, with not even a memento for me to hold.

'I thought you would give me a farewell gift,' I demurred in an attempt to hide my anxieties.

'What need of you for gifts? You have more rings than any woman I know.'

'Will you send word?'

'When I can.' A final warm but brief kiss, for he was already searching for his boots—the whereabouts of various items of clothing, tossed aside in urgency, more important to him than I.

But I knew he would not. What man ever did?

So he had left me.

But this was not the moment for such concerns and I thrust the memory aside. Philippa would go with the expedition to her marriage with King João of Portugal, to make an alliance between him and the Duke against Castile. I might never see her again.

'You can have this.' Philippa held out a gold-edged veil and matching ornamented chaplet which she knew had taken my eye. Had I not borrowed it on more than one occasion?

'Are you sure?'

'Yes. And I agree about the lute. Keep it, and play it for me sometimes.'

Emotion welled in my throat so strongly: to hide it I rose swiftly, crossing the room to take the instrument from her. But I didn't take it. I had barely reached her when my vision broke into facets of light and, fingers suddenly clumsy, I dropped the instrument, the strings complaining with a discordant twanging.

Oh…

A pain struck at my temple and it was as if all the blood drained from my head to my toes, leaving me cold and unsure of my balance. I staggered as little, pressing my fingers against my brow, eyes squeezed shut.

'Oh…!'

Nausea gripped me hard, before Philippa was there at my side.

'You are as white as my new ermine collar.' Her hands reached out to me.

I held on tightly to her arm, one hand now pressed against my mouth.

'I think you had better move your new ermine out of harm's way,' I gasped, 'or I'll vomit over it.'

Which she did, taking my warning seriously before she pushed me to lie on the bed, thrusting aside the satins and velvets, beckoning to one of her women to bring me a cup of ale.

'What is it? Are you ill?'

'No. Nothing.'

'She was dizzy yesterday morning, my lady,' Josselyn, Philippa's waiting woman remarked with unfortunate familiarity.

'I don't recall,' I said, pushing away the solicitous hands.

I tried to sit up, but since my head was spinning I sank back, grateful when Philippa produced a bowl for me to vomit into—which I did, then fell back on the bed again with a groan of final acceptance. I had denied this. It was not the first time I had been so discomfited, but I had rejected the fear that was growing in my mind as the truth was growing in my belly.

'Has this happened before?' Philippa was looking at me, on the alert.

'No.'

'Lady Elizabeth did not go to Mass yesterday morning,' Josselyn said with saintly disapproval.

'No, you didn't.' Philippa, frowning faintly, brushed my hair back from my brow. 'I recall.' Then waved her women away to the far side of the room. Too late for that, I thought.

'Lady Elizabeth has not broken her fast for four days,' Agnes added a parting shot, carrying the incriminating bowl from the room.

'Elizabeth…'

I sipped the ale cautiously, not meeting Philippa's eye, until she seized the cup, took my chin in one hand and forced me to face her, and I knew my secret was out.

'You might show some sympathy!' I tried.

'Sympathy? Tell me this is not what I think it is.'

'Then I won't.'

'But it is, isn't it?'

And I thought of the limited experience I had of pregnancies, wanted or unwanted, in a household that had not been blessed with such occurrences. There was no doubt. Constanza had only borne one daughter, but there was no doubt at all.

'Yes.' Retrieving the cup from my sister's grasp, I sipped again. My stomach seemed to be under my control so I pushed her supporting arm away. 'I must get up.'

'You can't *not* tell me.' Philippa's voice had dropped to a whisper, as if it were possible to keep my ignominious sin from the gossiping tongues of the solar. 'Not Jonty, of course.'

'Ha. Our brother might have pre-empted the arrival of Mary's new womanhood, but they were in love. Jonty still has no time for anything but his horse and his new armour and a flighty kitchen maid.'

'Then who? By the Virgin, Elizabeth…' I thought that if I had not been so ashen she would have shaken me.

I sighed, finding it impossible to imagine what she would reply. But say it I did.

'Then I'll tell you. You would guess anyway. This child that I carry is John Holland's.'

'What?' Little more than a squeak. 'No, you must be mistaken.'

'Do you think so?' Irritably I thrust her aside. 'How many men do you think I've taken to my virginal bed? For shame.'

'I didn't mean…' Philippa sighed. 'And of course you're not mistaken. How naïve of me.' A frown came quickly. 'Did he seduce you?'

'Oh, yes.' And I found my irritation draining away and that I was smiling, although there was nothing for me to smile at in my wretchedness. 'John is a master of seduction. But not in the way you mean.'

'You make no sense. Was it rape? Did he force you?'

'Certainly not. I desired it as much as he did.'

'Elizabeth!'

'I love him. I have loved him since he rescued me from the Tower. And perhaps even a little before that, but I was very young. And then when I went to return the gifts, the finches, I couldn't do it, and I knew that I was destined to be with him.'

'Holy Virgin! I warned you about getting singed. I didn't expect you to leap into the fire! What will you do?'

'At this moment I don't know, other than lie here and suffer.' I had fallen back on the bed again amidst Philippa's gowns.

'Does he know?'

'No.'

'You must tell him.'

'To what purpose? He'll be with you in Portugal within a matter of weeks.'

We stared at each other, the difficulties of my position looming large.

'Think of the scandal!' Philippa whispered.

'I can think of nothing else!' I closed my eyes as if it were possible to obliterate it.

'Elizabeth!' Philippa nudged me into awareness. 'You cannot allow Holland to go to Portugal without knowing that you are carrying his child.'

'And what do we expect him to do about it?'

'I have no idea. He was fairly efficient in getting you into the situation.'

Nor had I any idea. I could not imagine how we could escape from this scandal.

'A pity you had not thought of this earlier.'

So I thought. All I had thought about was the delight of each reunion with John Holland.

Her final words as she left me to suffer. 'We are not going to part as fast as we thought we were. You had better come with me to Plymouth. I'll say a novena for you.'

Her face was set. No sympathy there then. Except that she turned at the door and looked back, the faintest of smiles.

'I expect you'll find a way. You have a charmed life.'

At that moment, racked by nausea, I did not feel capable of magically producing any satisfactory outcome. There was nothing for me to do but order my coffers packed and accompany Philippa to Plymouth. And there I would have to face both John and the Duke.

★

Plymouth was in a turmoil of troops and horses and all the essentials from ale to weaponry for a protracted and hostile expedition overseas. Our entourage might have found difficulty in forcing its way through the masses but the Lancaster pennons had the desired effect. We were soon in the enclosed courtyard of the castle, no quieter or less turbulent, but with the promise of food and a cup of wine. My spirits and my robust health had returned and the journey, although long, had awoken my resolution.

What were the choices for me, a royal princess, contracted in a strategic but unconsummated marriage, yet carrying the child of her lover? My youthful husband had no power over me, but his family would be falling over their hems to express their horror, and what would the Duke say? More to the point, what would he do? His own marital adventures would have no bearing on his reaction to a daughter of Lancaster falling into foul sin. It was one thing for Dame Katherine de Swynford to bear an illegitimate child to the Duke of Lancaster, it was quite another for a ducal daughter to be caught up into the same trap. I considered my future.

It might be considered desirable to arrange a fast nuptial bed with my Pembroke husband, and then express amazement at my equally fast conception and a child born before its time. I imagined it had been done before in many a high-blooded family. The Duke could arrange it for me under the scowl of his disgust with a wilful daughter, and Jonty was now of an age to be effectively potent. It might save me from shame, and memories at court were short. Who would count the months of my pregnancy?

What if, instead, I were dispatched to some distant and discreet convent under the auspices of Lancaster, where the child would be delivered and cared for, with no one the wiser? I would return from my sojourn in the country as white as a sacrificial lamb and resume my interrupted marriage. Seven months in isolation, with prayer and contrition my only companions, might be considered a small price to pay.

And my child—John's child—handed to some foster family with a purse of gold to ensure its welfare and suitable education. I wrinkled my nose in disgust. I would not consider it a small price. I would consider it beyond my bearing.

'What's wrong?' asked Philippa, ranging up beside me.

'Not a thing.'

'You looked sour.'

'Your imagination, dear sister…'

Reluctant to parade my fears before her, I arranged my features into a bland appreciation of the countryside through which we travelled and continued to pick apart the close weaving of the tapestry of my life. It seemed to be a mass of entwined stems and smothering leaves, like a hop-bine at the end of the autumn harvesting, with no clear pattern at all.

Why did I not simply ask the Duke to arrange an end to my sham marriage? He had rarely refused me anything in all my life, indulged and petted as I had been, but that was in the matter of gifts and comforts, of clothing and jewels. I had been raised to know my fate in the scheme of Lancaster preferment, that I would, at my father's behest, wed a man who brought a fine name, authority and wealth. It would not be for me to choose, however eminent the man I set my eye on or however unsuitable I considered my father's choice for me. Had the Duke not refused to listen to my pleas when the Pembroke marriage was first mooted? For certain he would not be enamoured of so close an alliance with John Holland, even though he might be brother to the King. A dangerous man, the Duke had said. John Holland was as unreliable as an unbroken warhorse, a man still with a reputation to repair. No, the Duke would not rejoice at the prospect. And I no longer thought that I had the means to influence him.

There was only one certainty in my mind.

I must tell John. And then…

But there the unknown ran riot through my thoughts. I could imagine full well what my father would say, and I quailed at the prospect. But what about John? Enjoying intimate intervals of intense passion and avowals of love were all very well, but to conceive a child threw a dangerous flame into the nicely smouldering twigs of his ambitions. A conflagration such as this might not be easily extinguished. Would his desire to wed me vanish like the flame of a snuffed candle, or—the thought made my heart bound against my ribs—would he see it as a lever to move the stone of my refusal?

Not that I was in a position to concur with his demands. My heart plummeted again as I prevented a sigh, pinning my smile even tighter when the complications multiplied to swamp my nascent planning. Even if this child, born in full public view, was recognised as the bastard of John Holland, what did I foresee for my future? All I saw was isolation and shame and John far away in Portugal, perhaps not returning before the child could stagger to greet him on its own two feet.

If he had any sense, he might stay there for ever as a soldier of fortune. And what an escape that would be from a trap of scandal and an illegitimate child.

As for the condemnation of the Pembroke family...I could argue that I did not care what Jonty's family would say, but many would argue that there was no way out of that particular morass of public recrimination.

This was no good!

What use was it in allowing myself to be deluged in qualms and difficulties? What was it that *I* wanted? As a sudden shower of rain forced us to quicken our pace, I directed my thoughts into a path away from all the damage this pregnancy had created, for I knew exactly what I wanted. This child might unnerve me with its inconvenience, but deep within me was a sense of unexpected elation, a ripple of pure joy as if the child already moved in my womb, and an utter certainty. I wanted this child, and I wanted John Holland for my husband, a husband who was not hundreds of miles away engaged in a war that might keep him absent for months if not years. Once I would have obeyed my father, but no longer. My mind was set on where I saw my future happiness.

Yet still I desired my father's approval and, as far as

was possible with some diplomatic handling, I wanted the approval of the court. There would be no convent for me, no besmirched name, no bastard child, and no condemnation from the likes of Walsingham. I wanted no gossip in corners, no speculative glances when I entered a room. I wanted reinstatement as a Plantagenet daughter and Holland wife with no cause for me to blush. I was no loose court harlot. I would be Elizabeth Holland, and would hold my head high as I had done all my life.

All I had to do was ease events into motion to achieve it.

Nor was I in any manner daunted. Philippa would probably say that I was undertaking a campaign greater than my powers, but Philippa was never one to beard the dragon in its den. I would. I would tempt the dragon into the open and set it to work for me, even if it demanded unconscionable duplicity to persuade it to my way of thinking. How to go about this miraculous reversal of my fortunes kept my mind occupied over many wearing miles.

'There's Plymouth,' Philippa interrupted my intricate thought processes.

'Good,' I said, all traces of past nausea vanished, my wits sharp.

If I failed, it would not be said of me that I had not done my best.

*

Plymouth at last. A small town, much destroyed in the past through raids and fire, but the castle was intact and the port was thought to be most appropriate for the convergence of all needed for a major campaign. Dismounted, we were shown into a chamber barely larger than the buttery at Kenilworth, put aside for Philippa, but since I was not expected I could not complain.

Although I did. 'I suppose I'll have to share your bed.'

'Yes. And you should be thankful. The Duke might, of course, send you straight back to Kenilworth in disgrace which will solve your problem.'

In disgrace? I had already rejected that. 'I will not go.'

'It may not be your decision for the making.'

I chose not to reply.

We made our way into the living quarters, preventing our skirts from snarling on the edge of coffers and bundles of weapons and armour wrapped in linen, to a room over-looking the port where the Duke greeted us with harassed affection. Sir John was nowhere to be seen, even when I leaned to squint through the window to look down into the activity below.

'I did not expect you, Elizabeth,' my father observed with a lift of his brows. 'Should I have done?'

'I could not bear to be parted from my sister,' I replied, moving back into the cluttered room to sit on a stool. It was a relief that it had a cushion and did not move.

'I doubt we can house you.'

'Philippa has offered half her bed.' I smiled ingratiatingly when she frowned at me.

'You are astonishingly cheerful, all things considered!' she murmured as the Duke walked to the open door to summon a page with food and refreshment.

'What choice do I have?' I regarded her, eyes wide. I had

certainly not informed Philippa of my planning. It behoved me to appear troubled and helpless.

'About what?' the Duke asked, but Philippa deflected him, giving him her attention as she lifted a pile of documents from a coffer lid so that she could sit.

'You appear to be up to your ears in lists,' she said.

'Bills of lading. Always a nightmare at this stage in an embarkation.'

'So where is your efficient Constable, to take the burden from you?' I asked, refusing to respond to my sister's glance in my direction.

'I expect he's down on the wharf...'

'Your efficient Constable is here.'

John Holland walked through the door, carrying a flagon and cups he had waylaid. And I allowed my eyes to rest on him. What mood would he be in today? Would it be the mask, which I had seen often of late, of controlled indifference? A mask I now knew to disguise an uncomfortably acute brain and a raging ambition, a degree of self-preservation and a demonic temper. A turbulent character who would drive his own direction through life regardless of those around him.

But there was no mask today. Today he was the practical soldier from head to toe, garments plain and serviceable, the only decoration in his inlaid sword-belt. He smiled at the company, his expression one of courteous pleasure, pouring the wine expertly with his fine hands. My future rested in those hands.

How uncomfortable! But how impeccable I had become at hiding my thoughts, that initial leap of sheer delight at his presence in the same space. And he too, as if we had never shared the same breath, the same intimate four walls, flesh on flesh. He bowed with brief courtesy, all grace and deprecation, but barely glanced at me. I rose and curtsied with suitable decorum as to a court acquaintance. Philippa did the same but her eye on him was frosty.

'We are pleased to see you here, Sir John. I have heard much talk of you of late.'

I held my breath. If our Constable was surprised, he hid it well.

'I trust it was to my good name. Sadly, it rarely is.' His expression became sardonic. 'But, reputation aside, I will deem it an honour to escort you to your marriage, my lady.'

Philippa looked as if she might have said more but instead tucked her hand in the Duke's arm and drew him aside.

'Is Constanza already here? I would like to speak with her. I need some direction if I am to win King João's admiration when I make my first appearance.'

'He'll admire you whatever you wear,' he said, 'but Constanza will be pleased to see you. The coming child makes her lethargic...'

And then the chamber was empty but for how long? Servants were passing back and forth outside the door. A page sent with a message scurried past. I could hear voices echoing in the stairwell. John observed me from a careful distance. Suddenly there was no smile of welcome, rather a speculative gleam, and the stage was set for my performance, whereupon I must outplay the most skilful of mummers.

'Have you come specifically to see me, Countess?'

'Yes. Are you sorry?'

'Not sorry at all. Merely surprised. I had resigned myself to leaving without seeing you again. But now that you are here…' He broke off as one of the heralds strode between us, face imprinted with urgency as he tossed a muttered apology.

'Is there anywhere we can talk without interruption?' I ventured.

'I doubt it. I share a bedchamber with three others. I know a better place, if windswept.'

And with a little gesture he led me through narrow corridors, up a staircase that brushed my skirts on both sides and out onto the wall walk that allowed us to look down onto the little port. The wind tugged at my veil, threatening to tear it loose until I tucked the flighty ends into the high neck of my houppelande.

'I'll be relieved when we set sail. It's too crowded and the natives are getting restive at all the upheaval.' He pointed to where, below us in the street, the remains of a fracas was being sorted out with fists and the flat of swords by two heavy-handed soldiers.

I slid a glance, picking up his words. 'You are pleased to be leaving me?'

Leaning an arm on the parapet, John faced me, expression relaxed in bland lines. 'Did I say that?'

'I'm not sure.' I studied my clasped hands. 'It may be that you see it as an escape from an affair that has become a burden on you.'

'It may be, of course,' he agreed. 'How long does a court affair last, on average?'

'It's true they are fleeting,' I concurred. 'How many

weeks is it since we have exchanged even a word? What woman would not begin to feel bereft?'

'Or what man consider himself to be hunted by an importunate woman, when she arrives on his doorstep on the day before a campaign? He might of course find a longing for his former freedom...'

His gaze never left my face. Was this to be the end? Nothing but a court flirtation falling to its death on the sword of a military expedition? I did not believe it. He was playing with me. I kept my tone as sweet as honey in the comb.

'Have you truly no desire to kiss me, sir?'

At which John laughed, that infectious laugh that stirred all my senses as it lifted the gulls from the parapet into raucous flight.

'I would fall at your feet and kiss them as a token of my regard, except that it would be blasted all over the garrison within an hour and your father would be hunting me for my blood for trifling with his daughter.'

'Are you trifling?'

'Not I!'

'Then you should know.' I caught his gaze with mine, lavish with anxiety. 'I carry your child.'

His laughing face stilled, all fine planes and angles as he absorbed the news. The laughter was gone. I spread my fingers against the heavy material over my belly, my eyes dropped from his.

'A child, John.'

'Ah!'

He was thinking. I could almost sense the rumble and jostle of his thoughts.

'I am filled with trepidation,' I murmured. 'What do we do?' I bit my lip.

'Have you told anyone?'

'No. Only Philippa.'

'And what does she say?'

'That I was a fool.'

'What do you say?'

'I think she is right.'

Every part of me was tense, waiting as I felt his eyes narrowed on my profile.

'Do you regret our love?' he asked.

'I might regret the results of it,' I said sorrowfully. 'You speak of vile reputation. What of mine? I can hear Walsingham sharpening his quill and his tongue from here. What a gift I have tossed into his lap if he wishes to continue his campaign against the Duke. Or against you,' I added.

'No, he's forgiven the Duke. He is now hailing the Duke as a saviour of England and the perfect royal counsellor. Walsingham hates de Vere more than he hates Lancaster. But that's not important.' He looked at me, his eyes agate-bright, and I looked back.

'I think I am in despair.' I summoned a beautifully melancholy smile. 'We could make a secret match of it, of course...' I suggested.

'What? Abscond on the eve of the expedition? Wed in secret?' His eyes bore into mine, until I broke the connection.

'No. We could not, of course.' I bowed my head again in a parody of shame. 'It would be a great sin, to live as man and wife without the church's blessing. Would we burden this child with the bar of illegitimacy?'

'Of course we would not. What are you thinking?'

'I am thinking that I do not have much courage. That perhaps my choice must be a convent where my shame can be born in secret. That is what the Duke will suggest. Philippa thinks so.' And when there was no reply: 'The Duke will do all he can to protect the family name. Why would he listen to a daughter who has flouted the mores of society as I have? Such ignominy.' I felt, with some satisfaction, the dampness of a tear on my cheek.

I thought he might offer comfort. Instead he turned his back, hands fisted on hips, shoulders rigid, leaving me to regroup my resources.

Until he turned his head to look back at me. 'You were not made for the convent. We both know that.'

'I know,' I whispered. 'But it may be that I must, to hide the shame. How can I not regret...'

'No time for regrets,' he announced curtly to a pair of passing kittiwakes. 'My son and heir is growing larger with every passing day, until all the world will see the results of our lack of control. I do not want him born with all the disadvantages of bastardy. Nor do I want him born in holy disgrace in a convent.'

'But what can we do? Will you help me? I have no one to turn to...'

Abandoning the gulls, Sir John's regard became undeniably speculative, his mouth compressed and unsmiling. I held my breath.

'You have me, dear Elizabeth.' He was controlling his breathing. 'And I will have a true heir from you.'

'So do we abscond?'

All I received was a lift of his brows.

'I still see the convent doors opening to receive me…' I pursued.

'Not they! I doubt they would have you. Are you certain of this child? I see no despair in you.'

'I am certain, and well practised at masking my despair by now.' I flattened my palms, one on the other on my breast where my heart bounded with a solemn beat. 'I am desperately in need.'

'Then who better to answer that need than I? Come with me, Countess.'

And he bowed me from our windswept platform. I was none the wiser of what he would do, but if anyone could take the initiative and drive our path through thicket and swamp, it was John Holland. Without another word, forbidding in his silence, John led me back down the stairs and then in the wake of my father and Philippa until we came to the door to what proved to be Constanza's chamber.

'Stop!' I urged, pulling on his arm before he could raise a fist to the door as if I was in fear of the consequences. 'What are you doing?'

'Something we should have done weeks ago.'

So, on the eve of the campaign, when all was focused on events to take back Constanza's birthright, John intended to challenge the Duke. It would take courage, but if there was one man with courage and enough it was John Holland.

'I don't think I can do this,' I said in anguish, shrinking back as his hand closed on the latch, swallowing the fast leap of victory in my throat.

'What do you suggest? A fast coupling with Pembroke and a child born—how soon before full term?' Releasing the latch he cradled my face in his hands and kissed my lips. 'Better that it is ended and you wed me.'

I took a breath that caught slightly, but raised my chin. 'Then I think I should tell the Duke myself. I cannot imagine what he will say. A Plantagenet daughter with royal blood bearing a child outside of wedlock.'

His smile was wry. 'And you think I will allow you to face him alone?'

Pray God you don't! 'It might be better.'

'It would be a slight on my pride.'

'You will fight for me?'

'How could you doubt it? We will stand together. And then we will face the world.' He ran his knuckles down my cheek, then rapped them smartly against my temple. 'And you, my dear vixen, need play the distraught and helpless ravaged maiden no longer.'

Catching his hand in mine so that he could not rap again, I raised my brows.

'I don't know what you mean.'

His face was alive, a little devious and supremely beautiful, and I loved him for it.

My heart began to sing, even as I preserved my sanctimonious disapproval.

'You know exactly what I mean,' he murmured against my lips. 'When were you ever helpless and tearful? I have been reading you like a book. I know exactly how your mind is working.'

'And how is that?' allowing puzzlement to colour my voice.

'It was a tour de force, to play the distraught female to my dominant masculinity and desire to protect you.'

'You have been laughing at me!'

'Would I do that?' he asked briskly. 'Don't overplay your hand, Countess! Your father knows you too well. Leave it to me.'

He rapped on the door, while I allowed a light sigh of relief.

*

All heads turned as we entered. Not in surprise, but in welcome, although perhaps they had not expected John to be there with me.

At least he had released my hand.

'Come and talk with me about armaments, John. The women have immersed themselves into what they might wear in Portugal.' The Duke's eyes were keen, the beginning of a new campaign that might bring him his heart's desire. It touched my thoughts that my news would destroy all his satisfaction, all his immediate pleasure and fierce concentration in what he saw as the fulfilment of a long-held dream, to rule as King of Castile. Had not Richard already presented the Duke and Constanza with golden diadems? There they were, carefully packed for the journey. And here was I, preparing to coat the dream in dross. For that I was sorry, but what choice had I?

'Before I talk stores and weapons, sir. There is a matter…'

'What's gone wrong now?'

The Duke was pouring a cup of wine, holding it out to John, but instead of taking it, John stretched out his hand to me and I placed mine there.

'I love your daughter, sir. And she loves me. We have consummated our love and she is carrying my child. It is my wish to wed her, so that this child comes into the world with all the advantages of legitimacy as my heir. We need your blessing, and Elizabeth needs an annulment.'

There it was, stated in as short a time as it took to breathe in and out.

The room shimmered into stunned silence that could be felt on the ear. Constanza looked up, her needlework abandoned in her lap. Philippa had anxiety writ large on her face. My father looked baffled at a piece of news he could never have envisaged, then astounded. Finally bright with anger. His gaze moved from John to me and back again. With a brusque gesture, he drank the contents of the cup, placing the vessel at his side with a careful exactitude. To me he said with similar control:

'Is this true?'

'Yes.'

'How long? How long have you been lovers?'

'Since the King pardoned John last year.'

'I told you it must not be.'

'I know, sir.' Bearing John's warning in mind, I kept my answers brief but regretful.

'I did not expect such dishonesty from a daughter of mine.'

'I did not willingly deceive, sir.'

'And yet you did. How could you put yourself in so reprehensible a position? As for you...' He wheeled to face John. 'I have supported you, promoted your interests. And you repay me by seducing my daughter.'

There was a grey shade around the Duke's mouth. This was worse than I thought. Rage was there, tight held, but for how long? The Duke of Lancaster held up to ridicule by an errant daughter. A vital alliance with Pembroke destroyed by wilful passion. I knew his anger was rightly justified, but now was not the moment to retreat if I hoped to achieve anything from this clash of wills.

'Who is to say which man will take a woman's eye?' I ventured. 'This man took mine.'

'You are held by sacred marriage vows.'

'I have been held by them for eight years.' What use in dissimulation? 'How can I be expected to remain loyal to a child in an unconsummated marriage? I love John Holland.'

'It is a deplorable situation.'

John must have felt the trembling in my limbs for he drew me closer to his side. 'I cannot allow Elizabeth to take all the blame.'

'Oh, I agree. Your immorality has led my daughter to the brink of shame. Beyond the brink, by God!'

'It was no seduction, sir. I saw it as a wooing. I love your daughter and want her for my wife. She is the greatest prize I could ever win. I am honoured that she should give herself into my keeping. I can only ask for your forgiveness, and hope that you will lend your aid in ending a marriage that is no marriage.'

No regret, no apology. I held my breath.

The Duke expelled his in a grunt of disgust. 'It is a sacred contract, made with holy vows and not to be broken. It is an alliance that I value. Do I destroy that alliance for the sake of your misdemeanours?' He was cold, icily furious.

'Yes. That is what I am asking,' replied John. 'That you have the marriage annulled. It is not consummated. I see no difficulty. Then I will wed your daughter before there is any talk of the conception of this child.'

'No. I will not.'

'Please, Father...' I had known it would be bad, but not as bad as this.

'Be silent!'

'It is,' John remarked as lightly as if discussing some familiar aspect of the forthcoming campaign, 'as I see it, the only way to eradicate the promise of malicious talk at court. And it is what I want, to protect Elizabeth's good name. As I know you will wish also. Out of this debacle, for which I take full blame, Elizabeth is the one we must protect. I don't like the situation, but we can come out of it without wounding her or your own reputation, sir. Allow me to do what is right by your daughter.'

Constanza and Philippa simply sat, rigidly held. I had to admire John's silken words, the clever way he allied himself with the Duke to protect me. But would the Duke reject the alliance?

'It is not how I would have chosen to make my claim for Elizabeth's hand, but I want her, and I want this child.'

'I wish it too,' I said. The strangest way to accept a proposal of marriage, when I had done nothing but refuse for so long.

'God in Heaven!' The Duke flung himself into the only vacant chair in the room. 'I could do without this.'

And I knew that this was the moment to speak out.

'I repudiate my marriage to John Hastings,' I said, as if I stood before a man of law. 'I have no pleasure in a marriage that only exists in legal words.'

'And I would wed Elizabeth, with or without your consent.' John's hand was firm around mine as if he would anchor my thoughts and my words. There was no room for drama here, even though for me there was one final step in the drama. 'We are both of an age to make that decision. This child merely pre-empts the marriage vows we would have taken. The only problem is…'

'The problem is the existence of John Hastings and all his powerful connections. You hold my hand over a blazing fire, Holland. What a shattering dilemma you've created between the pair of you.' In what seemed a moment of despair, the Duke rubbed his hands over his face. 'Do I have a choice? To give in to a situation that appals me, or have my daughter's name dragged through the sewers by every common gossip in the land.' Surging to his feet once more, he strode to stand with his back to the window, head and shoulders illuminated in bands of golden light that came through the narrow aperture. 'I have been there. I know what it can do. I have felt the pain that it can bring. Do I throw my daughter to the monkish wolves, or do I undermine my integrity by breaking an alliance that has stood for all of those eight years?'

The tension in the room had built massively. We waited for his pronouncement. There was nothing more for any of us to say.

'By God, you are irresponsible, Holland. It's not as if you were young and thoughtless, like Henry in the first flush of youthful amours. You knew exactly what the repercussions of an illicit roll between the sheets could be. At least Mary was his wife...'

'No,' John said. 'We are aware of what we have done.' His demeanour was as cool as the Duke's was hot. Only I was aware of the underlying tensions for my fingers were being squeezed unmercifully, my rings digging deep. It was no small matter to challenge the Duke of Lancaster against his will.

The Duke prowled. Still we waited, the direction of my future life hanging in the balance of his decision. I glanced at John, but thought there was nothing more he could do, and this was assuredly not the moment for any intervention from me.

But then, with a little turn of his head, John smiled at me, the slightest curve of his lips.

'Perhaps there is an advantage in this union, sir. I am not entirely without influence,' John said evenly. 'My marriage to Elizabeth can only consolidate your relationship with the King. Perhaps together we can hold Richard to his true destiny.'

Clever. Superbly cunning, as well as politically astute. I should have known that John would have his full armoury manifest in making his bid for my hand. It was a clever point, cleverly made, and brought the Duke to stand before us.

'Can anyone hold Richard to his destiny? I doubt it.'

John nodded. 'It may be that we will fail, but we can at least try. Or I can, with your daughter at my side. You, sir, will be wearing the coronet of Castile. But when Elizabeth and I eventually return to England, it may be that we can influence an older and wiser Richard into the path of good governance.'

I saw my father consider this. I saw the moment of acceptance in his eyes, as I saw his acknowledgement of what John had done. Two resourceful men, each appreciative of the other.

'There's merit in what you say. So we need an annulment.' He grimaced, the lines on his face harsh, but the white fury had faded. 'You have a way with words, and much as I resent this debacle you've landed at my feet, I must see the sense of what you say. God damn you, John!' Inhaling sharply he rubbed his fist over his jaw as if he could smooth out the tension. 'All I have to do is to explain to the Pembroke connections that my daughter is not the sanctified vessel I, or they, had thought her to be. They'll not like it, but it can be done. There will be a price to pay but if I am prepared to pay it…'

How typical of my father. To cover the most difficult ground as fast and as easily as possible.

'As soon as the annulment is secure, you will wed,' he continued. 'Before we sail.'

There. It was done. Relief flooded through me. But not quite. Not quite yet. The future might still not be at all to my liking.

'And what of me?' I asked in parody of tremulous anxiety.

'Your reputation will be restored, Elizabeth. You will be wed to this man and the child will be Holland's son, without question. Is that not what you want?'

'But John will have sailed for Portugal. What of me then?'

'Return to Kenilworth until the child is born,' my father said dryly. 'You will be safe and comfortable with every nursemaid in the place at your beck and call.'

I looked at John, all solemn compliance in the face of my new betrothed. 'Very well. I will do that of course. I will raise this child alone. I will tell it how brave its father is, fighting in a just war, and unable to return to be with us. And one day, God willing, we will be reunited…'

John's stare was lucid and knowing, and I forced myself to return it, before he addressed my father.

'If I might make a suggestion, sir, to the benefit of all. That Elizabeth sails with us, in the household of the Duchess and Lady Philippa. This will remove her from any source of unfortunate gossip. By the time she and I return to England, after a successful campaign, the child will be long born and growing strongly. Any scandals associated with our rapid marriage will be well nigh forgotten and the child's conception of no interest to anyone.' He slid a glance in my direction. 'I presume this will meet with your favour, lady?'

Anticipation, thick and sweet, slid along my spine. 'I will come with you?'

'Can you think of a better idea?'

He was superbly solemn. So was I. 'No,' I replied, breathing shallowly, hiding my breathlessness. 'If you will allow it, Father.'

The lines in the Duke's face had relaxed and there was

a glimmer of a smile. 'I feel I have been manipulated by the pair of you. You have more political cunning in your bones, Holland, than a parcel of Scottish ambassadors. And now I must grease some papal hand with gold and get the annulment. As if I had not better things to do.'

I seized his hand. 'Thank you.'

'Don't thank me. I have been pushed into an uncomfortably tight corner.'

'I will make an inestimable addition to your family, sir.' John also clasped hands in formal alliance.

'Make sure you do.'

Philippa came to wind an arm round my waist.

'You are a cunning woman, Elizabeth,' she whispered.

'I don't know what you mean.'

★

And thus it was done, the idea that had been born in my mind as the towers of Plymouth had come into my line of vision had been carried out to perfection. I had known exactly what I had wanted, neither a hasty bedding with Jonty nor the cage of a convent. This child, so carelessly conceived, drove me to acknowledge what I desired, and I knew I would stop at nothing to achieve it. There was only one escape from shame or enforced seclusion or even from the interminable boredom of life in Kenilworth or Hertford as the respectable Countess of Pembroke, far from events that shaped the kingdom. Perhaps this child, that had become very precious to me, was not so much a disaster as a blessing in disguise.

If I could make it work for me. And I would. I had.

Persuasion. That had been the key to it. But it had needed careful handling, persuading two men who prized their authority as much as a gold crown to agree to my unspoken wishes. Would it be truly possible for me to draw these men into bringing my resolve to fulfilment, without their even knowing it? Why not? If I did not at least try, how could I succeed? It had taken all the patience I rarely lay claim to, and a degree of dissembling and skilful manoeuvring that I did. With solemn contrition, a sprinkling of tears, and reproachful uncertainty, I had used all the tricks of female helplessness, while all the time fighting for a future that would satisfy me. Would not any woman of considerable talent and a determination to influence her own future do the same?

And now I had it, all that I had envisioned, even a sojourn in distant Portugal during which Richard's court could forget my misdemeanours. Furthermore I had discovered how much John Holland desired me: enough to face my father on the eve of the expedition and fight with smooth words and even smoother arguments to win me.

Thus the Duke put the weight of the Lancaster name and influence into action and I achieved an annulment as fast as it took to send off a courier and hand over a purse of gold. At a time when all I desired seem to be coming to fruition, I found a moment to think of Jonty, who would discover his new unwed status by that same Lancaster courier. It seemed a harsh and cold manner to terminate our marriage. I thought I should have told him, but in the end, the official ending of the contract was all that mattered. His family would find him a more suitable bride of an age to wait for him. He was a matrimonial prize. There would be no difficulty.

Would Jonty miss me? I did not think so. I would remember him with affection. Now my thoughts were all for the future.

To my relief, my father was too preoccupied to do more than remark: 'He is a man with few morals but the ability to charm a frog from a pond. I see no happiness for you with him, Elizabeth. He is as dangerous as a sharp blade in the hands of an untrained squire.'

'But I love him.'

'And does he love you?'

'He says that he does. And I believe him.'

As for John, I saw very little of him since the Duke kept his organisational abilities engaged from dawn to dusk, but we met together in the castle's chapel, early one morning, to exchange vows in the presence of a very small and select congregation come to witness the marriage of Elizabeth of Lancaster to John Holland. No important guests, no ceremonial, no bridal garments, merely the sharing of the holy words, a plain gold ring, because John had nothing else to hand, and a nuptial kiss that was deceptively brief and chaste.

I marvelled at our achievement against all the odds, and I loved John Holland even more as my admiration of what he had done gained hold. The clever intellect, often masked beneath the outer glamour of soldier and courtier. His political vision for England. His courage in demanding me, in the face of my father's ire, with a cold logic that could not be gainsaid.

There was no happier woman in the kingdom than I.

*

'So you got your own way in all things, Madam Elizabeth.'

Plymouth was fading on the horizon as a stiff wind took our vessel on a spritely south-west course on our journey to Portugal. His voice in my ear, his hands locking me against the ship's rail as I looked up into his face. As my husband he was free to approach me in public without censure.

I smiled. 'Now why would you think that?'

'Don't play the innocent, mistress. You are a revelation in trickery, my love. You are as full of guile as a bag of foxes.'

I could not deny it. And what need, now that we were embarked? 'Would you rather I stayed behind?' I asked, sure of my love.

'What do you think?'

'I think I have never been more content.'

And I was. This was what I wanted. I could see nothing but success in this venture, where I loved and was loved. There were no doubts in my mind to sully my happiness. If I had ever doubted, those doubts had been swept away by John's shining certainty that he would have me as his wife, and I wanted to be with him, whatever the difficulties. Had we not managed to scale the most formidable of bulwarks, my existing marriage? He was my life; my present and my future. This was love, a depth of feeling that obliterated everything but the sense of his protection. His devotion.

John Holland was not without faults, but neither was I.

I thought we would never live at peace. We would know the clash of equally determined wills, of hot words and wilful disagreements. But equally I knew, his arms solid and supportive around me as the ship lifted and fell in the swell of the waves, that we would remain constant. Ambition might put its stamp on him, but I was an integral part of that ambition and always would be. Were we not dedicated to the nurture and support of the same family, the same King who was so close to both of us?

'What would you have done,' he asked, chin resting on my head, 'if I had agreed that you return to Kenilworth while I went soldiering?'

'I would have dressed as a man and followed you,' I replied promptly.

I felt him smile. 'I suspect you might have done. Fortunately there's no need, my wife. Have we not made all things to our liking? And now I think we should investigate the accommodations they have made for us in this creaking bucket. I expect it has a bed of sorts in it...'

With every word, every gesture, he drew me to him, like a moth to a flame, a wasp to a honey pot. Like a woman to a man who defied convention, who took fate by the throat and shook it so that it cowered in obedience, who beat his own path through life. A man who was good to look at, quick-witted and silver-tongued. What a future we would make together at Richard's court, when we returned home. John left me in no doubt that he would win his redemption and take his place at Richard's side as a valued counsellor, just as my father had done.

'You look happy,' he said. 'Like a cat who has lured its

prey and now has it under its claws.' And he kissed my fingertips as he drew me into the cabin he had discovered.

I flexed my fingers, interlinking them with his to rub along my cheek, smiling like the satisfied cat he called me, saying simply: 'My happiness cannot be measured. I have you to thank for that.'

'It is my pleasure.'

Our pleasure was mutual, and then we turned to look towards Portugal and our new life.

Chapter Nine

February 1387, Oporto, Portugal.

I sat in my chamber in the royal palace—Philippa's palace now—my thoughts with the Duke and John, my body at ease, happiness sitting as lightly on my shoulders as my loose silk gown, for I was not receiving guests. It had been an eventful month.

My father and John were away at war. Any attempt to enforce Constanza's claims on the kingdom of Castile through diplomatic means had been rejected by the present King so in retaliation our army, in alliance with that of King João of Portugal, had invaded the Castilian possession of Galicia to increase the pressure on King John of Castile. The campaign had gone well and Galicia had been taken. This much we knew. Would not Castile come to terms, conceding Constanza her inheritance? Thus the campaign would come to perfect fruition and John and I could return to England.

My mind was as much at ease as my body.

Not that I resented my surroundings. All was comfort, a gentle breeze stirring the air around me as one of the royal servants picked out a tune on a lute. I now recognised the songs and could hum the melody. I was not home-sick.

I lifted the baby from its cradle to my lap, where it slept on, still exhausted by its rapid entry into the world. I smiled, stroking the tiny hands, the perfect nails.

'You are the cause of a lot of trouble,' I informed the child, who yawned. 'What will your father say when he sees you?'

The baby was unimpressed.

'Let me tell you a few things you should know. Were you aware that you are part of a most pre-eminent family? Your aunt Philippa is now Queen of Portugal. You almost put in an ill-advised appearance in the middle of the wedding ceremony.' I laughed softly at the memory of my hasty departure from the proceedings. 'She is mar-ried to King João to make a strong alliance against Cas-tile. What a Queen she will make. She will have every virtue and the people of Portugal will adore her and sing her praises. She will never be the cause of scandal. Not like your mother.' I stroked the wisps of hair that escaped the baby's cap, dark tendrils, not fair like mine. 'Philippa is intent on loving her husband, even though she had never met him until they were within weeks of the altar, and she has discovered that he has a mistress. I could not be so sanguine, but then your aunt was always more tolerant than I.'

The baby slept, untroubled by the heat, or my essential information for the newest member of our family.

'And then there is your grandfather. The best man I know. The bravest. The most honourable despite his keeping a mistress. They are estranged, but not as much as they once were. You will meet Dame Katherine when we return to England. She will love you as I love you. But your grandfather—he is proud and ambitious for power, and one day he will be King of Castile. He will lavish gifts and affection on you, as he indulged me. His blood and spirit will be in you too. It is a great inheritance.'

For a moment I let my thoughts wander to the problems facing our forces, but what use in that? Nothing I could do would affect the outcome.

'Your grandmother you will never know. Blanche the fair. Blanche the beautiful and good. I barely recall her. Your grandmother by law is sharp and impatient and Castilian. She will have no time for you, but we must not be too harsh. She lost the child she was carrying within a month of our landing. She'll not bear another. All her hopes now rest with her daughter Katalina when she desired a son so badly. We have to be compassionate. She spends much time at prayer.'

'Your father.' And I smiled again. The baby's hair was as dark as John's. 'What do I tell you about him? Where is he now? Somewhere in Galicia I expect, but you must understand that as Constable of the Army his time is not his own and he cannot dance attendance on us.' I leaned to whisper in the baby's ear. 'I should warn you. He will care for you and nurture you, but he will always put his own interest first.' I mused aloud again to the backdrop of the sultry lute. 'Your father loves me, but he managed to be far away when you were born. Perhaps you look a little like him. If you are half as good a knight as he is, you will carry all the prizes at the tournament and turn women's heads. He turned mine. As well as rescuing me from certain death. I wish he were here now, so that…'

A hand brushed my shoulder, lightly.

'So that he could tell you about your mother.'

The voice and touch made me jump, but then all my senses settled into a steady hum of pleasure as battle-hardened knuckles brushed against my throat, yet I looked up, deciding to hide my delight, to punish him a little for neglecting me. Oh, how good it was to see him again. If I needed proof that my decision to risk marriage and this strange exile with John, it was in the sheer joy and relief that squeezed my heart.

'John! What a surprise to see you here. Was I expecting you?'

He signalled for the lute-player to depart. 'And a surprise for me too!'

He stooped to press a salute against my cheek, before taking the child from my arms, holding him with easy competence as he proceeded to catalogue my less endearing characteristics.

'Your mother is headstrong and obstinate, like an unbroken filly. She can be scheming and devious to get her own way. She has the pride of all her family, some would say the vanity too.'

'John…!' I remonstrated, at last.

John shook his head. 'She has more courage than any woman I know,' he continued. 'She has wisdom and integrity, and such a keen loyalty, you would not believe it. It shines like a shooting star in the heavens. She is the only woman I have ever loved, the other half of my soul.' Then added, lifting his gaze to mine so that I could read all the love shining there: 'You will forgive my lapse into poetic verbiage—unlike me, I know. I'm sorry I wasn't here.'

'But you are here now.' How I loved him. And in the long moment that his smiling eyes held mine, the bond, unbreakable, unequivocal, was refashioned between us. A little weary, still wearing travel-worn clothing—which made my heart leap a little for he must have come straight to me—he brought into the solar the aroma of horse and dust and sweat, yet he looked well. The strains of campaigning had not touched him. Nor had it blunted his wit.

'What do I call it? Is it a son?' he asked as the baby whimpered in its sleep.

'Yes. Can't you tell?'

'Not without unclothing him. He is very small.'

'He is only two weeks old.'

'How soon before he can hold a sword?'

'Not for at least another month.'

He placed our son back in the cradle and set it rocking gently with his foot, while his eyes fixed on mine with a raptor's fierceness.

'I thank God for your safe delivery. You were much in my mind.'

Which made me fall in love with him all over again.

'And what do we call our son?' I asked to divert attention from my flushed cheeks. 'Will it be John?'

'Too many Johns in this family. Richard. We will call him Richard. The King will like that. A final step in my reconciliation.'

'The future Sir Richard Holland.'

'I've set my sights far higher than that. I must impress Richard into ennobling me in gratitude for my services. Would you enjoy being a Duchess?'

Lifting me from my chair, he drew me into his arms, regardless of the unfortunate transfer of detritus from weeks of campaigning from him to me, to seal his homecoming with an embrace that reminded me of all the passion which had led to the arrival of this splendid Holland heir.

'Do you think I care?' I asked, when I could, for John was not content until he bore me off to my chamber where a tub of hot water led to much laughter and splashing.

'I'm sure you don't. You will always be Lancaster's daughter. But I do.'

Which confirmed everything I had said to my son about his father. But I loved him. Even when the heat and the insects wearied me beyond bearing I would be nowhere other than with him. The grime of campaigning suitably obliterated, we celebrated John's homecoming with languid kisses, followed by less than languid embraces as we rediscovered old wounds and abrasions, and many new ones. Which reminded me of the perils of warfare, and I gave thanks for John's return.

*

The lines on my father's brow deepened like furrows in a ploughed field with the passing of every week. Constanza, sharp and sleepless, devoted herself to prayer. Philippa wore her new robes with anxiety. John ate little and slept less.

My father's campaign to Castile, as many had predicted, proved disastrous for his and Constanza's long cherished ambitions. Philippa might be satisfactorily wed to the King of Portugal, giving us a strong ally, but any diplomatic attempts to enforce Consanza's claim to Castile died a terrible death, despite the initial success against Galicia. In a show of force our army invaded Leon, a kingdom owned by King John of Castile, only for despair to set in as our troops suffered. It was a time imprinted for ever on my memory, with its horrors of starvation, dysentery and heat that beat us into the ground. Our troops deserted, yet the Duke's determination committed us to further warfare.

Until John stalked into my chamber to announce in a tone that did not brook opposition or even discussion: 'That's an end to it. We are going home.'

It shocked me, took me by surprise. It could not be. 'No!' The first clash of our married existence.

'I say that we will.'

'We cannot leave. You have a duty here.' Would we really abandon the campaign? Abandon my father and the whole enterprise? Could the Constable of the army bow out of the whole enterprise with impunity?

'We cannot stay.' His face was set in even grimmer lines that were harshly delineated through loss of weight in the last weeks. 'I came here to restore my reputation. I never will. The war is doomed and the Duke's star is in the descendent. Every blind beggar at the church door can see that.'

I was not persuaded. Was this cold ambition or rampant realism? Could nothing be resurrected from our present failure?

Apparently not. 'It's over, Elizabeth.' He prowled from one end of my chamber to the other, the violence of his passing wafting the delicate bed hangings into a shiver of silk embroidery. 'We do nothing but waste men and money. It is indefensible to continue in what everyone must see as a lost cause.'

'But the Duke…'

John cast himself into a chair, then abandoned it to walk with increasing restlessness as he explained.

'The Duke is blind to reality. Ask your sister's royal husband. He sees the truth of it. He's reluctant to promise more troops to a campaign that can never be won. My only hope is to put myself back in Richard's eye and hope for a short memory and family loyalty to bring me back into his good books.' His stare when he halted in front of me was inimical, in case I continued to oppose him. 'Otherwise I will remain a poor, landless knight, selling his skills around Europe, barely able keep his wife in silk and his son in good horses as he grows.'

So both ambition and realism, it seemed. I added my own immediate problem to his shoulders for good measure.

'It could be worse than that, John. I am breeding again.'

Emotion warred in his face as he gripped my hands tightly to drag me to sit beside him on the bed. 'Even more reason to go.' And when he still saw doubt in my face. 'I know your reasons for staying. Your family will not travel back with us, but there is nothing here for me, and *my* increasing family. There is everything for us in England. That is where we belong. That is where we can make our mark and set down roots for our children.'

I could see his reasoning, impeccable as ever. Self-serving as ever, many would say. Yet, releasing my hands from his, I went to the intricately traceried window from where I could look out over the parched hills, the pale sky. There was a choice to be made, but was it so momentous as I had first thought? I would leave Philippa to rule Portugal beside her husband, but that I had always known and accepted. If the campaign failed, the Duke would make a settlement to preserve his dignity and he too would return. So I imagined would Constanza if she was denied her birthright. Henry was in England with his wife Mary and a newborn son I had never seen. Then there was Richard, who might have grown into a stable maturity under the influence of capable and loving Anne. I could renew my connection with Dame Katherine in Lincoln, who would be charmed by my son and the forthcoming child. All the family I knew and loved to welcome me home. Everyone I knew at Kenilworth, my favourite home. What was to keep me here?

Nothing. Nothing but the inevitability of failure. There was no difficult choice for me to make when family beckoned so strongly. Besides, John wanted to go home. He would never agree to leave me here and return alone, so why trouble myself over a decision that was already made in my mind and in reality?

I returned to stand before him.

'Are you sure about this?'

'Never more sure. I've already spoken with the Duke.'

'And he agrees?'

'Reluctantly, but yes.'

So all was arranged, with or without my blessing. But I could find no strong argument to offset the planning.

'We will go home,' I agreed, already mentally distancing myself from the silk-clad languid luxury of this Portuguese palace.

And that is exactly what we did, after a lachrymose farewell with Philippa, a more stringent one with my father, and with safe conduct to travel through Castile to Gascony where we took ship. And home.

'What will await us?' I asked, my hand tucked in John's arm as the coast of England came into view, a thin grey line on the horizon.

'Promotion for me,' John announced. 'Richard will award my loyalty with land and a title. He'll make me work hard for it, of course.' Anticipation had grown stronger in him with each mile we covered towards England.

And perhaps he was right. Any guilt I felt in what some would have said was a rat abandoning the sinking ship, any regrets at leaving Philippa, were swept away when we set foot on English shores, a bare twelve month since we had left. The Castilian problem would be settled without my presence. Now we had our own family to think of. Richard would welcome us, John would work hard to establish us, and all would be well. Our future unrolled before me, a time of royal approval when Sir John Holland would become one of the foremost men of the land.

There was nothing to ruffle the waters of my serenity.

Chapter Ten

September 1397: Windsor Castle. Ten years later.

'Now what do you suppose he is planning?'

'Probably something not to our liking.'

John's *sotto voce* query was accompanied by an increasingly frequent saturnine expression, his tolerance for his young brother fraying around the edges. Standing in a crowd as we were, I hushed him discreetly. Since the unfriendly affair at Radcot Bridge, ten years ago now, there were changes in our King. It was like waiting for a thunderstorm to break out of a summer sky, without warning.

John bowed as Richard's eye fell on him. I curtsied as the royal observation passed to me. A wave of obeisance followed the King's scrutiny. Richard had acquired heightened notions of his royal superiority.

'He has something in mind,' John continued, bending his

head as if to survey the more restrained toes of his shoes as Richard's attention moved on.

'I know he has, but who will be the victim?'

'The Lords Appellant?' John had returned to watching his brother, with cat-like narrowing of his eyes.

It would have to be. Richard detested the group of Lords Appellant, a small but powerful group, with a vicious fury. I sought out Henry's solid figure in the crowd, since he was one of the five, but my brother appeared insouciant, calmly unaware of any undercurrents. Or, as I presumed, giving a good pretence. We were all tiptoeing round our King, and rightly.

It had been a time of some anxiety, marking the years since John and I had returned from Castile, when Richard's infatuation with the charms of Robert de Vere had reached its dangerous height. I remembered De Vere as little more than a youth, charming Richard, flattering him in the courtyard when my father had given me one of my first lessons in the importance of political allegiance. Richard had been well and truly snared, and de Vere, grown into even more charming and ambitious maturity, had been intent on consolidating his power with weasel words in Richard's ear. And Richard, listening avidly, against all advice, had showered his favourite courtier with land and wealth, unable or unwilling to see the consequences. For as de Vere's hold over Richard grew, it stirred resentment amongst the lords and magnates who expected the honours for themselves. Including my brother Henry who joined forces with our uncle of Gloucester, as well as the FitzAlan Earl of Arundel, Mowbray of Nottingham and the Beachamp Earl of Warwick. Five influential men, a puissant alliance against the King, the Lords Appellant made their demands to rid England of the King's evil counsellors.

Would Richard listen? Would he distance himself from de Vere, now preening as Duke of Ireland, and allow the counsels of his great magnates in the form of a commission instead? He would not.

The result had been a battle, in the year before we had returned from Castile, where the Lords Appellant had defeated de Vere at Radcot Bridge, driving him into exile and forcing Richard into a bared-teeth compliance. So my brother and his associates had emerged triumphant with their curb on the young King's powers, but Richard had never forgiven them. Richard might smile and ask advice but he was biding his time. I hoped that his new child bride would take his mind from his woes, but my knowledge of Richard warned that our King would not be compliant for ever.

Yet in spite of the ripples on this political pond, this was a time of good humour and unity. Perhaps my suspicions were unfounded after all.

'It is my wish to award a prize,' Richard was announcing, 'as a token of my esteem and appreciation for those who have graced my festivities.'

Richard beamed at the assembled masses in the great dancing chamber at Windsor, all resplendent in silks and satins and feathers as was he. It was a celebratory feast, held by Richard to mark the ending of the session of parliament, and I had danced until my feet were sore. In those festive days and nights I sang to the lute and dulcimer and rode to the hunt, my heart tender, so great was my joy. Utter contentment, such as I had never believed would be mine, swaddled my emotions, as a mother would wrap her newborn child, for John was at my side and his satisfaction rubbed against me so that I acquired its glitter, as a silver bowl acquires a sheen from the polishing cloth.

There was no shortage of partners with whom to hunt or dance, or willing knights to lead me into one of the formal processions. Not that I needed any. Did I not have John whose love remained the brightest star in my heaven, and always would be? And my children. I smiled when I read Philippa's letters, bemoaning my lack of maternal doting. That was a thing of the past. I loved them dearly, this growing Holland family of ours, for as well as John's adored heir, born in the heat of Portugal and now an energetic ten-year-old with an energy for the tournament that reminded me of a young Henry, we had three daughters, and a baby son of two years.

'Who would have known that you would prove to be so fertile?' John had remarked as he held his newest son, another John.

'I'd rather we didn't prove it again,' I said, knowing there was no guarantee. Our love was as tight-knit as the day we had stood before my father and John had bargained for my hand.

What a superb family we were that autumn.

Richard, bedecked and bejewelled, recovered from the death of his beloved Anne three years previously, now had a child bride Isabella de Valois on whom to lavish glittering rings, and with her the glory of a new alliance with France to his name, which he much desired despite the dark mutterings at court.

Catching my breath from my exertions, I looked round the room, noting the scattered members of my family.

My father the Duke, returned from Castile, failing in his bid to snatch the crown for Constanza, who was dead and not greatly missed, for her final years had been sequestered. Free from matrimonial toils, my father had the previous year wed his life-long love at last. The scandal had raged through the court, but they were happy in their new-found respectability. And there she was, Duchess Katherine, utterly serene, until you saw the caustic gleam in her eye. She did not trust Richard either.

And there, proud and eye-catchingly groomed—when was he ever not? —Henry too was with us, still unwed after the death of Mary in the same year that Richard lost his own wife, but with four fine sons and two daughters, they added to the noisy celebrations at Richard's court.

And there was another face familiar to me as my own. My cousin Edward, heir to the York inheritance, now Earl of Rutland and Duke of Aumale and grown into his Castilian inheritance of good looks from his mother Isabella. How confident he was, and ingratiating, slipping neatly into the place in Richard's life left by the absent and now dead de Vere. Too neatly, some would say. Seeing me watch him, Edward grinned and raised a hand, before turning back to whisper in Richard's ear.

It was a golden time. A family united and reconciled. Truly a time for celebration.

And I? What of proud Elizabeth of Lancaster? Although

a wife and matron, I felt as young as I had been when I had first succumbed to the persistence of John Holland. My steps were as light and lithe as those of any virgin looking for her first love. The great ruby, given to me by my father on the occasion of my first marriage as a mark of his approval, flashed on my finger. That marriage was long gone and Jonty of Pembroke dead these nine years after a terrible accident at the Christmas junketings at Woodstock. I mourned the loss of his young life, but intermittently. My vision was centred on the present and the future. How could it not be?

John was my love, my future and past. Gone were the days when we were showered with disapproval for his pre-emptive taking me to his bed before the exchange of marriage vows. Earning his reparation in Castile, he was now frequently to be found at his brother's side, royal patronage his for the asking. When John led me into the dancing, his steps betrayed a confident swagger, for was he not created Earl of Huntingdon and I his Countess? He had been awarded Richard's recognition with this fine title, with lands and castles in Cornwall and a great house at Pultney in London where we could entertain in sumptuous luxury.

How foresighted John had proved to be in bringing us home from Portugal. There was nothing there for him, or in the disastrous war against Castile, but here he had been welcomed by Richard and forgiven his past sins. Not without self-interest of course: in the terrible aftermath of Radcot Bridge Richard needed family around him. He had needed support against the Lords Appellant. Wooing John to his side could only be to his advantage.

John smiled and bowed and flattered, making himself

indispensible as a good counsellor should. And thus I was once more a Countess. As for the authority to go with it: Richard had created him Chamberlain of England, an office stripped from Robert de Vere. So it seemed that our star was in the ascendant with Richard's determination to build a level of personal support that could not easily be displaced. John would be central to that support. Who could not admire the chain of sapphires with its white hart livery badge, the King's personal gift, that shone on John's breast, a mirror image of the chain worn by the King himself?

'You look happy, my love,' John observed as our steps brought us close in the dance.

'I am happier than you could ever imagine,' I said. 'And I will show you later, when we are alone…'

My father, worryingly aged since his return from Castile and his reluctant acceptance that the marriage of his daughter Katalina to the Castilian heir was the nearest he would ever get to his dream of this southern kingdom, was pleased to scowl on my new happiness.

'He worries me,' he announced, watching my husband move from group to group, listening, advising, nodding sagely.

'Have you withdrawn your regard from John?' I asked, not too concerned. 'Once you were quick to see his merits.'

'But I was never blind to his deficiencies. Look at him. All he sees is power. He'll make enemies.'

'He'll make friends as well. Did you not live with friends and enemies both?' My certainty that John would survive all vicissitudes could not be shaken. 'Were you not able to hold the balance between them and enjoy the benefits?'

The Duke's frown deepened. 'Beware, Elizabeth. He's casting all his eggs into Richard's basket. If you have any influence, make him see that sometimes moderation is the better policy.'

There was no moderation. I knew what Richard was doing, and why should we not be part of my cousin's empire-building? Strengthening his own support against those who would oppose him, as my father had done, as any family that valued its future supremacy would do. Our own children played their own role at Richard's behest, one of our young daughters already betrothed to the Mowbray heir of Nottingham. I saw no harm in it. We were the premier family in the land below the King. Why not make strong alliances with our daughters?

I kissed my father's cheek.

'You should be proud of your daughter and son-in-law.'

'I suppose I should,' he acknowledged but without much enthusiasm.

And when John rode in the lists with such éclat that showed no hint of fading, my father could do nothing but applaud and acknowledge the astonishing spectrum of his skills. As I did. Was he not at the height of his prodigious powers?

'Just let him keep his temper and his ambitions in check,' the Duke warned, 'and then we might all survive.'

'Don't you trust Richard?'

Diplomatic to the last, the Duke chose not to answer that, but his opinion was clear enough. 'If you smile on him and Huntingdon provides a steady hand at the helm...'

For my father's years of power as royal counsellor were

long gone. And so I smiled as rewards and royal patronage were heaped upon us, and John began to build Dartington Hall in Devon as a home fit for his new elevation.

Thus we basked in the sunshine of Richard's regard.

The music died away and Richard, leading the little Queen forward, called us to attention.

'It is my wish to reward those who love me and mine.'

I watched him as he handed Isabella forward, his face clear and unlined, eyes soft and full of gentle affection. There was no cat-like malice in Richard today. This marriage could be the making of him, with this young life to protect and nurture. We curtsied, bowed, a silence falling over us.

'Who is the best dancer amongst us?' He looked round the expectant faces. 'Which lady has the grace and elegance of my own white hind? What do you say, Uncle of Lancaster?' He looked at my father whose expression was a masterpiece of diplomacy.

'Who can say, sire. It would be cruel to choose from so many fair exponents.'

'But choose we must. And I know who will tell me the truth.' He leaned and whispered in Isabella's ear.

Isabella, all of seven years old, shook her head, eyes wide with apprehension.

Richard whispered again. Isabella whispered back. The crowd laughed indulgently.

'My wife has chosen, and I will agree.' He held out his hand, an open-handed gesture of pure friendship. 'We award our prize to the Countess of Huntingdon.'

I laughed, a little startled, disconcerted. The supreme

agility of youth was no longer on my side, so what had my royal cousin in mind? I glanced at John who was still playing the great magnate, his face a superb example of brotherly appreciation. That mask, when he chose to use it, was still difficult to penetrate.

'Come, Cousin.' Richard beamed. 'We await you.'

I stepped forward, as Richard drew a ring from his own finger and pushed it onto my thumb where it gathered the light from the candles and cast it out in flashes of azure light.

I curtsied. 'I am honoured, sire.'

'So am I, to have you at my court, my dearest cousin.'

The dancing continued around us.

What could possibly prevent Richard's reign from being one of the most glorious, with John as brother and counsellor? The Duke had said ours would never be an advantageous marriage, that it would be ill-conceived to ally myself with Holland. How wrong he had been. It had been like opening an oyster and discovering within it a pearl beyond price.

And yet...

'I think Richard is in a dangerous mood,' I said bluntly when Richard allowed me to retreat. 'When Richard smiles like that I always fear for our good fortune.'

'How can we be threatened?' John asked, taking my hand to take cognisance of my reward, a blue sapphire set in a heavy gold ring—far too valuable for such a prize. He seemed to have cast off his earlier doubts, and who could blame him in the face of such royal approbation? 'Am I not the most loyal of subjects?'

But I was not convinced. Perhaps the Duke's warning had sown seeds.

'You are, of course. But I swear I am not the best dancer.'

'Isabella chose you.'

'No. She didn't choose me. It was Richard. He has ulterior motives. The problem is, what are they?'

'He has indeed. Shall I tell you?' John teased.

I dug him in the ribs. 'Another marriage to plan for our infant children?'

'Would you object? A daughter promised to the Earl of Oxford's heir. Richard is mending fences on all sides.'

'You don't trust him either,' I said.

'No. But I think he wants to please me. Are we not basking in the gilded light of his regal gaze?' I heard the cynicism. John was as watchful as I, even though he shrugged. 'He is my brother and will not harm me. He has promised me an even greater prize. Richard will grant me the office of Chamberlain for life.'

It was a superlative end to the celebration.

'Will you support Richard against the Lords Appellant, if he asks it of you?' I asked as we made our weary way to our own accommodations. Richard's court demanded an unconscionable degree of standing around. What it was that put the thought into my head I had no idea, but I could not let it rest.

'Yes. Of course.'

I understood his reply. As Richard's Chamberlain he could do no less, but it would assuredly cause difficulties. It would bring him into immediate conflict with my uncle of Gloucester, and with Henry. And, inevitability, there would be an uncomfortable distancing from my father, creating more infinitesimal fault-lines in the family loyalties.

It threatened to gnaw at my contentment as the consequences of Radcot Bridge hung over us like a bad odour.

I would not think about it. There would be ways out of the conflict. There were always ways out of political dilemmas and we would find them. John would find them.

*

When there came a knock on the door of my parlour, one of the great chambers in Pultney House that I had designated as my own, I motioned to one of my women to open it to discover Master Shelley, our steward, accompanied by two figures, not yet reaching full adulthood, muffled in cloaks. One of the boys, the eldest by his height, stepped forward. The other boy, square and sturdy, merely scowled.

I rose to my feet, intrigued by these unexpected visitors, relieved to have something to distract me, for pleased though I was to have made my home at Pultney House in London, I was suffering pangs of loneliness. I had become used to John's comings and goings but sometimes I missed him when Richard's demands came first, as they must, and as they did increasingly often. Richard could never bear to be anything but first, and John had been gone for some weeks, quite where I did not know.

'We have guests?' I asked, brows rising. They were marked by signs of long and arduous travel, but there was about them an air of hauteur rather than of weariness. 'Is Lord John here?'

'My lord is here,' the steward replied. 'He says that we have additions to our household.'

So who were they? I walked forward. There was no sign of deference from the two youths as I beckoned them into the room, looking them over. They came reluctantly. What had we here? The cold light of fury in the eyes of the younger boy was unmistakeable, for all his youth. I found it faintly amusing that he should glare at me in so hostile a manner.

'Who are you?' I asked since they offered no explanation. The two boys were close to adulthood, unknown to me, yet the cast of their features and their light colouring suggested a family that I knew. Clearly gently born, their garments of good quality, they should have been raised to know when courtesy was due.

'You are old enough to show deference,' I remarked, when none was forthcoming.

It was the elder boy who spoke. 'I am FitzAlan. This is my brother.'

'Then welcome.' The FitzAlans were family of course, through blood and marriage, and these youths must be the sons of the Earl of Arundel. But why was their presence so acrimonious?

'I am Richard FitzAlan,' the youth stated again, voice icily clipped, at odds with his eyes ablaze with some fervour. 'I am Earl of Arundel—except that on my father's despicable death I have been disinherited. I have no wish to be here in the home of a murderer. I will show no deference. And you cannot make me,' he ended, youth and emotion overcoming dignity.

Everything within me stilled, as if at some presentiment of danger.

Arundel? Dead? Here was information new to me. I knew the Earl of Arundel of course, head of one of the most powerful and well-connected families in the land. I knew Joan FitzAlan, his sister, even better. She was Countess of Hereford through her marriage with a Bohun husband, and mother of Henry's dear lamented Mary. Through her descent from King Henry the Third which gave her Plantagenet blood, she had always been close to my father. The FitzAlans were a family to be reckoned with, if not of my own quality, yet here was this boy with such bitter accusations that made no sense.

'You should beware of loose talk, Richard FitzAlan,' I replied. And there was John, entering on their heels, his cool hauteur matching the boy's.

'I know what I saw,' Richard FitzAlan glowered at John, 'and our father is dead.'

'Dead as befitted a traitor,' he remarked.

'Murdered at your hand and that of the King.'

I saw how John tried to temper his reply. 'Shown mercy at the hand of the King.'

'Is execution mercy?'

'It's far preferable to the punishment doled out to most traitors,' John said with ineffable patience, eyes full of understanding. 'If it were not for the King's mercy, you would have watched your father hanged, drawn and quartered in public display.'

The youth paled. 'He was no traitor.'

'He took up arms against the King at Radcot Bridge.

That is treason enough. Now go with Master Shelley who will show you to your rooms. He will give you food and a place to sleep. We will speak tomorrow.'

'God damn you for your part in our father's death.' A vicious parting shot from the younger of the two as our steward ushered them out.

When they had gone, John and I stood and looked at each other, the curse hanging heavily between us.

'You could have warned me,' I said. 'Do I ask what all that was about?' Although I could guess some of it for myself.

'I couldn't warn you because I didn't know Richard's intentions to foist the brats on me. Richard has become a master of disguise.' John's features relaxed from recrimination into a wry smile. 'How long is it since I last saw you?'

'Too long.'

Stepping together in one mind, his arms were firm, his kiss a promise for later, before he stretched his long limbs into a chair by the fire with a sigh of utter weariness.

'What is all that about?' The FitzAlan news had stirred a dormant fear in me.

'Later…'

I sent for wine and food, rid the room of the women, and waited with impatience until he had slaked hunger and thirst.

'You have travelled far.'

'Yes. I don't want to see a horse or a saddle for the next se'enight.' I smiled as I went to sit at his feet and link my fingers with his when he beckoned. It was good to have him home. 'There's nothing to concern you.' He leaned to press his lips against a furrow that must still have been evident on my brow. Then said, as if he could not keep silent: 'Richard has begun his campaign against the Lords Appellant. We always knew he would.'

Of course it concerned me. For here was the retribution, that we had feared and that had come at last to assuage Richard's desire for revenge. Was Richard strong enough to emerge from this with his authority and his crown intact? He might well, but I feared for my father and brother. As one of the Lords Appellant, Henry would be fortunate indeed to escape, and here was news of the death of Arundel. My belly quivered with nerves. Meanwhile John was intent on ridding me of my fears, which did nothing but stoke them.

'You should be ecstatic, my dear love. You are now a Duchess and may wear a ducal coronet.'

'You are standing so high with your puissant brother.'

'I am indeed. I am now made Duke of Exeter for my services.' But the worry was there, underpinning the sense of fulfilled ambition. The line between his brows, probably matching mine, was thin and deep. Would he tell me the truth, the whole of it?

'Then tell me about the FitzAlan offspring who it seems are to live with us. And who despise the very air we breathe.'

'We have custody of them until Richard is satisfied with their loyalty to him. Which could be longer than he thinks. At the moment they're ripe for murder.' John sighed, absent-mindedly chafing my hands between his, frowning at some distant scene that still filled his mind.

'I gather that the Earl is dead.'

'Executed. Because Richard decided to strike at those who humiliated him.'

So I was right to be concerned. 'Did you know?'

'Yes.'

'And didn't tell me.'

'I thought it better not. You are too close for comfort to some of them.'

I took a breath. Henry must be safe, or he would have told me. And yet fear leapt into life. 'My brother?'

'No. Henry is spared so far. But it has been a bloody affair.'

And so he told me. I sat, a cup of wine forgotten in my hand.

'We always knew it would only be a matter of time, didn't we? Richard has had his revenge against three of the Lords Appellant at least. I was with him at Windsor when he made his plan, then went with him to Pleshey where he arrested your uncle of Gloucester. He also took Arundel and Warwick. Gloucester is sent to Calais to await trial. Warwick is under lock and key in the Tower. But he made an example of Arundel. Richard has had him executed on Tower Hill for treason.'

It was a bleak recital of retaliation. Richard FitzAlan, who had carried the royal crown at Richard's coronation, dead as a traitor.

'What about Henry? And Mowbray?'

'Still at large and unthreatened. For now.'

Blessed Virgin! Henry was safe, but not, I feared, for long. 'Is this good policy?' I asked. 'To execute a man so close in blood ties?'

'It will make any man who thinks of opposing Richard think twice.'

'And you are rewarded for your part in it.'

'I have been granted the honour of Arundel and Arundel Castle. And custody of the young FitzAlans, whom you will charm so that they will come to your hand like chicks to a bowl of grain.'

I could try. But I suddenly felt it was as if all the critical links that held our family together were unravelling under my eye, like an ill-stitched girdle. Where would it end? And where would I stand in the approaching upheavals?

'It worries me,' I said. 'It sets you at odds with my father and Henry.'

I am afraid it will set you at odds with me...

The thought stepped softly into my awareness, chilling me to the bone.

'I'm too busy carrying out Richard's orders to be at odds with anyone.' He leaned forwards, hands gripping my wrists as if he would force me to see the future as he did. 'All will be well if your father and brother allow Richard to wield authority as he sees it. I doubt he will attack Henry. He was not one of the main protagonists. He was very young at Radcot Bridge.'

'But if Richard continues to be driven by revenge, until every one of those who forced him to give up de Vere is punished...'

'It's all ifs, Elizabeth. Who's to know? We'll try and keep his thoughts and actions in moderation.'

'I wish Anne had not died. Isabella is too young to exert any influence on Richard. And,' I looked up into his face,

'I don't like this outcome. I don't like it at all. The FitzAlan boys are so angry.'

'As I would be in their shoes,' John admitted ruefully. 'We will do what we can to keep my brother on an even keel, and meanwhile try to prevent the FitzAlan youngsters from murdering us in our beds.'

Which brought another thought leaping into my mind.

'If we had been in England, would you have joined the Lords Appellant against Richard?'

John's reply was immediate, with no hesitation at all. 'I would have had more sense.'

I said nothing more, for what was there to say in the face of such distancing from the stance that the Lords Appellant—and my own brother—had taken? Little ripples of anxiety doubled and tripled to rob me of my delight in his return until:

'I've had enough of the FitzAlans, and of Richard.' His fingers around my wrists softened into a caress as he kissed his way along my fingertips. 'Come and welcome me back in true wifely style. I've been thinking patiently of our reunion for the past hour, and my patience has just expired.'

As an invitation it could not be refused, and so our reunion leapt from heat to heat as John lit the flames. Absence had its advantages.

'How long since we were together?' he demanded.

He found a need to reacquaint himself with every inch of my skin until I glowed like a storm-lantern on a dark night.

But as I lay sleepless beside him I was forced to acknowledge that all the ease of the days when I won the prize for dancing was gone. How trivial it had all been. Now this undercurrent of danger lived with us, when it was impossible to predict Richard's next move, his hand hopping this way and that on the chessboard. Had John always been aware?

I asked him.

'Yes. Richard is unstable. But he is my brother and for that, he deserves my loyalty.'

And that was what worried me.

★

'I am furious with him. At this moment I despise him! How did Richard turn out to be so viciously mean-spirited?'

At this moment, sweet as dripping honey, Richard was dancing with Queen Isabella.

How often did I say those words, or similar, as we continued to meet at court with all the pretence of an affectionate, united family? On this occasion it was my brother who bore the brunt of my low-voiced accusations. John had heard enough of them.

'You're safe enough,' Henry advised lightly, bowing as Richard's gaze touched on us, I spreading my skirts in graceful deference. 'I'm the one who has to watch his back.'

'Before God, Hal. Don't provoke him.'

Richard's interest had passed on.

'I? I'll not provoke. And what need?' As ever Henry faced the world with a stark realism, inherited from our father. Nearing his third decade, honourable and clear-headed, he had emerged from Mary's death with an inner strength, a pride in his children. A pride in Lancaster, his future inheritance, only second to the Duke's. 'If Richard decides to strike, he'll do it and answer to no one. Our uncle of Gloucester discovered that to his cost.'

'Just take care.'

'When did I ever not?' Squeezing my arm, he smiled. 'Good to know that you are on my side, sister.'

'But is that of any value to you?'

I might return his smile, wishing I might ruffle the ordered waves of his hair as I would once have done, if only to disperse his tendency to lecture, enjoying the intricate borders of his houppelande, flamboyant on sleeve and hem, for Henry had also inherited the Duke's love of ostentation. Yet knew I was right to fear what Richard might do. It was as if once he had tasted the sweetness of revenge with Arundel's death, he could not live without it, like a drunkard having enjoyed the rich savour of the finest red wine. Thereafter revenge teased Richard's tongue, ran in his blood. It seemed to permeate his every thought and for those of us on whom he frowned, there was no escape.

More hurtful, more agonising, the estrangement between John and myself grew, encroaching on our happiness, step by tiny step. I tried to understand. I tried to put myself into his shoes, but how could I watch him bow with awful reverence before his brother when Richard had had my uncle of Gloucester put to death in Calais, crying victory over the death of yet another of the Lords Appellant who had rid him of his blessed de Vere? Arundel executed, Gloucester murdered, Warwick incarcerated. Any man who was not a fool could see the pattern of Richard's vengeance. How long could Henry and Mowbray survive it?

And John? John remained silently, solidly as Richard's trusted counsellor.

'How can you support him in this?' I demanded on a hiss of breath, anger flickering like a will o' the wisp, even as I tried to control it.

'It is his right. He is God's anointed King,' John murmured.

'He had Gloucester murdered.' I was still struggling to accept that Richard had been party to the death of our uncle.

'As I am well aware.' John studied his linked fingers, for we were kneeling at Mass with the royal court. 'Richard says Gloucester died from natural causes.'

'Smothered in his bed more like. I doubt Richard's praying for his uncle's soul!'

'Then you pray instead!'

So, acknowledging John's reciprocal ill-temper, and knowing that this was neither the time nor the place to pursue my fears, I prayed, feeling as if I were standing between the two pans on a goldsmith's scales. While John was in the ascendant, lifted by Richard's elegant fingers so that he shone like a beacon, my own family seemingly fell, Richard's heavy palm pressing them down into obscurity. Into oblivion.

It would be Henry next. I knew it. Richard would discover, or create, the perfect opportunity to express his loathing of my brother. But how far would he go? Richard was still smiling on the Duke and his new Duchess Katherine. Would he dare attack the Lancaster heir?

'Can we do nothing?' I demanded of John after another

interminable day of Richard's demands that we show him
the reverence due to Almighty God.

'No.' He remained uncompromising. 'Not until we know
what Richard intends.'

'So you admit he is plotting something.'

'Yes. You know him as well as I do, Elizabeth. Look at
the gleam of mastery in his face. Richard might keep his
own counsel, but having dealt with Gloucester he won't rest
now.'

'I think you could try and deflect him.'

'And ruin my own position to no purpose?'

'Is that all you can say? Is that all you can think of?'

'You were pleased enough to enjoy my position at court.
To be Duchess of Exeter.'

Heat was building between us again, my anger no longer
a mere flicker of intent. It seemed I had a temper as strong
as John's when those I loved came under attack. It flared.

'But that was before Richard took a hatchet to his family.
That was before I see only blood and…' I stopped, before I
could say words that would not easily be undone. I felt like
an apprentice juggler with a handful of eggs. 'The Duke is
unwell,' I said instead. 'He could not bear it if Richard had
Henry murdered in the same manner as my uncle, smothered in his bed in Calais by some nameless assassin. I think
it would be the end of him.'

The Duke's recurring ill-health was becoming a concern
for us all, a wearing away of the once great strength. He
might deny it but the years were taking their toll.

There was no sympathy in John's response. It was as if I
faced a solid barbican that prevented me approaching any of

his finer feelings. 'I cannot turn Richard's mind, Elizabeth. Once it is made up… It took Radcot Bridge to get him to give up de Vere. And he's never forgiven those who forced his hand. He'll follow his own desires with or without me. All I can hope to do is temper his response to what he sees as justifiable use of royal power.'

How coldly realistic he was.

'I know. I know. I know your hands are tied. But how often did my father stand for you? How often did he plead your cause? How often did I? If you had any—'

He rounded on me.

'Don't say it. Don't go down that path, Elizabeth.'

If you had any love for me, you would at least try…

Nor would I ask: *did you have a hand in my uncle Gloucester's death?*

But I did, because I was in no mood to placate.

'No.'

One word in brutal denial. Family loyalties were dividing us, tearing us apart. We parted in a spirit of disharmony. For the first time in all the years that I could recall, when leaving to attend on Richard, John did not kiss me in farewell.

Chapter Eleven

A black year. A year of farewells and disagreements. How right I had been in my suspicions that Richard would act against my brother, for on a cold grey December day I stood on the shore at Dover and watched Henry step aboard the ship that would take him into exile.

All Richard's doing.

Fabricating a treasonable plot, magnificent in its complexity, Richard had waved the regal sceptre to banish Henry from England for ten years, Mowbray for life. Thus the final two Lords Appellant paid for their disloyalty to the Crown. In a fit of false generosity Henry's ten years were transmuted to six but it was little comfort.

I held Henry close in a storm of anger and grief which we both hid behind rigid shoulders and stern expressions. Here was no time for emotion. Our father might be racked with pain and remorse but his example was superb. The family of Lancaster would hold their heads high and wait for better times.

John did not accompany me to my bitter leave-taking.

And then, in March of the following year, I was standing in St Paul's Cathedral to watch my father's body laid to rest beside his beloved Blanche, the mother who was a fleeting memory to me. I was too numb to weep, too heart-broken to accept that he was gone from us. How could we continue to exist without the presence of that fine spirit in our midst?

Covertly I watched Richard as the choir filled the church with a glorious vocal celebration of my father's life. What was in his mind? I had no idea. Here to mourn his most royal uncle who had raised him and supported him as a child king, Richard's expression was perfectly governed into doleful lines. John stood beside him.

No Henry, of course. Henry dare not return, on pain of imprisonment and execution at the hands of his dear cousin. Philippa was far from me in Portugal.

I was devastated and alone.

And when it was over, Richard processing out with John at his side, there was Duchess Katherine. Silent and dry-eyed, she had weathered the ceremony well, I thought, until I was close enough to see the grief that flattened all her features. It was as if her former beauty were masked by a grey veil. The depth of sadness in her eyes struck hard at my heart. Here, with this woman who had been as much a mother to me as anyone, was where I would give comfort and receive it. Might we not weep together?

'I am so very sorry. If I find it hard to accept he is no longer here with us, you must find it impossible.'

The cathedral had emptied. Approaching, my heels click-ing on the tiles, sending up their own echo, I took the Duchess's hand but it lay cold and lax in mine, nor was there any welcome in her face. It came to me as a dash of cold water against warm skin. Whatever closeness had been between us in the past had somehow dissipated, when I had not been aware. Yet her reply was dispassionate.

'He suffered at the end, you know,' she said. 'In body and in spirit.'

'But you were there to comfort him.'

'Yes, I was. I did.' And then: 'You did not make it easy for him, Elizabeth.'

Grief, I had anticipated. The bitterness of pain. But not what was undoubtedly an accusation,

'The banishment of Henry destroyed him,' she continued. 'But your marriage to Exeter hurt him, too.'

It thrust me on the defensive. 'He agreed to my marriage.'

'Because you gave him no choice.' How judgemental her stare. 'It was never a marriage he would have conceived for you, but on the eve of the voyage to Castile, and with a shame of a child conceived out of wedlock, what could he do? He never believed that this marriage would bring you happiness. And neither did I.'

'He was wrong. *You* were wrong! John has given immeas-urable happiness.' I tried to reassure her, to reassure myself, when all around us was suspicion and enmity. How could she be so blind to the deep love that united John with me, and would hold fast whatever the future held in store?

'And can you say that you are happy now? With all

the acrimony between Richard and Henry, and Exeter his brother's most fervent supporter?'

She called him Exeter. How damning she was.

'Where do your sympathies lie in the ruinous dissention, Elizabeth?'

I could not answer, simply standing there, the cold rising through the thin soles of my shoes, but no colder than the hand around my heart.

'Perhaps it was my fault, too,' the Duchess continued, her tone reflecting the chill around us. 'I had hoped I had given you a keener sense of morality.'

I kept my regard level and unambiguous. 'Keener than your own?' How cruel I was in my personal hurt.

'Yes. Of course. I don't make excuses for myself. Or for the Duke. We did not live by the dictates of morality. But you, as a royal daughter, should have known better.'

Every certainty in my life seemed to have been cut away from beneath my feet, but pride in my Plantagenet blood held me firm. I was answerable to no one. Certainly not to Duchess Katherine.

'So I should have foresworn love and remained wed to Jonty.'

'Yes.'

'Would you have done that?'

'That is an irrelevance. You had a duty to your family, Elizabeth. You had a burden of conscience.'

I swept the argument aside with an abrupt, angry gesture. 'I love John. He wanted me and I wanted him. You of all people should understand that.'

'Yes I do. Who better? But where do you stand now, Elizabeth? With Henry banished and Exeter preening in glory of his new pre-eminence, where do you stand now? Beware, Elizabeth. Don't be blinded by the sun of Exeter's rising. Don't you see? Richard may never allow your brother to return.'

Had I not already considered this? I was not so naïve as to believe in my cousin's goodwill, but nor was I willing to admit any fault.

'He must allow it,' I responded, anger reined in until once again I was as cold as she. 'Richard has promised.'

'And promises are empty air in Richard's mouth. If he banishes Henry for good, will you still remain ecstatically hand-clasped to Exeter? You should never have wed him. You were always wilful and irresponsible, and I failed to change you.'

'I don't regret it. What right have you to put this burden of guilt on my shoulders?'

'I have every right. Because it is true. Your father grieved for you in his final days of pain, but you thought of no one but yourself. Was that not always the case?'

'No...' My grip on the slippery reins was becoming harder to maintain.

'I think it was. Now you will have to live with the consequences.'

'John will not abandon me. He loves me still.'

'I'll pray that it is so. My faith in Exeter's constancy is not as strong as yours. I have more faith in his driving ambition. And you can't argue against that, Elizabeth, however hard you try.'

On which caustic note she turned and walked away, the rift between us growing with every step across the heraldic animals that pranced across the patterned tiles of the cathedral floor. I would not tell her that I was carrying another child.

Alone, I was forced to acknowledge the truth in some of her accusations. I had always considered my own needs first. Had I indeed brought pain to my father? Perhaps I had, but the Duke had been the first to acknowledge John's value as soldier and leader of men. I would not regret those long ago events that I had fought so hard to set in motion. Anger built again. The Duchess had driven a sword between us, making me doubt myself. I could not forgive her, when grief for father and brother commanded every sense. So be it. I no longer needed Duchess Katherine in my life. I was strong enough to beat my own path and I would do it.

Yet my heart felt the sting of a physical wound as I left the empty church, where John was waiting for me.

'What did the Duchess have to say?' He took my arm.

'Nothing. We shared our grief.'

I did not think that he believed me as he led me to where our horses waited. His hand was warm and firm on my arm and his smile understanding as he helped me to mount. Whatever the clash of family and temper I would not let our love falter. I knew it was worth fighting for. One day all would be smoothed over and this new child, created in our reunion in the aftermath of Arundel's bloody end, would be born into a period of golden tranquillity.

In my heart I did not think I truly believed that either.

★

Somewhere in the distant reaches of the Pultney house, growing closer by the second, was a blistering rant of raised voices, the loudest that of Master Shelley, our steward. Unable to ignore it, John flung himself across the antechamber where we were removing our outer garments into the hands of our servants, to open the door.

'Now what? Do we have insurrection in our house?'

'Yes, my lord.' There was Master Shelley on the threshold, one hand gripping the arm of one of the FitzAlan boys, hard. Behind them walked his brother. 'Of a particularly invidious nature too, my lord. I've brought the culprit here for justice.'

Hat and gloves still in hand, John frowned at the boy. We had absorbed them into our household with our own children, the pages and squires, but indeed the young men were old enough, and resentful enough, to be put under the training of a Sergeant at Arms. It was John's intention to do so but had had little time to consider their future. Perhaps we had been tardy.

'Which one are you?'

The lad scowled back, his habitual expression. 'As if you care.'

While Master Shelley dealt him a cuff to his shoulder, I saw John take a breath, placing his hat and gloves gently on the chest, and knew he would strive to be patient with a boy whose temper had undergone no mellowing. Understandably, perhaps. John had been granted much of the Arundel inheritance, while these two young men were landless and penniless, dependent on our charity until Richard said otherwise.

'Mind your manners, FitzAlan. You know better than that,' John advised evenly.

'As if you care, *my lord*.' The curl of his lip was striking and crude.

'I might care if I knew what this is about.'

It was the younger of the two boys, as I knew. The more surly, the less amenable to what they undoubtedly saw as imprisonment.

'It is Thomas,' I said.

'So what has Thomas done?' John asked.

'This misbegotten creature. Caught pissing in the soup pot. I just prevented your cook from cleaving his head with the axe he happened to have in his hand.' Master Shelley, seething with righteous anger, dragged the lad forward. 'Not cowed by the lash of the cook's tongue, he swore he'd do it every day until you died of poison. And if that didn't work, he'd piss over the hog on the spit. And over your cook as well if he tried to stop him.'

I caught a reluctant gleam in the steward's eye. But there was none in John's as he addressed himself to Richard, the older boy who had taken a step forward.

'Well?'

The boy's eyes were as defiant as his brother's. 'I am to blame, not my brother, my lord.'

'I doubt it.'

'I swear that I am.'

'As heir to your father, would you swear on his innocence, which you claim so often and with such vehemence, that you were the one to defile my kitchens?'

Face flushed, the disinherited Earl's eyes fell.

'As I thought. You cannot take an oath on your father's good name, can you?'

Richard FitzAlan shook his head.

'Then let your brother take his punishment. At seventeen years he is of an age to do so.'

'I'll not be punished by you,' Thomas muttered. 'You have no right…'

On which note of defiance John raised his hand and dealt Thomas a flat handed blow that dropped him to his knees, while I, unwilling to interfere, moved swiftly to grip John's arm. Not that it was necessary. John's temper might be explosive on occasion but his blow had held more flamboyance than weight, and I knew that he had some compassion for the disinherited and orphaned FitzAlans. Their mother had been dead for more than a decade. I walked across to lift the boy to his feet, but he pushed me away.

'I'll be beholden to no one in this house,' he hurled his challenge from his knees. 'Not until the day of my death.'

'You are not beholden,' I tried. Surely reason would have more effect than a beating. 'You are only here until the King sees fit to restore your father's lands and titles to you.'

But John's patience was at an end. 'Would you dare to dishonour my wife? With behaviour more suited to a beggar in a gutter? Even he would know better than to contaminate good food. Get up. You are not hurt. You will make your apologies.'

'I will not.'

John hauled Thomas to his feet. 'Whatever gripe you have with me, this is the Lady Elizabeth's home and you will treat it and her with the courtesy I presume you were raised to understand.'

I saw the fire in the boy's eye. So did John.

'Do I strike you again for unpardonable ill-manners? Your father, a courageous man and a man of chivalry, would be ashamed of you.'

A blow that got home. Thomas paled and dipped his head.

'I will apologise if I must. I beg pardon, madam.'

'And you will not repeat your crime?' I asked.

'No, my lady. But I'll not...'

'That's enough, before you spoil it,' John intervened. 'Now get out, before I regret letting you off so lightly. But first...'

John sat on the chest and pulled off his bemired boots, holding them out to the boy. 'You can contemplate your many sins while you restore these boots to a state I would see fit to wear. By then I'll have thought of something else to take your mind from pissing in my food. And be under no misapprehension. If you are caught doing it again, I'll thrash you with my own hand.'

'You have no right to treat me in this manner.'

'I treat you no differently from my pages and squires, whose manners are far better than yours. I show them respect when they deserve it, which you do not. Get out of my sight.'

'I'll use hemlock next time!' And Thomas FitzAlan stalked out with a clumsy attempt at dignity that was heart-breaking. In spite of his crude manners under severe provo-cation, it wrung my heart to imagine my own children in a similar position if Richard, in some fit of uncontrolled pique, decided to take issue with John and take our own heir as hostage.

Richard FitzAlan bowed awkwardly. 'He cannot forgive. I don't think he ever will.'

'And what of you?'

He shook his head.

'There are many things we cannot forgive but must live with,' John lectured mildly. 'It will be best if you teach your brother some sense of diplomacy along with the courtesy. You should instill in him a sense of rightness. Under my jurisdiction I will give you the education and training due to your noble blood. But such crass discourtesy I will not tolerate.'

'Yes, my lord. No, my lord.'

John watched him leave the chamber, then laughed harshly, swinging round to face me, still impressive in spite of his lack of boots. 'I'm sorry to bring this into our house at a time like this. Perhaps I was too harsh with the boy.'

I wrinkled my nose at the revenge Thomas had seen fit to employ. 'You were fair. But they'll never forgive us.'

'It will be better for all concerned if I send them down to the castle at Reigate and leave them in my Captain's care. They can loose arrows at the butts as if it were my black heart. I should have done it before. They need physical duress to take their mind of their woes.'

'They'll not like it,' I observed dryly. 'Reigate was one of the Arundel properties.'

'I can't change that.' John shrugged. 'Where were we?'

'Looking at the impossibility of treading an equable path

between your brother and mine. We can't reach Richard any more, can we? It is as if there is a web built around him, and he sits within it, a monstrous spider spinning some malicious undertaking.'

'He'll not attack you. Richard retains an element of chivalry towards women.'

'I don't fear him.' I recalled Duchess Katherine's warning which had lain like a stone on my heart. Should I tell him of my fears? I was weary of keeping them to myself. 'If I am afraid, it is that our love cannot keep faith under such strains. How often do we seem to be on different sides?'

His glance was sharp, but he did not hesitate, reaching out to me to draw me close into a firm embrace. 'It will remain steadfast. Do we not love each other, as we always have? Don't let Richard stand between us.' He kissed me and soothed me. 'Henry will return and all will be well.'

'And you will remain as Richard's man?'

'Yes. Is it not for the best?'

Perhaps it was. Was it just ambition, or was it his own fidelity to those of his blood? Duchess Katherine was in no doubt that ambition ruled John's every move. I was not so sure. I could not think of distancing myself from my brother, so was it wrong of me to hope that John could abandon his? Perhaps it was. Perhaps I had been short-sighted to expect him to step away. All I could do was pray for Henry's return and Richard's acceptance of him as the new Duke of Lancaster. Which would heal all our wounds.

'Don't let this destroy us,' John murmured against my temple as he kissed me into acceptance. 'We always knew there might be difficulties.'

'But not like this.'

'You have trusted me in the past. Trust me now. Where is the strong-minded woman I wooed and wed? Where is the woman who made her way through war-torn Castile with enemies on every side?'

Where indeed? Sometimes I felt that she was a different woman in a different life, but there was only one answer I could make.

'I will keep faith.'

'My brave love. We will not let the world set us apart.'

In the privacy of our own chamber he removed my satin chaplet, then my robe. And all that was beneath.

Duchess Katherine was wrong. I was happy. And when John discovered, as he must, that I was breeding again, we celebrated anew.

★

18th March 1399, Windsor Castle

Another nagging premonition touched my thoughts. A flutter of storm-crow wings, where there should have been none. There Richard was, seated on his throne in the audience chamber, gloriously clad, golden circlet agleam. We, the esteemed members of his court, had been summoned for a pronouncement of importance.

Richard glowered. Despite the studied glamour of his accoutrements, the banners, the loyal subjects bowing the knee before him, Richard's mind was not in good frame.

As I rose from my deep curtsy, the deepest possible for only such was acceptable without a reprimand from our King, I looked across at John who stood a step behind

Richard's right shoulder, and raised my brows. John managed a wry twist of his mouth, the faintest shake of his head. He had no more idea than I what this was about.

Richard surveyed us, eyes travelling smoothly over every face, observing and noting, until he deigned to speak.

'It is my wish, as your Anointed King, that you, my loyal subjects, will in future address me as Majesty.' His voice, gentle, light-timbred, stroked over us. 'I deem it most fitting.'

Such majestic arrogance. I recalled addressing him as Wily Dickon in our youth when he schemed and cheated to win at games. Even on one occasion as Daft Dickon when he sulked and whined—for which I was duly chastised by Dame Katherine, as she was then. But so it must be, sour taste on my tongue or no.

'Your Majesty,' we murmured. And once again made the required obeisance.

'It is my wish that my closest friends,' he smiled as his gaze travelled over our august ranks once more, 'be addressed as Magnificence.'

My glance slid to John who preserved a stern expression, giving nothing away. His Grace, the Magnificent Duke of Exeter indeed.

'My very best of all friends,' Richard was continuing, 'the most noble Edward, now Duke of Aumale, my own dear cousin, shall henceforth be addressed by all here-present as my brother.'

I sighed surreptitiously. Had Richard summoned us all here simply to learn the new nomenclature of his royal court? I hoped that Cousin Edward was honoured by his adoption as royal brother. Of course he was. How he preened. How self-satisfied the smile that had more in common with a smirk. He reminded me more of his lady mother, the lascivious Isabella, now departed from our midst to heavenly realms, than he had ever done.

I returned the smile, for it would be foolish not to do so, but any inclination towards pleasure had vanished as the implications of what was happening here struck home. If Richard was adopting Edward as his brother, what did this presage about the future? Richard had no son, but nor he had a brother. Who might therefore step into the royal shoes if Richard failed to find a fertile wife in Queen Isabella as she grew to maturity? Edward as next King of England?

If Edward of Aumale was to be raised up, what was in store for Henry? There was no place in the succession for Edward, his father being a younger son of King Edward the Third. While Henry lived, Edward should not even have appeared on Richard's horizon as his heir. So what was it that Richard had in mind for my brother?

That, as I realised with a sinking heart, was why we were here.

'It is my wish to reward my friends. Just as I will call down my wrath on those who prove to be my enemies.' Richard showed his teeth in just the sort of crafty smile I had recalled. 'It saddens me to say, but in light of the treason committed against my sacred person by the house of Lancaster...'

My throat tightened,

'...I have deemed that the inheritance of that house be confiscated. I reward my friends well. The Lancaster inheritance is mine to make those rewards of value.'

By now every sense in my body was frozen in disbelief. This was Henry's birthright. Made forfeit to the Crown. Richard had no right…

'I had placed a limit on the banishment of our cousin Henry of Derby from this land. Ten years, which I foolishly allowed myself to be persuaded, out of pity for my dear uncle of Lancaster now deceased, to a mere six, for his plotting against my person. Now I revoke that decision. Henry of Derby is banished from England for the rest of his life.'

Silence fell, heavy as a crack of doom. And with it a shiver that could be tasted.

This was extreme.

This was unwarranted.

I dared not look at John. Had he known of this? But then I did. His expression was guarded, his eyes deliberately not meeting mine.

Yet was I entirely unaware? There had been rumours. I had wiped them from my mind, refusing to believe that Richard would take so unprincipled an action.

Richard's smile grew to encompass us all, as if not one of us would sense the implied threat to any man who fell from the King's high regard. 'It is my wish to bring glory to England. I am about to embark on an invasion of Ireland to bring the rebellious Irish Lords to book. What glory it will bring us as we grind them under England's heel.'

He raised his hands as if to welcome our acclamation.

'I have invited two young men to become part of my household, as if they were my own children, during these auspicious days,' and he beckoned to one of his attendants, who promptly ushered in those chosen for the honour.

Well, they were certainly of Richard's blood and mine, but my recognition of them brought no joy. The eldest was all but a man at sixteen years: Humphrey, son and heir of the late murdered Duke of Gloucester. And the second? My throat dried as I saw what Richard was doing. It was Henry's son, Henry of Monmouth. Twelve years old.

'We welcome them…'

Hostages.

As clear as the rubies in the collar around Richard's neck.

'It would be unwise for anyone of a discontented nature—not that I envisage such—to consider sending any letters abroad. All letters sent to Europe must first be approved by my Privy Council,' he was continuing gently.

Shock held me. Here was Richard at his most malicious.

Where did John's loyalties now lie in all this? How could he possibly condone his brother's actions in such injustice, such an overt piece of mischief against Henry who had committed no crime other than to be one of the Lords Appellant who protected the good of England and the removal of a royal favourite? How could John possibly see any rightness in this? The House of Lancaster, the royal blood of Henry the Third and Edward the Third, was being dismantled under our very eyes.

I was filled with dread, but refused to let it drain all my spirits. This was Richard, my cousin, albeit King. All I knew was that I must try to encourage his better nature, calling on old fealties, old friendships. If John would not support me then I must do it alone. Richard could not dismiss me out of hand. Was not our blood too close for that? Lancaster pride having no role in this, I must become a petitioner at the King's feet.

If John would not fight for Henry's inheritance, then I would. Surely Richard would listen and respond to ties of blood.

★

When the court emerged from its formality to mingle, sip wine and gossip in corners over the ill-luck, wicked vengeance or justified punishment against the exiled Duke of Lancaster, I, with purposeful steps, presented myself in Richard's path.

'Sire…'

Was this truculent man the same one who had awarded me the sapphire ring with unctuous grace? Now his face was set in sour disapproval, and I recalled his dictates. I should have been more careful.

'Your Majesty.' I curtsied low, head bent, praying that I was making up lost ground.

'My lady Exeter.'

The bleak formality was a warning slap. So was the abrupt gesture for me to rise. I had misjudged his earlier smiling mien, but I could not draw back. Not with Henry's future in England hanging in the balance. Ignoring the lurking presence of Edward of Aumale whose self-satisfaction nauseated me, I began:

'I have come to make a petition, Your Majesty. On your mercy.'

Richard's reply was bleakly hopeless under the smooth

delivery. 'I know what you will say to me, and I will spare you the need.'

'But Majesty…'

'The Lancaster lands are forfeit. The penalty for plotting against my person.'

'My brother is not guilty of so foul a deed…'

'In my eyes the guilt is unquestionable.'

'Richard, I beg you…'

And he took a step back as if my use of his name had within it a contamination.

'It would be better if you didn't, madam. And then I might forget that you are the sister of a traitor and would-be murderer.'

Richard presented his back to me. The ties of blood held no power for Richard.

And as I turned away, stepping round Aumale who murmured some meaningless words in sympathy, it was to see John watching. When I raised my shoulders in a little shrug, his face remained void of expression. For the first time since I had known him I felt a lack of compassion. Rather a disapproval. He kept his distance from me for the rest of the afternoon. Was this to be the pattern of our life?

*

'You shouldn't have done that.'

We had returned to the Pultney house in less than amicable mood.

'So I realise now,' I said. 'But I could not stand there and smile and drink Richard's wine as if nothing were amiss. I didn't notice you pleading Henry's cause.'

'Because I know it would be a waste of my breath.'

'I will write to Henry,' I declared.

'He will know already,' John observed.

'And what will he think, isolated in some rented room in Paris? Seeing his inheritance swept away, Richard gloating at the wealth that has fallen into his hands? Wealth to be given away, awarded as Richard sees fit?'

I stood in the middle of the entrance hall, not knowing what to do.

'He'll think that he's safer in Paris—if that's where he is—than attempting to return. If he's any sense.'

I could not accept that. All I could hear was Richard's condemnation and John's lack of interest.

'Richard hates him,' I argued. 'Richard has always loathed him. They are so different. Sometimes it is as if he envies Henry. They clashed as boys when Henry was the more confident, clever with bow and sword where Richard was not.'

'I don't know that.' John shrugged again, leaving me adrift with my worries. 'But he'll not let him return.'

Which made me decide. Opening one of the doors off this antechamber, I entered the Master Shelley's neatly-ordered domain where I found in a coffer means to write a letter.

'I will write,' I announced.

John had followed me to lean against the door jamb, but now he stepped close and took the quill from me. 'Don't. Don't encourage him to come back.'

'I want him to.'

'To what purpose?'

'To claim back his inheritance. What else?' I discovered my hands were clenched into fists. 'Do you forbid me? I wouldn't, if I were you. I am past good reason after the last few hours of Richard's vindictiveness.'

'It would be a declaration of war. You must not do it.'

'John—' Suddenly I had to know. 'Did you know what Richard would do today?'

We stared at each other, despair a winter cloak, deadening all other senses.

'Did you?' I repeated.

'Yes. I knew.'

'Why did you not tell me, warn me?'

He made no reply, simply casting down the quill, now mangled into pieces, whereas I simply covered my face with my hands.

'John. What will become of us?' My plea was muffled but clear enough.

'I don't know.'

'Is our love strong enough to stand fast?' No reply. So I asked what lay like a knife against my heart. 'If you had foreseen this rift between Richard and Henry, would you have wed me?'

How I dreaded the answer, that John would rather have stepped away from this conflict of loyalties. But he pulled me into his arms, to kiss me, though I could taste more than a hint of desperation in his lips.

'I would do it again. Tomorrow and tomorrow and tomorrow,' he said, voice rough.

'As I would wed you.'

But tomorrow might become desperate. There was a gulf

growing between us. Once I had constructed a bridge that we had crossed together. I feared that this chasm might prove to be unbridgeable.

★

I took no heed of John's advice. Dictate, rather. How could I remain silent and inert, leaving all to chance? Husband or brother? Brother or husband? It was an agonising decision but I wrote and paid a courier to slip out of England to Paris, where it was delivered.

A brief and emotionless missive:

John says—and John is much in the King's confidence—that it would be unwise for you to return, that Richard will not receive you with anything but ill will and it would not be to your advantage. That to return would end in your imprisonment and perhaps worse. Richard is not beyond wishing the death of our Lancastrian line.

Your eldest son Henry is safe but lodged in the royal household for your good behaviour.

I think you must make your own decision. John and I are at odds over this, but I cannot bear that you should be stripped of what is rightfully yours.

I thought, long and hard.

My advice would be to come home and claim your inheritance.

This was, as John had made plain, to encourage a declaration of war. I knew it, and yet what choice did Henry have if he was not to live a landless pensioner, without status or hope for his family, begging for handouts round the courts of Europe who would be merciful in memory of our father? Selling his skills in the tournament for the entertainment of the foreign aristocracy? That must not be.

And then all I could do was await a reply, thinking that he might, for the sake of his sons, err on the side of caution and remain silent. But in truth I knew my brother well enough to anticipate his next move.

There was a reply, pushed into my palm on a scrap of parchment.

I will return.

I did not tell John what I had done. For the first time there were secrets between us, dangerous secrets, as I grew heavier with my impending child. Consequently the disturbing news from Reigate barely registered on our troubled horizon. Richard FitzAlan was dead, the young disinherited Earl of Arundel wrenched from life by some nameless disease. He would never be reunited with his father's inheritance.

And Thomas?

With rabid opportunism, Thomas had escaped the somewhat lax surveillance and was, so our steward wrote—and good riddance to him—bound for Europe to join his uncle, the FitzAlan Archbishop of Canterbury, deposed by Richard and now in exile.

'One more weight off my mind!' remarked John. 'Although I regret the lad's death. I expect it will be laid at my door, but I can't worry about that now. I'm going to Ireland.' He grimaced.

'Now?'

'Now. Richard wants it. Perhaps not the best of times, but he has visions of ruling a great Empire. I hope he lives to see the day...'

John's sardonic observation made me think beyond the

death of intimate communication that seemed to have engulfed us. Did he know? Did he know that Henry would return? Of course he did. He would not be the political animal I knew him to be if he did not. But nothing passed between us. John kissed me farewell, bade me take the weight off my feet, and went to Ireland.

I barely thought about the FitzAlans, my own disparate family filling my mind from daybreak to nightfall.

'Don't do anything I wouldn't do.' John's eyes were fierce with his final instruction.

'No,' I said. Layers of lies, building up, while beneath my composed and affectionate farewell, I was aware of the turbulent anger that raged in my belly. Anger against Richard and his fickle intransigence, against John and his damned loyalties. Even against Henry who had failed to persuade Richard to see his own value as cousin and counsellor. When I wed John Holland I had thought my feet settled in a path that would bring me a life befitting my rank and talents. A presence at court in my own right, I and my family would be strong, ruling England well in a formidable alliance as my grandfather King Edward would have wished. As my father worked for.

But all my contentment, all my certainties were destroyed. As John rode out to accompany Richard to Ireland, I smiled bitterly at my youthful innocence when I had thought that all things could be managed by an intelligent woman, when I had manoeuvred to achieve the marriage I desired. How ignorant I had been. In the end female ingenuity and cunning could achieve nothing against the thrust of power and ambition and pragmatism, against fear of whose hands held the reins of power in the kingdom. I was helpless, forced to bow before a greater authority than my own.

All my happiness had been stripped away. Some days I thought I would never find the means to reclaim it.

★

There came for me a time of anxiety and waiting. I prayed. In better days Duchess Katherine would have been proud of my persistence, but the silence—she in Lincoln, I in London—continued between us. Her heart would be with Henry. As was Philippa's, whose letter-writing was prodigious. All I could do was pray.

But for whom did I pray?

For John, whose safety in Ireland was a constant stone in my shoe. For Henry who had done exactly as he had promised. Landing in England in Yorkshire at Ravenspur in the heat of July, he was marching steadily south, collecting men who had no good to say of Richard. Even for Richard, that he would see sense and come to terms, smoothing over the old rifts so that we might be comfortable again.

Impossible, of course. I rejoiced for Henry. I yearned for John. I prayed for this child that grew in my belly, that it would be born into a kingdom that knew peace, not warfare, for I could not see the future with any hope. I despaired for Richard, yet kept him too in my prayers.

And then rumours flew thick and fast, painting such vivid scenes, all through the long months of August and into September while I remained at Pultney. Henry fell to his knees to kiss the ground of England as the Lancaster retainers rallied in vast numbers to his call. Henry claimed no ill intent against Richard, but only to reclaim what was rightfully his, the inheritance of Lancaster. Richard returned from Ireland to Pembroke in a hurry, only to take refuge at Conway after a show of disgraceful cowardice.

And then the news I had hoped for, news of John, sent by Richard to negotiate with Henry, as skilful intermediary between King and invading traitor. A hopeless case, however persuasive John might be to reunite the two royal cousins, for Henry was intransigent and Richard, reluctant but helpless without strength of arms, forced into surrender. As for John, he was kept under surveillance in Henry's following as Henry marched to London with Richard as his prisoner.

England had fallen into Henry's hands, as neat as an egg into a cup. Henry was home and, with the King under his hand, the Lancaster inheritance was his for the taking. I shared a cup of wine with our steward, toasting my brother's success, and I was glad, but there was no lasting joy in my heart as the uncertain future rolled out before me.

Victory for Henry, and I should rejoice for him. But at what personal cost? Those closest to me in the world, my family, those I loved, had been shattered into separate pieces, like a costly Venetian glass dropped by a careless kitchen maid. Richard would find it impossible to accept Henry's power over him, nor would Henry be tolerant. Here were two ill-matched cousins who would never come to terms. Whereas John...how could John's pride survive being chained to Henry's side? Where were his loyalties now?

There was only one thought of comfort. There had been no bloodshed. They were all alive to work out some compromise. If I had been a naïve woman I would have believed this, but I knew that a Venetian glass, once smashed, could never be reassembled.

I longed for John's return and yet I feared it, for what would we say to each other? All I could do was wait, my increasingly ponderous body swathed in light silks until the day when Henry entered London in a superb display of triumph. Of course he would. Would my brother, raised from his cradle to know his worth as the Lancaster heir, do any other? And I rejoiced with him, for this was a malicious wrong being put right.

How could my mind be so appreciative of Henry's success, at the same time as utter desolation constructed a wall around my heart? I woke, my first thoughts to rejoice that all the vile events of the past were over and justice would be done. Richard would repent, Henry would take back his title and estates, and John would clasp the hands of both in friendship. And then I trembled, for I was alone in my bed and John's future lay hidden like a foul toad in the murk at the bottom of a pool. Justice for Henry could be destruction for both Richard and John. Would triumph for my brother destroy John's love for me? I could see no way through the tangle of my conflicting emotions.

'Come with me,' I would have said to John if he had been beside me, after I had kissed him into wakefulness. Would those days ever return? 'Come and throw yourself on my brother's mercy. He will understand. He knows the demand of family and will be magnanimous. Did he not welcome you with courtesy when you negotiated on Richard's behalf? Did he not listen with grave consideration, as if your opinions mattered to him? Richard's days as King are numbered and my brother in the ascendant. Come and greet Henry, at my side, for he will assuredly receive me with love. And you too. Am I not his well-beloved sister?'

That is what I would have said, but I did not know where John was.

Racked with helplessness, all I knew, all that I could cling to when I imagined the very worst of outcomes, was that John was no political fool. There was no unworldliness in his planning, rather a streak of pragmatism as wide as the seas between us and France, and he would be quick as the next man to detect when his chosen stance had no sure footing. If I could detect a lost cause, then so could John. To remain with Richard was certain disaster. How could John expect my brother to accept soft words from Richard when it was patently clear that those words meant nothing, merely sliding from his tongue as necessity demanded? No promise was binding to Richard, and my brother, with an army bellowing 'God bless Henry of Lancaster' at every opportunity, was under no necessity to negotiate.

Pray God John made the right decision. In the gloom of disillusion I considered John's future if he were to remain adamantly in alliance with Richard. Loss of land, loss of titles. Loss of power. Would it mean exile, as Henry had been exiled? And his heir? What of our son, Richard? Another boy to live out his life as a hostage for his father's behaviour.

A desperate existence for a man of pride and passion.

That would be my future too, as wife to an attainted traitor.

And what if the end was death by the axe, the ultimate penalty for those on the losing side? I could not think of that. And yet I must.

For me, now, all was to play for. It was for me to tread a difficult path, perhaps an impossible one, to do all in my power to reunite the two sides of my family, for which outcome I would fight with every breath in my body. Richard's days as King were undeniably numbered, but perhaps it was still possible to bring John and Henry together in some form of mutual agreement that would salve the pride of both.

If not, how could I live, torn between them?

If I had to make a choice…

No. It would not come to that. Never to that. I could not even contemplate such an agonising decision.

Meanwhile I had an appointment to keep.

Chapter Twelve

'Long live the good Duke of Lancaster!'

'God bless Henry of Lancaster!'

As the shouts became clearer, they jolted me. For me, the Duke of Lancaster was still my father, but time had moved on. What would my father have said about the overthrow of the young King he had fought so hard to shape and foster? Thank God the future was not ours to read.

I dressed as if for a celebration, but a solemn one, the folds of night-blue silk-damask capacious enough to flatter my increasing girth. Knowing Henry as well as I did, I knew what he would do as soon as he entered London. I knew which direction his steps would take for his motivations were as clear to me as my own. Duty. Love of family. Pride in his ancestry. Pride in his blood and what was due to the past. I knew where to wait for him.

Henry had made his entrance into the city through the great Aldgate, as I could tell by the cheering crowds, the direction of the increasing volume of noise. Exiled traitor turned hero, lauded as he and his victorious army marched through the streets, with the Mayor and Aldermen in festive array and fervent agreement. I had arrived at my self-appointed position early. I was so certain that this was where Henry would come.

But where was John? If he was with Richard still, would he be lodged in the Tower with him as a prisoner? If so, even more reason for me to meet Henry. I would kiss him in greeting then go down on my knees to beg for mercy. For John. For Richard.

I hoped Henry would be of a mind to listen and smile on me. It was no wish of mine to meet him on my knees.

I waited, the minutes seemingly endless, but I had not been misguided in my surmising. There he was, striding towards me, his metal-shod feet echoing in the vast space of St Paul's Cathedral, walking swiftly and alone along the nave towards the high altar. I drew back into the shadows. I would give him this moment alone. Had he not earned it after the months of uncertainty and anguish?

I studied him.

Acknowledging that the extent of parting had been good to him, I found my anxieties smoothing out, the tension in my body relaxing. At thirty-two years, Henry had grown into his strength with an authority to match. It was as if his experiences in exile had tempered his confidence and he wore it like a pair of velvet gloves, superbly formed in expert hands. I could not but admire him. He had staked everything on this return, no less than an invasion. Of course he had returned. What man of courage and of royal blood could accept such a monstrous decision to banish him for life, based on a weak king's whim?

So here he was, to reclaim his own inheritance—and more.

I knew where he would set his sights. As soon as I saw the proud tilt of his head, the sumptuous suit of chased and gilded armour, I knew he would wear the crown.

Henry knelt, exactly where I knew he would kneel before the altar, head bowed, hands clasped on his sword hilt, while all around him was silence, despite the nave filling up with Mayor and Aldermen, with Henry's friends. It was such a prescient moment, a moment of awful truth for Richard as well as for Henry.

There was no sign of Richard.

Henry rose, stood, head bowed still, then turned to walk slowly forward to where I waited in the sheltering bulk of a pillar, but his eye was not for me. All his attention was for the tomb where the old Duke, our father, lay at peace at last beside our mother Blanche. I could feel the tension in him beneath the composure, the need to lay his victory before his father. I let him go.

Magnificently carved, the effigies were crisp in their recent completion. A lance and shield hung above and I saw the exact moment that Henry raised his eyes to them, to the coat of arms of my father encompassing the golden leopards of England that hung flatly motionless in the still air. Henry's face was taut with emotion.

At last, sensing a need in him, I stepped forward.

'Henry.'

His eyes touched my face fleetingly before returning to

the likeness of the Duke. He was not surprised to find me here. 'I could not be here when he died,' he said.

'I know. I was here for you. And Duchess Katherine. We honoured him for you because we knew your absence was not of your choosing.'

Henry wept, tears racing down his cheeks while he made no attempt to hide them. And stepping closer, I wept too—for our loss, and for my brother, my face pressed against the metal of his shoulder, his arm around my waist. So we stood, the wretchedness of our parting swept away in that moment of recognition of the greatness of our father.

'I should have been at his side. I should have returned.' Despite the rigid plates of metal I felt his body shiver beneath my hands.

'He knew you could not. It was too dangerous. Katherine was there with him at Leicester. She arranged it as he desired. It was all done as you could have wished for.'

Henry wiped away the tears with the heel of his hand.

'Have you come to welcome me home, little sister?'

'I have. My heart is glad.' What of John? I wanted to ask. But this was not the time. 'Where is Richard?' At least I could ask that.

'I've sent him to the Palace of Westminster. Later he will be lodged in the Tower. And then we will decide.' He must have read my expression. 'All I wish to do is remove him from power. Nothing more. There will be no more injustice to harm the people of England.'

'And will you take the crown of England for yourself?' It was the question on everyone's lips.

'We must wait. All is not settled yet.'

Since it was as much as he would say, we knelt before the Duke's tomb and gave thanks for Henry's safe return, until, equanimity restored, we stood together, smiling, all the weight of family healing the past months of separation.

'You are well,' Henry stated, kissing my cheek. 'And near your time, I would say,' eyeing the swell of my robes.

'Yes. You look good on victory.' I reciprocated his welcome.

'And Philippa?'

'A doting mother.'

'And your children?'

'Thriving. Have you seen your four boys? They grow like saplings.'

Such closeness, but emotion shivered between us with the one name that had not yet been uttered. It was as if John stood between us, unacknowledged.

'Will you come with me to Westminster?' Henry asked, taking my arm to guide me along the nave. 'Tell me what you've been doing.'

Slowly we walked together towards the great door where the crowds were dispersing and where Henry's closest followers were awaiting him.

'They welcomed you,' I said, still astonished at the force of the acclamation.

'They did.' Henry paused, pulling me to a halt, the timbre of his voice chilling to match the air in the cathedral. 'But here is one who might not.'

I followed Henry's line of sight to the dark figure standing just within the door.

'Did you tell him to come?' he asked.

'No. No, I have not seen him.'

There, by the carved arch, in a little space as Henry's friends drew back, was my husband—not under constraint, and my heart leaped in relief. But then I saw his hand was clenched on the sword at his side, his face set like one of the carved statues set in the niches around me, grim and entirely unforgiving. And I saw the little scene as if from a distance, how Henry and I must appear, united against him. Perhaps that was the cause of his rigid jaw, the heavy lines bracketing his mouth. Did he think I had made a stand with Henry against him? The expression in his eyes as they touched mine stung me by their lack of emotion. Of course he recognised his own isolation in our close stance.

But oh, the relief at seeing him there, returned to me! I smiled, holding out my hand towards him in welcome.

John did not move one muscle.

Neither did Henry.

There would be no clasping of hands here.

I took a step, away from Henry, to stand between the two men, so that I might see them both. Did Henry feel no sense of duty, of past gratitudes for John's support for our father in those terrible days at Sheen, when Richard had accused the Duke of plotting foul murder? It might even be argued that John's timely intervention, seizing Richard's sword arm, had saved our father's life. John had been retained by the Duke, had fought bravely at his side in the Castilian campaign. But there was no recognition of past debts in Henry's eyes, as little as in John's. Both mature and seasoned in the use and abuse of power, both driven by ambition, they assessed each other. I might well not have been there. Their eyes held,

John's dark and stormy, Henry's clear with conviction. A challenge? A plea? I could not tell. All I knew was that there was no coming together.

In desperation I placed my hand on Henry's arm.

'Henry…will you greet my husband? He has come here of his own free will.'

'I will greet him when I know where his allegiance lies. When we last exchanged words of any length, he was the chosen negotiator for my cousin Richard.'

'And now you have my brother under lock and key in the Palace of Westminster,' John replied. 'Will you tell me your intentions towards him? He is still your Anointed King.'

'I am under no obligation to tell you anything, Exeter. I hold the whip hand here.' There was no doubting the threat in Henry's demeanour.

'So you will seize the Crown.'

'Whether I do or not, it is time for you to display your future fealty. Long past time. Are you for me or against me? I could send you to enjoy your brother's quarters at Westminster. It would be just retribution.' Henry's face broke into a smile, although not one to give me any hope. 'But for my sister's sake I will wait. I will leave you free to see the birth of your child. But after that, you assure me of your allegiance, Exeter, or I will strip every honour and title from you.' Suddenly the threat was rebounding from the stonework, frightening in its power. 'I am victor here. The sooner you come to terms with that reality the better.'

Henry shrugged off my hand, bowed formally and briefly, walking around John to rejoin his friends, leaving us, word-less, to follow in his victorious wake until I stopped John by stepping in front of him. For a moment I thought he would side-step and continue, but I grasped his tunic.

'Well?' I demanded.

'Well, what?' His regard was hostile. Here was no meeting of minds.

'Have you nothing to say?' The anxieties of the past days bloomed into a conflagration unfitting for our holy surroundings. 'Did it not cross your mind that I would worry myself to death? I had no idea where you were, whether you were safe. Why could you not send word, if nothing else?'

'Your concern is encouraging, Elizabeth. It has to be said that it did not seem to be worrying you unduly. Your reunion with your brother was touching. Most commendable.'

'Of course it was. Would I not welcome him? He has every right to be here.' Loosening my grasp, I smoothed my fingers over John's chest as if I might soften his anger. 'You have to make your peace with him, can you not see that? It would be political suicide to make yourself his enemy.'

'I already am his enemy it seems. He has a short memory.'

'He has not forgotten our family's debt to you, but he also remembers your sworn allegiance to Richard...'

'And Richard will be shut up in the Tower before the end of this day.'

'Henry will treat him honourably.'

'Are you so sure? I'm not. It would be in his best interests to obliterate Richard entirely. If your brother seeks the crown, a living king is a dangerous entity. Far better to destroy him.'

I paused to draw in a breath, as John voiced my own well-hidden fears. I could ignore them no longer.

'Is that what you would do?' I asked. 'If you were in Henry's shoes?'

'That is not what I said.'

'It is what you implied.'

'There is no reasoning with you. You are too close to Henry to see reason.'

'As you are too close to Richard.'

He exhaled forcefully. 'Am I vermin to escape from a floundering ship, to abandon Richard in his despair?'

'But if you don't leap overboard, you will drown with the rest.'

How impossible it was.

'Do I abandon one lord to whom I have sworn allegiance, to immediately bow to another?'

'Yes, if it is a matter of survival.'

'It is treachery.'

'Can you argue that Richard is a man to bring honour to England? To rule fairly, upholding the law. You cannot. You know he is self-serving. Unpredictable…'

'Will Henry, if he takes the crown, rule any better?'

'Yes.'

'How can you be so certain? And by what right does he claim the crown of England?'

And there was the impossible question, for there were others who stood before Henry and the succession to the throne.

Still I stood, smoothing my palms against his chest, sensing a lessening of his anger.

'I cannot argue this with you. Before God, John. If you love me, if you value our love and the stability of lives, for our children, accept Henry as your lord. You heard the Mayor and Aldermen, their words of welcome. Richard's time is past. We must accept that. Will you make a martyr of yourself, for Richard's sake?'

'And would you encourage treason?'

'It is not treason. Richard has agreed to give up the throne.'

'Only under pressure. He would never choose that of his own free will.'

He was looking at me, stern, judgemental, none of the old love in his face, rather a hard-eyed assessment that made me quail.

'What is it?' I whispered.

'I saw you standing next to Henry, before the old Duke's tomb. You were smiling at him. Your face was alight.'

'Because he had returned.'

'Even though you know his return will ruin me? The House of Lancaster cleaves together. I could expect no different.'

I raised my hands to let him go. 'I cannot talk to you.'

He left me, our life together in tatters, even though he returned with me to the Pultney House.

'John…!' I called, in a final attempt to lure him back to me, striving not to let my wretchedness harden the edges of my voice, as he strode past me to vanish round the turn in the stair.

He did not reply. He did not even turn his head.

And so he remained in the following days, a silent and

restless force who shut himself in his own chamber. For the first time in my life I knew real fear. Not the confused terror of the day in the Tower of London so long ago, but a fear that shook me to the essence of my soul. I was afraid, so afraid, that if John refused to accept my brother, Henry would surely destroy him.

John and I were impossibly estranged.

In my loneliness I spent the time in plotting. I needed a stratagem to work a miracle. A gift of power, of good omen, from the Duke and Duchess of Exeter to the newly returned Duke of Lancaster.

That was it, the perfect solution.

I saw my task with clarity: to bring some semblance of unity to these two formidable men, brother and husband, who could not, through the demands of family loyalty, meet eye to eye, hand to hand. To remove the conflict and prove that it was possible for them to co-exist with a degree of amity if not affection. To remind Henry of his debt to John. To show John that my brother would make a worthy king, of greater value to England than Richard could ever be. That it was only justice for Richard to give up his throne. And to show Henry that my husband would be a valuable addition to his body of counsellors.

And to bring back some healing laughter into our lives.

Quite simply I needed some meeting without politics and power, to allow us all to step back from the conflagration of Richard's overthrow and remember the good times.

A simple matter?

Impossible, but that would not stop me. I could not afford to fail. To do so would be to drop us all into an abyss of suspicion and growing conflict. Worst of all, I dared not talk of it to John. Therein would lie disaster. It had to be said that we were not speaking other than the habitual trivia of the weather and the state of the roads when the household met for meals. Our dining was a masterpiece of cold brevity.

How to do it? All it needed was a suitable framework within which I might work some form of clever female magic and bring them together.

My mentor was obvious. Not Philippa who would advise soft handling, which had patently failed already. Not Duchess Katherine who, if she were speaking to me at all, would advise prayer. I had no confidence in God's intervention in this fraught hostility. My mentor was Princess Joan, who had used her talents to negotiate between difficult men in conflict. She had not been slow to extend her capable hands and bring the warring parties together.

I could do the same.

I wished she were here with me to guide my hand but I knew enough of the workings of the two minds to undertake a reconciliation. Henry was as superstitious as most men. I could make use of it. And John had a strong streak of practicality. I prayed that Henry would smile and John would be receptive.

Holy Virgin, protect me from the pride in my family.

I wished Joan were alive to stand beside me. I missed her caustic wit.

*

A celebration.

I recalled the events of Richard's life when he was the

young heir, full of promise just before the death of our grandfather, King Edward. A particularly happy outcome was reborn in my memory, hosted by the City of London to show its support for the golden child that Richard was, and the golden King they hoped he would become. An event of colour and festivity and good omen. Could I not do the same?

Pultney House would be perfect for such a gathering, more intimate than one of the royal palaces but suitable for the great and good to gather. With John as host and Henry as guest, all overlaid with a soft ambience of music and good food and a little trickery, how could it fail?

I spent liberally. I was out to make an impression.

'And what do you hope to achieve?' John enquired with more cynicism than I liked when he caught me in communication with Master Shelley over the wine we would consume. I could hardly hide the preparations from him.

'Only a family gathering.'

'All united in amicable friendship, I suppose. Do we invite Richard?'

Richard, as we both knew, was still locked away in the Tower at Henry's behest.

'Go away if you cannot be practical.'

'Are you sure you should be exerting yourself?' he asked, his eye on my burgeoning belly.

'This child,' I remarked waspishly, 'at this precise moment is less trouble to me than you are.'

John left me to get on with it.

'You will be there,' I said, raising my voice so that he must hear before the door closed behind him.

'I wouldn't miss it for the world. It will be a miracle if it does not end in bloodshed.'

'As long as it's not yours…'

'Or Henry's. Which would you choose, my dear wife?'

I set my teeth, then got on with it.

I hired a company of vizored mummers to parade through the streets. Knight and squire, an emperor and a pope complete with retinue: cardinals and papal legates. Well over a two score, with their blazing torches they lit our courtyard to mark the victorious return of Lancaster, to smooth a layer of peace and goodwill over the country. Wine and ale and roasted meats were served in abundance. When the minstrels tuned their instruments our guests danced and sang.

John was a gracious host, Henry a courteous guest, I a heavily burdened hostess who spent much of the time in resting on a cushioned stool. But I allowed a sigh of relief, even though I was aware of the one absent face. Richard. A ghost absent from our midst.

It was time to add a little light-hearted frivolity to preserve the tone. Would not Princess Joan agree? I was certain of it.

The minstrels rested, the dancers drew breath, the mummers removed their masks, and I approached Henry with my youngest son of four years bearing a lidded basket, my eldest in well-drilled attendance.

'A gift for you, my lord, from the Duke and Duchess of Exeter.' My little son John had been well-trained. I managed not to meet husband John's caustic eye. He knew nothing of this.

Henry, feigning ignorance of the tensions around him, laughed as the basket rocked in my son's hold. 'Does it bite?'

'Only…' My son hesitated. 'Only rats, sir.'

Henry lifted the lid and lifted out a handsome black kitten. A sign of good luck. I knew it would catch Henry's interest. Did he not wear a brooch bearing the words *sanz mal penser*? His superstition even as a child had been a matter of mirth; a tunic that brought him good fortune in a practice joust had to be stripped from him after three months of constant wear.

'He is a symbol of prosperity, for you and the kingdom,' John's son and heir Richard added with excellent solemnity since this was beyond his brother. 'He will rid your house of vermin, my lord. His father is a good mouser in our kitchens.'

'My thanks to the most gracious Duke and Duchess of Exeter.' There was much laughter as Henry handed the little creature to his eldest son, Hal, who restored it to its basket when it began to squirm and mew. It was a good atmosphere. A little family moment of intimacy and pleasure, as I preened myself on my success, breathing out slowly in relief, my hand stilling the child in my belly. 'Does he have a name?'

Richard shook his head.

'He is for you to name, my lord, to mark this occasion.'

'May I suggest Deceit?'

There was the hiss of an intake of breath from around me, and my heart thudded as heavily as my unborn child's fist, for at my shoulder was the gracious Duke of Exeter himself, incomparable host, all semblance of graciousness wiped away. The whole room hung on the next exchange of words.

'Perhaps you recall the occasion,' my husband addressed my brother. 'When Richard received a set of loaded dice from the mummers who entertained him in the days before the Crown of England came to him. It was to allow him to win, which he did. And they cheered his victory, travesty as it was, because they looked forward to the golden age when he would rule. But the dice did not bring Richard good luck, did they? Just as I doubt the cat will rid you of all your vermin.'

I listened with horror, my face paling as it became worse.

'Do you mean these?' Henry asked. Like a gifted magician, he removed them from his purse. An eye-catching pair of dice.

'So you took his dice as well as his crown?'

'I removed a disease from England.'

'Which could be cured, with careful handling.'

'Which needed to be wiped out.'

'And will you wipe it out?'

'I am attempting to find a painless remedy.'

'Painless for whom?'

Upon which Henry made his departure in high dignity and a black mood. He did not take the cat.

'Could you not try?' I faced John as we were left to survey the debris of the ruined evening.

'To do what? Ingratiate myself with the man who would place the crown of England on his own head? You are so busy welcoming your brother that you do not even see my dilemma.'

'But I do…'

'I beg to differ.'

'There is no compromise in you.'

John left me, in a mood as black as Henry's.

The cat remained with me, in my kitchens, presumably named by my cook. What would I have named it? Despair?

*

I did not expect John to come to my chamber that night—why break the habit of all the previous nights? —nor did he. I waited and then could wait no more so wrapped my cumbersome state in a robe and went to his rooms.

He was asleep, head burrowed in the pillows.

It was in my mind to slide in beside him, as effectively as I could slide anywhere, and hug him back into a warm consciousness that might heal his wounds, but what use? Nothing I did could lessen his pain. It was his choice to be apart from me, and so I did not wake him, nor did I touch the shock of hair even though the urge to do so was strong. I did not know what to say to him that I had not already said.

By next morning he was gone, leaving only the hard words we had shared to reverberate in my mind, refusing to be laid to rest. They shattered the quiet rooms of Pultney House, made even quieter from John's absence. Where was the love that had brought us together, that had given us the strength to defy convention and demand that we be man and wife? An uncomfortable worm of guilt curled in my belly. John had accused me of selfish disregard. That Henry's achievements overwhelmed any thought I should have for John's intolerable position. Was it true? Was I so selfish?

I did not think so.

But still the worm churned and destroyed as the day of Henry's coronation drew closer.

Why could John not come home so that we might talk?

Had I driven him away?

So relieved had I been at Henry's acceptance by those who could have stopped him, I had presumed that John would follow the same course. But Richard was John's brother, for good or ill. Now all I could do was wait.

My bed remained cold and empty.

*

'Is my father here?' Richard, my son, John's heir. To witness this most momentous of occasions.

'I don't know.'

I strained to look over the heads of the lords of the realm. There were some seats vacant. That was my first thought, and my fear. One of them would most certainly be that of the Duke of Exeter.

In the Great Hall in the Palace at Westminster, the lords were gathering, all wishing to be part of the proceedings, and I would be there, with John's heir, to bear witness, wherever John might be. No one would be able to accuse my son or me of disloyalty to the new King. As a woman I was not invited. As the new King's sister, no one would deny me the right to be there. Nor in the seat I had commandeered at the front. Probably the state of my pregnancy made the stewards unwilling to dispute the fact with me. No one, least of all me, wished this child to be born in the middle of the ceremony.

'I can see one empty chair,' Richard said.

'That is the one occupied by the Duke of Lancaster. It is your uncle's now. It has never been occupied since the death of your grandfather.'

'The throne is empty too.'

The throne, draped in cloth of gold. Vacant. For we had no king. Not yet. King Richard, stripped of the right, incarcerated, had willingly resigned his powers, if anyone believed in such an unlikely eventuality. And because there was no king, the writs for a parliament had been withdrawn. This was no parliament but an assembly to ratify Richard's deposition and confirm the inheritance of his successor.

But where was John? If John absented himself on this most important of days, his estrangement with Henry would be complete and beyond my healing.

'What will happen if Father does not join Henry?' Richard whispered. A percipient boy, now twelve years old. He had heard much of what was talked of at home.

'I don't know.'

'Will my uncle Henry execute him?'

'No. They will talk about it and come to an acceptable conclusion.'

Lies, all lies—but I could not put fear in my son's eyes, the fear that kept me from sleep.

'What will happen to my uncle Richard?'

'I expect Henry will allow him to live comfortably in some castle away from London.'

'It would be dangerous to let Richard live. It would be better if he were dead. Better for Henry.'

It was as if a hand tightened around my throat and my belly lurched at these words that I had heard before, yet never expressed with such innocence.

'Is that what you would do?'

'I might if I were King. My uncle Henry might.'

'Then we must talk him out of it, mustn't we.'

'But he will be King. He will have the power.'

So I knew. I made a clumsy turn in my seat to look at my son's solemn face. He grew more like John every day but had a sweetness of temper that was increasingly fleeting in John. Even my son saw the political demands this situation could make.

The doors of the Hall were flung back. Here they were.

'What if…?'

'Hush, now.'

I leaned forward to see between the ranks.

Two mitred heads as two archbishops came in solemn procession. So Henry had the blessing of the church. He would be relieved.

'Look…' Richard nudged me with a sharp elbow. 'He's brought them.'

Slight figures, pacing solemnly with formal dignity. Henry had brought his four sons to make their own claim for the future. Henry and Lionel, John and Humphrey, ranging from fourteen to ten years. Henry had an eye to the impression his family would make on a country starved of heirs in the last years.

'I wish I could be with my father. I wish I could walk at his side as his heir.'

Richard's eyes were glowing. He really believed that John

would take his place in the procession. Such youthful hope that I had not the heart to destroy.

I only pray your father is here at all.

I could not say it, but held Richard's hand tightly. His father might be a foresworn traitor before the end of the day if he did not see fit to fill his vacant seat.

A man walking alone. At first I could not see but then because of his burden I knew. It was Sir Thomas Erpingham carrying a great jewelled sword. The Lancaster Sword, Henry's new sword of state. The one Henry had carried at Ravenspur in the campaign that brought him to victory. A sign of power.

Who next? My knees were weak, my breath shallow. I was hoping against hope.

'Please God...' I murmured.

But here was Henry. So John had not proclaimed his allegiance after all.

I gripped Richard's hand in a death grip, forcing myself to concentrate on the sight of my brother walking slowly forward, the Italianate armour replaced today by dramtic damask in blue and white, Lancaster colours. A calm, an assurance, a determination that his ambition would be thwarted by no man, was imprinted on the old paving by each careful step. How proud Mary would have been. And Philippa should have been here to see this moment when Henry placed the House of Lancaster upon the throne of England.

An intense loneliness struck home. Henry walked alone. So might I.

Henry took his place in the seat reserved for him as Duke of Lancaster. But not in humility. I knew that. And as he sat, he raised his eyes to mine. No smile but an infinitesimal nod. He had taken back his own. He had had his revenge for the campaign against my father. He was returned, and now the whole Plantagenet inheritance was at his feet for his taking. I could imagine my father's pride that what had been so mindlessly stripped away was now restored. But as I saw Henry's eye traverse the assembled lords, saw him note the empty seats, my joy crumbled, a vast expanse of fear swelling in my chest until it had taken over the whole space.

John was not here. His absence had been noted. Henry's enmity would be assured.

Richard nudged me again. There were footsteps. The procession had not quite come to an end. I could no longer look.

'Look…!'

And to stop him assaulting my ribs again, I did.

I sighed, deep and long, sweat clammy along my spine in spite of the chill in this place, for there in solemn formation, abreast so that they filled the space between the seats, strode three vividly clad nobles wearing ducal coronets. I knew them all.

The Duke of Surrey, John's nephew. The Duke of Aumale, York's son and my own cousin. And…

The Duke of Exeter.

He had come. He had come. John was here.

'It is Father.'

'I know. I know.' How I wished to shout it.

But events were continuing as a backdrop to the loud beating of my heart, the relief that was heady enough to compromise my balance. Even tears threatened. All I had hoped for had come to glorious fruition. What had finally persuaded him? I did not know, but John was here, for all to see. For Henry to see.

'Is it the will of everyone present that Richard's resignation be accepted?' the newly returned Arundel Archbishop of Canterbury demanded of the lords.

I did not listen to the arguments, the charges against Richard, knowing that they would be heavy indeed. All my attention was on John, to note his response. Could he feel my stare? Did he know I was there to give him strength, the support he had thought I had withdrawn? He gave no sign. How hard for him to listen to the denunciation of his brother.

'Is it your will?'

'Yes.' The lords assented.

The tension in the great chamber was wound as tight as a bow string. The throne of England was empty. Who would take it?

Henry stood.

Was Henry's right to be King of England in Richard's stead acceptable?

'Yes.'

The acclamation shattered the tension.

I watched John's lips repeating the short affirmations with the rest of them as Henry was led to the throne where he knelt, prayed and sat amidst the cloth of gold to another roar of acclamation, which was picked up in cheering in the streets and courtyards outside the palace.

I did not listen to the sermon. All I could see was

Richard's ring glinting on Henry's finger and the rays of sun creating bars across the floor, across his tunic, and John standing at his side with the other nobles of the realm.

Henry spoke. I listened. Henry was always good with words.

I stared at John, willing him to look up. To feel my love and goodwill. I stared until his eyes lifted to mine.

I was too far away to make anything of his expression. His face was a mask, pale and still. Eyes dark with images I could not imagine. Who knew what emotion moved him as his brother was stripped of his anointed kinship. But he was there. He was there. He had made his allegiance public in the most obvious way. That was all that mattered.

I held his gaze until he looked away.

*

We stayed in the apartments set aside for us at Westminster, John spending time to answer Richard's endless questions. Except for one.

'What will happen to the King. The old King?'

'That is in your uncle's hands.'

'I know. I know that, but…'

'Enough!' But not harshly. Reluctantly Richard took himself off to bed.

'Are you satisfied?' It was a question flung at me with just a hint of venom, enough to make me careful. All was still not right between us as John dropped into the high-backed chair, stretching out his legs to cross his ankles, for there was no relaxation in his posture, rather an intense weariness covering an emotion I could not read, as if he had done what he knew he must but had no pleasure in its completion. And indeed there was none, as his bitter statement made clear. 'I condemned Richard's actions with the rest of them. I stood with Henry at the legal acceptance of his filching of the crown. I agreed to it. God damn me for it! As he undoubtedly will.'

'John! No...!' So it remained as bad as that for him.

'He had no right.'

I moved to stand before him, and for the first time since we had entered the quiet room, far away from the festivities, his gaze lifted to mine and held, because now we must face the gaping chasm between us. My heart trembled for him, for us.

'Yes, to answer your question. I am more than satisfied,' I said. 'I could not ask for more. Nor can Henry. He could expect nothing more of you than you stand witness at his coronation, whatever past dregs of allegiance might remain. You have done all you can. And I thank you for it. I thank you from the bottom of my heart.'

All John's energy that had carried him through the long day seemed to have drained away.

'Thank God for that. At least something has been achieved today. The King and the King's sister are satisfied at last.'

Again it hurt. A sharp blade against my breast. Nor could I blame him, for I had given him little peace, but this was no time for retaliation, rather a time for healing old and new wounds. And so, clumsily, it had to be said, I sank at his feet, enclosing one of his hands in mine. How cold it was. How chillingly, unnervingly unresponsive, and I knew it was a withdrawal I had to break, but was not at all certain how to go about it. Nor was I certain of any success.

'I think that was the most courageous thing you have ever done,' I said, and meant every word of it. 'I could not imagine…'

'Ha! The hardest, certainly. I listened to you.' He smiled sharply as my brows rose. 'I always listen, even if I don't always act on your advice. But I saw that I must. For you, for my sons. There is no looking back, is there? Richard will never regain his throne. The future is with Henry and it is my duty to make a place for me—for us—in the new reign.'

He lifted my hand to his lips, a small gesture of reconciliation. Small but worth a golden crown to me. The shard of ice in my heart began to melt a little, and the fear began to dissipate. 'The question is, what will Henry do with Richard?'

'Is he still at Pontefract?'

'Yes. Out of sight, out of mind.'

I did not tell him of his heir Richard's considered opinion, which matched his own exactly. Instead: 'It will work itself out. Henry says he will allow Richard to retire to a castle of his choice. It is what Richard wants. I do not think Henry is planning bloody revenge.'

'Then he would be a fool. And Henry is not a fool. You know as well as I that to leave Richard alive would be to leave a constant danger in the realm.'

'But he would not…'

'And then, the next question, which I defy you to discover a trite answer for, is what will he do with me?'

Another twist of the knife. 'Why should he do anything? You have taken the oath.'

'Because there are those of us who still have to answer for our past loyalties to Richard. To our role in the death of Gloucester. Arundel too. I think Henry will not be the man to let this go unpunished. I doubt he will let me go scot free.'

'You were not in Calais when Gloucester was killed.'

'But I was with Richard at Pleshey when Gloucester was arrested. I was with him when Arundel was taken. Will Henry turn a blind eye?'

I thought as I sat. 'Perhaps not, but you are too valuable to be cast aside. Henry sees that. He must see that.'

'Pray God you are right.' At last there was a lessening of tension in the line between his dark brows. 'And I think we have talked enough.'

I smoothed his hand. 'Thank you.' I kissed it.

'For what?'

'For not destroying what we have.'

His reply was a jolt to my senses. 'What do we have, Elizabeth?'

Struggling to overcome this rank cynicism, I knew that I had to build anew. 'A love that will overcome all things,' I urged. 'A new life to celebrate.' I placed his palm on my belly. 'Soon.'

For a long moment he studied me. 'Do you believe that?'

'Of course. Do you doubt me? My love for you?'

'I have thought that the present conflicts have drawn our love thin, like morning mist. With a hole in it that an army could be driven through.'

'Forgive me if I have been thoughtless, careless.'

'You have.'

'I would never put Henry before you in my heart.' A long moment. So long that I felt my limbs begin to tremble. 'Do you not trust me?'

And at last John leaned forward, cradling my cheeks in his hands, and kissed me gently, so gently on my mouth.

'Of course I trust you. Pray God Henry allows us to live in peace to enjoy it.'

We went to his bed where his lips were soft, his hands so fine on my body that my tears flowed when he folded back the linens with such careful precision, when he turned his attention to clasps and laces, then to his own clothing. Here at last were compassion and understanding. Whereas in those lonely weeks I thought that my heart and body had been carved from marble, he kissed me and held me until I became flesh again.

'It has been a long trial for you and a longer waiting. Rest with me until your strength returns. Let me comfort you,' he said against my loosened hair. 'Let me give you solace and hope.'

I rested. And when I could command my breathing once more, and his kisses became a demand rather than a gentling, I allowed myself to be seduced from the hard reality of brutal loyalties to the softness of pure physical pleasure, discovering a return of the old depth of feeling in him, and an answering response in me that I had dreaded might be damaged for ever. No endearments, no poetry, no promises for the future—how could there be? —only a lightness of touch that allowed me to forget for a little while. And so, I believed, did he. My sheets were no longer cold. We enjoyed our reunion, even if John had to stretch his arms to enfold me, before we lay quietly together, not speaking, merely glad that the rifts in our life together appeared to be healed,

All would be well. All *would* be well. I would strive every minute of every day to make it so. The old tapestry had changed, had been reworked. The stitches were still new, but they would settle into the old weaving until the patching could not be detected. But it was not the old tapestry. It would never be the same.

We were resolved it seemed. A line drawn beneath the terrible events of the past.

But I knew in my heart that I would never see my cousin Richard again.

★

The next morning John was up betimes. He had, I knew, been awake for some hours, thinking thoughts that I had done nothing to disturb. Better to let sleeping dogs lie, I decided. There was nothing more that we could say to each other, and weariness had overcome me at last.

'Where are you going?' I asked drowsily as he donned garments suitable for a day's travel.

'Never mind. Get dressed and come down to the courtyard. And don't dally. Put on sensible shoes and a travelling cloak.'

I did as I was bid, too low in energy and spirits to argue. I heard the noise first. The clamour of children's voices. And there they all were, the whole Holland brood awaiting me. I surveyed my family, the weariness draining away. Richard was already mounted, as was Constance, now eleven and inheriting all my restlessness as she vied with her elder brother at every opportunity. Elizabeth at ten and Alice at seven were ensconced with their nurses in one of the travelling litters. John was in the act of scooping up his namesake and placing him there too.

I smiled.

For there was a separate palanquin, sumptuously curtained, heaped high with cushions, all for me.

'I thought you might appreciate some privacy,' John remarked, coming to take my arm.

'Where are we going?'

'To Dartington.'

'Dartington…!' Did I need so long a journey into the west?

'You look tired.'

'And I won't be tired travelling?'

Without comment he led me to my transport, before taking hold of my shoulders and speaking severely as if he thought I might still resist.

'You have had enough. Too much, in fact, of your family pulling you apart. It has to end. Henry can fend for himself, and we need time away from court. You have this new child to consider. We are together, and we are going home.'

It all but reduced me to a bout of weak tears.

'Do you agree?'

'Yes.' And then: 'What about Richard?'

'We can do nothing for Richard, so what point worrying endlessly? We will go to Dartington and live there in peace for a little time and make it a home for the future.'

I managed a watery smile and sniffed a little. 'Until you grow weary of rural solitude and want to dabble in the political pot again.'

'Yes. Until that happens. We will not argue about it today.'

'But you probably will tomorrow.'

'Probably. And if I don't, you will.' Wiping my tears away, his smile was tender, lingering, with all the love I remembered from the past, until the girls' chatter broke in. 'Get in the litter, woman. My intention is to be at Dartington before this child is born.'

He kissed me, and then again, reminding me of how few impromptu kisses there had been between us of late. I would not allow it to happen again. The future might still be clouded, but for me, and I thought for John too, it was a day of restored happiness.

Chapter Thirteen

'Build me a new Kenilworth,' I said to my husband in a perverse moment of homesickness.

And that is what he set out to do on the vast estate in the soft fields and wooded inclines of Devon, all glowing stone and seasoned timber, high windows letting in the light much as those in the Duke's banqueting hall.

'I will build you a bower of roses too,' he promised, in romantic mood.

'I doubt you'll be there to sit in it with me.'

In unity we might be, a seamless calm of love restored to us, but neither of us was of a mind to sit in a rose bower. Did we expect to live in a mood of everlasting happiness and contentment?

Yet why should we not? John directed his energies to the building of Dartington, into long discussions with the vast array of craftsmen needed to create a house for a great magnate while I gave birth to a large, placid child, a son, whom we named Edward after my grandfather. The child watched the dust motes dance in the sunshine above his cradle, snatching at them with tiny fists. Did he know of the period of rebellion and upheaval that accompanied his growth my womb?

'He looks as if nothing will disturb him,' John observed as Edward slept under the eye of one of his nurses. 'Pray God nothing will.'

His prayers were not to be answered, since Henry had decided to repay John's difficult loyalties by imprisoning him at Hertford and then bringing him to trial with the rest of the lords whose past leanings—in effect their support for Richard—gave my brother cause for concern. Had John's ultimate defection from Richard not been enough? No, it had not.

'Do you have to do this?' I demanded of my brother, young and malleable no longer, when I abandoned children and domestic life and rode hot foot to abrade him at Westminster.

'Yes.'

'John forsook his brother to support you.'

'I'll not dispute it, but it's time to make an example of those who turned a blind eye to Richard's misuse of power. Which means Exeter's involvement puts him at the top of my list.'

I knew he meant the death of our uncle of Gloucester.

'An example?' As so often in those days my blood trickled icily.

'Don't worry. I won't kill him.'

'Well that's a relief to know!'

'All I mean to do is show my magnates that loyalty to me would be their best policy.'

It all left a bitter, lingering, taste in the mouth and John was quick to spit it out.

'What more does he want?' John snarled as, ultimately released without physical harm, he rode fast to Dartington—as far from London as he could get, he growled—where he stood in the middle of our new courtyard and dragged in a breath of free air. 'I stood there with the rest of the sycophantic minions, through the whole of his damnably long-winded coronation. I took the oath. I perjured myself, after taking the damned self-same oath to Richard. I try not to think about my brother, still locked away in God knows what conditions in Pontefract. I have proved myself the perfect, loyal subject. Does that warrant my imprisonment?'

'Henry thought it did. Are you going to come in or will you continue to shout your ills to the whole world?'

He had not yet moved past the new door lintel.

'Ha!' John's glance was speculative, his mood still sour. 'And what about you, my dearest wife? Were you worried for my safety?'

'Yes. Henry promised he would not kill you.'

'You went to see him to plead my cause?'

'No, of course I didn't. I left you to Henry's tender mercies! Why would a wife plead her husband's case?' Tucking my hand in his arm, taking his gloves and hood to cast on a chest beside the door and setting myself to unpick the edges of John's understandable disgruntlement, I drew him into one of the new rooms, where he would find warmth and wine and comfort. He looked sharply worn with weariness and irritation. 'Be thankful he didn't lock you in a dungeon in the Tower and forget about you.'

'I'm thankful for nothing,' he replied, although he had the grace to smile a little, a wash of colour on his cheekbones, as he allowed me to lead him in. 'Your brother has taken the shears to my titles and estates fast enough. Did he learn that little trick from Richard? Your son will not be Duke of Exeter, lady. I'll be lucky to hold onto Huntingdon for him. And what income we'll have…your brother has confiscated the Duchy of Cornwall.'

'I'll speak to Henry,' I offered, without much hope.

'And beg for me again? You will not!'

'Then I will not.'

After all we had salvaged, I could see our relationship falling into pieces again in front of me. Yesterday I had been awash with fearful desolation, not knowing when I would see John again. Today I was full to the brim with relief that John was free and returned to my governance, yet attacked with a whole new set of anxieties. He had not even kissed me in greeting. Not even touched me, although he had not resisted when I took the initiative. So although it was in my mind to set off for London, to rage against Henry once more, I pushed John to sit and poured him wine, shooing a curious Elizabeth from the room.

'I don't think that Henry will punish you more.'

John refused the wine. 'How would you know what is in his head?'

'I hope I do. I always did. He's afraid that there will be a rising against him unless he shows a firm hand. So those

who were close to Richard have to be held up as an example
of what happens to a man who makes the wrong choice.'

'Do you support him in this?' His regard was not amenable. 'I should have expected it.'

Looking down at where he slouched in his chair, all I
could do was sigh.

'All I'm saying is that Henry fears that if he does not
watch his back…'

'He has a right to fear it.'

Such a small comment, so seemingly inconsequential,
spoken without heat. But uttered by a man grey-faced and
eyes red-rimmed from long days of travel, it smote at my
understanding. I stared at him. He looked back at me, eyes
bleak and cold.

'John! You wouldn't.'

'Wouldn't what?'

'I don't know! Take up arms against Henry. Engage in a
conspiracy…'

'Why wouldn't I? What have I to lose?'

'Your head, for one.'

'Would you care?'

Never had I known him so blighting, his words so uns-
paring of my sympathies. Not even in the days before
Henry's coronation. And as I took in the lines that marked
his mouth and brow, I faced a sudden insight of impending
disaster. I was once more tossed back into the morass of fear.

'How can you say that?' My tone as bleak as his. 'You
know I love you. I have always loved you and always will.'

Still his trenchant gaze held mine. 'When Richard was
arrested, the crown stripped from him, you rejoiced.'

'I rejoiced that he no longer had the power to cause harm. Because he had hounded my brother and father, robbing Henry of what was rightfully his in the Lancaster inheritance. He had been instrumental in the murder of my uncle Gloucester. Yes, I rejoiced.'

'When Richard was incarcerated in Pontefract, you were quick enough to sing your brother's praises.'

'Henry deserved it.'

'When Henry was crowned you glowed with satisfaction.' The accusations came thick and fast, his voice gaining power. So did mine.

'Why should I not? Henry had every right.'

I felt as if I were on trial, but I would not retreat. I had done all those things, rejoicing that a mishandling of justice had been put right, even when I knew the hurt that John must feel.

'When Henry has Richard done to death by some foul means, as I've no doubt he will at some opportune moment, will you celebrate then?'

Which effectively silenced me. Not just his words but the vicious emotion that had come to inhabit our new home as accusation followed counter accusation.

'No. No, John. He would not. Nor would I rejoice.'

But I was not so sure. John was half-right in his charges against me, and it stung.

John sighed, some of the anger dissipating, to be replaced by what I could only think of as despair. 'I think he might very well. As do you, if you'll be honest with yourself. If he's feeling vulnerable, he'll rid himself of any rival. And that means Richard, with or without the crown.' And then the despair thickened, his face becoming raw with emotion. 'He is my brother, Elizabeth. You have faith in yours, God help you. How can I not feel it a mortal sin to betray mine? I betrayed Richard because I could not tolerate his lack of judgement, his poor government. It had become impossible to support a man who showed such cowardice in his flight from battle. I made the choice, but it tears at my heart, Elizabeth. Can you understand that?'

'Yes. Yes, I do. But I can't mediate between the pair of you for ever.' I had a sudden vision of myself, old and grey, still trying to keep the peace between two recalcitrant men whose grey hair should have brought them wisdom, and hadn't. 'Don't you see? It destroys me too.' And in a final plea: 'I cannot bear that we are once again cast into this cauldron of distrust.'

'Of course I see.' And at last he raised his hands in a gesture of supplication. 'Perhaps it would be best if you take no notice of the diatribe of the past ten minutes. I am weary.'

I knelt at his feet.

'I have been afraid for you.'

'I know. I don't doubt you, Elizabeth. I never will.'

But sometimes I doubted myself, my own capacity to love this difficult man, and yet I could not imagine my life without him. A familiar emotion stirred within my breast, heating my blood.

'You haven't kissed me yet.'

'Then I must remedy so great an omission.'

He pulled me forward to kiss me, with all the old possession, yet even in the heat of his kiss, I sensed that his thoughts were elsewhere.

'Are we at one?' I asked, when I could.

'I think so.' A remnant of his grin. 'As your husband should I not be able to command your fidelity?'

'You do. Would I betray you?'

'No. Not willingly. Not knowingly.'

We sat in silence for some time, hands clasped, as the sun moved round and filled the room with a blessing that unlocked all the tensions. Until I looked up and saw the cause of his stillness.

'You are sleeping,' I murmured. The carved leaves in the wood behind his head might not be the most comfortable, but his eyes were closed, his breathing even, the lines of strain fading.

'Forgive me,' he stirred. 'Hertford was damned cold. I think Henry hoped to freeze me into submission.'

'I thought you were intending to be submissive.'

'So I am.'

But I did not believe him as we stood, his arms banding fast around me.

'What do we do for the Christmas festivities?' I asked.

John groaned against my throat where his lips were pressing a row of increasingly urgent kisses.

'Henry and the children will be at Windsor,' I continued. 'Do we join them? It will look too particular if we don't. I think we should go.'

'What else?' It was not quite a sneer. 'We'll celebrate and put on a good face between the dancing and the tournament. Perhaps someone will have the good fortune to run our sanctimonious King through his gut with a lance.'

I did not like the image but I kept the moment light. 'But not you.'

'No. Not me. Now come and reintroduce me to my newest son.'

'He has lungs like a blacksmith's bellows.'

And John laughed. Arm in arm, we were reconciled. The love we shared remained strong, if not untouched. Did I ever regret the life-changing step I took when I rejected the tranquillity of the Pembroke marriage for the upheavals of my life with John Holland? No. He was still the one true love of my life, the solid foundation of all my happiness. And beneath the strains of family rivalries, I knew I was his. He would always be driven, always ambitious, but I had known that from the start, had I not? Perhaps I truly saw it now for the first time. But I was older and wiser and, with good fortune, would keep his ambitions from destroying us. Did love make a woman less selfish? Perhaps it did.

I must be circumspect, treading carefully, to keep the peace. Not impossible as the reign settled and loyalties were no longer questioned at every step. Perhaps the New Year festivities would help to calm the family storms.

*

'Well, here we are. About to step into the lion's den. Let's hope the lion is asleep.'

John leaned from his saddle to draw back the curtain of the travelling litter that had kept the younger children contained, as it had when we left London before the birth of Edward. We were at Windsor.

'Will we see lions?' Elizabeth asked.

'Not here,' John said, then to me: 'Is King Edward's lion still alive?'

Taking a firm grip on Alice, I shook my head and led the long walk from the lower ward to the royal apartments.

'But a King will need a lion to protect him from his enemies,' I heard Elizabeth announce.

'Your Uncle does not need an lion. He has your mother to roar for him,' my caustic husband replied, but there was laughter in his voice and I smiled. It was an image that pleased me, and John's mood augured well for the occasion.

We had travelled from Dartington to Windsor, the children excited and John making a good face of it as we settled into our accommodations. For me, in spite of all assurances to the contrary, a strange hovering uncertainty invested the rooms, thick as a miasma over a noxious marsh, however much they might be festooned and tricked out for the masques and merriment that Henry had planned.

Henry, trying hard, was warm and welcoming.

'Elizabeth. Huntingdon.' Clasped hands. A fleeting kiss on the cheek. A sup of warm ale and a cushioned settle after days over rutted roads. All was as it should be, and Henry's greeting was the perfection of a welcoming and generous host. 'It's good to have you here. It is a time for family to rejoice and celebrate. We have much to celebrate. It's time to put the past behind us.'

How benign. I preferred Henry when he was boisterous. It had been many years since I could read his enthusiasms, his expressions. The smiling lines on his face might have been engraved with a knife.

'Of course we would come,' I said, returning his embrace.

'I could not refuse your invitation, sire' John added, careful of ceremony. 'An invitation to a royal property is a rare and fine thing.'

He had not been invited to Hertford. That had been a compulsion under guard. I nudged John as Henry turned his head. I could sense that John seethed behind the benign exterior, but he shrugged and, as he had promised me, set himself to play the role of loyal brother to the newly crowned King.

'I have had a lifetime of experience,' he had observed dryly. 'I will do it to perfection.'

Pray God he meant it.

We hunted and hawked, enjoyed the mummers and minstrels, the games of the young people. The name of Richard was not mentioned, and although his absence hovered over us, I relaxed into the family traditions of the past. It was so easy to slide into the court life that I knew, all gossip and ostentation and unthreatening friendship.

*

We had been there barely a week, celebrating early Mass in the great chapel of St George as the family did, our children in a row, fidgeting under my eye and that of their nursemaids. Until Charlotte, sharp-eyed as ever, leaned across brother John:

'Where is Father going?' she whispered during the priestly preparations.

'Your father isn't going anywhere. He has promised to take you hawking along the river since the ice is too thin for skating.'

'He is,' Richard, on my other side, said. 'He ordered his horse to be ready. He wouldn't take me with him.'

I considered. 'Perhaps it's an errand for the King.'

And perhaps it was not. I turned my head, but John was nowhere to be seen. Where was he going, at this moment, when a Mass was to be held in commemoration, for the quiet rest of Mary's soul and that of her ill-fated first born child.

'Is he still here, Richard? In the Castle?'

'I don't know.'

'Yes.' This was Elizabeth. Did all my children listen to adult conversations? 'Father said he had to…'

I hushed her as heads were turned in our direction. 'Stay here,' I ordered. And I left with a genuflection. What an excellent time to choose for some purpose I could not define. Had he intended to tell me? I thought not.

I found him in the stables, already shrouded against the winter cold in felt chaperon, a fur-lined cloak, however unfashionable it might be, and heavy gloves, one foot in the stirrup. There was a squire, a page, but no escort.

'John!'

He abandoned his reins to his page and approached, his hands held out to take mine, quick repentance in his face.

'Forgive me, Elizabeth.'

'I'm uncertain what I have to forgive you for as yet. Where are you going?'

'London.'

'Why?'

He pulled me out of the path of his squire who was leading a spritely animal from stable to courtyard. At the same time, I could only note, he manoeuvred me to where we could not be overheard.

'Why are you going to London,' I repeated. 'When you should be with me, kneeling with everyone else to give thanks for God's blessing on our King and his family?'

For a split second he looked away, his brows meeting heavily, but any discomfort was momentary, for within a breath he was planting a kiss on my lips and rubbing my cheek with the back of his glove.

'A matter of business. I doubt I'll be missed.'

'I think you might be.' And then: 'Is it legitimate business?'

His smile was quick and assured, before becoming a grimace of disgust. 'Of course. Did you not know? Your royal brother, my love, since he has stripped us of the duchy of Cornwall lands, has made a gift of them to his eldest son. I need to see my man of law. There are legal matters to attend to before the transfer to Prince Henry. Not something I appreciate, but a necessity.'

'I'm sorry.' I could understand John's irritation. Yet my suspicions were still lively, my fingers curled like claws into the fullness of the fur edging of his cloak. 'I don't like this,' I said. 'You are taking no escort.'

'There's no need for concern. I'll be back within two days. Now return to the Mass and pray for me. And our children.' He all but pushed me through the stable door.

'And for the King?' I asked dryly.

John kissed me, firm enough to shut me up, but fleeting. 'Certainly for the King. What could harm him now that he wears the Crown and we are all loyal subjects?'

'John…'

He shook his head, mounted with habitual fluid grace, and rode out, leaving me to disbelieve every word he had uttered.

★

But true to his word, John was back in our midst within the two days. Eyes bright, face flushed with cold, he strode into the chamber where we were gathered to enjoy an afternoon with chess and frivolous gambling, lifted me off my feet and kissed me. There was a rustle of laughter around us.

'Did you miss me, Countess?'

'Not at all. Too much going on here to miss someone so unnecessary as a husband.'

Henry strolled across towards us.

'It must have been important business.'

'It was. The little matter of my erstwhile Cornish estates.' John's reply was brittle but at least brief. 'And now I must make my apologies to my wife, who is still scowling at me for abandoning her to all this indulgence.'

I laughed, suspicions momentarily allayed by the light mood. 'It's good to see you back, my lord.'

He took my hand. 'Come and tell me what you have been doing.'

He led me from the room, indulgent comments following us. Yes, I had missed him. His return filled me with hot desire, but I was troubled by that air of shimmering excitement about him. A nervous energy. Whatever the legitimate business, it had stirred his blood, which had excellent repercussions, for he restored the intimacy between us with verve and drama, reminding me of the early days when we still had much to discover about the passion that held us. John kissed and caressed me into insensibility, and as all my fears were swept away, I reciprocated in kind.

'I must leave you more often,' he groaned when I had destroyed all his self-control with a crow of delight.

'Don't you dare!'

I proceeded to relight all the fires anew.

'What's Henry doing?' he asked as, slowly, with some youthful endearments, we put our clothing to rights, John taking it upon himself to pin my hair into passable order beneath a simple veil.

'Planning his grand tournament. He has in mind something spectacular on the lines of his grandfather's extravaganzas.'

'Perhaps I'll offer my services.'

'Which will surprise him. But please him as well, I think. Are you truly reconciled to him?'

'Why not? He could have had my head. Many say I should be thankful it was only my dukedom. I can live with it.'

'I'm sorry about the Cornish estates. I know you valued them.'

'I'll live without them. But not without you.'

It was the sweetest of reunions, touched with all the magic of the seasonal glamour. Yet it did not quite smooth out my days and I found myself watchful, wakeful, alert for any wrong step in the pattern of the festivities.

And then I saw it.

I saw it from the vantage point of the gallery when Elizabeth and Alice had given their nurses the slip. What had all the appearance of a clandestine conversation, four men tucked into a quiet corner, heads close together over a cup of wine. Standing perfectly still I looked down. John was instantly recognisable. With him was his young nephew Thomas Holland, the Earl of Kent after the death of John's brother Thomas two years ago. And there was my cousin Edward, former Duke of Aumale, demoted to Rutland, another of Richard's friends suffering a stripping of titles and land, as both John and Thomas had. All three close associates of Richard in the past, but seeing them in intimate conversation surprised me. I had not thought there was much in common between Edward and the Hollands. Edward was a mere twenty-six years to John's forty-seven. They had had little to say to each other when Richard was King, but here they were in some heart to heart. John was doing all the talking.

The fourth of the group was a young man with a fashionable bowl crop, over-long sleeves and chaperon, face shielded from my view, but playing a part in the deep discourse, until a group of courtiers came too close and the contact was ended, the unknown man slipping away as if on an errand. A final murmured comment, then with a laugh as if it was a trivial matter, easily abandoned for more entertaining matters, John and those remaining joined the boisterous throng raising their cups to cheer on the revellers who were reminiscing over their hunting exploits. But not before I saw a screw of paper change hands between John and my cousin Edward, to be tucked smartly into Edward's sleeve.

All in a matter of moments. It might never have happened. But it did. It was probably entirely innocent, but there was something about their watchfulness, the speed with which they brought their exchange to an end. And, as the anonymous youth departed, my eye was caught by a glitter of silver and enamel. A livery badge, if I were not mistaken.

I made my way from the gallery to join the revellers.

'What did my slippery cousin Rutland have to say?' I asked my husband with grand insouciance.

'Rutland?'

'I saw you talking with him. And your nephew.'

John replied easily enough. He would always match me for composure, guilty or innocent, a past master at masking his thoughts. 'Nothing of moment. Whether they will take part in Henry's grand tournament. I wagered I would beat Rutland into the ground.'

'I'm sure you will.' I awarded him a smile. 'Who was the young slave to fashion in your midst?'

'A squire. Rutland's. By the Rood, Elizabeth. Why is that important?'

'I don't know. I don't like what I saw.'

'What did you see?'

'Four men in a suspicious huddle, that broke up as soon as you were no longer alone. And before you ask, I was leaning over the gallery.'

He breathed a laugh. 'You're imagining things.'

'I don't think I am. I'd say you were plotting something

that must be kept secret.' I paused, to see the mask descend on John's features.

'There was no secrecy.' He was obdurate.

'No? Then why did I think I saw—and now I am sure that I did—Richard's livery badge of the white hart pinned to Rutland's squire's shoulder? Very unwise in this climate, I'd have thought.'

'An affectation, I expect. I didn't notice. It had no meaning, but I agree it was unwise.'

As I detected the slightest hesitation before this response my heart plummeted. The more I was drawn into this accusation and denial, the more fearful I became.

'Why would Rutland's squire wear...'

'Don't!' John's hand was hard around my wrist. 'Don't speak of it.'

'Why not? What are you involved with?' Our voices had fallen to a whisper. 'I think it's a conspiracy. I just don't know what you're conspiring to do.'

John surveyed the room, then drew me into the centre of it so that we were surrounded by courtiers and children and he could see if the gallery was empty of interested audience. Safety in numbers, for this was no place to discuss insurrection.

'So I can't hide it from you.' Keeping his voice low, his smile was wry. 'I didn't think I could. You're too clever by half, Madam Countess. So this is it.' He must have seen a flash of fear in my eyes, for he tightened his hold. 'There's no cause to look aghast. It's not as bad as you think.' He kept a smile in place as if we talked of nothing but the delights of each other's company. 'We are of a mind to persuade Henry to come to terms with us.'

'Who is of a mind?'

'Those he put on trial for their allegiance to Richard. Those he casually stripped of land and title, even though they had forsworn Richard in the end.' Despite all his efforts, the smile faded. 'We hope to encourage Henry to promise restoration of land and titles and promotions. We plan to bring Henry into a…' He paused on a little laugh. 'Into a frank and meaningful discussion, when we meet for the tournament. He will be full of festive goodwill.'

It sounded feasible enough. 'Is that all?'

'That's all. What else do we need to do? Aumale, reduced to Rutland, is as keen as I. So is Thomas who wants the dukedom of Surrey restored to him. There are others.'

Now I understood. 'You discussed it in London.'

'Yes. A group of us met in the Abbot's lodging at Westminster Abbey where we could come and go without too much interest shown. We made our plans, and that is what we will do.'

'When?'

'The Feast of the Epiphany, when Henry's in a magnanimous mood after the tournament. There's nothing to fear, Elizabeth. Henry will listen and see sense. He will reassure us and we will bend the knee in recognition of his generosity. Does that put your anxieties to rest?'

'And the squire?'

'A courier. Faceless enough to carry information between us without rousing suspicion. Except in the mind of my wife, it seems. That's all. It was a mistake, his wearing the white hart. I should have reprimanded him.'

John kissed my hands while I turned the thoughts over in my mind. The beat of his blood in his wrists was regular and steady. If he was disturbed by my accusations, he was hiding it well. And then a thought...

'Would you wear the white hart still? When you ask for Henry's goodwill, will you ask for the release of Richard as well?'

'No,' he replied gravely. 'We will only ask what Henry will be prepared to concede. Are we not pragmatic? Richard's release would be a step too far.'

Eminently reasonable. I studied his face, the well-loved features, the smile that still warmed my blood, the curve of his mouth that could reawaken all my desire.

'Well? Surely, my love, you don't suspect me of foul play.'

'No. No, of course not.' It allayed my fears, but only a little. 'I don't like such secrets. I don't like the thought that Henry is under some species of threat, that I know about it and he does not,' I said sharply.

'He will not be harmed.'

It was enough. It would have to be, and I would keep the secret, because John asked it of me.

*

But it did not allay my fears to any degree. They built and built inside me until I could barely contain them beneath a façade of festive joy and unbridled merriment, such as was expected of the Countess of Huntingdon.

'You wouldn't,' I challenged John again, unwilling to put

into words what I feared, for how would he reply if he could see the dread images in my mind.

'No, Elizabeth. Whatever it is you suspect I might do, I wouldn't.'

'It's not that I suspect...'

'I can see it sitting on your shoulder like a bird of ill-omen. We're here to laugh and make merry. Let us do it.'

I could get no more out of him, and allowed him to pull me into a dance that demanded more vitality than elegance. And I laughed, enjoying the wicked light in John's eyes as he forced me to keep step.

But the thoughts, the impressions would not release me, creeping back to take control as soon as I caught my breath.

So the plan was to force a discussion with Henry about his future behaviour towards those he had punished. It might hold the weight of logic on first glance, but with deeper reflection, what would be the point of that? Would Henry respond to such a discussion with the subjects many already considered to have been treated with unwarrantable leniency? Not the Henry I knew now. As the newly crowned, untried King of England, Henry had his muscles to flex. He would not bow the knee to his subjects in open discussion, as if they were merely deciding on the best route to take in a hunting expedition. Did John and the other lords who considered themselves to be dangerously exposed to further royal encroachment really expect to put pressure on Henry with any degree of success? I could not envisage what they actually hoped to achieve. If Henry was of a mind, he might smile and agree and promise all they wanted. Whether he would keep such a promise was more than I could guess, and the lords would have no redress if he did not.

More likely they would all end up locked in close quarters in the Tower.

My mind continued to scurry through the increasingly dark corridors. If the lords' intentions were of so minor a plotting, why the need to go to London to do it? Why not decide and discuss over a cup of ale and a hot pasty, or during a run of the hounds? Why not simply stop Henry on his return from Mass and request a royal audience?

I could not rid myself of doubts. Well, of course I could not. The version John had given me was as full of holes as a moth-ridden tunic.

Then there was the little matter of Epiphany.

This was what was troubling me. When I asked John when this negotiation with Henry was to be, the Feast of the Epiphany, John had said. And for a moment I had thought he regretted telling me, not because I was unable to keep a secret, but because of its significance which he must have known I would espy. Was it a coincidence? I did not think so. This day, the sixth day of January, was the day of Richard's birth. As I knew. As John knew.

A day of some significance, then.

Despite John's denial, the lords might intend to use this auspicious day to ask Henry to deal more favourably with Richard, to release him, even if it meant sending him into exile where he would be no danger to Henry's hold on the crown.

They might.

But Richard would always be a danger to Henry as long

as he lived, whether in prison or fixed in France. As even
my son had seen, Richard alive was a danger. Richard alive
and at large was a danger twofold. I frowned at my abandoned embroidery, re-creating instead the little scene in the
hall from my vantage spot in the Gallery. John, Thomas and
Edward and the squire. The squire looking round, looking
up as if some untoward noise had taken his notice.

The squire gained in significance as I imagined, again and
again, the little group I had seen from the gallery, but why
he should I was not altogether sure. Except that he did not
even look like a squire. His bearing towards his companions
had certainly not been that of a squire. I could see no reason why some nameless, faceless squire should be included
in a discussion between the three great magnates. Nor was
he a mere courier, a carrier of messages, but one who was
engaged in the conversation. What had he to do with what
they were planning?

My suspicion grew blacker and blacker, urged on by some
inner intuition born of a lifetime of political intrigue. Princess Joan, I knew beyond doubt, would be calling into question the whole episode. But what was the purpose behind
it all? Not a discussion, not a negotiation. It was simply not
logical. So was it to be an uprising, an insurrection plotted and directed from the Abbot's lodging at Westminster,
to do more than engage in polite conversation with Henry.
Would they take him prisoner? And if so, was it their plan
to release Richard and reinstate him on the day of his
birth?

My flesh shivered at the images in my mind, for if they
took Henry prisoner, would they be content to keep him

alive? And then what of his four sons? As Henry's heirs, they might suffer the same fate.

You go too far, I abjured myself. Your imagination is too lively. What evidence have you for this?

None. None.

And yet it gnawed at me. There was more heavy truth to it than the tale John had told me, and if it were true, it placed an impossible decision at my feet. Conscience demanded that I tell my brother of my fears, however unformed they were. As sister and subject I had a care for his welfare.

But as a wife, my loyalty was to John. He was my love, my life. I had promised my silence.

Love, oh love. Betrayal was a terrible thing.

To keep my tongue between my teeth might result in Henry's blood being spilt on the tiled floors at Windsor. To reveal the plot might equally result in death for John and the lords as perpetrators of treason.

Blessed Virgin…

Remonstration with John would have no effect. I danced and sang and flew my hawk as if there were no burden on my soul. I watched as John laughed with Henry, as he engaged in rough sports with the royal lads. As they flew their arrows at the butts or rode in mock tournaments, the younger children shrieking with joy.

How can you do this? How can you plot their deaths?

I didn't know it. I had no evidence, only the thoughts that prowled and refused to let me be.

But the longer I thought about it, the more sure I became. Every magnate punished by Henry would be at the Epiphany tournament. All present under the guise of festivities. All outwardly well disposed to the royal court but with conspiracy in their every breath. When I could keep silent no longer, conscience all but demanded that I pull John from the next bout of practice swordplay and force him to listen to me. But what would I say to him? In my fevered mind I imagined the conversation.

'Would you kill my brother? Would you plot his death? And the four boys you have just encouraged to beat you at the archery butts, winging your arrows astray so they can have the joy of victory against a fighter of renown?'

'In God's name, Elizabeth. Do you think I would be party to such a monstrous outcome?'

'I think you would have no alternative. I think Henry would never co-operate, and so to liberate Richard, my brother's death is exactly what you would engender.'

And in my mind John would slide into deadly revelation.

'Then so be it. If you demand the truth, then here it is. Henry's death has become imperative. What would you have me do? Give my silent consent to Richard's ultimate fate at Pontefract? My conscience will not condone such an act. We will release and restore Richard. The true anointed King.'

'But Henry is my brother!'

'And Richard is mine.'

What to do? Betrayal of one to save the other? Was blood thicker than water? Or love stronger than family? Who to betray?

If I did neither and let events play themselves out, would that not be the simplest path for me? But it would be the coward's path and the death of Henry would be on my soul.

John had talked of conscience. Mine refused to let me rest. It was like watching a rock teetering on the edge of a precipice above our heads. When it fell, who would be crushed?

I didn't know know that Henry's death would be the price of Richard's release, but I feared it would. The highest of prices.

I sat and shivered in my chamber, mistrust for everyone and everything swelling into vast proportions, before donning a green damask robe and mask to play one of the dragons to John's St George in Henry's mumming play. Henry might revel in it, as did our grandfather, but throughout the drama I felt like a grinning death's head, the one question beating at my mind as St George made mock sallies against me with a wooden sword: what do I do?

★

It was on the fourth day of January, two days before the Feast of the Epiphany, that the deluge hit us. Rumours rattling from wall to wall, Henry's court was thrown into a seething mass of claim and counterclaim, while Henry was launched into a whirlwind of action. To do nothing would be to invite catastrophe. The tournament, which he had planned to mark the Feast day with such meticulous care, was a thing of the past. All festivities were abandoned, Henry collecting his sons and a heavy entourage, bristling with weapons.

I did not even try to pretend that I knew nothing of it. My worst fears were being brought home to roost like a flock of summer swallows.

And were confirmed when Henry hammered on my door.

'You will come with us,' Henry commanded, occupying the doorway to my chamber, armed to the teeth with sword and dagger, his upper body protected by a brigandine.

'Why? Am I in danger?' I did not think that I wished to accompany him.

'Not you. It's my blood that they seek. Do I need to ask where Huntingdon is?'

'I don't know.'

Nor did I. What we all knew was that at early Mass there had been a remarkable absence of faces from the ranks of courtiers at Windsor.

'I want you where I can see you,' Henry snarled.

'I would not work against you, Henry.'

'Your husband's in the thick of it. I'll keep you with me. Leave the children here. I've no quarrel with them. *I* don't murder children. Get what you need to ride to London and be ready in a half hour. If you are not, I'll come and get you.'

I did as I was told, my mind, when it could break free from galloping terror, gripped by the possible repercussions. John had left Windsor with the other recalcitrant lords to undertake whatever it was that they had planned and that John had refused to tell me. John had not said goodbye. He was gone before dawn, his squire and pages and a group of liveried men with him and his horses. So was his armour gone when I searched his room. He had gone without telling me. I did not think I could ever forgive him for that. But what could he have said that I had not already guessed?

Anguish was a cold hand on the nape of my neck. Whichever side came out of this conflict as the victor, I would be in mourning.

Better that I was in London than here at Windsor if there was any chance of my stopping what seemed to be the inevitable. When I mounted my horse as required I spoke not one word of my fears for, clearly, Henry had no thought for me or my worries. If he fell into the hands of the rebellious lords, there would be no mercy for him or his sons.

★

We rode. We rode through the night on some long, never-endingly circuitous route for it seemed that Henry expected an interception. If the lords hoped to waylay us, they would never track Henry's path. For hours we rode in silence. There was nothing to say between us, until a late dawn was breaking as we came in sight of London where we were met by the Lord Mayor with the warning that the rebel lords had six thousand men in the field.

'Led by Huntington, I presume,' Henry commented.

The Mayor did not know, and I vouchsafed no reply. I thought he was probably right.

And then there was no time to think, for it was simply a barrage of orders, issued by Henry in a tone that no one would disobey. To close the ports. To summon his followers to raise an army. The boys to be dispatched to the Tower. And I with them.

'She does not leave,' he ordered the brisk escort sent with us. 'Nor does she receive visitors. Other than that, ensure that the Countess is housed with all she requires.' And then, as he turned his horse's head, Henry swung back to me. 'I'll bring his head to you on my shield. That will save you having to make any future choices over where your loyalty might lie.'

Turning to follow my escort I made no response. What could I possibly say to him? This was Henry, my beloved brother, intent on destroyed the man he knew I loved. This was Henry driven by vicious practicality to demand John's life. I understood why. Of course I did. Treason could never be condoned, but never had I thought that Henry would threaten me with such savage consequences.

Then you were a fool, I chided, in bitter acknowledgement. There could never be any other outcome. If Henry laid his hands on John, John would surely die and I could have no redress. My heart, my mind, my soul were full to the brim with the agony of truth.

Next morning, after a wretched night in company with the image Henry had painted for me, I was told, when I badgered the Constable of the Tower for news, that Henry had marched out of London with an army at his back to face the rebels. Where John was I had no idea.

All I could imagine was their meeting on the field of battle.

I despaired at the outcome.

*

Where is he? Where is John now?

The one question that leapt again and again in my mind, and for which there was no answer.

Rumour trickled through to us, none of it good. How could any of it be good for me? The rebel army, faced with Henry in person and a solid force of loyal troops intent on fighting to the death, disintegrated and fled. London remained solidly behind my brother. The revolt, the uprising, for that is what it clearly had become, was over without the spilling of one drop of blood on a battlefield.

So far so good. Henry was safe and John was not dead. The royal boys, rejoicing at the news, would live to be reunited with their father. But what I knew beyond any argument was that John would never be reunited with me. How could Henry forgive him for such blatant rebellion that had threatened to bring conflict and bloodletting to England?

It was Henry who brought the news, still in armour but without his shield or its dread burden. I let him tell the boys, allowing him to assuage their fears. I had expected elation from him, but instead there was only a cold and weary determination to stamp out any future repetition.

'I will have peace in this land,' he said to me.

'I pray you will.' I was as cold as he. 'What of Huntingdon?' I asked, deliberately formal.

All I got was a hitch of one shoulder.

'Did he go to Devon? To Dartington?' I asked.

'We have not heard of him in Devon. There were no forces raised there against me.'

'So he is alive. He is not your prisoner.'

In spite of everything, relief was trickling through me.

'Not yet. But not for long.' The weary chill was suddenly submerged in a roil of hot anger, Henry's face flushed with it. 'The most noble lords who dared defile my realm are running for their lives, but they'll not get far. The squire, Richard Maudeley, who they were using to pose as Richard to rally the masses has already been taken and hanged for his sins. A clever ruse, don't you agree? Same build, same fair skin, same hair colouring. Put him in armour with a gilded helm and who would know the difference? The good citizens of England would see their rightful King once more walking amongst them and flock to his standard against me.'

So I had been right about the squire, who had been there for a purpose and had paid for his part with his life. The revolt was over. Henry was safe. I should be rejoicing with the rest of them.

I could not.

'Are you not at least relieved?' Henry demanded bitterly, easily reading the ferment in my mind, in the white tension of my interlocked fingers. 'The plan, as I now understand it, was to cut me down at Windsor in the heat of the tournament. And my four sons with me, clearing the path for Richard's return. As bloody a plot as I could have envisaged.'

'Yes. Of course I am relieved.'

I could manage no more now that the true savagery of John's conspiracy had been placed before me, merely repeating his words.

'You are hardly enthusiastic.' He turned on his heel and marched to the door. 'Here's a piece of news for you. I hear that Huntingdon is in London. If he tries to make contact with you, we'll take him and kill him. There will be no clemency, so don't waste your breath in begging.'

*

If he was in London, where was he? He would never try to go to ground at Pultney House. It would be watched, far too obvious a bolt hole for a rebel with a price on his head. Nor would he come here to me at the Tower.

If John was in London, there was only one possible place to my mind where he might seek sanctuary. The Abbot's lodging at Westminster Abbey. Henry did not know that the Jerusalem Chamber had been the conspirators' meeting place. That is where he might take refuge. But with no hope of mercy from Henry, what was he thinking? Was he planning some escape route? Perhaps it had already been put in place, for fear the revolt would fail.

Henry being preoccupied with the stamping out of any further pockets of loyalty to Richard gave me some space. A cloak, a hood, a horse at my disposal, my authority as royal sister imposed, and unaccompanied except for a page in royal livery, I set out to cover the short distance from the Tower to the Abbot of Westminster's lodging.

*

When I gestured to my page to knock on the door, it was not immediately opened. Nor at his second insistent rapping.

At last: 'Who is it?'

I motioned to the page to reply, which he did, his voice trembling with nerves.

'The Countess of Huntingdon. She is here to see the Earl of Huntingdon.'

The door was opened by one of the Abbey servants, anonymous in his robes, allowing me access into the abbot's parlour, and for a moment I simply stood on the threshold and looked. Magnificent tapestries, superb linenfold panelling, an ornate fireplace welcomed me. Was this where the lords had plotted? Had all this grandeur been witness to the detailed planning that would have brought a bloody end to my brother? A plot as treacherous as it was possible for a plot to be: no well-mannered debate between Henry and his disaffected lords who feared there would be further retribution against them tucked up their King's capacious sleeve. No frank discussion over the future of Richard, their rightful king, imprisoned in Pontefract. In this, the Jerusalem Chamber under the auspices of Westminster Abbey, they had met in secret to piece together a terrible revenge.

And now, as I had thought, it contained one of the defeated rebels, the Earl of Huntingdon, surrounded by signs of a hasty departure.

My page dispatched beyond the closed door, we stood and looked at each other. How could I ever forgive him for what he had planned? And yet the relief that he was here and unharmed was strong enough to make me light-headed. How could love and despair exist so strongly in the same heart, twisted into an unbreakable cord? He had misled me, lied to me. Yet what point in berating him, or allowing my anger free flow? It would do no good.

John's face was expressionless, his hands filled with leaves of parchment, as I waited for him to attempt the impossible and explain.

'Elizabeth.' There was no welcome. His eyes glinted in the candlelight but not from pleasure at seeing me. 'I did not expect you.'

'I don't suppose you did. Why did you do it?'

'To save Richard.'

'At Henry's expense.'

'It was the only way.'

Neither of us moved one step. I was not sure that I could cross the Abbot's tiled floor towards him, nor he to me, so great was the distance between us, so deep the chasm. I could not be compassionate, and yet I understood. There was no hope for Richard now. There was only one means by which Henry could rid himself of this dangerous man who would always be a focus for rebellion. John knew it too as he stood, the documents still in his hand. I could see it in the tightening of his mouth into a thin line.

'Our failure has signed Richard's death warrant.'

'Yes.'

'And mine too, I don't doubt.'

'Yes, if you are caught.' What point in deception? We knew it to be so.

'Are all our forces defeated?'

'Yes.'

'We misjudged Henry's speed in collecting an army. And London's loyalty.'

'They don't want war.'

'And were promised reparation if they fought for Henry. We had nothing to offer them. It was a risk, and we failed.'

Even now he was well-informed. And how incongruous, the stark observations of our conversation, set against the luxurious furnishings of our surroundings. How could one be so bleak, the other so sumptuous? But the furnishings were of nothing compared with our words, which sounded a death knell to our love.

'Where are you going?' I asked.

'I have passage on a ship. To take me to France.' He began to stuff the pages into a saddlebag.

'Would you have told me?'

'No.' He raised his head to meet my gaze. 'I imagine you despise me.'

'You would have killed my brother.' I slid around the question he had asked. 'You always meant to.'

'Yes.'

And I discovered that tears were running down my cheeks.

'Why are you weeping?'

I could not say. I did not know, except that my life was falling apart and the light in it extinguished.

'I go within the hour to catch the tide.'

'The weather is bad with high winds.' How could I be so practical when he was leaving me, when my reason for living was like a battlefield of devastation?

'I can't stay in London.' The silence drew out. 'Can you forgive me?'

'I don't know.'

He held out his hand but I did not move. When I could not step across the dark pit he had created, John allowed his arm to fall to his side.

'I don't know what to say to you,' I whispered. But I could not let it go, because I needed to understand. 'You gave your allegiance to Henry when he took the crown. Would it have been so hard to continue to be his man? What was so very different? I know your loyalties to Richard, but you had accepted that his rule was damaged, that he was no longer fit occupy the throne. That Henry would make a better King. You could have stood at Henry's side, as his adviser, his well-loved counsellor. What had changed for you?'

'Different? Changed?' Eyes opening wide, a glint of light, John considered the sumptuous surroundings with scorn. 'There was no difference. Yet everything suddenly changed for me. It would have been the simplest of matters to let events take their course. To let Richard go to his incarceration and death—'

'You have no evidence of that!' I broke in.

'—for I see nothing less than death for him,' John continued as if I had never spoken. 'I could have worked for a return of my titles and lands from a grateful Henry, and taken a stance on the side of power and military might. How painless it would have been to accept office under the banner of Lancaster, mimicking the affection of a close-knit family.' The sneer took me aback. 'I thought I could do it. And then I could not. My little sojourn in Hertford as Henry's prisoner made me aware of my vulnerability, and of my true allegiance. And if *I* was vulnerable, how weak is Richard? It was not right, Elizabeth. I could no longer pretend that it was.'

In spite of the anguish that was building—for was this not indeed farewell between us? —I forced my mind into the paths that John's was taking:

'But was Richard right in his judgements? Was he a better man than Henry? If you had murdered Henry and released Richard, would your brother have ruled England with fairer justice than my brother? There is no evidence of it. Rather of the contrary, I'd say.'

He sighed. 'Probably not, but Richard is King by true inheritance. Where will we be if might is allowed to have its day? Do we accept that a king be usurped by a powerful man with an army at his back, simply because he is the stronger?'

'Not any man,' I urged. 'Henry has enough royal blood and more to make him eligible. He is our grandfather's heir by royal entail and male descent. It is his right to be King.'

'And there are many who would question that right!' Frustration gave fuel to John's arm as he flung the packed saddlebag to the floor. 'The whole Mortimer faction will be crying foul on Henry's claim.'

Which I knew. Descended from my dead uncle Lionel, second son to my grandfather, the Mortimers had a sound claim, except that it ran through a female line which old King Edward had overstepped in his entail.

'And you know full well,' John was continuing, 'that Richard chose the line of your uncle of York to succeed him.'

'Of course I know. With Cousin Edward smirking with regal pretension.' Still I would argue Henry's cause. This was no time to be distracted by Edward of Aumale's posturing. 'Henry's claim has the force of law behind him. He has the right to rule through our mother's blood too, from Henry the Third. It is a claim that is hard to resist.'

'It's hard to resist because Henry has men who'll fight for him in their own interests! But does that make it legal?'

'Yes. To me it is entirely legal.'

As John, furiously, marched to the end of the Jerusalem Chamber to collect his outer garments, animadverting bitterly on the cunning words of lawyers, I scooped up the saddlebag and waited for him to return to me. Which he did in the end, to stand foursquare before me.

'I know there is no bending you,' he said. 'But let me speak to you.' And at last, anger draining away, I saw grief and regret in the flat planes of his beloved face. 'This is the last time we might see each other. If the fates smile on me, and bring me safe to a foreign shore, will you come to me? Or will spending the rest of your life with me be more than you can bear? If I have indeed destroyed your love for me, then I must accept that we will never meet again.'

Against my will, the beat of my heart quickened. Still at this eleventh hour, he was offering me a choice.

'You never make life easy for me, do you?' I said

'No. We never thought it would be.'

'Would you want me with you?'

'Yes. You are the heart of my heart. That will never change.'

I loved him so much. In spite of everything, I loved him. I suspected I always would. But would I willingly go with him into exile? Would I leave my children and follow John into an uncertain existence in France? An exile that might never be rescinded? The alternative, the terrible alternative, was never to see him again.

Could I refuse him—and myself—that final vestige of hope of living together?

Reality rushed through my mind to cool my heated thoughts and show me what it would mean. He would never again be there at my awakening, or in the final hour of my day. Never would we ride together through pasture and woods, a hawk on his fist, the hawk no fiercer than he. Never would I see the golden lions of his banner in a tournament heralding his incomparable dexterity of hand and eye. Never again would I know the brush of his fingers against my wrist to set my blood pounding into desire. Never would he shower me with opinion, inviting my response as if I were an equal, not a woman to be kept in the background.

John smiled a little at my silent presence as if he could read my thoughts. And I was stabbed with love and desire that heated me all over again. Remaining apart from him was no alternative at all. My decision was made, chasm or no chasm.

'If you can get word to me, I will come to you,' I said.

'It will mean being an exile.'

'Then I will live in exile with you.'

In spite of everything, I could not let him go.

'You don't have to decide now. Wait until I can send for you.' His lips twisted into a smile that was barely a smile. 'Will you allow me to kiss you in farewell?'

I stepped across the abyss and there I was, enfolded in his arms as I had been so often in the past.

'It was wrong and the outcome is dire, but I would do it again tomorrow,' he said.

Honesty was what I expected from him. That appalling honesty.

'I know. I can't condone it or excuse it, but I do understand. Keep safe, my dearest love.' I would not weep again. He did not need my tears. 'You must go.'

I offered my lips and he took them, his hands cradling my face with so much love and understanding that for a moment I could believe that the hot breath of treachery was a fantasy, but when he released me, it was to confront a cruel parting, the need to be gone stark in John's face.

'I will love you for ever,' he promised, brushing a wayward curl of hair from my temple in a final gesture.

'As I will love you.'

'I will never forget you as you are at this moment.' His fingers rested against my cheek, my lips, my brows, as if he must retain the image of them for a time of drought.

'Nor I you.'

'God keep you, my dear love.'

'And you. I will keep you in my thoughts.'

Such a simple confirmation of what we had been to each other, before he left me there, striding off through the environs of Westminster towards the Thames. I could have gone with him to the waterside, but better that I leave him without any further chains around his neck. What would I have done, stood on the riverside and waved to him in farewell?

Before he left, I give him a purse of coin. All I had.

'Go! Be safe!' Guilt colouring my words so that he must surely understand, but with a courtly little bow he left me.

Holy Virgin, keep him safe. Holy Virgin, give me the strength to withstand our parting.

★

'Who?' the guard barked, holding up a lantern.

'Elizabeth of Lancaster,' my page replied soft-voiced but still arrogant on my behalf. 'Allow her to enter.'

There was no hesitation.

So I returned to the Tower, no longer surprised how a

few coins and being sister to the King could open doors. My face, my status, were well-known. In present circumstances, uncertain of its reception, I took care not to breathe the name of Huntingdon.

Once more within, my page dismissed, I leaned back against my door and allowed the full horror to wash over me, my love for John battered by my knowledge of what he had done. What he could envisage as just revenge for what many saw as remarkable leniency. What was the loss of a title weighed against the death of the male house of Lancaster?

But could I condone Henry's killing of Richard? Any childhood affection for Richard had long faded but he was still of my blood, and Henry's too.

But he will not.

I thought he would. I kept out of Henry's path, not difficult since he was still occupied with the final bloody consequences of the Revolt of the Earls.

Keeping close in my rooms I prayed that the Blessed Virgin would bring John to sanctuary. That he would make landfall somewhere in France, and that one day I might be united with him. For in spite of all, my love for him had bonds of steel. Yet even as I offered up prayer after prayer, outside my windows storms raged, dashing my hopes that he would reach safety. More like his ship would founder and he would be dashed to death on the rocks or dragged down beneath the indifferent waves.

I would never hear from him again and I would never know his fate.

My knees were sore as my fingers clicked over the beads of my rosary, repeating petition after petition, not least for peace within my own soul that I knew I did not deserve, until at last, in hopeless despair, I sank back to my heels.

'I can pray no more.'

All I could do was wait. Knowing my children to be safe at Windsor, I determined to stay in London until I knew, for better or worse. I kept to my chambers, the only thought in my heart being that to hear no news was not all bad. The storm winds had abated, bringing a strange calm. John might even now be secure and at liberty in some French port.

Chapter Fourteen

Three days after I had said my farewell to John, there was a fist driven against my door and a royal official was admitted.

'My lord the King requests that you attend him in the audience chamber.'

Since the official avoided my eye, anxiety destroyed my hard won calm. For Henry to make this an official meeting—and I could imagine his advisers flanking him as he delivered the news—I could only imagine what it would be. The official did not appreciate my hesitation.

'My lord the King is hard pressed and would see you now, my lady.'

I would not be hurried. 'Tell the King I will attend on him shortly.'

'But my lord the King is…'

'Tell the King I will present myself in his audience chamber as soon as I am fit to be received into his presence.'

'It is momentous news, my lady.'

'It may be momentous, but five minutes more will make no difference.'

I needed time. To dress carefully, to plait and cover my hair. To compose my features. To order my senses. I would not fall and weep at Henry's feet, whatever the provocation. Nor would I show him any signs of neglect from my days of prayer and sleepless nights. I would attend this summons with all the pride of a daughter of Lancaster. It was, I decided as I chose a jewelled caul, all I had left. And if John was alive so that I could bargain with Henry for his life, I would do it from a position of well-groomed dignity.

You know what he has to tell you.

I could imagine Henry's sense of accomplishment as I placed a Lancaster livery collar on my shoulders, even if his victory was at the behest of the tides and an alien coast.

John is dead.

And thus I went about my preparations with an iron-like will, governing every sense, every emotion, my face as smooth and bland as new whey.

John was assuredly dead, his body brought ashore by the wind and tides, and Henry would be in celebratory mood. I was sunk in the blackest of desolation, but no one would read it in my face.

*

Henry was not smiling. Perhaps it was out of some residue of compassion for me, but I could no longer think along those lines. Acknowledging that we had drawn too far apart for compassion, I curtsied deeply, noting the counsellors that stood with him, those who had made the politic choice and abandoned Richard to his fate. I knew them all, but this was between me and my brother.

'You wished to see me, my lord.'

My announcement was as bleak as a winter morn, but no bleaker than his.

'I have news of Huntingdon.'

I waited for the blow to strike.

'He was driven ashore. Onto the Essex coast.'

'And he is dead,' I said, my lips stiff so that forming the words was difficult. 'Is his body found?'

'Oh, yes, Elizabeth. He is found. Huntingdon is very much alive and well.'

My heart leapt with such force, the relief so great that I could barely contain it. All I could do was offer a silent thanks to the compassionate Virgin. Until reality struck with the sinister truth contained in the news. I looked up at Henry, where he stood above me on the dais, all my fears coalescing into one solid mass beneath my heart.

'So he is in your hands.'

'Yes.'

'He is your prisoner.'

'Yes.'

I looked at Henry's face, trying to recall the rounded smiling, mischievous features of Henry as a boy. Leaner, older, stamped with authority, this man was King of England and I must never forget. I must learn my new role in this relationship. He was King and I was subject and supplicant. More than that, my husband was a foresworn traitor and in his power to dispatch to the executioner.

'You know what I must do, Elizabeth.'

Oh, I did. I did.

'You will put him on trial. For treason.'

'Yes. He risked all in a foolish gamble and lost. The full force of the law will be used against him.'

I simply stood, absorbing what this would mean, obliterating from my mind the horror of it if Henry insisted on the full penalty for a traitor, to hang, draw and quarter. Execution would be a more compassionate alternative.

'I'm sorry.' He did not sound sorry. 'I know how this will affect you.'

Did he? Had he any idea how important this man was to me, in spite of everything I knew about him? I ran my tongue over dry lips. I had said that I would not weep or plead. Yet I begged.

'Can you find it in you to have mercy?'

'He would have had me and my sons hacked to death on my tournament field.'

'He was afraid for the life of his brother.'

'Or was he afraid for his own safety? I treated him with justice. I punished him with a light hand. And this is how he—and those like him—repay me.'

'He took the oath of allegiance to Richard.'

'He took the same oath to me as well. And it meant nothing to him.' The sardonic savagery was a wound in my side.

'He would return to your side if you wooed him.' What an empty gesture that was, and yet I would say the words. 'I beg of you, my lord.'

'I will not. Nor can you expect it. Here we have an oath-breaker of magnificent proportions. I will never trust him again. There is no value in this discussion, Elizabeth.'

Still I would not let go, even though I knew in my heart that there was no hope. Never had I seen my brother so recalcitrant, yet I fell back to childhood usage.

'If you have any affection for me, Hal, show mercy.'

'It is out of my hands.'

'Where have you sent him?' There again, a little leap of hope. If his new guardian was open to persuasion… could I at least beg that he be allowed to escape again, and this time arrive safe at some European strand? Surely that was the best outcome for everyone.

'I have placed him,' Henry said as if weighing every word, his eyes on mine so that I could not miss the implication, 'in the custody of the Countess of Hereford at Pleshey.'

And at that, in spite of all my good intentions, I wept. In the presence of Henry and the counsellors and the royal officials. I wept. Nor did I cover my face, but let the tears roll uselessly down to mark the damask of my bodice and spike the fur.

'Why would you do that?'

'Why would I not? The Countess of Hereford and the FitzAlans deserve some satisfaction.'

It struck against my heart, crushing every final grain of hope, and I turned on my heel. Without permission I left the royal presence. In that moment I never wished to see my brother again.

★

The Countess of Hereford had John in her power. If John was in the clutches of Countess Joan of Hereford, then all was surely lost to me, and to John. I returned to my rooms to begin preparations for a journey full of the worst foreboding.

And yet once I would have travelled to Pleshey with such joy, for Countess Joan was a blood relative, a confirmed supporter of Lancaster, even showing herself to be a good friend to Duchess Katherine before she was made respectable, offering her a loving sanctuary for the birth of her daughter Joan, out of the Countess's deep affection for my father. A devoted mother to Mary de Bohun, Henry's ill-fated wife, Countess Joan had proved a warm and comfortable presence in my own childhood. Pleshey Castle figured vividly in my memories, a place for exciting New Year gift givings and Twelfth Night revels. Countess Joan could never be accused of giving less than whole-hearted support to the family of Lancaster.

But Countess Joan was a FitzAlan by birth, and there was the thing. Countess Joan was sister to Richard FitzAlan, Earl of Arundel, who had been the first to be called to account as the most outspoken of the Lords Appellant, the most critical of Richard's mistakes. Countess Joan was aunt to the two FitzAlan sons whom we had housed with so much ill-will on their part. The FitzAlans had been transformed from strongest allies into most bitter enemies.

How could I blame them? Richard had made a bloody example of Richard FitzAlan, his head struck from his body on Tower Hill. Now my blood ran cold as I dredged up the details of those terrible days. When the Lords Appellant had been taken prisoner, it was John who was standing at Richard's side. When the Arundel estates were forfeit to the

crown, it was John who received them at the grateful hand
of his royal brother. Who had been given the magnificent
fortress of Arundel Castle? It was John.

As John rose in power and prestige at their expense, the
FitzAlans fell, the young dispossessed Earl even losing his life
while in our keeping.

And would that John's pre-eminence at their expense was
his only crime in the eyes of the FitzAlans. My mind hopped
from sin to even worse sin. For a vengeful Countess there
would be far more to weigh against John's life. Countess
Joan's elder daughter Eleanor had been wed to the royal
Duke of Gloucester who had his life crushed out of him
in Calais. When Gloucester had been arrested at Pleshey,
who had ridden at Richard's side? John might not have
been involved in the deed in Calais, but he was complicit in
Richard's planning to rid himself of those who had attacked
his royal dignity. Who was more often than not seen in the
ascendant in those years of Richard's power, recipient of
Richard's patronage, and at the expense of all others? It was
John.

I rode out from the Tower with violent death and John's
complicity in the FitzAlan downfall as close companions.
Would the Countess ever find it in her heart to have mercy?
I did not think so. John's involvement, however slight, in
Gloucester's death would have been made worse in her eyes
by the death of his and Eleanor's little son Humphrey a matter of months ago, followed by Eleanor's rapid demise from
a broken heart.

I could imagine the gleam in Countess Joan's eye with
John Holland under her dominion, hers the choice over

him, of life or death. I could imagine her response if I begged for mercy.

'Do you realise what your damnable mis-begotten husband has done to my family?'

And yet I would go to Pleshey and beg. I would call on her as one woman to another, as one woman torn by grief and despair to another. I would do all in my power, as my father's daughter. And as the daughter of her great friend John of Lancaster, would she turn me from her door? Surely she would discover some vestige of compassion in her heart.

I would not abandon all hope before I had even tried.

I went to Pleshey.

★

I walked into Countess Joan's beautifully appointed parlour, all so familiar, announced by her steward as if I were the welcome guest I had been in the past. I had had the whole journey to decide what I would say, and still I did not know. John's actions seemed in the light of the Countess's sufferings indefensible. And yet I trod carefully. I did not yet know how she would receive me. If it was with past affections it might make all the difference. All hung on the spin of a coin so I curtsied as expected towards one of my father's generation and family, a lady of influence as broad as her hips and brow.

'I am grateful that you would receive me, my lady.'

'I was expecting you,' she said, turning from where she had been, at the window, clearly watching my arrival. Her face was wiped clean of all expression, but at least I was not faced with rampant hatred.

I stood before her impressive bulk, hands folded neatly, gaze level in polite respect when my mind was in furious turmoil. 'I had to come.'

'To plead a lost cause.'

'To ask you to at least listen to me, my lady.'

'And why would I do that?'

'Because of past loyalties and deep friendship I believe you would give me a hearing.'

And I did believe it. Surely there was some element of reason in this clever, political woman's heart. Some tiny seed of reason, of compassion to which I could appeal, to win John his freedom. Surely here was some means to escape if I kept my composure and argued with some line of clear logic.

'I suppose that you would say,' the Countess said lightly, 'that it was my duty, and my own inclination, to give you a hearing, in light of my long-standing friendship with your father.'

'It is what I had hoped.'

'We were always close.'

'As I know.'

The faintest of smiles touched her lips and I had the sensation of a lightness in my heart. Perhaps hope was not quite dead.

'What do you suppose that John of Lancaster would advise in such a case as this?'

'To have mercy,' I replied promptly. 'He held my husband in high regard.'

'So you say. Sadly your brother the King holds him in utter contempt.'

So I said what I knew I must. 'I beg of you, for my sake, out of all the love you bore for me and my family, to show compassion for a man who did nothing but obey the orders of his own King, of Richard. To whom he had taken the oath of allegiance.'

The smile had vanished from the Countess's lips. Yet she laughed, a light trill of derision, and as the laughter died away I felt a presence at my back. The Steward had not closed the door and someone had entered with silent footsteps. Now he came to stand at the Countess's side, turning slowly to face me.

And all the hope that had been building, one tiny stone on another, collapsed in absolute ruin as his eyes held mine. There would be no compassion here.

The last time I had seen this young man he had been a youth, a sullen youth, barely grown out of childhood, placed with his brother in John's care after the execution of his father. A disgruntled youth who had expressed every desire to disrupt our household, and had carried out a childish revenge.

Here was no child.

Here was Thomas FitzAlan, now the dispossessed Earl of Arundel on the death of his brother Richard from some malevolent fever in our keeping. Thomas who had escaped from Reigate Castle and fled to Europe where he had sworn his allegiance to my brother.

And here he was, to extract ultimate vengeance for the death of his father and brother. And somewhere in this fortress, kept under lock and key, and the key doubtless in the hand of Thomas FitzAlan, was my husband.

'I see you are returned in triumph, Thomas FitzAlan.' I broke the simmering silence.

He was nineteen years old but looked older than his years with his new responsibilities, his high-necked houppelande full-skirted and stitched with bright silks, worthy of Henry himself. In his hand a velvet hat and a pair of jewelled gauntlets. So Thomas FitzAlan had become my brother's pensioner until his estates were restored to him and was enjoying the King's open-handedness.

'And I will take my revenge.' He did not even need to gloat.

How could I possibly have seen this eventuality? In all the choices I had made, I could never have foreseen this. The weight of repercussion on heart became suffocating.

'Then I will not beg you for mercy, as I would have begged the Countess.'

'No. For I will not listen. John Holland is a dead man.'

★

They allowed me to see him, even when I thought they would refuse. How they enjoyed my impotence; there at Plesh y had no power to demand entry into whichever noxious room in which they were keeping him, but at last, with a glance at her nephew, to cow him into reluctant submission, the Countess summoned a servant to conduct me.

'She deserves that much at least,' she snapped when Thomas demurred. 'For her brother's sake.'

If she thought it would intensify my pain, she was wrong. Nothing could do that. The days of familial closeness were long gone, even as I inclined my head in a semblance of gratitude. As a young girl, intent on my own personal happiness in my supremely privileged world, how could I ever have guessed that my marriage to John would destroy all my confidence, forcing me to bestride the great divide between two warring families? Conflicting loyalties wounded my heart at every turn when I was forced to cast myself on the mercy of those who would have no mercy.

'Enjoy your farewell.' The Countess was exultant in her triumph. 'You will not see him again. Or not with the capacity to engage you with honeyed words. It is hard to speak with your head severed from your body.'

My breath caught, my whole body rigid, my hands flat against my waist where my heart thundered. Death. Execution. Taken utterly by surprise, I could not think how to react. The decision had already been made. My journey, all my pleas had been for nothing. I had been right to fear the worst.

Still I harnessed all my willpower. 'This is wrong. There has been no trial,' I observed with cold dispassion in contrast to the Countess's fervour.

'What need? His guilt is proven by his flight from justice. The men of Essex will gather when I summon them, and they will see justice done.'

Her assurance swept me into utter despair, aghast at what her words implied.

'How can you even consider letting the mob run wild? Did we not see the dangers of uncontrolled demands for what the men of Essex considered to be fairness?'

Images of London, The Savoy Palace burning to destruction, flickered through my mind as a monstrous backdrop to my present woes. I heard the cries of terror of those snatched up from the Tower and done to death on Tower Hill without trial. Would Henry, who had almost fallen victim to the mindless bloodshed simply because he was his father's heir, risk such uncontrolled rebellion undermining the law and order of his own kingdom? Countess Joan had no compunction in using the weight of the mob in her own interests.

The Countess remained unmoved. 'There will be no lack of control. The men of Essex will speak with a fair voice under my guidance, never fear.'

'And you will persuade them of what is fit and fair, if they stumble in their choice.'

Anger at Henry burned brightly. Henry who had so cleverly shuffled off his responsibility here. He would bear no guilt for John's death, but would emerge as white as a new untrammelled snowfall, while Countess Joan and Thomas FitzAlan willingly shouldered the responsibility in his stead.

'And you will receive a suitable reward at my brother's hands,' I said to Thomas FitzAlan whose face wore an appallingly self-satisfied smile.

The smile became a grin. 'Why not? Henry has already knighted me. When this rebellion is put down, I will receive possession of my inheritance. I'll be Earl of Arundel, as is my right.'

It was all hopeless. And yet: 'I ask for clemency. The Earl of Huntingdon does not deserve to die at the hands of the mob.'

'Who was there to grant my father mercy, to vouch for his good name? Or to speak for my brother, too young to die at Huntingdon's hands?'

'Huntingdon was not responsible for your brother's death,' I returned, knowing the accusation to be groundless, hoping my cold assurance would have an effect. 'He was not at Reigate, as you well know. Your brother was never ill-treated in our household. What you say is an infamous calumny.'

It had no effect. Viciously casting his hood and gloves at my feet, as if issuing a challenge to combat, FitzAlan seized the thread of vengeance and spun it out to create a master-piece of bloody intent. 'Huntingdon treated me as a slave. My brother died of the foul handling he was given. And you talk to me of compassion and clemency. Save your breath. Besides, this is treasonable talk. A traitor deserves no con-sideration. For you to argue the case, my lady, would only be disloyal to the King, your brother.' He gave a hoot of laughter. 'Holland will pay for making me clean his bloody boots!'

Nothing less than a smirk accompanied the final truth and the use of my title with such lack of respect. These FitzAlans had all the power here at Pleshey. Had I fallen to my knees to grovel at their combined FitzAlan feet, there would be no moving them. Holding fast to a hard control that I would need to carry me through the next hours, I would beg no more, since there was no mercy in this room.

I managed to curtsy my thanks, eyes downcast to hide the burden of hatred that filled my chest so that I could scarce breathe. They might rejoice at bringing John low, but they would get no more satisfaction from my misery.

★

I was led by a silent individual, more guard than servant from the weaponry attached to his person, to one of the towers, not a dungeon as I had feared, but, except that it was not below ground, little better. Thrust into the room without ceremony, the heavy door was locked at my back, leaving me to blink in the shadows.

Shatteringly cold, severely under-furnished, almost light-less with windows little more than arrow slits, this was a part of the original stone structure that had undergone no refinement over the years. No fire warmed the dank air that stank of long disuse and blood and rodents. There was a bench, a coarsely constructed stool. There was no com-fort here. I could barely see across the room, only conscious of a movement as a figure rose slowly from the roughly-constructed bed against the far wall.

John, once Duke of Exeter, reduced to this. King's brother, King's counsellor, locked away in filth and neglect. All he lacked were the chains. It was as if I could see the axe poised above his neck, if that is what the Countess was pleased to grant. That he might be torn apart with animal fury by the promised mob was too much for my mind to encompass. Despair and grief entwined in my belly with the stench, so potent that I could not at first speak. There was the reek of incipient death in this room, and it silenced me.

It was John who broke the silence, John who was never afraid to put into words his worst fears, to face the danger head-on. Was it not always so?

'Elizabeth.' It was little more than a sigh. My belly clenc-hed. I had not thought that he might already be injured.

'Yes,' I replied.

Because he remained as far from me as he could get, his
back flat against the wall, hands splayed there at his sides, his
beloved features were impossible to discern, but I could hear
the rasp of pent-up anger as he demanded, almost savagely:

'Why are you here?'

'To see you.'

'I don't want you here. If you bang on the door, my winsome jailer will return and release you.'

It was not what I expected, but then, what had I hoped
for? Not that he would welcome me with open arms, but
this was rejection after our tentative promises in the Jerusalem Chamber. I took a single step forward.

'I will not go. I am come to appeal for the life of my
husband. I am come to beg the Countess for mercy.' Until I
could sense his mood, I could not speak of my failure, even
though in the end I knew I must. There was no room for
untruths between us, nor would he believe me. 'I am here
because I could not stay away. Did you think I would hide
behind Henry, seeking his goodwill by abandoning you?
You are my husband, for good or ill. It is my duty and my
care to plead for you.' I took a breath. 'I am here to plead
for you out of love.'

There was a long pause before he found the innocuous
words to reply.

'Then I should be grateful, should I not? For no one else
will.'

How cruel truth could be. After that brutal assessment
John did not move. The shadows remained motionless as if
even his breathing was stilled.

And then: 'You will not succeed. But you know that.'

I could not deny it. And how lacking in emotion he
was. I knew I must take care not allow my own to over-
flow and drown us both. Driven by an urge to be practical,
to bring some lessening of the pain in that bleak confine, I
turned and hammered on the door, which was immediately
unlocked. So the guard was waiting outside. Perhaps even
listening, although what he might learn that could further
damage John's cause I could not imagine.

'Didn't take long, mistress. The goods too damaged to
satisfy your needs?' His grin was as obscene as was the implication. And I feared what I could not see.

'Long enough to be ashamed at the state in which the
Earl of Huntingdon is kept,' I said. 'I wish for candles.'

'It might be better if you don't...' I heard John murmur.

'I've got no orders.' The guard remained unabashed.

'Fetch them. Fetch wine and bread. The King my brother
would not have this man kept in this condition. And he will
surely hear of it...'

For a long moment I thought that he would disobey.

'Would you defy me?'

'Not I! As you wish, mistress. On your head be it.'

With a guffaw at his own wit, the man departed, returning with two rush lights, a flagon of wine and two cups,
but no bread. No matter. I took them without a word
of thanks—I was beyond thanks—and he locked the door
again.

At first I busied myself, placing the lights in their brackets,
but when their flickering illumination showed what had
been hidden, all I could do was look at John, horror seeping
into my bones. Someone had already applied a punishment

to his unprotected flesh and enjoyed the task. Clothes stiff and begrimed from his days at sea and the beaching, that was the least of it. There was blood on hose and tunic, for had he not been severely manhandled? Hair dark and matted with filth, bruising along his jaw and beneath one eye, blood dried and smeared, it was clear to me that he had been given no attention. I thought the fingers of one hand, curled clumsily into a talon against the stonework, were broken. Someone had already taken revenge with a heavy hand, but not enough to rob him of his senses. They wanted him alive and aware. Nothing must be done to strip away the suffering of the final punishment to come.

Sorrow, slippery with regret, welled up in me, and I swallowed hard, but he must have seen what I could not hide, for his smile was twisted, resembling more a grimace as his damaged muscles resisted even the slightest movement.

'I doubt I'm good to look at. I said it would be better without light, but you never listen, Elizabeth. You never did, so you'll not start now.'

I would not argue with him. Instead I crossed the room, stopping only to pour a cup of the wine, and pushed him gently to sit on the bed where he subsided with a groan. With difficulty I helped him to bend the fingers of his less damaged hand around the cup and aided him to drink, surprised when he did not demur. He was weaker than I thought.

'By the Rood, that's poor stuff,' he grimaced.

'Your jailor doesn't care about the vintage. When did you last eat?'

'Feeding me is not one of the Countess's priorities. As long as I am on my feet to greet my executioner…'

'You need food. I will arrange it.'

'No.' Not all his strength was drained. He stopped me by dropping the cup and clasping my wrist, even though the effort made him gasp.

'This is the end, Elizabeth.' A flat, hard statement of truth. 'We'll not prolong it with fine wines and fair repasts.'

Tears of despair collected on my lashes, guilt stabbed hard at my heart, but I transmuted it into anger. 'In God's name, John, why did you not listen to me? I warned you what might happen. Did I not advise you to use more subtle means than an uprising?' Emotion was not too far away, lodged like a mouthful of dry bread in my throat. 'Why would you not listen to me?'

'Because you spoke with your brother's voice,' he observed laconically, the same reasoning that we had already tossed, endlessly, between us. 'And I, in the end, could not betray mine. Leave it. If you need a deathbed confession from me, that will exonerate me of my sins, I can't do it.' There was the defiance, still strong, despite the wounds and abrasions, the damaged voice. I could not look at the bruises that already encircled his throat as if fingers of steel had been pressed there, presaging what lay ahead with the kiss of the axe. His voice became a harsh rasp. 'It is too late for that.' His eyes slid to mine. 'Someone talked. Someone leaked the plan to Henry. He was ready for us. He knew the date and the time.'

My breath faltered.

'How could that be?' he asked.

All I could do was stare at him.

'Not that it matters,' he continued. 'Here we are, and I must face the consequence of my so-called treachery. If a man lights the conflagration of treason he has to accept that the flames can burn him too.'

'John…'

'No. Don't say anything. There is nothing more to say.'

And stopped me with his broken fingers against my lips.

'Elizabeth. No. We are past all that. The choices have been made, the decisions taken. An ill wind brought me back to these shores, into the arms of waiting fate, and fate desires my death…'

His voice trailed away into silence. And there was the future after all, crowding in on us with its foul breath.

'I swear I will do all I can to make fate step aside,' I promised as my gut churned with nausea.

John's smile was raw. 'Just sit with me. Or does my appearance disgust you?' He tried to retrieve the cup and swore. 'My hands don't work too well.' It looked as if someone had stamped on them. 'Tell me something I can hold fast to, to the end. Something that is good and indestructible and redolent of past happiness. About the children. About Dartington. About anything but…'

'I cannot. I cannot talk of any of this.' Although I remained seated with him, in the face of his courage, my brave words meant nothing. 'All I can see is…' My breath hitched, my blood was cold as death.

'All you can see is my death.'

'Yes. I can do nothing.'

The sneer was back, well marked beneath the crusted

blood and bruising. 'Will Henry not make a final bid to save me to please his well-beloved sister?'

'Not so well-beloved. Henry refuses my pleas and has handed the jurisdiction to Countess Joan and Thomas FitzAlan.'

'Ah! So Thomas is here.' There was the smile, the old charm that wounded me with its brilliance. That he could still smile was beyond my fathoming.

'You have not seen him? I thought he might have been responsible for the blows.' Gently, regaining control, I smoothed his damaged fingers between mine. Two of them were broken.

'No. Some of his minions though. I expect he has vengeance in mind for the boots. Does he blame me for his brother's death?'

'Yes. And yes, the boots remain a black memory. I suppose in his eyes it was a brutal punishment to make him clean them as often as you did.'

'He needed discipline. Better than beating him.'

'I think he might not agree. A beating would not wound his dignity. He has an amazing capacity for dignity for a youth not yet reached his twentieth year.' How could I talk of such trivia, when these might be the final words we exchanged? But I did. 'Thomas looked down his nose at me as if I were a cockroach.'

'I have some compassion for him. Who would not? His father did not deserve execution.'

I took a breath, astonished at a depth of magnanimity that was beyond my encompassing. 'I will never condone what he has done to you,' I said, and raised his ruined hand to my cheek, pressing a kiss into his palm. 'There. And I said I would not weep.'

'Nor will you. Tell me about the others. Those who joined with me to see justice done. No one will tell me…'

I could not lie and so I told him of the outcome that had swept them all away. 'Thomas Despenser is dead. Your squire is hanged. Your nephew Thomas died at Cirencester, together with the Earl of Salisbury. Their heads were sent to Henry in a basket…'

Why was I telling him this?

'What about Aumale? Or Rutland as I should call him? Is he dead, too?'

'No.' I frowned, remembering. 'He was with Henry when I last saw him. I'm almost certain…'

And yes, I was sure of it. He was there in the group of counsellors when Henry had informed me of John's incarceration at Pleshey.

'Was he now?' I saw the familiar surge of anger in John's eyes, but it was short-lived. There was no time for anger now. 'A strange change of heart on Henry's part for his ingratiating cousin,' John admitted. 'I doubt he'll use it for me.'

'Ah, John! I can't talk of this.'

'I have brought you nothing but misery.'

'And such happiness.' I kissed his cheeks, his closed eyes, his lips, the lightest of caresses. 'Such amazing happiness.' I felt the forbidden tears on my cheeks after all and made no attempt to wipe them away.

'I wish with all my heart this had not come between us. I know you say I was intransigent. Perhaps I was. Forgive me, Elizabeth.' He laced his fingers of his good hand with mine, as best he could, lifting them both to wipe away the moisture. 'It has caused so deep a rift between us. But I think that perhaps we are, at last, at one.'

'Yes.'

'You must never think that I love you any less than in those halcyon days when I wooed you.'

'My love for you, even when I hated you for what you were doing,' I admitted, 'is indestructible.' How long ago it was since we had last exchanged such words of devotion, and I regretted it. 'Forgive me for not understanding. For letting Henry force a path between us.'

A fist hammered at the door. 'Five minutes to make an end.'

I flinched, driven again to honesty. 'I can do nothing, John. I have failed you.'

'But you can do so much.' With the minimum of movement, he placed one arm around my shoulders, drawing me to rest against him, one hand clumsily pinioning mine against his chest as his voice dropped into an urgency that no amount of anguish could destroy. 'Listen. Listen to me. You can stand for me beyond death. When I am dead, my land will be forfeit, my titles, my inheritance. You must fight for them, Elizabeth. Fight for what is mine, for our children. They deserve recognition, good marriages, preferment at court. Their blood could not be better, from royalty on both sides. Don't let their father's misjudgement drag them down so that they live in penury and shadows for the rest of their lives. Richard should be Duke of Exeter. The girls should make good marriages. Promise me. Rail at Henry until he concedes at least this. The axe that severs my head from my body must not be allowed to hack away at the future of our family. Our children are Henry's own family through your blood. You must stand for all of us.'

Once again any response was frozen on my tongue. I had not expected such cold acceptance. But why had I not? John would not pretend, not with me.

'I will fight,' I promised, at last.

'Go to Dartington. Hold possession of it as long as you can. Henry will not turn you out. Take the children there. They will be safe.'

'Yes. I will do it.'

'It's a beautiful place. I had hoped that we would be there together. Make it a good home. Plant the gardens.'

'I hate gardens.'

'But you will do it because I wish it.'

'I will do it.'

All the things we wanted to say that we could not say. All hidden beneath this futile exchange about the existence of paths and plants at Dartington. My soul raged within me. 'Before God, John...'

'No!' His hand closed more firmly around mine. 'Promise me.'

And I was driven to make that promise, my hand flat against his heart.

'Yes. I promise. I will make Dartington the home you would have wanted and I will ensure that Richard becomes Duke of Exeter.'

'And you, my love, my light. You should marry again.'

Lifting my head from his shoulder so that I could look

at him, every sense was stilled into stiff rebellion. 'I will not.'

'It is not in you to remain alone. You must be a sensible woman.'

'I will never love again.'

'You do not need love for a good marriage. Besides, who knows what the future will hold for you. You must wed again. You will make some man a good wife.' The minutes of time were fast flowing away. 'And now you must go.' Gently but with such firmness, he pushed me away, and I allowed it.

'I'll speak with the Countess again. Even with Thomas FitzAlan.' I hesitated. 'And whatever the outcome, I will stay to the end.'

'No!' He took my shoulders and shook me, despite the pain to him. 'Look at me.' And he shook me until I did, holding the anguish in my eyes with his. 'You will not stay. If you never obeyed me in anything else, you will obey me in this. Do you hear me? I don't want you here when I am led to the block.'

I clung to his wrists. 'I can't go…'

'I don't want you to be here.'

I stared at him, understanding.

'I don't want you to see me. I want you to remember me as I was when I rode in the tournaments and won your heart. That is the picture I want you to paint for our children. Elizabeth, the best thing I ever did was woo you. Now go before your presence unmans me.' He pulled me to my feet and kissed me. Hard and sure. 'My heart and soul. My dear wife.'

He all but dragged me to the door and brought his fist down hard on wooden panels in one final blow with a groan of agony.

'Tell my sons that I did what I thought I must. What I thought was right. I would do it again tomorrow. Now go!'

I could not do it. Not yet.

'There is something I must tell you first...' The words had flown from my lips before I could stop them. Knowing, accepting at last that we would never meet again on this side of the grave, the need for confession was a heavy hand on my heart.

'No!'

The power in his denial startled me, but I was not deterred, despite the fear of what I might see in his face. 'I must. On my soul, I can't let this remain unspoken between us because...'

'No, my dear one.' The force had gone, overlaid with an intense fatigue that I could not combat. 'There is nothing that you need tell me that I do not already know. All that matters is that we loved and that we still love. Sometimes life puts too great a burden on us. Now go. Go to Dartington, my very dear one.'

A final kiss of mouth against mouth.

'You were always, and always will be, the best woman I know.'

And as the door opened, he pushed me through, and closed it himself.

I stood outside the door, palms and forehead resting against the unforgiving wood.

I left Pleshey with no farewells. It would need a miracle to save him, and I did not think I had any recourse to any. All I could do was be obedient and do as John asked. To tell his sons of his glorious reasoning for so foul a crime of treason, and keep possession of Dartington.

Determination carried me back to Westminster.

Only when I was back in my rooms did a tidal wave of guilt thrust me to my knees.

★

1400, Dartington

John is dead.

How does a woman know that the man she loves is dead, that he has taken his last breath? I know it, even though there has been no courier from Henry, no message of vengeful satisfaction from Pleshey. Still I know it in my heart, which continues to beat with the same steady rhythm. How can that be, when the one man it beats for no longer inhabits this earth? I will never see him again. He will never walk across the room to gather me into his arms when he returns from some king's business. He will never ask me what I have been doing that might have set the cat amongst the pigeons.

How long will I be able to recall his smile? He could barely smile at me in that room so redolent of pain and violence at Pleshey. I know I must hold on to my memory of the deep-set corners of his mouth, the gleam of self-awareness in the dark of his eye. I must remember the fall of his hair, the fluid, almost insolent manner of his stride. I must remember for all the years of my life that are left to me.

I love him. I love him despite his temper, his ambitions, his ill-fated choices. I love him because of them, because that is John Holland who wooed me and won me and would not let me go.

Don't tell me that he would have brought my brother to his death. I know it. Don't tell me that he was not worthy of my love. He was, he was! And I know why he made that fatal choice. John's betrayal of his own brother was an ignoble affair that he must put right. I cannot forgive him for his plot of vicious murder, but I can understand. Does he not hold a mirror up to my own soul? I have discovered that we are all capable of betrayal. Its consequences lie within me, every hour, every day. My love for John remains as strong as the day I placed my future in his hands and told him I carried his child.

Death is in the cold dank ground, in the bare trees, frozen into motionless acceptance in these January days. I cannot envisage spring and new life.

I am in cold despair.

I think of Henry, when he was my brother Hal and dear to me. The images of childhood race through my atrophied mind. Henry with a book in his hand, Henry with his armour covered with gilding, with a hawk on his fist, with a new sword, riding at the tournaments with verve and dash. Henry protecting me at the Tower when the rebels broke in. Henry anxious for my happiness. My brother whose affection had been part of my life, unquestionable.

I am estranged from Henry. I have nothing to say to him.

I cannot weep. My heart is a solid stone in my chest. My blood is sluggish. Every step, every movement is an effort.

I have no feelings, nothing. I have been robbed of all my joy, for my love is dead.

★

'You didn't ought to be doing that, mistress.'

'I know it.'

Casting aside the mattock with a hiss of frustration at my clumsy handling of it, I resorted instead to a pair of shears.

'Some would say as you shouldn't be cutting that rosemary at this time of year, mistress,' the gardener persisted.

'And they'd be right about that too. Damn them.'

The edges were blunt, and I was inexpert—when had I ever tackled such physical work in my whole life? —but I continued to wield the shears, to the sad detriment of the shrub, while I was invaded by black despair and even blacker fury. I could barely breathe for the constriction in my throat.

What a fool I was. What an unutterable fool.

'Maybe I'll do it for you, mistress.'

I looked up at the man who tended the gardens and saw my presence in the herbery as an intrusion. And a destructive one at that.

'No you won't. I am not incapable. Go away. And take the children inside with you. It's too cold for them out here.'

I saw them watching their mother, wary of this woman they barely recognised in her woollen skirts and furious application of garden tools. They were all there in a little huddle, except for baby Edward. I could not blame them for keeping their distance.

Attacking a plant of rue—by the Virgin! there would be no rue in my garden! —I reduced it to a few hopeless twigs.

'You need help, mistress.'

'I don't.'

Had I not promised? I had promised and I would do it.

He retreated when I picked up my mattock again, only to lurk behind a bush to keep an eye on the mistress who appeared to have taken leave of her senses.

Taken leave of them? I felt as if every sense I had was hammered into a coffin.

No! Not that!

The denial howled in my head.

Earlier in the day, numbed by shock, I had shut myself away in my chamber, until I realised the futility of that. I could ride out, hunt. I could ride and ride until I was exhausted and my mind blurred with it so that I could sleep and forget. But I would imagine that he was with me, riding beside me as he had done so often. I would hear the hooves of his horse, see the wind lifting his hair, hear his laughter at some comment passed between us. How could I ever ride for pleasure again? I needed an occupation to drain my energies rather than that of my mare. An occupation John would never have undertaken.

When had I ever turned my hand to physical work other than the setting of stitches? Playing the lute. Singing. Dancing. That is what I was made for. But today I needed some back-breaking work that would demand my concentration and my strength.

Yet, the inertia of grief laying its hand on me, I would still have remained shut away in my private chamber, until Alice ran in, a roughly constructed birdcage clutched in her eight-year-old hand. She danced on the spot, holding the occupants high for me to see.

'Look what the chapman has brought. He says they are for me, if we give him a silver coin.'

I stared in horror, seeing myself, in different circumstances, holding a gilded cage of singing finches.

'Take them out!' I shrieked, before I could stop myself.

'But Mother…' Alice's eyes gleamed with quick tears.

'I'll not have them here.'

Taking my daughter by the hand I strode unseeing through the beautiful rooms of the house that John had built, through the kitchens and out into the enclosed courtyard beyond. Once there I knelt beside Alice, taking the cage from her and opening its door, lifting it high to encourage the pair of birds to fly free, which they did. Wiping away my child's tears with the edge of my sleeve, I gave the only explanation I could.

'They did not deserve to be shut in a cage. They will be happy to be free.'

Alice sniffed, not understanding, and in a sense neither did I. All I knew was that I would never again have a pair of singing birds. Nothing to remind me of my treacherous husband's glorious wooing of me. Or my own treachery.

Alice and I continued to kneel in the puddle-ridden courtyard, watching them go.

My household must have thought that I had run mad.

From there, face frozen, I had taken myself into the herbery on this dire January day, simply because I could think of nothing else. My only knowledge of herbs was the use of them to perfume my coffers or produce a healing draught.

What did I know about working in the earth, about cutting and shaping? I had donned garments more suited to physical work, but to what avail? My fingers wept with blisters and my hems were ruined with mud but my anger remained as bitter as the rue I had just eviscerated. My mind lowered as dark as the clouds gathering to presage snow as I recalled John sending me a package of rue.

I rested momentarily on my knees, oblivious to the destruction of my skirts. I thought Henry would pardon him. I thought that in spite of John's inexcusable treason, Henry would use his royal prerogative to grant John a pardon. For my sake. For the love he had for me. And because of the love I had for John. Could not Henry lure John back into the Lancastrian fold with soft words and generosity? My brother would not rob me of the man who meant more to me than my life. His compassion would be overwhelming and he would forgive.

I had held fast to that when my heart was heaviest. Or had I? Had I not always feared the inevitable? Retrieving the shears, running my thumb along the blades, I scowled at the line of blood that appeared. Had I truly believed that Henry would be magnanimous? Gradually learning that generosity was rarely the answer when political power was in the balance, I had come to know the penalty paid by those who played with fire. I knew full well the price to be paid in the interest of alliances and loyalties and political manoeuvrings. I had been a political bride to a child because the alliance was too valuable to be snatched up by someone else.

And Henry. Henry had been banished for his flirtation with the Lords Appellant. Still very young, only on the edge

of the fatal alliance against the King, Henry had been banished and had had to fight for his inheritance. Richard had
had no compassion for him or for my father. And so Henry,
now shouldering the authority of Kingship, had cut down
those who had dared to rise against him. Many would say
he had every right to bring down the power of the law on
the heads of those who plotted insurrection.

Even after that final meeting with John, wretched in despair, I had clung to a futile hope, speeding a letter to Henry,
a final last minute appeal, when I had fled from Pleshey.

To my well-beloved brother Henry,

*You can never accuse me of disloyalty. I do not question your right
to rule or your power to defend your life and that of your sons. I
will always remain your loyal subject.*

*But if you have any love for me, have mercy on John Holland.
Save him from the vengeance of the FitzAlans.*

Your loving sister…

My cheeks were wet. Not tears, my denial continued.
Merely the icy rain that had begun to fall. In desultory fashion I hacked at a clump of decaying foliage that I did not
recognise, but which the rising scents told me was sage.

I stood, oblivious to the gathering wind, for the first
time in my life admitting my loneliness and the need for
a confidante. When had I ever needed the consolation of
a woman's advice. But now, when I was estranged from
everyone, Princess Joan was dead, Katherine was hostile and
retired into widowhood in Lincoln, Philippa in regal splendour in Portugal.

Yet not entirely true. Philippa had written to me, but I
had added it, unread, to the little pile of unopened letters

from her, unable to tolerate her lectures or her pity even if they were doused with love.

Never had I felt so isolated, so alone, so wretched. I had no practice at being alone.

'Well, you had better practise hard now,' I berated myself. 'For who else is there to listen to you?'

Because the reality of my situation had struck as hard as the winter ground under my feet. I could not talk to Henry. Men driven by ambition rarely listened to their womenfolk and Henry, having usurped the crown, had enemies enough to deal with, without having to listen to the demands of his sister. And what could I now demand?

John was dead.

In my damp misery I howled, refusing the warmth of Constance's arms about me as she was driven to give comfort to this mad woman who was her mother.

He had banished me. He had died alone.

I could formulate no plan. No plan at all.

I despised Henry and the Countess of Hereford and Thomas FitzAllan, all in equal measure.

A gust of wind brought the sound of distant hooves clattering into the stable courtyard and for one foolish moment my heart leapt. He had come to me. He had been released after all…

The truth caused me to fling down the shears and cover my face with my hands, for suddenly my own misery was cast into nothingness by the acknowledgement of John's death. He would never come to me again. And what terrible choices he had had to make, standing between his own brother and his wife. How was it possible for a man to determine the direction of his heart when faced with such a dilemma? And I had made it so difficult for him, torn as I was between equally divided loyalties. My choice was no easier than his.

Did I feel guilt?

Yes. Yes. And yes. It seemed to me that I was frozen in a wasteland of unending, unforgiving agony from which there was no escape.

The gardener emerged from his woody seclusion, leading a man I did not know. A herald, as it soon became clear. One of Henry's superbly appointed couriers, tabard gleaming in the dank gloom. Which was warning enough.

Facing him, still on my knees, I dared him to react in any manner to my appearance. Nor did he. He bowed. 'My lady.'

'You have come from the King.'

'Yes, my lady.' His solemn face showed no recognition of my strange state, even when Constance plucked at my shoulder. The rest of the children had vanished.

'And your message? What has the King to say to me?'

'My lord requests that you return to court.'

'And why is that?' Unable to control the bitterness that welled within me. 'Does the King intend to parade me before his loyal courtiers as the wife of a traitor?'

Which he wisely ignored, handing me instead a document heavy with seals and signatures, the red and gold shining against my mud encrusted hands. Perhaps my face was also smeared, but I did not care. Legal, official, the weight of the document made my heart sink.

'Tell me, or do I have to read it?'

'It is to inform you, my lady, of the confiscation of all lands, possessions and properties of John Holland.'

He was not even given the respect of his title. There would be no title, no inheritance for my children. No advantageous marriages, for who would desire a landless child of a proscribed father as mate? John had seen it all. We would be cast as beggars on my brother's charity.

Why have you done this to us, John?

Suddenly I was so angry with him.

And yet inordinately I felt laughter forming in my chest, dispersing my fury, and would have laughed aloud if it could have bypassed the constriction in my throat. For this ground I had been digging, these plants that I had been destroying, no longer belonged to me. All had been taken away. I was homeless, even more bereft than I could have believed. I would have to throw myself on Henry's mercy and be dutiful and dependent on him for the rest of my life.

At last I struggled to my feet, holding the document as if it were a poisoned chalice.

'And to whom does the King gift my lord's properties?' All in all I was proud of the calm tenor of my voice.

'I know not, my lady. The confiscation will first be ratified by parliament when it meets in March. Until then the estates will become royal property.'

'But free for the King to use, to reward those whose loyalty is beyond question.' The Countess of Hereford would be high on his list. And Thomas FitzAlan. I caught a slide of pity in the herald's eye and straightened my spine, snatching at dignity. 'My thanks for your news.'

'I will escort you, my lady.' Yes, there was definitely pity, even as I faced him with disdain. 'There's something else you should know, my lady...'

'Another message from my royal brother?'

'No, my lady.' He inclined his head, not meeting my stare. 'It's not his doing, but you need to be aware, if you're going to London. I wouldn't want it to be a shock for you. As it would...' And, uneasily, compassionately, he told me, yet in deference to my need as I dug my fingers into his arm, spared me nothing in the telling, of the true span of Thomas FitzAlan's revenge.

It was like a blow of a mailed fist to my chest. Dropping the shears, I hitched my skirts, abandoned the herbery to the gardener and Henry's herald, and fled towards the house, every breath difficult, every thought suffused with ultimate horror. Despite the threat of snow, despite my heartsick state that had kept me inert for so long, I packed my coffers and ordered my horse and an escort.

Chapter Fiveteen

Dry-eyed, driven by a raging fury interlaced with fear, I forced myself to travel on, throughout the whole of the following day and night without respite, stopping only at the roadside for bread and wine that I could barely swallow, while all the time in my head shrieked the voice that despite all my efforts I might be too late. I knew the hour and the day when this abomination would be perpetrated. I must be there.

John's inevitable execution, the gloating delight of Thomas FitzAlan, the cold implacability of the Countess, then the stripping away of John's title and lands, all had been a weight that I would bear with all the composure I could summon to my aid. But this—this final, inexorable degradation—drove me to risk my safety on the roads, to honour John at the last, to make this final bid to restore some tiny—some would say worthless—vestige of dignity to my dead love. It would be very little but it would be something.

How could Henry have allowed it?

Nor was I alone in my self-imposed mission.

'I am coming with you. Whatever you say.'

There was a severity in the dark gaze. Constance, at eleven years, had all the obstinacy that had driven me at that age.

'You will remain here, Constance.'

'I will not. This is no longer our home. Richard, as the eldest, will remain and order the young ones about until it is decided where we will live. But for now, I will go with you because you should not have to do this alone.'

There, in my daughter's insistence, was John's clear, unadorned logic that almost brought me again to my knees. So she had been listening.

'And who else is there to go with you?' she added. 'I have already packed what I need. I am ready.'

For the briefest of moments we eyed each other across one of the half packed panniers, Richard standing at Constance's shoulder in silent agreement. Travelling fast with a small escort, I did not need the added burden of my daughter, but her mouth had shut like a wolf trap, her brow furrowing with her determination so that she resembled even more closely her father at his most recalcitrant, and because I did not have the energy to resist, I had given in. There would be a refuge for her in London before I kept the dread appointment. She must not be there.

It was as if she read my mind.

'I will be at your side. Whatever it is that calls you to London, you will not face this alone.'

I did not argue, but I would not allow her this experience.

Now as we rode through the streets of the city towards the Thames, time was running out for me, and there was nowhere I could leave her in safety, unless in the sanctuary of some church. I could not think or plan ahead, my mind stunned with what awaited us. In the end I had no choice but to keep her with me, praying silently that my daughter's Plantagenet blood, and the strength of will of Princess Joan, would come to her aid. She was too young for such a cruel lesson as this.

And here we were, beside London Bridge before dawn, before the predictable crowds gathered.

'Wait here,' I said, pushing a little ahead of my escort, including Henry's herald who had refused to allow me to come alone, onto the bridge itself, clenching my reins in freezing fingers.

'I did not intend that you should be here, my lady,' he grunted, the herald's mount keeping step.

'Would I stay away? You do not know me.'

'I know you for a brave woman.'

'Then pray God my courage holds true.'

I knew it would not be long. Exhausted we might be, our mounts foundering beneath us, but we had arrived in time. My escort shuffled restlessly when I waved them back. Not long now.

For a half hour, while the winter sky lightened imperceptibly to a livid grey, we sat our horses and shivered, Constance insisting on keeping this strange vigil at my side. And then the sound I was waiting for, the striking of shod hooves against stone. More than one horse. As if in some strange anticipation, mist rolled over the surface of the river, coating the streets in rime, hiding the opposite bank where, from the north, the horses and their riders drew closer.

They came to a well-disciplined halt, four of them.

Automatically I reached out to take Constance's hand and held tight, dismay building fast in my chest, berating myself for what I had allowed.

'You should not be here,' I said, my voice suddenly loud in the mist, until I forced it into a harsh whisper. 'I should not have allowed it. It is not fitting…'

'Nor is it for you. But if you must, so will I.'

'Do you know?'

'I do now.' I could see tears spangling her cheeks and knew they were mirrored on mine. 'You should have told me.'

'Perhaps…'

'But you tried to protect me from seeing my father as the traitor he is.'

'He is not!'

'Thus the world sees him.'

'I know. But I would not have you remember him like this.'

'I remember him as a father who laughed with us and let my brother claim victory over him with sword and lance. I will be brave.' Her glance was keen. 'I'll not demean you. Or his memory.'

And I managed to smile, a bright, clear smile at my redoubtable daughter who carried her father's blood so valiantly.

'Then we will be brave together, as we try to prevent this travesty. But I think we will fail.'

Three of the men, now obvious in their familiar livery, emerged through the mist into the centre of the bridge. The white swan of the de Bohuns shimmered as if touched by magic. The livery of the Countess of Hereford.

'It is not right,' I whispered.

'No,' Constance murmured her mind running in tandem with mine. 'It's not right at all. It should be our own Holland livery. Could they not even give him this respect?'

Her maturity astounded me. But of course they would not: John had lost all such rights, all claims to dignity and recognition, when he had lifted his sword against the King. For Constance, I must be her shining example, not a whimpering creature, awash with useless emotion.

'We will be dignified as Plantagenet women and do what we can.'

One of the men dismounted. Two kept watch despite the silence and the shrouding mist, one nodding in our direction but making no move towards us. Who would see resistance from two anonymous cloaked and hooded female figures? As for the royal herald, he would be expected to heartily applaud their actions. Then the man who had dismounted was un-strapping a pannier from his saddle.

I dismounted, walked forward. Slowly. I would not retreat from this. This was why I was here. My mind cried out. *john, my love. I was with you in spirit even though you forbade me. I am here now.*

'Halt.' The command rang out and I halted. 'Go away, lady.'

'I will not until I have fulfilled my task.'

'You have no task here.'

I continued until I was within arm's length, aware of Constance behind me when her heels clacked on the wood. I spun round.

'Go back.'

'I will not.'

I could hear a hoarse rasp in her breathing, even as every one of my senses was focused on the pannier in the man's hands.

'Give that to me,' I said.

He grunted, a disbelieving laugh. 'Who are you?'

I pushed back my hood. 'I am Elizabeth of Lancaster.'

He exchanged glances with his companions.

'I am Countess of Huntingdon. One time Duchess of Exeter. Sister to your King.'

The man's features settled into a harder line, or so it seemed in the growing light, as if he had been warned, but he inclined his head with some respect.

'Give me that,' I repeated.

'I've orders to follow.'

'Whose orders? Who gave the order for this?'

'The King's orders.'

'The King will not punish you. He will not know if you give it to me.'

'So what do I tell King Henry when it disappears?' The man's teeth showed in a fierce grin. 'That some passing thief purloined it? That it was spirited away by some ghostly apparition, or carried off by a starving gutter cur?'

'I care not.' I held out my hand. 'If you have any mercy in you.'

I would beg.

'No, lady. On the spikes at London Bridge, he said. On the spikes it goes.' He grunted. 'Or the Countess said. Same thing.'

It was indeed. She would take her instructions from Henry, but she was not beyond pursuing her own needs. Perhaps she had listened to her nephew, Thomas. How bitter was her revenge. The words, spoken so callously, forced me to face the truth of what I had come to see, and for a moment I closed my eyes. I did not want this.

'It's best if you're not here, mistress. And the young girl.'

Mistress! He had reduced me. The wife of a traitor had no worth. As I felt Constance's hand tug on my cloak, I drew in a raw breath, aware of the beginnings of a little crowd of townsfolk, voices carrying with excitement that would enrich the boredom of their day. Would I indeed flee, powerless as I was, leaving my mission incomplete?

'Let me look,' I said.

He shook his head.

'Let me see him. I'll make no trouble for you. One final time, on your mercy. Then I'll go and let you complete your work.'

He shrugged. In the end he cared not, as long as he could carry out his orders and leave, or go to a tavern with his companions to drink after their long journey and forget this unpleasant outcome with a woman who pestered them and should know better. Yet he had no heart for an argument with me.

Before I could even prepare myself, he thrust his hand

into the covered pannier and lifted out what I had come for. The head of John Holland.

I breathed slowly, in and out, aware of choking down a little cry of grief.

And then I forced myself to stand, to look, refusing to miss one detail, except for the jagged rawness where the axe had done its terrible job. I took in the fall of hair, bloody and matted where it had dried, filthy with dust, sparkling with the salt in which it had been packed. The closed eyes. The wax-like face, all expression drained except for the line dug deep between his brows that even death could not erase. The lips pale and thinned, white as the rime on the bridge supports. John had not died at peace. All the love and life and fervour that had carried him through the years of life had been cruelly obliterated.

That I had expected—the imprint of suffering and of a violent and brutal death—but not the ravages of crows and other birds intent on carrion. How his beauty had been disfigured, marred by beak and claw, and I gasped, nausea rising swiftly, making me step back, only stopping when Constance's grip moved from my cloak to my arm where it tightened. I felt her turn her head away but I couldn't, even as I took her in my arms and pressed her face against my shoulder.

'Don't look if it hurts you. Don't remember him like this. It is enough that you are here with me,' I murmured and pushed her behind me.

'Holy Virgin, intercede for him,' I heard her whisper.

And with my daughter's show of grace, my courage returned, and turning back, I touched him, smoothing the dust from his damaged cheek, pushing aside the wayward hair, so limp and lifeless. With the edge of my cloak I tried ineffectually to wipe the dried blood from his cheek.

'How can this be?' I asked.

'The Countess ordered the exposure on a pike at Pleshey, my lady.'

I had been reinstated. Perhaps he was impressed that I had not fallen to the floor in a faint or screamed my agony.

'John…' I whispered.

'Go home, lady. Go home to your children. Remember him when he was alive. If you choose to remember a traitor at all.'

'He was no traitor to me.'

My love. My dear love. How could I not stop you before it came to this?

Stony faced, I looked up at the spikes where the heads of criminals and miscreants were exposed. I would not weep, even though birds were already hovering in anticipation, coming to land on the parapet.

'I will fight for your title, your inheritance,' I repeated my previous oath even more fervently. 'I will fight for your lands. I swear that I will. I will give Henry no peace until he restores what is the rightful inheritance of our children.'

Drawing up my hood, I wrapped the cloak tightly around me as if to curb my shivering that was nothing to do with the cold, then I turned away. I could not watch this final horror. Yet how could I leave when there, at the end of the bridge, was a face I knew, a man who had come to watch the final disposition of the traitor's head. And to gloat.

Constance's hand remained hard on my arm.

'Where now?' Constance asked.

And I was brought back to my senses.

'To the King, of course.'

To Henry, because he was my only hope.

★

I had not seen Henry since the day the air had snapped and sparked with our temper and I had marched from his presence, vowing never to see him, never to speak with him again. I would never humble myself before him, arrogant King that he had become, and beg for anything ever again.

How futile some vows, how empty. After what I had just seen on the bridge in the misty half-light, and knowing what I had left behind there, I strode into Henry's presence as if I had seen him only yesterday. He might refuse me. As King he had that power. But I would not make it easy for him. I was his sister and he had a duty to hear me. All I had left in the world was my Plantagenet pride, but that was all I needed in my demand for justice. I could not save John's life but I could argue the case for fairness and rightness, and because every feeling in my body seemed to be dead, every argument would be from my head, not from my heart. I did not think that I would ever weep or laugh again. There would be no emotion in this meeting.

And that would be a good thing. There had been far too much emotion between us.

As I stalked through the rooms and anterooms towards one of his audience chambers at Westminster, pre-empting any announcement by his chamberlain who fussed at my side, my path crossed that of Edward of Rutland, coming in the opposite direction.

'What are you doing here?' I snapped. The last time I had seen him was in close company with John, heads together in a conspiracy. Or perhaps he had been with Henry when I had been told of John's capture. Had not John asked about him? It did not matter. Here he was, silk-clad and beautiful.

'I could ask you the same thing, Cousin,' he replied, but did not stop to hear my answer. 'The King is in a particularly good mood today.' His voice died away with a light chuckle. 'He's received good news of your late husband…'

I had no time for Edward and his opinions, for there was Henry, turning his head in expectation as I entered. His whole body stilled. It was not me he was waiting for, as was made clear when he turned fully to face me, away from his magnates and bishops, with an expression that might have been carved from stone.

'Elizabeth.'

'My lord.'

I might be excruciatingly formal but did not curtsy. Nor, even though we were within the space of a hand-clasp, did we make the sign of greeting. There was no familial welcome in Henry's eye. But then, neither was there in mine.

'You have been absent from my court,' he said, almost an accusation. 'What brings you here now?'

Did I want this conversation in such a public arena? It did not matter. Nothing mattered but the one terrible image that filled my mind.

'John Holland is dead,' I said.

'So I am informed.'

Henry showed no satisfaction, no pleasure in it. But it was done and by his orders.

'Will you receive me, the widow of a traitor?'

I was in no mood to be conciliatory. The sight I had left on London Bridge had destroyed any finer sisterly feelings, for there, at the end, out of the mist, had been a face I detested, a man I would have hounded to his death for what he had done, seated arrogantly on his magnificent horse, glorying in the culmination of his deliberate campaign. For a long moment we had stared at each other, before, rejecting me as a woman of no importance, he directed his attention to the matter in hand.

It had taken Constance's hand on my arm to drag me away.

'I will receive you,' Henry replied.

His tone was light but I thought he had aged. I supposed that plots against a man's life could do that. Perhaps I, too, showed signs of the passing of the years. Grief and anger could leave their mark.

'What is it that you want of me?' Cool, watchful, there was no anger in him today. I supposed that he could afford to be even-tempered for the rebellion was over. 'If I can heal the rift between us, I will. I have no wish to be estranged from you, Elizabeth.'

And so, needing no further invitation to air my grievances, I began, like a man of law.

'My husband's lands are declared forfeit.'

'As they must be.'

'My children are disinherited.'

'It is a risk that Holland took.'

Nothing that I did not expect.

'So you would have my children landless as well as father-less. I am here to ask, as your sister, for restitution.'

'I have not changed my mind, Elizabeth. Treason has its penalties.'

'And I ask you to reconsider, Henry. I ask for royal clemency.'

How many times had I been forced to put aside my pride and petition for John? My throat was raw with it, my belly sore. But this would be the final time and I had vowed that I would.

'I want you to recognise the man who was once the most loyal of friends to you and our father. I want you to recognise the man who once saved you from certain death, and restore his titles and inheritance. I beg that you, for all that you have been to each other in the past, will restore his titles and inheritance.'

'No, Elizabeth.'

'You forgave John Ferrour, the soldier who rescued you, even though he was part of the Earls' Revolt. You released him and pardoned him because he shut you in a cupboard in the Tower of London and saved your life.' I saw Henry blink, that I should know of it. 'Why can you not restore the inheritance of the man who gave Ferrour the order?'

But Henry had his wits about him. 'Because Ferrour was a soldier who followed orders. Holland was the instigator of the plot to cut me down. There's a vast difference, Elizabeth.'

I read the implacable will, the pride in his own inheritance, the sheer strength of which I had always been aware, so that it was as if I faced my father again, with all the arrogance of a royal prince on his shoulders, braced against me. Even his eyes were hard, like agates, as the Duke's had been when his will was crossed. Today Henry was very much Duke of Lancaster, and I saw that my plea fell on stony ground. Perhaps he was even more King of England in his cold enforcement of justice.

And then the door of the audience chamber opened, the chamberlain approaching, and with him the man I had last seen on the bridge, who now walked to bow to Henry with the sleek smile of a snake in anticipation of a reward for a job well done. It was he who had brought John's head to London. It was this man for whom Henry was waiting. Here was my enemy at Henry's side with all the confidence of a chosen counsellor, as I knew he would be. Thomas FitzAlan, friend to Henry, who would soon be restored as Earl of Arundel.

'It is done, sire,' he said. 'The traitor Holland is dead.'

Henry's reply was brusque. 'I am aware. You did not receive my orders?'

'Sire?' FitzAlan's smile faded, his expression becoming a perfection of misunderstanding.

'That Holland was to be escorted here to London, to the Tower.'

All my attention was grasped by this one statement. FitzAlan was unperturbed.

'No, sire. The Countess and I received no such direction.'

Henry's lips thinned. 'Then I must thank you for the speed with which you dispatched an enemy of the peace of my kingdom.'

'Indeed, Sire. The mob was most insistent that death was the only penalty.'

'And I don't suppose you worked over-hard to change their mind.'

'No, Sire.'

Henry managed a regal smile. 'I will speak with you later. You will receive your reward.' And then to me, with no smile. 'We will talk privately.'

'We certainly will!' I managed as he gripped my arm and drew me away from FitzAlan and the curious magnates and clerics. I wrenched away from him, yet thumped my fist against his shoulder. So much for lack of emotion. 'You changed your mind.'

'Yes.' An infinitesimal pause. 'And no.'

'Why?'

'Because my damned sister looked at me as if I were vermin beneath her feet.' And here was emotion too. Henry's eyes were alight with it, a strange mix of irritation and compassion. 'I would have imprisoned him for you. I might have regretted it, to leave him alive to plot again, but I sent the order. Does that satisfy you?'

'Oh, Hal!' He had cared after all, but doubts still swam in my mind and I could not order my thoughts into line. 'Do you believe FitzAlan? That your orders did not reach Pleshey in time?'

'No. He took it upon himself.'

'And will you punish him? For rank disobedience?'

'No.'

No of course he would not. Did I believe my brother? Here was another brutal lesson for me in the reality of court politics. Henry might have ordered that John be spared and brought under his own jurisdiction, but he would not punish the FitzAlans who had effectively rid him of a man he could not trust. Henry would not mourn the outcome. Even better, John's blood was not on Henry's hands. Here, with a level of cunning that must be open to a clever king, my brother was confident enough to return my gaze without difficulty.

I could detect no guilt in him.

I knew all about guilt. I knew too much about it.

Fleetingly, I wondered if Henry would manage the death of Richard in similar fashion, so that others would be blamed, but the outcome would be to Henry's benefit. Probably he would. Here before me were the workings of the mind of a pragmatic King rather than a loving brother. For the first time in our lives I thought Henry to be less than honest.

'Have you nothing to say?' he demanded.

I felt empty, unable to thank him as he clearly expected, but I knew what it was I wanted and what I could achieve.

'I have this to say. John's head is displayed on London Bridge at this very moment,' I accused. 'Is that by your consent?'

He sighed. 'Sit with me, Elizabeth.'

'Not until I have justice. You have refused the titles and land for my children. I want John's head. I want it taken down from the bridge, to be restored and buried with his body. And I want it done today before further carrion ravages.'

'Why should I?' Henry's face was set. 'We have had this

argument before. A man who turns against his King knows the risks. His head will be exhibited to put fear into the hearts of all men who would rise up against their anointed king. Why should I make an exception?'

'Because the choices were too difficult for him to make,' I replied without pause. 'How impossibly hard it is for a man to abandon his brother. His heart was raw with it. I know it is hard for you,' I pursued, swallowing against the knot in my throat. 'But have mercy. I have been there, to the bridge. I have seen what they have done.'

'No, Elizabeth…' He looked at me aghast.

'Yes. I was there.' And with a little shrug of despair I allowed my emotion full rein at last, so that I did argue from my heart, the words spilling over us. 'Who could show him that final respect but me? There is no one to bear witness to his passing. But, in the end, I could not, coward that I am. I could not stand there and watch them put his head on a spike for the carrion to destroy. But *he* could.' I flung out my arm in the direction of the young man who had wreaked havoc in my life. 'FitzAlan could, in vicious revenge. Surely you are better than that. In God's name, Henry…' I dragged in a breath. 'Because I am your sister. Because it hurts my heart to see what is become of us. Because I ask it of you. For all that we have lived through and experienced together. Because of that I ask you to give me John's head.'

Hands fisted on hips, Henry looked over towards the little group of magnates. What was he thinking? That it would be a mistake for such a show of apparent weakness?

'Henry! Would it matter so much to you? For me it would be of greater value than this.' And I flourished my hand, where our father's great ruby flashed on my knuckle. 'You were not always so intransigent.'

And there was the faintest warmth of a smile.

'How can I refuse?'

Still I was uncertain. 'I don't know. But you might.'

'I will not.' He took hold of my hand with its great jewel and kissed my fingers. 'This is what I will do. I will grant you restoration of Holland's head. I will have it taken to Pleshey, to be buried in the church there, with his body.'

I drew in a breath at the magnificence of it. 'FitzAlan will not agree. Or the Countess.'

'It will not be for either to decide.' Still he held my hand. 'It will be sent to the Master of the collegiate church at Pleshey, under my seal, and they will give your husband a seemly burial. Will that suffice?' His grip tightened. 'Let this be the end of it, Elizabeth. Let him be buried and rest in as much peace as his soul can find. I doubt it will be much.'

'I will pray for his soul,' as some measure of relief was spreading through me at last.

'Of course you will.'

'What about me? My children? Will you restore the land that is theirs by right?'

But of course he remained adamant. 'No. It is confiscated. It is how the game is played out, as you well know. You are free to make your home with me, and I will give you an income to compensate for your loss. I cannot have my sister wearing rags. Just look at you.' His eyes flickered over my travel-worn garments, but any humour was gone when they returned to my face. 'You should not have gone to the bridge.'

'I had to be there. You should know that. I loved him. As you loved Mary.'

A shadow passed over Henry's face. 'How can you compare the two? Mary was all goodness. Holland had a soul forged in hell.'

'He was driven by loyalty to his brother.'

'He was driven by loyalty to his own interests.'

'We will never agree, will we? My heart is broken.'

His smile was wry. 'It will mend soon enough.' He kissed my cheek, and then the other. 'Let that be an end to it. You are my dearly loved sister and I will care for you.'

I did not wish to be cared for. Had I not all the resources to order my own life? But I would go back to court. I would fight for the rights of my children and I would try to live in equanimity with Henry because he was my own blood. I would raise my children to honour their father, for whom blood mattered more than life, who was ambitious and hot-tempered but who was also a man of surprising integrity. I would raise them to honour him and respect the King their uncle. I could do no more.

What of me?

All I had left was my pride and a deep raging guilt that would stay with me until death. I discovered there were traces of John's blood on my fingers. It seemed horribly fitting.

As I was halfway across the chamber, Henry's voice stopped me.

'It is my intention to base my household and the children

in Eltham. The palace pleases me. Come to Eltham. Come and live with me there, and we will try to rebuild what we have destroyed.'

Obviously an olive branch, if to my mind little more than a twig. Because I could think of no better plan, and I lacked the energy to refuse the gesture, that is what I did.

*

Richard was dead, at Pontefract. My first cousin, the man I had known from boyhood, had tolerated, sometimes despised, sometimes pitied, was dead. The boy who had been crowned with gold and anointed with holy oil was no more.

It came as no shock to me. No one spoke of it but every soul at Henry's court had anticipated Richard's demise. Nor did it touch me much, beyond a brush of regret, a sadness that his youthful promise had ended in imprisonment and an end that might or might not have been self-inflicted. Grief and tears were no longer within the scope of my emotions. I had expended far too much sorrow, and now felt as dry as a husk at autumn's end.

We heard that he had deliberately starved himself, refusing all food and water and taking to his bed, willing himself to death since, having lost his crown, he had nothing to live for. I did not know if I believed this. It did not sound like the Richard I recalled, even at his most wayward, and said as much to Henry.

'Why not?' Henry was unimpressed. 'He was refusing to eat when I took him prisoner at Flint Castle. He said he feared he would be poisoned. Whatever the cause, he's dead and, if I'm honest, his absence is a weight off my mind.' He returned my stare. 'There was never any love lost between us. Don't worry.' His voice was harsh. 'I will see that he is buried with honour. If I could ensure Holland's burial with some dignity, I can do the same for Richard.'

I was not convinced.

'Do you feel no remorse?' I persisted as I stood beside Henry in St Paul's Cathedral where Richard's body, brought from Pontefract, at last lay in state. My royal cousin's face was white and thin in death, at odds with the thickly embroidered pall that Henry had caused to be placed on the coffin. The white harts with their gilded collars brought back memories of happier times but now merely appeared doleful.

'Remorse? For a self-inflicted death?'

And that was the end of it, apart from paying chantry priests to say a thousand masses for the repose of Richard's soul and the removal of his body to King's Langley. I knew it was not a subject for discussion. If Richard had died from foul means, my brother was distancing himself from all responsibility. It was not a new idea to me, nor the fact that Henry had grown beyond me, the weight of his new authority constructing a bulwark between us.

I did what I could. I offered prayers for Richard's soul, and in the end I wept a little, but whether for Richard or for Henry I could not say.

'You were right, John,' I murmured against my clasped hands as I knelt alone in Henry's chapel at Eltham. 'I can't condone the death you plotted for Henry and his sons, but you saw the future well enough. Richard's death was inevitable. You could not have saved him.'

Silence walled me in. There was no sense of John to comfort me.

'Forgive me, John. Forgive me for everything.'

If I hoped to feel a sense of peace, it did not come to me.

Chapter Sixteen

June 1400, York

'I suppose that I am summoned here for the sole purpose of your keeping an eye on me.' I might have donned my public face of gracious enjoyment, but my voice had the edge of an executioner's axe.

'Yes. Why else?'

Henry, hair ruffled by a flirting breeze, was exhibiting a whole tapestry of irritation, although not necessarily with me, except that I was the nearest target for his ill temper. And I could see his justification. Who better to be recipient of Henry's mounting fury? Here I sat, a widowed sister with questionable loyalties, recently released from an ill-matched union with a traitor.

'Do you expect me to behave in some outrageous manner? Perhaps to wed the first comely man I see, regardless of his allegiances?' I asked with a winsome and entirely false smile.

'You might just. If only to spite me. You've done it before, after all.'

The deep friendship that had once flourished was harder to re-establish than we had imagined. A member of Henry's household, chiefly at Eltham, since January, I suffered from growing boredom and permanent grief. Henry, sound of judgement, solid of stature at thirty-three years, was beset with problems and short of patience. Perhaps it was time for me to show a little magnanimity.

'I am here to support you,' I said.

'And so magnificently clad.'

'Are we not here to make an impression?'

Smoothing the sun-warmed miniver that lined my over-sleeves, I yawned, raising my hand to shield my eyes from the sun at what was only the beginning of a very long after-noon, and fidgeted with the little ivory hand-fan that Henry had given me in the days when I was in his favour, brought back from his journey to the East. My women, equally rest-less, chatted and pointed, encouraging me to participate in their air of festivity. At least it would start soon. The herald had donned his pleated tabard, sweat mantling his brow at the weight of it in this heat, and was hefting his trumpet, merely waiting for the royal command to blast the combat-ants into action. I remembered the days when I could barely sit still, so great was my excitement. I remembered the days when...

I closed my eyes, except that I could see the scene painted on my inner lids. I had seen it so often before. I had seen it when it mattered that the knight of my choice rode to victory. When John, my beloved John, ruled supreme in the lists and I, clothed in bright silks and garlanded with flowers and jewels, could award the wreath of glory to the man who owned my heart.

It did not matter now. Nothing mattered.

The trailing skirts of my houppelande might be opulent, the embroidered blue and gold vibrant in the clear light, my hair plaited into a caul under a light veil as fashion dictated, but my spirit remained in the blackest of mourning, as if my thoughts were enclosed in a deep well. The six months since John's murder—for that is how I would always see it—had done nothing to lift the cloud that shrouded every thought. I was here at York, only under sufferance because my brother demanded it. Henry was doing a lot of demanding of late, but I thought that he was not without compassion for me.

'It would help if you at least looked interested, Elizabeth.'

'I will look interested when you will agree to restore my son's lands and titles.'

Henry grunted in exasperation. 'When will you tire of asking for the impossible?'

'Never!' Nor would I. It would be my life's work. My fingers tightened on the fragile handle, so that I handed it to one of my women. It would be regretful if I broke it. There was of course a limit to Henry's compassion. Clad in regal splendour for the occasion with velvet and ermine, Henry, determined to put on a good show in spirit and ceremonial, angled an unmistakable warning in my direction, his eyes fierce. 'It would be a blessing for us all if you appeared to be enjoying the celebration of what will be a notable coup against the Scots.'

Enjoy this display of arms, arranged purely to keep the knightly contingent of Henry's army content through swordplay and brutal force? It was in my mind that I would never find enjoyment in my life ever again, until the day of my miserable death.

'Well, I am not.'

'I recall the days when you loved the drama of it all.'

Uncomfortably, his thought mirrored mine. I recalled the days when John rode with such style, when his smile, as he received the prize could creep in and steal my heart. I remembered when the golden lions on his banners drew admiration from all. Now the banners no longer flew and I did not want to be here. I shivered as a chill breeze from the north whispered over my skin.

Much as the chill overtures from the Scots had cast a blight on Henry's ambitions.

We were in York, complete with a vast army and all the necessary accoutrements for an invasion, to persuade the Scots to make a lasting peace. Faced with a hostile France on one side, on the other a palpable unease in England after the Revolt of the Earls, Henry determined to secure his northern border. The Scots were tardy in approaching the negotiating table, but Henry hoped his military presence in York would speed the feet of the negotiators.

'I do not see that my interest or otherwise will make any difference to the outcome of these negotiations,' I said.

'That's because you're thinking with your emotions, rather than your head. Before God, Elizabeth, you have lived long enough at court to know the value of a smile and an open hand to win favour.'

I shrugged with less than elegance. 'The decision of the Scots will not be influenced by my sitting at your side, but I will do it,' I snapped. 'I will smile on your knights, Henry. I will pray for the success of your venture. But don't expect any depth of enthusiasm. I don't want to be here.'

'So where do you want to be?'

It was a question I could not answer. I did not know.

Henry gestured and the herald blew the summons. The knights began to muster.

'Smile, Elizabeth.'

Still I did not, fixing my gaze on the armour, glinting hotly, but as I sensed Henry frowning at me, I turned to meet a distinctly speculative stare.

'What?' I said. The speculation seemed to be very particular

'Nothing.'

'I think you've some plan in mind that I will not like.'

'I have no plans but to keep my army commanders from either attacking each other or going home out of sheer boredom.' Henry took my hand in his and drew me close, to plant a brotherly kiss on my cheek, murmuring in my ear in a deliberate distraction from the political to the personal:

'When did you not enjoy the prowess of a young knight in battle?'

'I am too old to admire young knights in battle—or old ones, for that matter.'

'You are never too old. Unless you would wish your-self into an early grave.' His fingers tightened around mine. 'Think of the future, Elizabeth, not of the past. The time for mourning is over. Holland has been dead for six months. There has been too much death.'

Did I not know it?

'I know your hurt. Take what pleasure you can from the day. It is important to me that the day goes well. Will you help me?'

And my heart went out to him, recognising the request he would have made from Mary if she had lived. Except that he would not have needed to ask. Mary, soft-hearted Mary, would have known his needs and responded with a loving heart. He was missing her as much as I was suffering from my own loss. It was six years since her death, and for a moment I saw that he too wished it could have been his loving Mary who was seated at his side, dispensing her goodwill on all.

'You should wed again,' I said, before I thought. Henry might not like me treading in his personal affairs. I knew him much less well than I once had. Being King had given him a gloss of power, of battle-hardened authority, that built a barrier between him and his subjects, but he did not seem to mind and his smile became the same grin I now saw on his son Thomas's face.

'I know I should. And who's to say I won't? So should you.'

'Never. I will not wed again.'

And his face softened. 'Now that would be a great loss for some worthy knight. But since we are both bereft, we will work together to make this country strong and secure. Won't we?'

I could not reject his overtures. He was my brother and he needed me. The bloody deeds of the past were not all of his doing.

'Yes, Henry. We will.'

And at last, as a good sister should, I set myself to look as if I were enjoying the clash of weapons, the straining bodies, the magnificent horseflesh. But I did not like the idea of a worthy knight in my bed. I did not like the idea of any knight at all.

★

The tournament began. In a concerted will to defeat the boredom of a long wait while diplomacy took its endless time of discussion and counter-discussion, the knights and their entourages set to with an enthusiasm. Hanging about was not good for discipline, nor was an uncertain outcome. This feat of arms would drain excess energies, allow the English knights the satisfaction of victory or the humiliation of defeat, and give the combatants something to talk about in their ale cups rather than the stalemate of the Scottish negotiations. I had to admit to Henry's good policy.

Retrieving my little fan, plying it briskly, I relaxed into laughter and comment as England's finest soldiery demonstrated its prowess. This was not the ostentation of my grandfather's tournaments when he, the old King, had fought with his knights, masquerading in velvet and feathers. This was a makeshift event, Henry on the brink of war and short of money. But it had an air of colour and festivity and as such was to be enjoyed.

The storm cloud lifted infinitesimally from around my heart.

With casual interest I began to note who had come to

show their skills, picking out a helm that I recognised, a heraldic emblem fluttering bravely, a particular jousting horse. The lions and *fleur de lys* of the Beauforts, the azure lion of the Percy family that Henry was carefully cultivating. The royal red and gold and blue of Henry's two eldest sons, Henry and Lionel. One day my sons would shine at such a contest. Provocatively, since I no longer had claim on it, I had left my children surrounded by their own household of chaplain, governors and nurses at Dartington...

And my breath caught. There. Another lion, rampant and gilded, gleaming in the bright sunshine.

I should have expected it, but strangely I had not. Now I found my breathing shallow, my heart thudding hard beneath the soft folds of hot velvet as I worked to preserve an expression of disinterest. I had managed, without difficulty, to avoid this creature, but there he was before me, all glamour in his father's gilded armour, proudly astride a bay stallion, larger than life. Thomas FitzAlan, now Earl of Arundel and restored to the FitzAlan inheritance with all its potential for power as an accepted associate of the King.

'You cannot avoid him for ever, Elizabeth.'

Henry had seen the direction of my hostility.

'Not when you show such favour to him.'

No, I could not avoid him, but neither could I prevent a leap of pure joy when, the contest underway, the new Earl was efficiently dislodged from his saddle and, in one to one combat, beaten to his knees by a well-aimed sword in the hand of some nameless knight. I had no compassion for his lack of years at nineteen. I would have had his head hacked from his body. When he was helped limping from the field, I watched him go, hatred masked by a bland face.

'How can you not despise him?' I asked.

'I cannot afford to despise him. I cannot afford to despise anyone. The FitzAlans have lineage and breeding. They are too potentially powerful to have them estranged from my court.'

I looked across to where the knight who had bested FitzAlan was catching his breath before launching again into the fray. I did not know him, nor did I recognise his banner. A lion rampant, ducally crowned, with a border *bezantee*, dramatic in black and red with a golden star on its shoulder. Silently wishing him well, my eye moved on, then returned as he took his sword from his squire and strode back to pit himself against one of the Percy faction. Unlike FitzAlan, his armour was plain and well-worn, no gilding here, the dents catching the sun to refract into glints of light as he remounted.

And again my breathing was compromised but in quite a different manner.

There it was, the same skill, the same grace that had characterised John Holland; a fluid deportment, a perfect co-ordination between hand and eye that brought him victory against any knight who opposed him. Agile, fleet-footed, there was no one to compare with this unknown knight. It could be John, restored to all his old inimitable prowess.

I took a deep breath. This was beyond foolishness, to be so moved by an ability to thrust and parry, to disarm, before clasping hands with the beaten foe in recognition of the fallen man's courage. It was not John. It would never be John again.

My fan had fallen still in my lap.

I berated myself again, my cheeks flushing in the heat as I realised that I had been regarding the knight with the rampant lion for the last handful of minutes, and at last my breathing began to settle and common sense dealt a healthy blow to my demeanour. This faceless man did not attract me. There was no obvious similarity between him and John, neither in stature nor in manner of fighting. This man was taller, slighter, fighting with an elegant composure, far different from John's magnificent aggression. Even though he wielded the great sword with impressive talent, this knight could not wound my heart as John had done.

And then there he was, this unknown knight, urging his mount into a controlled canter towards our pavilion.

'Who is he?' For want of something to say. And because, in truth, I was interested in a man who could exhibit such skill.

'John Cornewall. A knight from the west country,' Henry replied.

'I don't know him.'

'He's the son and heir of younger son, so out to make a name for himself. He's a man I would have at my side.'

'You would have every man at your side,' I remarked, recalling FitzAlan.

'What King would not? Besides, I like Cornewall's style in combat.'

The knight, his armour even more worn than I had anticipated, hauled his mount to an impatient standstill before us and, still helmed, bowed before me.

'I would carry your guerdon, my lady.'

A clear voice, light of timbre, even from the depths of the unadorned jousting-helm.

I smiled politely, as I must. 'I do not know you, sir.'

'Here is my emblem, my lady.' He gestured to his squire who rode up with the emblazoned shield.

'But I would not give my guerdon to a faceless knight, sir.'

Upon which he removed his helm and handed it to the squire.

'I am Sir John Cornewall, my lady. I would be honoured to fight in your name and carry your honour to victory in the lists. If my face is pleasing to you.'

Any lingering thought that this knight bore even the smallest similarity to John Holland was instantly obliterated. Sir John Cornewall was a young man untouched by hard experience, his eyes the palest of blue, like a winter sky touched by frost; his hair, already plastered to his skull with damp heat, had the fairness of flax as it curled around his ears, while his skin was pale with an unlined smoothness. His mouth was well-sculpted but unsmiling, his nose blade-narrow. A handsome face, all in all, if austerity and rigid self-control was pleasing. And there was the soft accent, from the west, that brushed my senses. Deep within me, I acknowledged an attraction to this man with such perfect manners, an interest that any woman might feel towards a handsome knight, even if her heart was dead.

'My lady?' I realised I had been staring. 'I would fight for you,' he repeated, 'if you would honour me.'

And I felt Henry's elbow nudge me where my arm rested against the carved chair he had provided for my use.

'Of course, Sir John. The honour is mine.' How very difficult it was to use that name, but I did, and on a whim, struggling to slide it over my knuckle, I held out a ring that Henry had given me at some past New Year's Gift Giving. 'God give you victory, sir.'

He bowed again, removed his gauntlet and slid the ring onto his smallest finger. Then, replacing gauntlet and helm, he took his place with the rest of the knights.

I tried hard not to allow my eyes to follow him.

'That was generous,' Henry murmured under cover of my women's chatter. 'A veil or one of your endless knots of ribbon would have done just as well.'

'Is he not worth more than a veil?' I asked languidly augmenting the breeze with my little fan. 'Besides, I wager that he will win, and I'll get it back.'

'Are you so sure? I think he'll keep it.' Henry did not look at me but seemed to be inspecting the disposition of officials on the field.

So I watched this man whose allegiance Henry would win as the contest continued in a more restrained show of arms, in which Henry's two eldest sons could compete. Henry at thirteen and Thomas at twelve would be doughty fighters: my brother's pride shone like the noon sun as they played their part. They carried themselves well; John Cornewall even better, who allowed the princes to display their skills before the inevitable disarming. He was a man of compassion. Or, if I were of a cynical turn of mind, a man of few financial resources using a clever ruse to catch the King's eye. He won, of course, defeating all comers. Throughout the heat of that afternoon, Sir John Cornewall rode with all the glittering mastery of a knight from the magical books of my childhood, snatching victory from the prestigious French and Italian knights who challenged him.

I stayed for Henry's presentation of prizes.

Did my chosen knight surprise me? Not with the innate dignity with which he accepted the Order of the Garter, bestowed on him by Henry in recognition of his upholding England's reputation against foreign competition. Not by his splendid courtesy to all who applauded his achievements. But yes, he did baffle me in the end when, the Order of the Garter blazing in the sun, Sir John returned the ring to me with a gallant gesture, kneeling, the ring resting in his palm as he offered it, the sapphire gleaming with blue fire from its depths. Even paler, fair face strained and hair dripping with sweat from his exertions, he bowed his head so that his emotions were hidden from me.

'I place my victory at your feet, my lady.'

'My thanks, Sir John. Your fought superlatively well.'

What it cost me to say that. I had to set my jaw to use the same name and title as John Holland. I expected that my expression was stony when he deserved my praise, but it was beyond my tolerance to comply.

'It was my desire to uphold your honour, my lady.'

'Then it is right that you should be rewarded.'

He looked up, eyes glassy with exhaustion, face smeared with dust.

I could not smile at him, nor did he smile at me.

'Good fortune, Sir John,' was all I said. 'The prize is yours to keep.'

I let him keep the ring. It was indeed very valuable and perhaps I should not have done it, but he had fought well and it would have been churlish of me not to reward him. What did this golden-haired knight mean to me? Nothing. He never could mean anything to me.

I left before Henry awarded the rest of the prizes. I could not sit and wallow in self-pity, stirred with fury into a lethal mix as each brave knight knelt to receive his king's commendations and a purse of gold coin that Henry could ill-afford to give. John should have been there if he had made a pragmatic rather than an emotional choice. John should have been there if Henry had allowed himself to be generous. John should have been there if I had not...

Too close to home. Far too close.

I allowed myself to feel the old hurt that never left me, and that night, in my dreams, my hands were drenched in blood.

*

The jousting ended on a high note of male pride and knightly boasting but Henry sank into sour despondency with no news, good or bad, from Scotland. Supplies, I was led to understand by the tone and colour of his language, were running low, a disaster if the Scots refused an alliance and Henry was forced to call their bluff with an invasion.

'The goodwill from the jousting will die a death overnight if we're left sitting here on our arses for the next month!' Henry snarled when the couriers arrived yet again from the north with no news.

All we could do was sit tight at York and wait, until Henry could discover sufficient resources, or wring them from the reluctant purses of the richest noble families in his army. Meanwhile he chose to host a banquet to celebrate the victors of the tournament.

'Pray that if I'm open-handed with roast venison and enough wine to swamp their grousings, they'll forget their grudges and stay for the next feast I can muster.'

Perhaps it all had the air of desperation. I did not fully comprehend all the difficulties in the stalled negotiations, and Henry remained as silently dour as the Scots except to say: 'They're playing us for bloody fools, keeping us kicking our heels here. I've a good mind to invade tomorrow and prod King Robert with my sword until he does homage.'

'Well, that will encourage him,' I observed. Then took my lute and my needle to one of the spacious rooms in Greyfriars in the city where we were staying and prepared to wait with him. With a banquet in mind, in the absence of a wife, I would be Henry's hostess, which pleased me well enough, for the accommodations at the Franciscan Friary were suitably sumptuous, and it gave me something to occupy my mind other than my interminably festering woes, as Henry found need to remark.

'I, too, have lost friends to death or divided loyalties. You are not alone in your grief. Your face would curdle the milk in the churn.'

I balked. 'You allowed my husband to be done to death. Do I rejoice?'

'No. And I'm sorry for it. What more can I say?'

And again seeing the lasting sorrow for Mary mould his face into harsher lines, I hugged him as if he were still the brother of my childhood. We were both alone and must support each other. It would never be the same, I would never trust him as I once had, but he was all I had.

'I will organise your feasts,' I promised, 'your wine and your venison, and we will tie your friends to you with shackles of music and food and celebration.'

'It will get better.' Henry returned my embrace. 'Loss will lose its sharp edge.'

'Of course it will.'

Neither one of us was convinced.

We feasted. Where did Henry find such a wealth of plat-ters? Commandeered from those who sat to eat from them, or from the rich merchants of York who had been invited to join the knightly throng. We sang songs of victory and love and knightly endeavour. Henry's minstrels were in good heart and well paid for their efforts.

We danced. Or that is to say, Henry's guests danced. I did not. Had I not vowed never to dance again? My feet felt as heavy as my heart. Meanwhile John Cornewall, lithe and sprightly without the confines of his armour, could dance as well as he could joust, nor was he short of partners.

'Will you dance?' Henry offered.

I shook my head. 'I am too old to keep my breath in this measure,' I said as the dancers beamed and sweated in the torchlight, instantly regretting that I sounded like Constanza who had disapproved of anything that lacked the stately elegance of Castile. I was not so old.

Reading my mind, Henry grinned. 'You can still dance better than anyone I know. You always could. Why don't you?'

'I am thirty-seven years old, Hal.'

How the years flew past, how the web of lines gathered beside eyes and lips. I turned away from him. I did not like to think of the days when I had won the prize at Richard's court. I would not talk about Richard, or John, not today when Henry and I were in amiable alliance. Henry, it had to be said, was not short of women who were more than willing to dance with him. A King of England without a wife, a young man with royal blood and attractive countenance, was a desirable entity.

'Come with me, if your advanced years will allow it,' Henry said, and seizing my hand he led me from the noisy environs of the dancing into an unoccupied spot where he procured a cup of wine for me from a page who responded to his raised hand.

'Elizabeth…?'

'Hmn?'

'There's something I need to tell you…' He paused, then hesitated longer.

'Tell me what?'

For a moment I thought my brother looked ill at ease, eyes sliding to mine, before sliding just as swiftly away. Henry was never sly, so it took me aback. Then he tossed off his wine and made a wide gesture with his empty cup as he looked beyond my shoulder.

'Never mind solemn matters. Here's a notable fighter wishing to claim your hand since the musicians have retuned and the blowers caught their breath.'

I turned, knowing instinctively whom I would see, and of course it was John Cornewall, making his way through the throng with the same skill and ease as he showed on the tournament field, and the same determination.

'Why do I get the feeling that you want something from me?'

'I have no idea. You are too cynical.'

Indeed I was. In these days my brother did nothing without a purpose. 'It may be he wishes to exchange some news with you, Henry,' I observed. 'Something relevant to your Scottish troubles.' The knight's face was certainly grave enough.

'I think his mind is on dancing rather than war.'

'So am I of a mind to dance with him?'

'It would please me if you did.'

So I was right. Henry was building alliances. I turned to the knight who, hand on heart in true chivalric mode, newly-won Order of the Garter on his breast, bowed to me.

'Have you come to talk with my brother, Sir John?' I goaded gently. 'If so I will leave you together.'

'By no means. It is you I seek. Will you dance, my lady?'

I cast an arch look at Henry as I replied. 'My brother the King should have warned you. I do not dance, Sir John.'

'I am informed, madam, that you dance superlatively well.' Now I glanced at Henry with frank irritation. I knew who had supplied that piece of information. 'I had hoped to tempt you to add your expertise to this August occasion and dance with me.'

Such a self-assured request, those light eyes holding mine with no shyness. He might be young but he had all the confidence in the world. I felt an urge to ruffle that perfect poise, and so stepped onto dangerous ground with a little thrill of expectation. How would he react? I would be interested to see if this put an end to his need for my company.

'Once I danced, Sir John, but no longer. Since my husband's death I do not have the heart for it. The manner of his death has robbed me of all joy.'

In brotherly disgust, Henry grunted and strode off. I waited to see if Sir John would follow.

'If you will not dance, will you sit with me?' he invited, his manner lightly courteous. Why would he wish to sit with me? Would nothing deter him? And I felt a desire to repulse him, to see what was behind that cool façade. And to foil Henry's planning.

'No, Sir John.'

'We could converse.' No, he was not deterred. 'We have many acquaintances in common.'

'I expect that we have. But it is my wish to return to my women.'

Sir John laced the fingers of his hands together and studied them, giving me ample opportunity to admire the fine texture of the hair that curled onto his brow.

'Can you not be persuaded, my lady?' Quickly, smoothly, he raised his eyes, to catch me watching him, but took no advantage of it. 'It might be that you enjoy the experience. Why would you wish to be the only lady here present with-

out a knight to partner her or devote himself to her comfort?'

His persistence ruffled me. 'No, Sir. I will not. Forgive
me if you think me discourteous…'

Upon which he offered me a suave, if perfunctory, bow.
'Lady Elizabeth of Lancaster could never be ill-mannered.
I will not inflict my presence on you further.'

No courtier talk here. John Cornewall left me to stand
alone.

I felt myself flushing under the sardonic response as he
retraced his steps, leaving me to walk slowly back towards
the dais where my women sat and gossiped, admitting my
discourtesy. What had driven me to be so rudely uncivil?
And I felt the heat in my cheeks deepen for did I not
know the answer. I had admired him at the tournament.
I had found his solemn pronouncements, his careful gravity,
even his cool self-assurance appealing, and immediately felt
tainted by disloyalty. What right had I to be intrigued by any
casual acquaintance when my heart was still consumed by
old loves, old emotions, old bitterness? Was I not betraying
my beloved John all over again? I could not. I must not. This
anger at my own shallow appreciation of this talented knight
had been rapidly transmuted into sharp-tongued boorish-
ness, and I was now angry all over again, for did I not know
better than to inflict my own guilt on an innocent man?

Yet it pleased me beyond sense that he was wearing the
sapphire ring that I had given him. It pleased me less that he
danced with every attractive woman in the room, and every
one of them younger than I. But I was hardly in a position
to complain, was I?

He did not ask me to dance with him again. He was not a man to hound me until I complied. He was nothing like John.

★

The banquet and dancing over, I dispatched my women to the rooms the Friary had allotted to us before taking one final survey of the Great Hall. All was in order and could be left to Henry's Chamberlain. Indeed Henry was still there, speaking with him, still fired with some enthusiasm, while I was weary and covered a yawn with my fingers. Perhaps tomorrow I would go to Dartington. There was nothing more to keep me here. If Henry had no word from the Scots I imagined that he would bring an invasion in short order, and I would be superfluous. I did not know whether I was relieved or disappointed.

Just weary, I decided, as a shadow fell across my path.

'My lady.'

I recognised the voice, and wished he would go away. I hadn't the energy for further exchanges.

'I am about to retire, Sir John.'

'Then I will not keep you. Except for this.'

Taking the sapphire stone from his own finger, he held it out. I regarded it, and him quizzically. Why would he do that? Did he not want to keep so valuable a gem? Surely it could not be my refusal to dance with him, he could not be so petty. But so be it. When I made to take it from him, he took my hand, gently but firmly enough, and pushed the golden circle onto my own finger.

My hand felt nerveless in his, the ring suddenly weighing

heavily. The air around us was breathless, heavy with portent. I was always quick at reading portents.

'Are you returning it?' I asked to fill the sharp little silence. There was a ripple of warning here for me. Please let it not be what I suspected. 'It was given willingly, Sir John.' My voice sounded breathless even to me.

'I am returning it,' he replied, keeping my hand in his. 'With intent. I am honoured, my lady,' he said, 'that you have agreed to give your hand in marriage to me.'

The air stilled around me into a suffocating pillow, and I stared at him. Words failed me, or suitable ones at least. How had he come to this conclusion? And then I knew. I knew it as if it was written in blood on the white linen of the tables that had still to be cleared of the debris. It was Henry. It was all Henry's doing. Building alliances, that was it, and here I was, to become an essential stone in the fortress he was constructing. Henry, my loving brother, had given my hand in marriage without even speaking to me of his cunning little stratagem. He had committed me to be wed again to this ambitious knight from the west, whether I wished it or not.

'My lady?'

Sir John bent his handsome head to press a kiss on the ring that presaged so much.

'But I have not agreed.' With an inelegant tug, I pulled my hand from his, and he did not resist.

'I was of the understanding that you had. My lord the King has granted me your hand, Lady Elizabeth,' his composure perfectly unaffected by my refusal.

'My lord the King had no right,' I retorted as the enormity of what Henry had done struck home. But of course he had. He had every right, and as King of England his rights had taken on even greater significance. If I allowed it. 'I did not know,' I said, a ridiculously obvious statement that stirred my irritation to raw anger.

How could he not have told me? Warned me? Surely he would not take my compliance for granted. Yes he would! But even if he did expect my obedience, I could not believe that courtesy would not have prompted him to tell me. To tell me why. So that was why he had been ill at ease. It was this—this *deal*—he had struck with John Cornewall, probably over the ale cups between one joust and the next. I was nothing more than my brother's gift to the victor of the day. Not allow me to present you with the laurel wreath, or even this purse of gold, or even the most prestigious Order of the Garter, but let me give you my sister. She will make you an excellent wife, if you disregard the little matter of her lack of lands and her dower because her husband was attainted for treason and executed, his head adorning London Bridge. Take her. It will get her off my hands. I won't have to watch her every step. And it will give you, Sir John Cornewall, a reason for being loyal to the crown. Is that not an excellent bargain for both of us?

And I was shaken with a blast of fury. I had been married once at my father's behest. I would not meekly comply again at the dictates of my brother. I had no intention of wedding any man when my heart was cold and wounded.

'The King has not informed me of this,' I repeated, icily obdurate. 'Was not the Order of the Garter enough for you?'

'I am honoured by the Order of the Garter, but your hand

in marriage is an even greater honour. Is this marriage not to your liking?' he asked.

'No, it is not. It seems that my opinion is irrelevant.'

'I would not choose to wed a reluctant bride.'

'Whereas I, Sir John, will not marry any man. I have been a widow for less than six months.'

He considered this. 'Some widows,' he remarked contemplatively, 'are new brides within a week of their husband's death.'

Some widows, quick to jump into another bed, did not love their husband.

I was too proud to say this. Instead, sliding the glimmering ring from my finger, I offered it back to him, balancing it on my palm. 'I will not, Sir John.'

He did not take it. 'Am I repellent to you?'

I observed him, taking my time to assess what I knew about him, as if that would make a difference to my decision. Which it would not. An ambitious knight, seeking promotion and preferment since his family's straitened circumstances would bring him no satisfaction. A well-mannered, well-tutored knight who was rapidly making a name for himself in court circles. A handsome, courtly man with a subtle use of words. No, he was not physically repellent to me, but the circumstances were. And anger leapt and leapt again as I saw the truth in the situation, that Henry considered that he had every right to decide on my future.

I turned my shoulder to him, to look across the chamber busy with servants, quartering it until I discovered Henry now surrounded by a handful of his counsellors and captains. As if sensing my hostility, he turned his head to hold my gaze with his own. He knew all about this conversation. He had done it without my knowledge or my consent, because he had been uncertain of my reaction, as well he might. Oh, he had the right to do it, but I thought there was a closeness between us that had been partially mended, that he would never take such a step without considering my wishes.

I had been mistaken. To win a man's loyalty to the crown, once again I had been chosen to play the major role.

For a moment I almost crossed the chamber to challenge Henry, to deny his right, to refuse what he had done to me, but the look on his face was one of implacability. Nor would I draw attention to my position, or shame him in the regard of his counsellors. Instead, pride strong in me, I addressed the man at my side. The man who expected to wed me.

'I will not wed you, Sir John.'

'Am I so bad a choice, my lady?' he pursued.

Any choice was bad, however good his features, however smooth his tongue. I could not do it. Well-mannered and chivalrous he might be, I would not wed him. There were many women who would castigate me for a fool, and indeed in other circumstances, in another life, I might just…

A thought struck me with the force of a mace.

'How old are you, Sir John?'

His brows lifted at so personal a question, but he told me.

And I laughed. I laughed loudly enough to draw the attention of every man and every scavenging dog in the room. And then I stopped, my hand to my mouth. It was ill mannered to laugh when the victim of my laughter had no idea why.

'No,' I repeated. 'I will not marry you. I will not marry you at my brother's behest. There is nothing in this marriage for me and I am no tournament prize for the taking.'

Not waiting to see if he would argue against this, ignoring Henry, I left the ring, which Sir John had not redeemed, on the table and left the hall.

But before I climbed the stair, I looked back. What woman would not? Hands fisted on hips, Sir John Cornewall studied the floor at his feet. Then he retrieved the ring and pushed it onto his own finger, apparently neither embarrassed nor discomfited at my pronouncement. Did he think I would change my mind, or that Henry would bring his will to bear on me? For a young man without powerful sponsors he had an astonishing confidence, but he would find no compliance in me.

I walked with great dignity up the stairs and locked myself in my room.

*

The next morning I was up betimes, dressed, orders issued almost before daybreak. I considered departing without a word to anyone, but the emotional turmoil that had rumbled throughout the night, keeping my mind alert even though my body craved sleep, refused to let me act the coward. My brother deserved to know what I was doing and why I was doing it. It need not be a protracted meeting, or a particularly private one. We would not air our linen in public. What it would not be was pleasant.

'Good morning, Elizabeth.'

I caught him, superbly groomed, every inch the King

despite the early hour, in the brief hiatus between Mass and his reception of his Scottish couriers. He had been smiling at some comment made by his steward, but his welcome was tempered by the time I was within speaking distance. Oh, he was wary, and it was in my mind to shout and rail at him for his deception. The night had given me much food for thought.

Was I actually invited to York, to take precedence at Henry's tournament and feasting with this marriage in mind? Had this been his plan all along, to make John Cornewall known to me, so that his undoubted expertise in the tournament field would melt my cold heart and encourage me to leap into his bed after a fast blessing of the church?

I was chillingly aloof. I enjoyed every inch of Henry's discomfiture.

'Good morrow, my lord,' I said, drawing on my gloves. 'I am here to inform you of my departure.'

A frown coloured his eyes. 'Where are you going?'

Which I ignored. 'I am also here betimes to inform you that I have refused the offer made to me by Sir John Cornewall at your prompting. I expect you know by now.' I could see that he did from the wash of colour over his cheekbones. 'I might have received his offer of marriage more sympathetically if you had discussed your plan with me. Or even asked my preference.'

'I knew your preference. I knew you would refuse. What point in discussing it?'

'And I have refused.'

'Elizabeth!' Annoyance was high, but there were too many interested ears in the crowded accommodation of

Greyfriars and Henry lowered his voice. 'Reconsider,' he urged. 'It is in my mind that...'

I refused to allow him to take my hands but stepped smartly back, away.

'I will not. I know that I am part of your overall scheme, but I will not. Nor will I return to your court since I cannot trust you to put my wishes before your own.'

'You will if I command you! I have promised your hand to Cornewall.'

'Then let's hope you do not command me. For you will be disappointed. I trust you will discover some means of breaking your promise. I expect you can promote another willing bride to enhance his status and win his gratitude.'

And I turned on my heel.

'Elizabeth! We are not done with this conversation...'

'But we are. We no longer have anything to say to each other.'

'Have you forgotten? You are penniless without an annuity from me. You are dependent on me for—'

'How could I forget?' I returned so that the whole chamber could hear how I was treated, and spelled it out for him with furiously bitter words. 'I am penniless and homeless. My thanks, Hal. I will not stay here to be assessed and prodded like a carcass set for the spit when you choose my next husband. I have more pride than that, and I deny you the right to determine the future direction of my life. You robbed me of my last husband. I will not take another at your hand.'

'I do not give my permission! You will remain here.'

'I am not asking for your permission.'

'Elizabeth!'

I simply stood and faced him.

'Where are you going?'

'I deny that it is any of your concern. You have destroyed my goodwill.' I curtsied deeply. 'Good day to you, my lord.' And, with brisk footsteps, I left him to fume and restructure his plans. I would not be part of them. I had been manipulated by the men of my family before. If I wed again it would be my own choice.

I swore I would not.

Chapter Seventeen

Out of that one satisfying blaze of anger towards my brother and his knightly protégé, my need for a confidante had emerged as an overwhelming compulsion. All my life I had been strong, in the confidence imbued in me by my royal blood, by privilege, by unimaginable wealth. The protective arms of my family had banded around me so that I knew I would lack for nothing, and, when there was conflict, I was assured that my father would listen and not condemn me, even if he would not always change his policy in my favour. Many would say that I was too much indulged. Perhaps I was, but my father's judgement was fair and honest.

Now my father was dead and my brother bent on his own singular path to securing the throne. Who to turn to for advice, for honest opinion? For comfort?

No, not comfort. I rejected comfort. There was no consolation for me. My choices had been made, disastrously, irrevocably, and now I must bear the cost because only I could. There could be no excuses, no redemption. There never could be. The burden on my soul was great, but did I not deserve it?

Yet still I felt the desire to sit and talk, with a cup of wine and no pressures of time, to a woman who would listen and respond as she saw fit rather than offering the platitudes she thought I would wish to hear. I grimaced at the truth of that. Who would be honest with me, sister to the King? There was no one in York. To whom would I open my heart? Not for the first time I wished that my sister were not so far away.

No point in wishing.

There was only one woman. Initially, my mind rejected her, unsure as I was of my welcome, but her calm beauty even in old age and her measured accents returned to haunt me, so much so that I made my decision, just to rid myself of an uncomfortable presence that lectured me in my dreams.

Perhaps it was time I made my peace with her.

Never one to give confidences to my women, not wishing to be burdened with their chatter, I travelled with one young girl in attendance and kept my own counsel as I rode east from York, with a small entourage of two grooms and a quartet of men at arms. Oblivious to the flat expanses of the vale and then the uplift of the ridge of low hills, I spent my time in mentally listing what I would talk about when I reached my destination. How my spirits wallowed as my mind lurched from one thought to the next, casting each aside as an impossibility.

My loss of John, that absolute loss for which there was no remedy, waged war against my inner peace.

My fear of loneliness as my children grew and age touched me. Though that would not be an issue if I remarried as Henry wanted me to.

Which led to another intimate fear that I would reveal to no one: that I might love again and so betray John. How could I risk that?

My resentment towards Henry that he should deal with my future so fast and so ruthlessly without either my consent or even knowledge. Being preoccupied with the recalcitrant Scots was no excuse, after all our lives together, all we had shared, rejoiced in, and suffered. Henry could no longer be a confidant of mine.

Yes, there was only one destination in my mind, and how simple a journey it was once I had set my mind to it.

★

'If you are here to see me, Elizabeth, the world must indeed be standing on its head.'

'I think it is,' I said.

'Are we at war? Or is it a crisis of the heart?'

'Both,' I replied, more sharply than I had intended. No, this was not going to be easy.

'Then you are welcome.'

The woman, standing in the doorway of the scrupulously arranged parlour actually curtsied to me. Her tone was even, if a little caustic, as I recalled that it could be when she was faced with insurrection in her charges, but her eyes were not unkind and the smile that lit her face was genuine in its warmth.

'Should not I show respect to you?' I asked. Still there was an edge to my voice, product of this unusual meeting, unusual circumstances. 'I have been stripped of my titles, whereas my father saw fit to clothe you in utmost respectability.'

'You should, of course.' She laughed softly. 'But your blood is of far greater value than mine.'

This was better. Acknowledging the gleam in her eye, I copied her neat gesture, then stood and observed the woman who had had more influence on my life than she would ever know.

'Come in and be at ease, and sheathe your sword,' she invited with all the old grace.

I stepped across the threshold, followed her into her private parlour, thinking how like her it was. The highly polished wood, the expensive hangings, the signs of female occupation with books and embroidery and a lute, all overlaid with a fine elegance and an essence of style that was very much her own. She was of course a wealthy widow, and free to indulge her tastes and interests as she pleased.

'Please to be seated.'

Nodding to dismiss her servant, she moved to pour me a cup of wine while I divested myself of hood and gloves, disposing of the items on a coffer beneath the window, beating the dust from my skirts. She was assured enough of her own status that she did not come to my aid. Nor did I need it.

So we sat and regarded each other, not yet at ease. She

had not kissed me in welcome as once she would have done. Nor did I kiss her.

I thought that she had aged since I saw her last but her comeliness was not disfigured in any way by the fine lines of grief and experience. As for grey hair I could not tell. She wore a plain linen coif that drew the eye to her broad brow and to her eyes, full, as I now saw, with compassion. Her hands lay in her lap, loosely linked, abjuring the cup of wine and her feet rested on a little cushioned stool.

How composed she was in her widowhood. Unlike me.

'Well, Elizabeth? You have not come all this way to Lincoln for the pleasure of looking at me, now have you?'

Dame Katherine de Swynford as I first knew her. Now Dowager Duchess of Lancaster. My father's sometime scandalous mistress and finally his wife, the woman my father the Duke had loved enough to keep by him for almost thirty years. The woman who was once my governess and who I believed had loved me. In spite of our sharp exchange over my loyalties to John, I knew—I hoped—that still she held me close in her heart.

Was that not why I was here?

But still I hesitated, inexplicably uncertain. Had I not come here for truth?

'It is many months since I last saw you,' Katherine said, to soften the silence. 'Are your children in good health? They will be well grown...'

We had never been as close, Duchess Katherine and I, as she was with Philippa. I felt her disapproval of John and my choice of him even now hovering between us, and resented it, for neither of us was without sin. And when I had demanded by what right she could criticise my choice, when she had lived in an adulterous relationship for all the years I had known her, all she could say was that at least her sin was with a man of honour. That John could never have a claim to that.

The hard words of the past raced through my mind, resentment building anew.

Ultimately Katherine sighed. 'Why have you come to see me, Elizabeth? Is there so much lingering bitterness between us over your choice of Holland that we cannot now find common ground?'

And I knew. She might have been a scandalous whore in Walsingham's eyes but Katherine was the most devout, most clear-sighted woman I knew. In the corner of the room was her own prie-dieu, with a rosary and Book of Hours and I would swear they were well used. Katherine would give me her guidance.

'You look weary,' she said.

'So do you.'

She smiled faintly and I knew she felt her years. 'Two widows, sharing a cup of wine.'

I grimaced. 'I feel old!' Yet I felt the tensions in my neck and shoulders begin to lessen.

'Not as old as I, I assure you.' Her light laughter was a blessing. 'You are a young woman with all your life before you. Now tell me why you have come, and if I can I will help you. Then you can go away again and we can both be comfortable.'

Direct as usual, but she smiled, and I found that I was returning it.

'I am not sure,' I said at last. My mental list-making had been for nought. 'I'm not even sure that I should have come.'

'I think I might guess,' she said, and stood with a smooth serenity that denied her years. 'Come with me. I'll make it easier for you.' And taking my arm she ushered me through the door and out into the cathedral close. 'You'll not need outerwear. It's warm enough for a little walk. Leave your woman here. We don't need protection in Lincoln.'

'Where?' I asked, suspiciously, ready to resist. Was she going to pray over me in the cathedral? I had had enough of prayers that left me empty with despair.

'You'll see. Just enjoy the scene.'

And then we were in the streets, making our way downhill through the shops towards the market stalls. All was bustle and prosperity, the daily task of buying and selling coupled with the exchange of news. All around us was the clink of coin, the exchange of goods.

'Perhaps I will buy some fish.' Katherine lingered by a stall where she was obviously well known.

I looked askance. 'If you do, I'll not walk with you!'

'What's wrong with a fine carp? You've suddenly become over nice. Your father once offered to buy me oysters in the market at Leicester.'

Again, the laughter in her voice soothed all the raw edges in my heart. 'And what a scandal that caused.'

'It was not the oysters. It was the horse.'

'I remember.' It was my father's indiscreet hand on Katherine's bridle, openly in the streets of Leicester, that had drawn too much unwelcome attention and dragged Katherine's name in the mud as witch and seductress.

There was no need to say more, for those days were long gone. Any number of people greeted Katherine, asking after her health. We walked slowly side by side, light comment passing between us, nothing to do with my purpose here. I could not define her intention but allowed her to take the lead. And then we climbed the hill again, back to the looming bulk of the cathedral.

'We will go in.'

'I have no wish to pray. I have prayed enough in recent weeks.'

'Then we will sit and talk.' Unperturbed, she led me towards the Lady Chapel where we sat in the cool tranquillity. 'We will not be disturbed. I am well known here.' Katherine disposed her skirts into seemly folds. 'One day I will be buried here.' I glanced sharply at her, wondering if I had been misled by her smiling composure. 'But not yet. I still have my health.'

For the first time, sitting close to her now, I saw the weaving of lines beside eyes and mouth. She would always be a comely woman, but there was evidence of suffering. Did I not recognise it?

'You miss him,' I said.

'Every hour. Every day.' No drama, merely a statement.

'I miss John,' I stated.

'I know. I did not know if you would wish me to speak of it. Our words were harsh, as I recall.'

'I loved him so much.'

'I never judged you. The Duke and I simply thought that

he would never bring you happiness. And I was right, wasn't I? His defection from Henry put you in an impossible position.'

'Yes,' I admitted. 'But oh, he brought me such happiness as well. And I thought you did judge me, in allowing him the intimacies of marriage. And in bringing grief to my father. That is why…'

'That is why you cut me off. You always were intolerant, Elizabeth.' She stretched out her hand to touch mine. 'How could I be judgemental, when I had committed the exact same sin? But enough of that.' She squeezed my hand then released it. 'Perhaps, two *femmes soles* as we are, we can now heal a few wounds. This is a place of contemplation and sacred thoughts. Of honest confession. Tell me why you are here.'

So I did.

'Henry has given my hand in marriage.'

'So soon. But I am not surprised. I thought that might bring you to my door.'

'Did you know?' I reacted with a sudden burst of barely suppressed frustration, despite the sacred place. 'Had he told everyone but me?'

This time she closed her hand around mine to still me.

'No. How should that be? I live retired from the world. But common sense tells me that that is what Henry would do.'

'I did not see it!' Or had I? 'Perhaps not so soon, at least.'

'What will you do?' she asked. 'Is he a personable man?'

'I care not whether he is personable or not. I won't obey. I have already told Henry.'

'You were always short on patience too. No…' As I made to stand and leave. She pulled me back to her side. 'Do you want my advice or not?'

'Yes.' Resentment at Henry's decision, and the Duchess's easy acceptance of it, still filled me to the brim.

'Then think about this. What did you see when we walked through the town?'

'I don't understand.'

'What did you *see*?'

'People going about their daily affairs. The busy market-place of course. The purveyors of fish.' I wrinkled my nose.

'Go on.'

'It was noisy and busy and provincial. How do you stand it when you could live in London? At court? At Eltham?'

'It suits me well. Use your wit, Elizabeth.' All formality was gone and there, despite the lines and the age marks on her hand as it gripped mine, was the familiar sharp intelligence. I felt like the young Elizabeth failing to learn her lessons all over again. 'It is a picture of peace and prosperity. Provincial if you will, but one of satisfaction and confidence. Yes, there was poverty, there are always beggars, but there were townsfolk with money in their purse and nothing better to do than dress in their best and gossip over the latest scandals that have nothing to do with either of us. Is that not so?'

'Yes,' I agreed.

'That is what Henry sees for England. It is what he wants for this realm. Would you have it rent by war? Peace destroyed by rebellion and bloodshed and poor government at the hands of an ailing King or an ill-advised one too young to make good choices? There have been troubles enough in recent years. Don't you recall the bloody scenes in London when The Savoy was destroyed? Of course you do. You saw and experienced the results of treachery and disharmony for yourself, and so did Henry. But Henry is no longer his own man. He is King of England, and a young untried King, at that. And one with a dangerous inheritance. Don't you see how difficult his position is?'

'Yes.' Of course I did. The seeds sown by Princess Joan so many years ago had fallen on fertile ground. I knew exactly the rumblings of discontent in the country, which might erupt into open rebellion unless Henry played diplomat and statesman.

'Rebellion. Disaffection. Revenge on every corner if he's not careful. There are those who will never forgive him for the death of Richard.' She glanced sharply at me. 'Can you honestly say that you can forgive him, completely and wholeheartedly, for John's death?'

Could I? Completely? A question I had shied away from, but my own guilt smote me hard and I sighed. 'I do not know.'

'There are many who will plot and scheme to remove Henry from this day until the end of his life.' She made the sign of a cross. 'God keep him safe.'

'Amen, indeed.'

'And what can he do to strengthen his own position? Very little unless he can widen his power base and win over all those who are willing to be won over. And how will he do that, if even his own sister is reluctant? You know all the answers, Elizabeth. You have seen it in action in the hands of a master of the craft for the whole of your life. Why can you not see it and admire it in his son?'

'Of course. My father knew how important friends were. He used patronage and friendship.'

'I never knew any man to equal the Duke in giving gifts to secure the loyalty of those around him.' Katherine smiled wistfully.

'And he used marriage,' I admitted.

'And marriage. Philippa's marriage to the King of Portugal was for one purpose only. As was yours to Jonty, God rest his soul. And now Henry needs all the friends he can get.'

'And I am part of the plan.'

'Indubitably. But you know all of this, Elizabeth. You always were selfish, and I think you have not changed.'

I flinched but raised my hand in salute, as if she had just struck home with the sword she had accused me of wielding. I could not deny it, could I?

'For a woman such as you, with all your royal blood, there will rarely be freedom to choose the man you will live beside. You did with John, un-foreseeing of the outcome, which brought you nothing but pain. Why should you expect similar freedom again when Henry has such need of his family? His own children are young and he does not have the advantage of a wife. He needs you and he needs your support. How can you be so closed-minded?'

Silently I sat and considered, not liking to be told what I already knew.

'Are you considering yourself to be a martyr?' Katherine asked sternly.

'Perhaps.' It was exactly what I had thought.

'Nonsense. There is no martyrdom in you. Your happiness was destroyed by political necessity. Your contentment with John could never be maintained when there was no possible compromise between Henry and Richard. Between the three of them you were destined for heartbreak.'

How bleak it sounded, this clear vision of my marriage, torn apart by political fealty and power struggles that had refused to be healed. I could feel tears gathering, and swallowed against them.

'Now you have to be generous. You have to see yourself as part of Henry's plan for England.'

'You never were,' I managed, my voice raw. 'You were never part of my father's plan to win support or popularity.'

'Just the opposite in fact.' The twist of her lips held much remembered pain. 'I was sacrificed for the greater good when Walsingham drew blood. I had no power to meld men into an alliance. But you have, with all your Plantagenet breeding.'

I studied my linked fingers. 'Henry should have asked me.'

'Of course he should, but he has much on his mind. He is the King and he has a will stronger than steel. He is more like his father than you might guess at.'

'You know much of what is going on.'

'I keep my ears open and receive many letters. It occupies my mind. You have allowed yours, Elizabeth, to be submerged in grief and selfishness.'

I drew in a breath.

'So what now?' Katherine asked, refusing to allow me to wallow in the sins I had just accepted. 'You know what I would tell you. Is he so unattractive?'

'No. He is young and handsome and courteous. He fights well. As a jouster he could almost match John. He can dance and sing. He has a chivalrous way with words, and I doubt he would compel me, as John did. I suspect he is everything a woman could ask for in a husband.'

'Then that is a blessing. I do not know this paragon.'

'He is too young to have come within your orbit.' And I told her what I knew of the age of John Cornewall.

'Age smooths all furrows,' was all Katherine said. 'He is not too young for you now. Shall we pray? It will bring you peace, and perhaps the ability to make the decision for your future.'

I resigned myself to it, but instead of the peace that Katherine wished for me, all the old guilt that I had managed to hold at bay washed over me. I covered my face with my hands and breathed hard against the tears.

'What is it, Elizabeth?' The gentle sympathy was almost my undoing.

'I have such a weight on my heart.'

'Then tell me.'

'I cannot.'

'Then tell the Virgin.'

'I have told her,' impatience robbing me of courtesy. 'My guilt remains as heavy. I think she will be weary of hearing me.'

'The Virgin will never be too weary. Her compassion is infinite.' Now Katherine had turned to face me, eyes stern and unyielding, all her old authority restored as if I were a young child under her governance again. 'Kneel before her, Elizabeth, and tell her what is in your heart. I command it. It is the only way to restore some measure of peace to your soul. As much peace as we are ever gifted, as sinners in this sinful world. The Blessed Virgin does not expect you—or me—to be perfect and without stain, but if you are truly repentant for what it is that troubles you, she will not turn her smile from you. I swear it. It is the only way, my dear child.'

Her solemn assurance settled over me despite my doubts. How could I reject her promise of such comfort, and when her hand pressed down hard on my shoulder I found myself kneeling before the statue, hearing the soft clatter of Katherine's feet as she allowed me this time of solitude. I had told her that I had made my confession, but not of all that I had done, only of my sorrow.

'And tell the Blessed Virgin everything!'

I heard her final admonition echo through the spaces around me. So, as a child in obedience I would do it, bowing my head as I murmured the familiar words of petition, of a lost faith, for how could she have mercy on what I had done?

'Hail, Holy Queen, Mother of Mercy, our life, our sweetness, and our hope. To thee do we cry, to thee do we send up our sighs, mourning and weeping in this valley of tears. Turn, then, most gracious Advocate, thine eyes of mercy toward us…'

The familiar prayer whispered into silence. Now I must speak for myself. Lifting my gaze to the calm face above me, my lips parted, then closed, for there it was in my mind's eye, a slide of one vivid scene after another, robbing me of words. John, smiling and persuasive, telling me of the plot hatched in the Jerusalem Chamber at Westminster to persuade Henry to deal more openhandedly with his troublesome magnates, his words and voice reassuring that no harm would come of it.

And then my own slow heartbreak, not believing for one moment that it would be so simple a matter as arguing the outcome to a fair compromise, ending with a handclasp and goodwill on all sides. My despair that I could not persuade John to step back from what could be a disaster, for Henry and for him. The arguments I had used grew once again with intensity in my mind, and I saw myself kneeling at my prie-dieu in another place, another time, asking for the Virgin's guidance, doubting every attempt I made to reassure myself that John meant no harm. How right I had been to suspect the true substance of the plotting.

I pressed my hands flat against my heart, as the scenes came faster and faster.

For there I was, standing at the door to Henry's private chamber, my hand raised to lift the latch, but unable to do so as I reconsidered my choices once more. To speak or remain silent. To stand by brother or husband. Did I knock and enter? Or did I retreat and pray that all would end well, my family reconciled?

And then at the last, my decision made because I could not walk away and pretend that all was well, I entered. I could not have Henry's death on my soul, and so, swallowing all my doubts, there I was, knocking and entering to stand before brother.

'I know of a plot, of sorts. I think it is to destroy you.'

Thus I told Henry, in hard, cold words what I knew and what I feared. I betrayed John Holland and told Henry all I knew, to stop the plot coming to its terrible fruition. And after the telling I had pleaded that my brother would forgive John's treachery. That he would safeguard Richard's life, for was he not of our own blood? That he would diffuse the plot without bloodshed. Even now I could see, in my mind, Henry taking my hand and, as he held it tight and kissed it, he had promised that all would be well.

But all was not well. All would never be well again. John and Richard were dead.

Then, as the scenes faded, my confession to the Virgin began, haltingly at first, but not once did I look away from her painted eyes, so beautifully azure like the cloak that fell in folds from shoulder to feet, eyes that would or would not judge me.

'I was to blame for John Holland's death. I betrayed him. I took vows as his wife, I loved him more than life, but I betrayed him to Henry. I knew enough of the planned rebellion and in the end I could not allow my brother to be killed. John said it would not be death, but I knew how these things worked and…'

For a moment I lost the words I wished to say in a morass of renewed despair, but then continued.

'I blame myself for John's death. I knew there would be retribution against John, but I thought I could persuade Henry to be pragmatic. He promised me. But it was impossible in the end. The FitzAlans would claim their revenge and Henry did not care enough to stop them. He said he did try, but I'm not sure...I think when power is in the balance, no man can be trusted.' I gave a little hopeless shrug. 'Perhaps I made the wrong judgement. I could not let Henry be done to death, but it was John and all the rest who paid with their lives. And Richard, too.'

There it was. The weight of my guilt must be carried with grim fortitude to the day of my death, in endless punishment. No priest could give me absolution. I would never rid myself of my betrayal of him. Almost, almost I had confessed at the end, in that dreadful room at Pleshey, but he had not let me, and I had been too afraid of the horror I would read in his eyes.

'I knew how much hatred was directed against John by those who would destroy King Richard and all he stood for.' I could not stop. Having started, it had to be said. 'I was beyond foolish to believe that he could escape the bloody revenge taken against him.' I took a breath, my tongue passing over my dry lips as I confessed the worst. 'I think that John knew I was the one to betray him, but he never said. He was hurt and angry, reduced by physical pain, but he never accused me. I cannot forgive myself. I don't deserve forgiveness.'

There. It was said, despite the knot of tears in my throat, and I bowed my head in true contrition. I had wept so little, and now it seemed I could not stop.

Silence stretched out around me, a daunting stillness when I had hoped for a sense of release, nothing but the air moving as a distant door opened and closed. When I raised my head there was no change in the serene features turned to her baby son. One hand, opened in welcome, made me speak again.

'I ask forgiveness. I can ask no more. And that John will know what I did and why, and he will find it in his heart to forgive me too.'

The serenity did not change, nor did the texture of cool air on my skin, but I continued to kneel, watching the light cast coloured mosaics over the Virgin's robes, until soft footsteps grew closer, and there was Katherine sinking to kneel beside me with a catch of her breath at the rude advance of age.

'Well?'

'I told her everything.'

'And do you feel her peace and compassion in your heart?'

I shook my head. Relief, yes, that I had at last spoken of it, but no peace.

'It's John, isn't it?' Katherine said.

I turned my head to look at her, absorbing the implicit knowledge in those keen, intelligent eyes, and I instinctively stiffened, but there was no condemnation there.

'Oh Elizabeth, I know you better than you know yourself,' she murmured. 'There are many who would praise you for what you did.'

'I betrayed John,' I said simply. 'I betrayed the man I loved to his death.'

'Yours was not the hand that slew him. Did you not fight for him? Did you not beg for his release? I can't imagine that you didn't.'

I closed my eyes tight to shut out all the memories. 'I sent him to his death. I was party to it, however cunning your arguments.'

'He put himself there. He knew the risks and took them. You can't blame yourself.'

'He would not expect his wife to destroy him.'

'Look at me,' she admonished, taking my hands in hers, holding them palm to palm within her own. 'He would not blame you.'

'How do I know that?' Grief built again within me.

'You have to trust, Elizabeth. In the love you had for Holland and that he had for you. And in the Virgin's incomparable mercy.' She tightened her grip a little when I would have pulled away. 'There is nothing I can say to alleviate your hurt, is there?'

'No. Nothing.'

'This I will say. If you had not spoken out to Henry, you would have been mourning your brother here today. And his four sons. Is that what you would prefer? Would that have been any easier for you to tolerate?'

Nothing here that I had not already considered. 'No.'

'There is no easy way out of this for you. But the Virgin will give you her peace. And then you must forgive yourself. You cannot live with this for the rest of your life. It would not be good for you, Elizabeth.'

For a little while we simply sat until I was calm again.

'Come and stay with me.' Katherine smiled, and at last she leaned and softly kissed my cheek, the gentlest of caresses. 'Is this young man of Henry's choice a man of strong will?'

'I think he might be,' I said. 'Why?'

'Just that he would have to be a man of strong will to take you!'

Which made me return the smile, if wanly. 'John had. John stood up to everyone to wed me.' And the tears flowed again, for all the hurts and travails of the past months. 'He would not let me stay with him when he died.'

'And quite right, too. Remember him in life, not in ignominious death. He would not want that.'

No, of course he would not. Katherine drew me into her arms, keeping her clasp light in case I resisted, but I did not.

'I will espouse my widowhood,' I announced at last when I was worn out with weeping.

'But not for too long. Don't let the past overshadow the future. I know how easy it is to do that. Who would know better?'

I returned with her, with some degree of peace, and for those days in Lincoln I let my mind rest. Had I been touched by the Virgin's forgiveness? I did not think so, but neither was I torn by such vicious guilt. I had no more decisions to make other than where I would go when I left. We were simply two women from different generations recalling the past. Healing in its way.

Chapter Eighteen

I must pick up the reins of my life again. If nothing else, in those tranquil days in Lincoln Katherine had taught me that there was no going back and I must step into the future. First I must go to Dartington, despite all the memories and the simple fact that I had no right to be there. I did not think Henry would mind.

How welcoming were the children, overwhelming me with their chatter and demands, the younger ones as yet unknowing and untouched by John's absence. Richard, who seemed to have grown a hand span in his new authority, was grave, until the energies of youth returned and so did his laughter. Constance touched my hand in some stalwart level of communion and I hugged her close. Alice and Elizabeth concentrated on the rough-haired puppy that had replaced the singing birds in their affection. John prepared to take himself off to inspect the new horses in the stable until I dissuaded him. Baby Edward watched from the arms of his nurse, exhibiting toothless gums in formless chatter.

And then there was nothing more for me to do but sit in my chamber with the future brooding like a summer storm that was approaching, clouds dark over the trees to the west. Princess Joan had seen the approaching clouds and tempests so many years ago, and I had paid her fears no real heed. I hoped she would forgive me, and acknowledge that I had done all I could to preserve the strength and unity of my family. I had failed, but I had done all I could.

Now my future stretched before me, pitifully empty, and I dreaded it. It was as if John's death had made me see my life, unrolling like a new and priceless tapestry. But whereas a new tapestry would glow with vital colours, inhabited by busy men and women beautifully clad, enhanced with birds and flowers and creatures of the chase, my life flowed before me, old and grey and formless, without colour, no points of interest, void of happy emotion as it had become apart from my children.

Was this what I wanted? Was this to be my life, in the rural fastness of Dartington, alone, without company or conversation, with nothing to do but oversee my Steward's running of an estate that was not mine, judging myself anew day after day? Oh, I could take on John's mantle as lord of this manor, but was that what I wanted? Would I be satisfied with an annual descent on the royal court when my brother summoned me for Twelfth Night festivities, an ageing widowed aunt to Henry's sons, under constant requests to wed again, a royal bride whose blood was more important than her face?

A bride whose ability to carry another child might be fast vanishing as the years took their toll.

I was thirty-seven years old.

Or would a convent open its doors to me in the end, to allow me spend the rest of my days on my knees in penance? Surely that would be preferable, but I could not think so. I was no more drawn to a cloistered life than I had been when faced with an illicit lover and an inconvenient quickening. That was not the future I would grasp.

A thud of a fist against my door caused me to look up, and there was my steward with a written instruction in his hand.

'There is a package arrived for you some time ago, my lady. It's stored with all the documents. Shall I have it sent here to your chamber?

'No. I'll come to your room.'

It would give my thoughts some direction.

One box, the bill said. For delivery to the Lady Elizabeth of Lancaster. No mention of its contents. Was it some items I had left at York, sent on by Henry? I could not imagine Henry being concerned enough to restore some trivial possessions to me when the imminent invasion of Scotland would take up all his energies. And why use my unwed style? On discovering it, it was not large but well travelled. My steward set the coffer on the floor at my feet, where, intrigued, I knelt beside it on the tiles.

I opened the lid.

Then did nothing but sit back on my heels with my hands resting on the sides as my curiosity froze into mind-numbing shock.

Had this been done deliberately? Was this nothing but another FitzAlan ploy to twist the knife in the wound against all connected with John Holland? I could think of no other reason for this box of bloodstained and torn garments. From the heraldic device on the breast of the tunic, they had belonged to John. When had he last worn them? Were these the rags he had worn in the room at Pleshey? I did not know, could not recall, but they were a testament to his final days of hardship and cruel handling.

Carefully I lifted them, setting them equally carefully aside for it seemed wrong for me to mishandle them even as I flinched from the stiffness of filth and dried gore beneath my hands. There was nothing of value beneath. There would not be, of course. Anything of value from John's person would even now be in the coffers of Thomas FitzAlan. So why send me something so worthless in the eyes of the world, but so agonisingly painful for me?

'What do I do with them, my lady?'

I shook my head, then extracted a thickly folded piece of parchment which, originally slipped down the side, now fell into the bottom. As I recognised the writing on the superscription my hands clenched so the document crackled.

Why was it not destroyed too? And then I knew. It was addressed to me as Elizabeth of Lancaster, royal sister of King Henry, rather than Elizabeth Holland. John left nothing to chance. He had done all in his power to make sure it reached me.

To be left in the keeping of Henry, King of England.

That had ensured its continuity. It had been read, of course, that I could see, but although the original seal had been broken, it had been resealed with Henry's own. So it was Henry who had the chivalrous intent to get John's final words to me. For a time I kept the letter held between my two palms, horribly uncertain. But how could I not read it? And since it had not been destroyed, it clearly contained nothing of importance. I opened it and began.

My most beloved Elizabeth.

The letters were crudely formed. I could imagine John struggling with his damaged hands, which was proof enough that this was of great importance for him to send me these final thoughts. John rarely wrote, preferring the might of the sword to the pen. I must read it, read it to the end, even though there was no preamble to soften the blow.

I know what you did.

I forced myself to read on.

I know what you did and why you did it. I know you too well, how much love there is in your heart for me but also for your brother. You were raised to value the bonds of family and I swear you learned your lessons well. How could you not do all in your power to save Henry's life? My tale of a polite discussion was a poor one, but the best I could do when you discovered the plot and challenged me with it.

I don't blame you. I should have known when I told you—it was my mistake. I should not have burdened you with a secret you could not keep, but I did because I was afraid that you would set in motion events that would destroy our conspiracy. Not that it would have mattered in the end.

This is what I would say to you, my love. You must never believe that you were in any way to blame for my death. It was not you who told the detail of our intent to Henry. You did not know enough to undermine the whole scheme. There was another who did. It was Edward of Rutland, one of our own number. He played the traitor. I know this because FitzAlan found delight in telling me, that one of our own conspirators was responsible. Henry used him as a spy, while Edward had his eye on the restoration of his title of Aumale. Henry knew about the plot, and the full truth of it, long before you told him.

I know you will say that your betrayal still cannot be excused. I say that it can. You had your reasons. Are we not all bound up with indestructible chains of fealty? Now you must forgive yourself, as I forgive you.

I can hear your voice so clearly, refusing to be absolved. But I say to you: I forgive you. I take the burden from you. My death is after all at my own door, for I made the choice of Richard over Henry. See how magnanimous I can be in death.

Before my hands stiffen beyond repair—not that it will matter after tomorrow—I will say this. You should wed again. You were not made to live alone.

I will remember what we mean to each other until the last breath in my body. You are the light in my life, the most precious jewel of all my achievements. As long as my heart continues to beat in my body, know that it holds fast to you, as I know that you will continue to love me, whatever the future holds for you.

You have so much to live for.

Remember, for my sake, that the capacity to love does not die when the lover dies.

My breath heaved.

Until I became aware of my steward with a cup of wine at my elbow. Gratefully I took it and drank. And then the final scrawl, as if his energy and dexterity had deserted him.

John Holland, Duke of Exeter.

The title that was no longer his but which he had chosen to use at the end, a final act of defiance.

I impressed the page with the tips of my finger, as if I might still sense his presence, the force of his mind behind his written words. And perhaps I could, for how much truth was enfolded in John's final testament. We had both been challenged with the same dilemma: to choose love or duty. How glorious it would have been to choose love. But neither of us was free to do that, and so in a strange mirroring of each other, we had chosen duty over family, and in so doing we had destroyed what we loved most. Yet here it was, plainly stated. John's indestructible love for me, and mine for him.

And at last, at last, a comfort settled over me, softening all the edges in my soul. No tears. I had wept enough and more. Here was a strange joy that John had understood my imperfect reasoning and, even when all the horrors of a violent death had been waiting for him, he had had the greatness of spirit to acquit me.

It was Edward. Oh, I was not without blame, but it was my cousin of York who had betrayed the plotters, telling every detail of their intent, for no other motive than to put himself right in Henry's eyes and receive recompense. Was it true? Of course it was. Edward was the only one of them who had not been punished, but instead was received once more at court, ostentatiously busy in Henry's confidences. If I needed any evidence, there it was. Henry had used our cousin for his own ends, and Cousin Edward had seen a chance for his own ambitions. My little cousin who had the skill of falling on his feet: adopted as Richard's brother but turning his allegiance fast enough to Henry. Trusted by John in the Revolt of the Earls, but wooed by Henry to turn evidence against them.

I despised the ground he trod on. But my hatred of Edward could wait for another day, for that was not all. Folded within the page of John's letter was the briefest of notes in Henry's hand.

I hope this eases your broken heart and your conscience, Elizabeth. I am in haste to Scotland. You might find it in you to reconsider John Cornewall as your husband if he returns from this debacle intact.

Henry had taken the time to do this for me, beset as he was with his own problems. Understanding why he had done it, my heart melted towards him a little.

Finishing the wine, I made my excuses before retiring again to my chamber, where I opened my jewel coffer to retrieve the broken pieces of John's worthless silver heart, given so long ago when we had nothing to think about but the attraction between us. How could he have guessed its terrible foreshadowing? Once, fancifully, I had thought of having a silversmith mend it but it had never been done. It would never be restored now. Was not my own heart still broken? But both halves were in my keeping, and one day they might be healed.

I lifted the pieces of silver to my lips, just once, before replacing them in the coffer.

Is forgiveness possible, John?

Here was for me the truth in the mirror that John's letter had held up so that I might see my soul. I could face the most painful question of all: would I make the same choice again, if presented with the same dilemma?

Yes, I would. Because to put my love for my husband before my integrity and duty towards my brother would have been to condone the death of Henry and his sons. How could I have lived with that burden on my conscience? Yes, I would make the same decision again, even though I now knew that Henry's political ambition took precedence over his brotherly affection for me. I was betrayed on all sides, but yes, I too was capable of betrayal.

How tainted was royal blood.

'Is forgiveness possible, John?' I asked again, aloud.

He thought so. It was his last and most gracious, most precious gift to me. I touched the veiled head of the little statue of the Virgin on my prie-dieu. I felt her forgiveness at last.

★

In the following days I read John's letter until I could repeat it word for word, waiting. And then, with the arrival of the news I had been anticipating, I prepared to travel north again. The Scottish campaign was over; Henry and his army were returned to England.

I forgive you, John had written.

Could I forgive myself?

Perhaps, at last, these days blessed by the gift of John's absolution had proved to me that I could.

For the briefest of moments other figures were there to accompany me as I made my arrangements for the journey, ghosts from the past keeping pace.

Jonty, as I had known him in his youthful enthusiasms, would have raced around, into everything, his enjoyment a noisy entity in this quiet place. He was always a boy in my memories. He always would be.

Richard, even before he wore the crown, would have had no interest at all, abandoning such mundane tasks to those in his employ, while he sought out someone to impress and admire. As King of England he would have demanded an entourage worthy of his greatness.

Whereas John, my beloved John, would have prowled like some caged beast in the royal menagerie, ever-restless, exchanging ribald comments with his men, laughing at shared memories, giving me no rest until I abandoned whatever took my time, to join him in some expedition or engagement. He would have lured me, flattered me, employing all the charm he possessed until I remembered why I had missed him so desperately during his absence.

For a moment, just a shadow caught by a blink of an eye, John was there at my side. It was always John who was with me as I rose at the beginning of each day. The one true centre of my life, the bane of my life, who had shattered the bond between us because of loyalty to his brother, as I became estranged from him through loyalty to mine. How complex were constancy and fidelity when they would seem to be the most unambiguous truths in the world, how full of pain and regrets. John and I would have loved and argued and lived until old age, and I would not have been standing here, adrift, at Dartington, if conflicting honour had not dragged us down.

But that was in the past. Here in my mind were new

possibilities, new ventures. Deliberately, heart-wrenchingly, I drove John's ghost away.

The capacity to love does not die when the lover dies.

I would never love John less, but maybe it was possible to find affection again. My passion for John would not be diminished if I allowed myself to take this step into the future.

So many ends to be taken up and mended, if my Plantagenet pride would allow it. Like my ageing tapestry fraying from careless use, it would need careful stitching over a lifetime. Or, I decided, it was more like a palimpsest, where the manuscript was scraped clean, the old words removed, new ones rewritten. Here was the future for my re-writing, forming in my head with bold strokes, and I knew it was what Princess Joan would have done, with utmost conviction.

Go to Henry. Make your peace with him. Petition again in moderate words for lands and titles for your sons. Allow Henry to arrange good marriages for your daughters. He will listen to you, he must listen. And then go to Pleshey to acknowledge the burial of John Holland and let him rest in peace, so that you, too, can find peace.

And there was more, crowding into my thoughts, emerging from my own intuition.

I would be icily tolerant of Thomas FitzAlan, as a political necessity. I would try to be decorous in the company of the Countess of Hereford. I would grit my teeth and speak with my cousin Edward as if the hatred in my belly did not exist. I would do that, all of that. The grief and guilt that had wearied me, numbed me, had lost their hold and I felt strong and sure at last. Henry needed to hold on to this kingdom and I would not hinder him.

Yes, I would do all of those things, through duty and sisterly affection, but what of me and my life? And at last I smiled a little for there would be a man at Henry's side. John Cornewall, a bold knight with perfect manners, a knight with only twenty-five years to his name, younger even than Jonty, whom I had rejected as a child when I was full grown at seventeen. How strange the circles of life. But the years had moved on and the difference in life span between us was not so great. Here was no untried boy: here was a man metalled in battle, a man with strong views and ambitions to match.

I might be a path to power and wealth for this man of my brother's choosing, but I thought it would not be an unsatisfactory bargain between us. Burdens were to be borne as lightly as possible. Love? I did not think so, but respect and graciousness were not to be disparaged in a coming together of man and wife.

Would he forgive me the ill-manners of our parting? I thought that he would. He might even ask me to dance again. And, with an unexpected surge of life within me, of new hope, I thought that I might accept.

★ ★ ★ ★ ★

ACKNOWLEDGEMENTS

All my thanks to my agent, Jane Judd, who, from the beginning, was willing to take on my fixation with medieval women. Her continuing support and enthusiasm for me and the voiceless women of the English Middle Ages are beyond praise.

Also my profound thanks to Sally Williamson at Harlequin MIRA, who burrows under the skin of my characters with as much tenacity as I do. Her insight is invaluable. And to all the staff at Harlequin MIRA whose professional commitment has enabled Elizabeth of Lancaster to live again.

And my thanks to Helen Bowden and all at Orphans Press. Their expertise in dealing with website matters, genealogy and maps is exceptional. I could not manage without them.

INSPIRATION FOR *THE KING'S SISTER*

My compulsion to write about Elizabeth of Lancaster, younger daughter of John of Gaunt and Blanche of Lancaster, was born out of my own initial ignorance about her, followed by a visit to the Church of St Mary, a tiny rural church in Burford, Shropshire, close to where I live.

It all began when I was invited by a local historical society to give a talk on her life, together with a guided tour to her tomb. Being an 'incomer' to the area, I was forced to admit that I knew nothing about her other than her parentage and that Katherine Swynford had been employed as her governess. A personal visit to her tomb was essential.

And there she was, the heroine of my new novel. I think I knew it as soon as I saw her effigy, clad regally in red with a purple cloak trimmed with ermine. Her hair is fair, her face oval and her nose long. Plantagenet features, I suppose. She wears a ducal coronet and her hands are raised in prayer, an angel supporting her pillow and a little dog holding the edge of her cloak in its mouth. She is quite lovely.

But to write about her as a heroine I needed to discover more. And how little there was, either in contemporary sources or modern historians. But one comment, written in 1994, intrigued me when it damned her with the only opinion given about her as 'frankly wanton and highly sexed.'

Was there nothing more to say about her than this? And was this simply based on the fact that she had three husbands during her lifetime of fifty years? And that John Holland, her second husband, 'was struck down passionately, so that day and night he sought her out' while she was still not free to wed him? I expect that it had a bearing on the judgement, but surely there must be more to say about this daughter of Lancaster.

And then I came to appreciate the political setting in which

Elizabeth lived in 1399 and 1400, the years of the overthrow of King Richard II by Henry Bolingbroke, who became Henry IV, followed by the Rising of the Earls in which John Holland, the Duke of Exeter, half-brother to King Richard, was implicated. Elizabeth was in the very centre of this maelstrom. First cousin to Richard, sister to Henry, wife of John Holland, how difficult were family loyalties for her within that setting? What would be her role in the dynamics of this vital Plantagenet family?

What a marvellously emotional story this would make, mapping the pressures of blood and loyalty and duty when a family was torn apart by ambition and poor government.

This was to be the story of Elizabeth of Lancaster, the king's sister.

AND AFTER THE FINAL WORD IN
THE KING'S SISTER...

Elizabeth married Sir John Cornewall in the late summer of 1400. A large portion of the Holland properties, including Dartington Hall, was restored to her. In 1404 a gratified Henry restored to Elizabeth her dower.

She lived until 1425, dying at Ampthill Castle, built by John Cornewall, at the age of fifty-one years. She made no more dramatic appearances on the historical stage. She was buried in St Mary's Church in Burford, Shropshire, one of John Cornewall's family properties, by her own choice, and where her tomb can still be visited today.

Henry remained King of England until his death in the Jerusalem Chamber at Westminster Abbey in March 1413. He was succeeded by his son, who became Henry V. Henry eventually remarried to Joan of Navarre in 1403. It was a happy marriage, but they had no children together.

Sir John Cornewall, created Baron Fanhope by Henry IV, died on 11th December 1443 at Ampthill Castle in Bedfordshire. He was buried at Blackfriars Preachers, Ludgate, in London. Sir John Cornewall and Elizabeth had two children together:

John Cornewall, born around 1403, died in December 1421. He was only seventeen when he was killed at the Siege of Meaux, standing next to his father, who tragically witnessed his son's head being blown off by a gun-stone.

Constance married John FitzAlan, 14th Earl of Arundel and died in 1427 without children.

Sir John fathered two illegitimate sons, John and Thomas, whom he recognised in his will.

As for the surviving children of Elizabeth and John Holland:

Richard died at the age of eleven in late 1400.

Constance, Elizabeth and Alice all made advantageous marriages and had children.

John was eventually restored to his inheritance and became Duke of Exeter.

Edward made his name in soldiering.

FOLLOWING IN ELIZABETH'S FOOTSTEPS...

🗡 🔲 🗡

Tempted to travel? Feel an urge to follow in the footsteps of Elizabeth of Lancaster, even if it's only through the internet or travel guides, from the comfort of your armchair? Here are some of the best locations associated with them.

Kenilworth Castle

The jewel in the crown for the Lancaster family. We think of Kenilworth in connection with Elizabeth I and Robert Dudley, when much building was undertaken, but much of the pre-Tudor construction was planned by Elizabeth's father, Duke John of Lancaster. This is where Elizabeth would have spent much of her young life. Kenilworth was the scene of her first marriage to John Hasting, Earl of Pembroke. Visit the magnificent Great Hall and dream...

www.english-heritage.org.uk

Windsor Castle

Elizabeth spent many days at the royal courts of her cousin Richard II and her brother Henry IV. Although the Court travelled frequently, Windsor was a favourite place for both kings, so Elizabeth would have been well acquainted with Windsor. The initial major reconstruction of the castle was done by her grandfather Edward III.

www.royal.gov.uk/TheRoyalResidences

Tower of London

This was very much a royal residence and Elizabeth would have spent time here.

en.wikipedia.org/wiki/Tower_of_London

Church of St Mary, Burford, Shropshire

Discover Elizabeth's final resting place in her magnificent painted tomb in this tiny church near Tenbury Wells. It is the only physical evidence we have of her and is not to be missed.

en.wikipedia.org/wiki/St_Mary's_Church,_Burford

Pleshey Castle, Essex

The scene of John Holland's execution in 1400 still exists, but is much ruined, with banks and ditches and very little stone-work. Much of it is not open to the public.

www.pastscape.org

Unfortunately there is so little to see connected with Elizabeth's life. Many of the castles and houses associated with her have been destroyed or replaced by eighteenth- and nineteenth-century building.

The Savoy Palace

Utterly destroyed in the Peasants Revolt. But the Savoy Hotel is built on the site and, viewed from the Thames, it gives a superb idea of the extent and dominance of this incredible building that was completely laid waste. One of the finest palaces in Europe, with a wealth of valuable items collected by the Duke of Lancaster, it remains a matter of great regret that it is lost to us along with all its treasures.

Dartington Hall

John Holland's new home was derelict by the 1920s, when it was rebuilt as the present Dartington Hall.

Burford Manor

The present Burford manor was erected in the reign of George II. Some remains of an earlier manor, presumably that of Sir John Cornewall, have been discovered in the gardens and beneath the present manor after an archaeological investigation.

Pultney House

No trace remains.

The Church of Holy Trinity, Pleshey

The church was rebuilt in the eighteenth century and contains no trace of the burial there of John Holland.

Ampthill Castle

More famous now for its associations with Henry VIII and particularly Katherine of Aragon, who was living there when news reached her of her divorce, Ampthill Castle in Bedfordshire no longer exists. Katherine's Cross marks the place where it once stood.

www.ampthillhistory.co.uk

QUESTIONS FOR YOUR READING GROUP

1. What do you think of Elizabeth of Lancaster? What appeals to you about her, and what doesn't?

2. John Holland makes an unusual hero. A complex character, with a notorious and turbulent temper, he had more enemies than friends in his day. Is it possible for us to understand Elizabeth's love for him?

3. 'Frankly wanton and highly sexed.' Does Elizabeth deserve this epithet by a modern historian?

4. Elizabeth's first husband was a child of eight years, when she was adult at seventeen. Such diversity of age was not un known. Can we understand her impatience with this situation, even though she might accept the need for a dynastic alliance?

5. What is the driving force behind John Holland? Can we believe that his wooing of Elizabeth and his love for her were genuine? Or was it purely ambition?

6. At the centre of this story is the heartbreak of Elizabeth's loyalties in the aftermath of rebellion. How would you have reacted? Do we praise her or condemn her?

7. We meet some old friends. What role does Katherine Swynford play here? Would her own lifestyle have had any influence on Elizabeth's view of morality and marriage?

8. How hard do you think it was for Elizabeth to accept her part in the outcome of the Epiphany Rising? Is it possible to come to terms with guilt of such major proportions and move on with your life?

9. Henry IV was faced with a difficult kingdom, suffering unrest in the wake of the overthrow of Richard, as well

as financial weaknesses. Does this help us to understand his uncompromising stance with regard to John Holland and his sister?

10. Elizabeth accepts her role in her brother's new kingdom, the lot of many medieval women. But did she have more independence than many?

11. Apart from Elizabeth and John, which character in *The King's Sister* appeals most strongly to you?

CONTACTS

If you would like to keep in touch with my writing, the images and events that give me inspiration and my thoughts on all things medieval that catch my interest, do visit me:

Website: anneobrienbooks.com

Blog: anneobrienbooks.com/blog

Facebook: www.facebook.com/anneobrienbooks

Twitter: @anne_obrien

Pinterest: pinterest.com/thisisanneobrien

Loved this book?

Visit Anne O'Brien's fantastic website
at **www.anneobrienbooks.com** for
information about Anne, her latest books,
news, interviews, offers, competitions,
reading group extras and much more…

Follow Anne on Twitter **@anne_obrien**

www.anneobrienbooks.com

London, 1938.
Meet Daisy Driscoll, the
working class orphan whose
luck may be about to change…

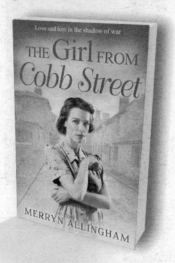

The war has just begun when Daisy meets and falls
madly in love with Gerald Mortimer. But when
Gerald returns to serve in India as a cavalry subaltern,
Daisy is left alone once more and, unbeknownst
to Gerald, pregnant with his child…

Wed by duty, Daisy struggles to adjust to life with her
new husband and soon discovers that Gerald is
in debt, and tragedy is about to strike…

www.mirabooks.co.uk

POLAND, 1940
A FAMILY TORN APART BY WAR

Life is a constant struggle for sisters Helena and Ruth
as they try desperately to survive the war in a bitter,
remote region of Poland. Every day is a challenge to
find food, to avoid the enemy, to stay alive.
Then Helena finds a Jewish American soldier,
wounded and in need of shelter.

If she helps him, she risks losing everything, including
her sister's love. But, if she stands aside, could
she ever forgive herself?

HARLEQUIN®MIRA®

www.mirabooks.co.uk

DI Richard Poole returns in this brand-new murder mystery from the BBC1 series *Death in Paradise*

Aslan Kennedy has an idyllic life: leader of a spiritual retreat for wealthy holidaymakers on one of the Caribbean's most unspoilt islands, Saint-Marie.

Until he's murdered, that is.

While the case appears to be open and shut, Detective Inspector Richard Poole is convinced that the evidence he's presented with doesn't quite stack up. In fact, he's certain that the person who's just confessed to the murder is the one person who couldn't have done it…

www.mirabooks.co.uk

*There was a moment when
Ivy Heartley could have told the truth.
But she didn't.*

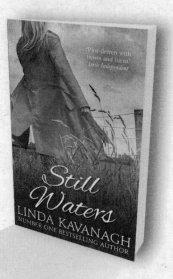

Now she's burdened with a terrible secret—
something so awful that she must constantly live
in fear, since its disclosure could destroy her
marriage, her career as a popular soap-star, and
turn her own son against her.

Will she ever be able to forget what happened?
Or will her past destroy her future?

www.mirabooks.co.uk